After Major Bianco's death in the Headquarters dining room, a detective from the military police—a dour redhead named Fallon—interviewed Kaufmann for all of ten minutes.

Q. Did you have lunch with Bianco a lot?
A. Only now and then.
Q. Any idea why anybody might want to murder him?
A. I don't know if he was murdered. I don't even know what he died of—do you? Maybe he was poisoned. With my sandwich. Maybe somebody was trying to kill me. Have you given that a thought or two?
Q. Any idea why anybody might want to murder Anna Krim, the waitress who waited on you?
A. Oh, God. Anna, too?
Q. Let me know if anything else occurs to you, will you, buddy?

Then Kaufmann's next informant dies . . . And Kaufmann realizes his own clock is ticking!

Tor books by Jack D. Hunter

The Potsdam Bluff
Tailspin

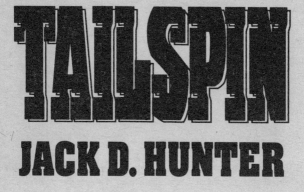

TAILSPIN

JACK D. HUNTER

TOR

A TOM DOHERTY ASSOCIATES BOOK
NEW YORK

TAILSPIN

Copyright © 1990 by Jack D. Hunter

A Tor Book
Published by Tom Doherty Associates, Inc.
49 West 24th Street
New York, N.Y. 10010

Cover art by Tom Daniel

ISBN: 0-812-50970-6

Library of Congress Catalog Card Number: 89-48634

First edition: June 1990
First mass market printing: August 1991

Printed in the United States of America

0 9 8 7 6 5 4 3 2 1

The author is most grateful for the technical counsel of

Col. Lester Personeus, Jr., USAF (ret.)

whose long and outstanding career as a military pilot and air power strategist was in great part made possible by his survival, in 1944, of twenty-five B-17 missions over Hitler's Reich.

Author's Note:

The turbulence initiated by Adolf Hitler in the third and fourth decades of this century caused me eventually to surface as one of the special agents assigned to the 970th Counter-Intelligence Corps Detachment, Headquarters, United States Forces, Europe. There, from the spring of 1945 through the subsequent bitter winter and into the fall of 1946, my buddies and I dealt with the melancholy realization that, although World War II had ended, World War III now impended.

This novel vignettes how things went for those of us who worked out of General Eisenhower's headquarters in Frankfurt am Main during those eerie days when surviving tyrants very nearly went for broke. The central characters are, of course, fictitious. And yet they aren't, because they typify that handful of anonymous men and women who, for no measurable reward or personal recognition, endured fearsome perils and anguish with an oddball blend of valor, rage and insouciance.

This piece of work is dedicated to them.

J. D. H.
St. Augustine, Florida

WEDNESDAY
5 September 1945

FOR YOUR EYES ONLY!
(All attachments)

File No. STH5826   5 Sept 45

To: Brandt
From: Gladiator

Subject: Operation "Tailspin"

1. See attached photo of classified (secret)
   memorandum directed to G-2, USFET, by
   Margaret Sunderman, a special auditor for CG,
   Army Service Forces, Washington. Sunderman
   has been working secretly on TDY basis at Hq,
   8th Air Force, Wiesbaden, since end of Pacific
   hostilities on 15 August 1945.

2. Also see photos of memos to G-2 from Capt. E. M. Bianco, former OSS operative, Northern Italy.

3. Note that Sunderman and Bianco have independently come upon aspects of "Tailspin" and urge full probe by Criminal Investigation Division, European Theater.

4. Please advise as to how to proceed.

FOR YOUR EYES ONLY!

PHOTOCOPY   SECRET   PHOTOCOPY

To: G-2, United States Forces European Theater
From: M. F. Sunderman
      Army Service Forces, Washington
      (TDY Wiesbaden)

30 August 1945

1. Theater-wide audit of salvageable aircraft reveals significant discrepancies. At least seven bombers of type B17G (serial nos. attached) scheduled for Stateside storage from TO&E, 8th and 15th Air Forces, have disappeared from inventory since 16 August 1945.

2. Also missing: 73 crates spare parts, 410 HE bombs (100 and 500 lbs.), 1000 cases .50 cal. mg ammo.

3. Pattern suggests criminal diversion to black market that can have occurred only with enabling participation of high-ranking military personnel.

4. Urge immediate referral of this matter to Criminal Investigation Division, Military Police, FBI.

PHOTOGRAPHY   SECRET   PHOTOCOPY

Code Zeus: DECODE
23 August 1945
To: AC of S, G-2, USFET

Sources interrogated Northern Italy report rail and truck shipments of aircraft parts, ordnance, via Kufstein, Graz, and Udine. Said to be directed to Communist partisans, but I can offer no confirmation as yet.

Bianco

COPY   COPY

Code Zeus: DECODE
25 August 1945
To: AC of S, G-2, USFET

Reliable partisan informant says undetermined number of B-17 bombers, parts, ammo are being shipped to city of Udine, Italy, and its province, stored at unknown facility by personnel of undetermined nationality. More later.

Bianco

FOR YOUR EYES ONLY!

File No. 22083A   5 Sept 45

To: Gladiator
From: Brandt

Subject: Operation "Tailspin"

1. Must stress the transcendent importance of this matter. We cannot afford to have anyone in ETO military establishment outside our group gain knowledge of "Tailspin" at this point.

2. The only individuals privy to our plan, besides you and I, are "Chocolate," "Mint," and "Licorice." Any and all others must be considered to be a threat.

3. Therefore maximum surreptitious effort must be made to divert or neutralize Sunderman and Bianco. The importance of this cannot be overemphasized.

4. Handle at once. Urgent.

FOR YOUR EYES ONLY!

1

Stalin had not invaded Western Europe and swept to the English Channel after all, thanks to a secret meeting in Potsdam, at which Harry Truman had assured the generalissimo—nose to nose, with only interpreters present—that one step into the U.S., British or French Zones of Occupation would get the Muscovite's ass smithereened. So went the disappointed gossip among certain headquarters denizens of rank and privilege and school ties who were never so much at peace as when the nation was at war. The members of this clubby stratum were key among those who composed and conducted the assorted loony tunes issuing from the United States Forces, European Theater—acronymned USFET. As such, they dealt daily with the paper blizzard that swirled into Frankfurt from Washington and London and Bern and Moscow and Tokyo, and because they were major contenders in the executive oneupmanship Olympics it was simple off-duty reflex for each to pass along whatever arcana might suggest his closeness to Eisenhower, the archetypal one-upper. Since a Stalin move to exploit the Western European political vacuum had been smugly anticipated by these cognoscenti, it was with ashen face and trembling lip that G-2's Lt. Col. William B. "Fatso" Gruber assembled the group in the command staff officers' club at Schloss Kronberg to whisper of events at the Potsdam summit conference. The group sat in silence, each dealing in his own way with the understanding that Truman's bantam pugnacity and Stalin's timidity in the face of what Stateside papers were now calling "the A-Bomb" portended an early return to dreary civilian careers. The portent was certified by Gruber's additional bad news: G-2 himself would soon suffer the Academy man's equivalent by being ZI'ed—returned to the Zone of the Interior—so as, it was rumored, to take command of that great limbo in the Maryland hills, the War Department Intelligence Training Center. And, as a sorry consequence, he was about to break in his successor in Frankfurt—the disgustingly competent, outrageously popular and adroitly political Colonel (soon to be Brigadier General) Amos T. Donleavy, much admired by the Pentagon for his ability to perform inside the trade as a by-the-book hard-ass while performing outside as a cuddly, pipey Uncle Fudd adored equally by congressmen and clodhoppers. As Gruber put it, "The sumbish out-Ikes Ike, for crissake."

Beyond Gruber's claque of headquarters doomsayers, most of the others comprising USFET's bulk—those millions of Andy Hardys whose preoccupation was the transformation of GI cigarettes into Nazi ceremonial daggers and relatively sanitary poontang—were happily and drunkenly oblivious to the storm clouds of impending peace. For them, browsing as they were among the charms of equally sozzled "Frawleins" from the North Sea to the Tyrol, Stalin and his thwarted geopolitical machinations were of as much concern as the temperature extremes on Jupiter.

Kaufmann, because he was a mere major and a counter-intelligence staff officer, was excluded from Gruber's circle and, because he was college-educated and had a manageable sex drive and a vague dislike of those given to turpitude, was generally unqualified for membership in the bottomside masses. His office was sufficiently critical and influential, however, for him to pick up the jungle drums that told of the secret confrontation at Potsdam and Stalin's subsequent subsidence. Being unconcerned with war-mongering and/or hedonism, he was one of the few among USFET headquarters personnel to have given the rumbling much thought. Once he had, he was by no means convinced that Stalin had withdrawn to his cave to sulk.

Because if there was anything Joe Stalin wasn't, it was timid.

"Something's going on," he said aloud, staring into his coffee cup. "Something wretched."

He was lunching alone, as was becoming standard these days. Most of the old crowd had already shipped out for the ZI and most of the new crowd were fuzz-faced sightseers who had spent the war years in saddle shoes and letter sweaters and, now equipped with ROTC commissions, had come to Germany to do the Conqueror's Strut among the ruins.

"You wish something, sir?"

"No, Anna. I was merely talking to myself."

Anna Krim was his favorite waitress. She took her work very seriously and, because she was a child and sensationally round here and there and had ice-blue Nordic eyes, she usually managed to look marvelous while doing it. But today her teenage beauty was overcast.

"Are you all right, Anna?"

"Sir?"

"You don't seem yourself. You seem to be upset, worried about something. Is something wrong?"

Her smooth cheeks reddened and her eyes showed sudden tears. "No, sir."

"You certainly look upset to me. Is there anything I can do to help you?"

She hurried off, disappearing through the service door.

He subdued the impulse to follow after her and to hold her in his arms and demand to know who was abusing her. All he could possibly get out of that would be more of her

evasions and the kitchen help's suspicions that he was a
dirty old man trying to exploit a nubile youngster's broken
heart. And perhaps he would be, in the sense that he might,
in some sick variation of narcissism, be playing to his own
loneliness, his own share of the soldier's chronic hunger for
sympathy and tenderness.

So go and weep, Anna-baby. Cry your goddam eyes out.
Kaufmann's got his own problems.

His table was in an isolated corner of the Farben Casino's
sunlit rooftop, a spread of concrete and dusty potted plants
fashioned into something resembling a California cocktail
lounge. It offered a dramatic panorama, with the moonscape
rubble of Frankfurt in the foreground, the Main River mid-
distant, and the blue foothills of the Taunus range dotting
the far horizon. A soft autumn breeze stirred in the trees,
and there was the smell of woodsmoke. Kaufmann considered all this broodingly: How many Hansels and Gretels
and grandmas and pooches and canaries still sprawled in
undetected pieces under those dunes of broken masonry?
Eisenhower had ordered the 8th Air Force's bombing crews
to spare the Farben Building complex so that he might use
it as a headquarters once "The War Against the German"
(as he and his topsiders put it so preciously) had been won.
The crews, legions of Smilin' Jacks in crushed hats and
leather jackets and Mennen's after-shave, had done precisely that—so efficiently that, while barely a twig had been
broken in the Farben's fancy landscaping, the blocks of
homes across the bordering street were now toothpicks and
gravel. A tribute to American know-how, he thought wryly;
German bombers blow hell out of London, killing nannies
and tots and parakeets in wasteful willy-nilly, but good ole
Yankee ingenuity enables *our* bombers to blow hell out of
Frankfurt, killing only *certain* nannies, et al. What a
crummy world.

He sighed. "Well, you keep your eyes on the gutter, you
never see the stars."

A shadow fell across the snowy table linen and a baritone
beside him asked, "What the hell's that supposed to mean?"

"Oh, hello, Bianco. I didn't know you were there."

"I spotted you from the bar. How's tricks?"

"Odd you should ask. Sit down. I got some questions."

Bianco took the chair opposite and made a business of lighting a cigarette. The sun, directly above, enlarged the shadows around his deepset eyes, transforming his Neapolitan features into something skull-like. Augmenting the effect was his slightly mocking, toothy smile and the tight-drawn, leathered texture of his skin. "So what's on your mind, Kaufmann?"

"Did you see today's Balkan Desk summaries?"

"Uprising in Yugoslavia. Albania. Bulgaria, Greece. Even parts of Turkey. It's become routine." Bianco blew smoke at the Frankfurt skyline.

"Right. The whole damned Balkan Peninsula—everything between the Adriatic and the Black Sea—is Commie gunshots and Molotov cocktails. And now the mess is spreading west into Northern Italy, according to this morning's update. Very mean, very large scale."

Bianco tapped his cigarette above an ashtray, and the sunlight glinted on his signet ring. He stared off at the distant hills, his face showing the sadness that comes to one who, having survived long-term peril, wonders if the struggle to live had really been worth it. "Hell, man, like I say: that's been going on for weeks now. Months. Tito's got a wild hair. For him, Yugoslavia ain't enough. He's running for king of the universe. And his fever is proving to be contagious among anti-Establishment types everywhere in southern Europe and the Middle East. So why should Italy's lunatic fringe be immune?"

Kaufmann leaned forward, elbows on the table. "Tell me something, Bianco. Why would I draw so many blanks when I ask about northern Italy these days? I mean, two weeks ago I'm reading a routine memo from one of my field hands on TDY in the Udine-Friuli provinces, north of Venice. He writes that while pursuing a G-2 matter on a farm outside the city of Udine he stumbled onto a gang of locals loading a civilian truck with U.S. Army Air Corps aerial bombs.

Inventoried and accountable high explosives stolen from a GI warehouse and worth a bundle on the black market. He reports the matter to me and to the MPs and the CID in Rome, then returns to his own work. Felonious theft; a criminal thing, not intelligence stuff. Routine as hell. But it bothers me. The bomb theft, coupled with the Balkan hell-raising spreading into Italy at the top of the Adriatic, gives me this great big uneasiness. And so I relay the report to the 15th Air Force in Foggia, and I am given a half-hearted thenkyew, and a dial tone. So I run around like Paul Revere to the 8th Air Force in Wiesbaden, where the Air Force Theater commander hangs out. Another thenk-yew-bye-bye. Next I run to the Italian and Balkan Desks, G-2; the Italian and Balkan Desks, CIC; the British MI-5 Liaison Officer; even the damn Eastern Mediterranean guy in Naval Intelligence. I warn everybody that some of our heroic Americans down there might be stealing and dealing—turning a buck by burgling heavy-duty weaponry from U.S. warehouses in Italy, then selling it to Italian Commies who ship it east across the Adriatic to their Balkan counterparts. But all I get by way of reaction out of the various Desks is the full-circle treatment: 'Sorry. That's an Air Force matter. You have to take it up with the Air Force.' And when I take it up with the Air Force, the Air Force doesn't want to hear about it.''

Bianco shrugged. "So what do you expect me to do? I'm just the OSS Liaison guy. Caretaking a dying agency. I am a man without clout.''

"Tell me what's going on down there.''

That earned an amused glance.

"Well,'' Kaufmann persisted, "you were with an OG team working with the Italian Resistance. Who in hell would know more about Northern Italy than you?''

"You've been fussing at me about the Balkans. Northern Italy is not in the Balkans.''

"Come on, pal, don't you start getting slick with me, too. Resistance-wise, there was a lot of coordination, mu-tuality of purpose, that kind of thing, between the Tito people and the Communist partisans from Trieste on down through Venice and all the way to Bologna, for cripes sake. I've been working the European dark side for four years, and right now I'm wondering what's going on in the whole goddam Adriatic area—the Balkans on the east, Italy north and west. There's no reason for those armed uprisings to be continuing the way they are. The Germans are licked; they've been evicted from all of those countries. The Japanese signed surrender documents last Sunday. Provisional governments have been established in all war zones. There's a peace on. But the Commies keep shooting. Picking off good guys. Why? What can they get by assassinating good guys that they can't get by not assassinating good guys? And why are so many of our own security people so damned indifferent to all of it, even to the fact that the buggers have taken to stealing aerial bombs?''

Bianco's brown eyes revealed genuine curiosity. ''Why are you so worked up over this, Major? Your assignment is counter-intelligence, the g-2 German Desk.''

There it was: the question he had asked himself many times over. Why indeed. In his honest moments, the answer was apparent. With Hitler's legions now a horde of tatterdemalions in demob processing camps from the North Sea to Vienna, German military intelligence operations were inert. Therefore, since his job was to spy on and outwit German spies, his desk, formerly an Alp of memos, advisories, message flimsies and Washington effluent, was today a mahogany skating rink. And with inactivity came boredom, and boredom was most surely followed by the Killarney Vapors.

Sired by an immigrant German language professor who had settled in Philadelphia with a wife derived from lace-curtain Irish Bostonians, Kaufmann was a mixture of Teutonic industry and guile and Old Sod intuitiveness and melancholy. And soon after Potsdam—soon after his desk had become barren—this dark blend had risen from wherever it lurked in his id to become an omnipresent twinge, like that in a sensitive tooth. Experience had shown him that the only cure was business, or lacking that, some kind of busy-ness. Not for him were drinking or wenching or golfing or butterfly collecting; he could no more abide a calculated waste of time than he could endure the boredom which inspired it. To flee boredom and its vapors he must pursue a course— be it ever so tangential—that could somehow add to his total capability as a professional. This day he was specially driven, belabored by a vast uneasiness, an unspecific suspicion of things unnameable.

But how do you explain such things to a man like Major Bianco? You don't. You lie. "G-2 has asked for a study."

"Big deal. G-2's always asking for a study. He doesn't go to the latrine without he asks for a study first."

"Come on, pal. Quit stalling."

Bianco stubbed out his cigarette. "Well," he said, "you ask me, the unrest throughout the whole area down there began when we—the OSS—saved Waffen SS General Karl Wolff from a partisan firing squad. Wolff, as you know, was commander of all German forces in Italy, right under Field Marshal Kesselring. He was about to be executed when we got word from Allen Dulles, OSS chief in Bern, that we were to save Wolff's ass at all costs. We did. We snaffled the Nazi bastard right out from under their little red noses. But soon after that came all kinds of hell, with the outraged partisans going off on killing orgies the likes of which you wouldn't believe."

"Why were you ordered to save Wolff?"

Bianco shrugged. "Who knows? I think it was part of the Sunrise thing."

"Just what was that, anyhow? I skimmed the advisories when it was going on, but I didn't keep up on it, being so wrapped up in the hunt for General Gehlen and the other intelligence spooks of the Wehrmacht's Eastern Front."

"I'm not sure myself, but it had basically to do with a surrender Wolff was trying to set up. He had a war crimes rap pending against him, and I think he was trying to buy his way out by turning over his German troops in return for some kind of personal amnesty. Who knows what the complete story was? Wolff knows, certainly, and Dulles knows, but Dulles is not exactly a gabby guy. So it'll be a cold day, sure enough, before either one of them tells all. Right?''

"Intuition tells me something big is about to happen. It makes me nervous when something-bigs happen."

"I can't see getting nervous just because some ragtag Commies are running around, shooting hell out of pizzerias and mayors. Now, Eisenhower's threat to bust any officer or dogface for fraternizing with the Germans—that's something to get nervous about. I'd sure hate to give up my fraternizing with Irmgard." Bianco moved his eyes around in a parody of evil conspiracy. "Have you *seen* that lady?''

"Everybody sees Irmgard. Trying to keep her a secret is like trying to hide the Graf Zeppelin in your garage."

"You've got to admit she's pretty, though."

"So was the Graf Zeppelin. But pure hell to get your arms around."

"Ah. That's just the point. Irmgard puts her arms around *you*. And you sink without a trace into ten acres of female mystery."

For all his reputation as a keen staff major and former guerrilla operations man, Bianco thought with his scrotum. Even so, he had been useful now and then, assigned as he was to OSS Liaison and inclined to gossip about that hotshot spy agency, and ordinarily Kaufmann would welcome this kind of impromptu contact. Today, though, his sense of impending doom would not long accommodate Bianco's tales of tail, and so he dabbed his lips with his napkin, stood up, and said, "Got to run. Big meeting at one."

"You haven't even touched your sandwich."

"Take it to Irmgard. To seal your piece treaty."

He went down the marble stairs and joined the line at the cash register. The lunch crowd was thinning. Busboys were already clearing the general officers' mess on the mezzanine, and the ground-floor field and company grade officers' mess was dotted with lingering shoptalkers. Irony dwelt in these high, sunny rooms, where a Viennese string quartet accompanied the cultured murmurings of the military elite.

Daily, surrounded by plate glass reaching to the sky, by parquet and chromium and stainless steel and leather, all of it polished to a surgically clean luster and redolent of fine rich foods, the olive drab chieftains would loiter here, rationalizing their hooky with brandy and pseudo-professional discussions of how best to dismantle the Third Reich. None took note of the raggedy-assed kids in short pants and dirndls who would poke through the GI garbage cans in the alley outside.

So what if the Krauts *are* crying for their mamas? Teach the little Nazi war goddam criminals a lesson. Right?

Right, Kaufmann thought sourly. Meantime, have another filet mignon, Colonel, sir.

A clattering sounded on the grand stairway. Kaufmann, startled, turned quickly, catching sight of the lanky German headwaiter and two military policemen—the pair that stood ceremonial guard when Ike or his generals were chowing down—racing two steps at a time for the rooftop dining area.

His sense of dread peaking now, Kaufmann was drawn into the gaggle of curiosity seekers swirling up the stairs in the cops' wake.

Intuition had not failed him.

It was Bianco, all right.

Slumped in his chair, Kaufmann's sandwich on the table before him, half-eaten.

"Let's get a doctor up here," the MP sergeant called officiously. "Quick. Somebody call a doctor."

"No rush." The corporal dropped Bianco's wrist.

"He's dead?"

"As a doornail."

2

A detective from the Farben Compound military police securitys section—a dour redhead named Fallon—had interviewed Kaufmann for all of ten minutes.

Q. What was your relationship to Bianco?

A. Working acquaintance.

Q. How long have you known him?

A. Since July, when Supreme Headquarters Allied Expeditionary Force became United States Forces Europe Theater and settled into the Farben Building.

Q. Did Bianco have any enemies?

A. An estimated ten million Germans and any number of P.O.'ed Italian Communists.

Q. Can we be serious, buddy?

A. No local enemies to speak of—he seemed to be generally well liked.

Q. Did you have lunch with Bianco a lot?

A. Only now and then.

Q. Why did you have lunch with him today?

A. I didn't. I was eating alone. He just happened by and sat for a time, chewing the rag.

Q. About what?

A. A thing I'm working on.

Q. What kind of thing is that?

A. It's confidential.

Q. You know I can get clearance if I need it, don't you, buddy?

A. I assume as much. But I'm not free to tell you anything on my own.

Q. Did he act unusual—say anything unusual, show any signs of strain?

A. No. Strictly shop talk, a few jokes about Ike's non-fraternization rule. Girl stuff. Like that.

Q. Any idea why anybody might want to murder Bianco?

A. I don't know if he was murdered. I don't even know what he died of—do you? Maybe he was poisoned. With my sandwich. Maybe somebody was trying to kill me. Have you given that a thought or two?

Q. Any idea why anybody might want to murder Anna Krim, the waitress who waited on you?

A. Oh, God. Anna, too?

Q. Her body was found in the Casino cellar an hour ago. Electrocuted. It could have been an accident, caused by a faulty wire. But maybe not. We're keeping an open mind.

A. Oh, God.

Q. Let me know if anything else occurs to you, will you, buddy?

A. Sure.

Kaufmann completed the workday in his silent office, mostly standing at the window and staring out at the Farben parkland, with its tidy trees and trimmed walkways and sissy flowerbeds. He caught his reflection in the windowpane, superimposed on an enormous spreading oak that graced an arc of driveway. An Everyman's face, chronically somber.

A girl (what was her name? Betty? Betsy?) once asked why he so rarely laughed. Because his father had taught him he should always be polite to ladies, he had tried to answer, but then, as now, he found that there were no words to describe the deep, sorrowful disappointment he felt to be living in a world that cared more about—spent more on—image and acquisition than it did on helping. Those petunias: they'd been set out there by some Kraut gardener under orders of some porky Quartermaster sergeant seeking to brown-nose the mightiest military commander in history, a conqueror unsurpassed in his technical ability to slay and destroy and who was about as likely to stand for a moment, admiring the petunias, as he was to dance "Swan Lake" before a joint session of Congress.

The abandoned little girl, poking tearfully through the garbage-spattered rubble down the hill: what could have been done for her with the U.S. taxpayer dollars it had taken to hire the gardener, find the petunias, buy them, transport them and get them into the goddam ground? Eh?

The world itself: what could have been done for it with the money spent by all the nations to trash a hemisphere and kill tens of millions who wanted nothing more than to be let alone in the scrabble for a decent living? Eh?

Laugh? Who in Christ's name felt like laughing?

At precisely five o'clock, approximately a half hour after all the other offices had emptied, he went to the coat rack, took down his service cap, placed it on his head, just the right angle to be out of cadet-square and not quite into jaunty, turned off the overhead light, and, throwing the door lock, stepped into the twilight of the empty hall. Not altogether empty. A young woman in trim officer greens, the silver bar of a first lieutenant on her WAAC overseas cap, stood there, fist raised.

"Why don't you pick on somebody your own size?" Kaufmann said.

She blushed—her face was pretty, in that way women who sing alto in church choirs and wear gingham aprons while baking cookies for the USO are pretty—and lowered her fist. "I was about to knock, sir. Are you Major Kaufmann?"

"What can I do for you, Lieutenant—?"

"Raines, sir. Molly Raines. Of G-1 Personnel Records Station. You know?"

"I was vaguely aware that G-1, being the army's personnel division, has a personnel section. I was not at all aware you were in it. Which proves my father's contention that a boy like me would simply have to evolve into a dull, unobservant and luckless man."

"Oh. Well. I—I see you were about to leave. I'm sorry I'm so late, sir, but I'd like to talk to you about something. I can come tomorrow—"

"I was going for a drink. Want one?"

"Well—"

He closed the door, tested the lock, then strode off, heading for the Paternoster—that peculiar endless chain of elevator cars that ran up and around and down like an out-of-shape Ferris wheel. "Come along, Raines."

"Where are we going, sir?"

"To the Casino. I'm told that they make an excellent martini there. Actually, I'm a whiskey man, but the supply officer last week received eighteen tankcars of Gordon's gin and we've all volunteered to help him bring it down to a more manageable gallonage."

Her pace slowed and she drifted astern. "I'll come to your office tomorrow, sir. I'd rather not go to the Casino—to be seen with you there."

"Ah. You have heard about my luncheon partner. You are afraid you, too, will not survive my company."

"Well, I'm really not worried about that, sir, but the things I want to discuss are sort of touchy—secret even—and I'd rather not have so many ears around. You'll be the object of a lot of stares after what happened this afternoon."

He stopped in mid-stride and turned to give her a lingering evaluation. "You really are serious, aren't you."

"I've been noticing some strange stuff lately, and I'm not sure what it means. It could be nothing."

"But obviously you don't think it is nothing. You think it is Something. Capital letter."

"Yes, sir."

"Why me? Why not take this something to your boss?"

She shrugged and made a small motion with her right hand. "I can't say without being—tactless. Let's just say you seemed to be the one I should talk to, sir."

"So come back to my office. People make too much of alcohol anyhow."

Kaufmann was one of the few officers above the rank of shavetail who was really comfortable with the idea of women in the army. Perhaps it was his lifelong admiration of his mother, or maybe it was that, to him, most army women looked like earnest-faced Brownie leaders who somehow would step in and straighten out this goddam mess around him. Whatever, he privately admitted that most women were a very great deal tougher and smarter than men and not nearly so profane and smelly and therefore easier to endure over the long haul, especially in six-by-six truck convoys on hot rainy days. Early in his military career they had symbolized safety; American women must be kept out of harm's way, except in rumble seats and tourist cabins, of course, and when a U.S. servicewoman was anywhere within fifty miles of him he'd felt assured that he was still in civilization and unlikely to be elevated to sainthood by a browsing artillery shell. This fantasy had dissipated quickly with his first London blitz, when, after a particularly bitter raid, he'd come upon the bodies of two nuns and their gaggle of school kids. He had been sweaty, trembling and nauseated for three weeks, and forever rid of the delusions which had been fed to him in a boyhood's worth of Saturday afternoon picture shows. Yet military women still pleased him, and this pink-and-cream first lieutenant across the desk, all neat and proper, skirt at knees, legs together, shoes shined, boobs discreet, at ease in his one comfortable visitor's chair, pleased him very much indeed.

"Also, Fräulein Leutnant, womit kann ich dienen?"

"Sir?"

"German for 'It's your nickel.' "

She gave him a level, den-mother stare. "As you know, Major Kaufmann, the rapid demobilization of our forces here in Europe has caused a lot of rather severe personnel problems, vis-à-vis jobs to be done and people to do them—in every command, theaterwide." She cleared her throat delicately, in the manner of a speaker who has memorized her material and is pausing for an inward scanning of Paragraph Two. "For this reason, most of us in the Personnel Section have ourselves been assigned additional duties, which often overlap with the assignments of others and take us into territories quite new to us." She paused again to dredge up Paragraph Three.

"Do you always talk like this, Lieutenant?"

"Like how, sir?"

"Like a field manual."

She blushed again, and again Kaufmann was pleased, because so few people could blush anymore, having committed all the deadly sins, broken each of the commandments, and come routinely to live like horses' asses.

"I'm trying to be concise, sir. I don't want to take up too much of your time."

Kaufmann sniffed. "Time, Raines? You say time? My God, woman, I don't have anything else these days. While you and your colleagues are getting double duty and going into territories quite new to you and all that rigmarole, I am a man without a raison d'être—a staff major who asks questions that get doors slammed in his face and whose only employment for the foreseeable future is answering the questions of a crab-faced redhead MP detective who wants to ignore anything that might make him miss his boat to Hoboken. So please, to keep me from going insane, kick off your shoes, rest back, light up a Lucky, and tell me the story of your life."

Her blue eyes registered interest and compassion, not too much to be phony, but just enough to communicate genuine appreciation of his uncomfortable situation. "I'm sorry you lost your friend." This, although in rough context to her expression, seemed to be blurted spontaneously, like an unexpected burp. She added, somewhat anticlimactically, he thought, "So suddenly. Tragically. It must be very difficult for you."

"He was an acquaintance, nothing more. And the only difficulty it's causing me is the fact that he died while eating my sandwich—a liverwurst on rye, pickle on the side. The army is having trouble forgiving me for that."

"Aren't you having trouble with the shock of it? The death of a man you'd just been talking with?"

He gave her a look. Where had this woman been? How could someone in uniform, in a war, even if on the remotest rim of it, be capable of such a question? "This isn't the first time someone has expired on me, mid-conversation. I don't get torn up about it anymore. Especially with a fellow who snaffles other people's liverwurst sandwiches."

She looked embarrassed. "That was silly of me. I meant the question to be sympathetic. It came out wrong. I'm sorry."

"As I say, we were hardly Damon and Runyon."

"Pythias."

"Eh?"

"It's Damon and Pythias."

"Good idea. Let's find a bar and get pythias."

Unable to recoup, she became redly silent, and because he saw she wasn't one who took easily to kidding around, he got back to the subject. "O.K. So what's up?"

"Part of my job since the end of hostilities has been to keep a daily status report on the disposition of German military prisoners—prisoners of war. You know: numbers, ranks, units, where captured and when, detention centers assigned, that kind of thing. It's compiled by the POW Section, then forwarded to me so that I can condense it and append it to the Theater Summary sent up each morning to

AC of S, G-1. In the past couple of weeks—since the middle of August, actually—I've noticed something rather strange.'' Her gaze went bluely out the window to take in the petunias.

''Strange?''

''Certain Luftwaffe aircrewmen are being screened out of the herd and sent to a new holding pen near Dijon.''

''To France? You mean, wherever they're under detention, they're being transferred to France?''

''Wherever. Oberursel, Haidhausen, Aschaffenburg, Wiesbaden, Augsburg. Some of them have even been sent to Dijon from Scotland and the Tyrol.''

''Why? Did you ask anybody?''

''Yes, I did. I asked my superior, Colonel Daley, who said I should ask somebody in G-2, since there must be some kind of technical aviation interrogation going on. But I pointed out that if that was the case it'd be much easier to have the interrogators move around than to move a crowd of Germans and their guards, and Colonel Daley said either to forget it or go to G-2, he was going to Schloss Kronberg for a drink and a movie.''

The lady was not above a bit of catty irony. Which raised her enormously in Kaufmann's already considerable esteem, physical attraction-wise. ''I take it you don't care much for Colonel Daley.''

''Is he a friend of yours, sir?''

''I wouldn't know Colonel Dailey if he fell into my soup.''

''Well, then: Colonel Daley is a ten-cent, wind-up poophead.''

Now here was a Brownie leader to be reckoned with, by God. ''This is the, ah, tactlessness you were mentioning?''

''I'm afraid so, Major.''

''So what's next?''

''So I went to see the G-2 officer we deal with the most, that's Colonel Roop, G-2 Personnel, and asked him if he knew anything about a special detention center for Luftwaffe POWs and when I finally got to see him—he seems to be always out on the Officers Club crap-shooting range, or something—he told me it was all news to him and why didn't I check with the IPW Section at Oberursel, where they're interrogating the top-level Nazi war crimes suspects. I called out there but they wouldn't put me through to anybody higher than the main office message center, some snotty sergeant with a French accent that sounds put on, who said I should write a letter to AC of S G-2 and let it drift down through the thicket until somebody who knows something might answer. I did, but there hasn't been any answer, and it's been almost three weeks now.''

"Well," Kaufmann said, "you really should allow four months for answers to letters around here. The urgent ones, that is. Routine isn't quite so fast."

"But last week I got a call from Maggie Sunderman—she's a tech sergeant in Air Force Documents Processing, over at Wiesbaden—and she said she'd seen my letter and could we talk privately. We met at the Bahnhof Red Cross Center, like we were transients, sort of, and wouldn't look courtmartially, an officer and enlisted woman meeting for social purposes, you know?''

"Have you worked with Maggie before?"

"No, sir. That's an interesting thing. She told me she saw my letter in her section's Classified Communix bay, right on top of a stack of documents due to be destroyed that afternoon. And she thought about it a bit and it seemed to fit into something queer she'd been noticing. So she wanted to see if there was anything else I was picking up that might dovetail with the thing she was working on."

"What had she noticed, Raines?"

"She's been doing a study of aircraft inventories and dispositions for the Strategic Bombing Survey and she's picked up an odd pattern. Twelve fully airworthy and regularly maintained B-17's—carried on the 15th Air Force Foggia inventories as replacement or backup ships and scheduled for eventual transfer to ZI warehousing—have disappeared from the inventories. Practically brand-new airplanes missing, along with all their documents. They were there, then they weren't. And her attempts to clarify with the pertinent commands have either been ignored or have been diverted to the office of General Vickery, chief of Air Force Special Operations at Wiesbaden. And inquiries there have met with nothing but, well, hardnosed doubletalk. Even crazier, two of the aircraft serial numbers show up on a list of planes sent to Russia under Lend Lease—which President Truman blew the whistle on last spring, for Pete's sake, and which never, at any time, specified B-17's for Russian use. When she checked with General Vickery's office, which ties in with Lend Lease, the General himself got on the line and told her to mind her own—I won't use the word he used—business. And the very next day the serial numbers for all twelve planes disappeared from the master aircraft status report. And then she said a very odd thing.''

"Like what?"

"She said, 'The whole thing is a clear-cut case of C-rations. I can feel it in my bones.' She said it sort of to herself, like. As if she was thinking very hard.''

"C-rations?"

"C-rations."

"Why would she say that?"

"I have no idea, sir."

She fell silent, seeming to reconsider everything she'd just said. Kaufmann thought about it for a time, too, then asked, "Does Maggie have a copy of the documents for the missing planes? Any other lists, or papers, or whatever?''

The lieutenant shrugged her handsome shoulders. "I can't say, sir.''

"Well, she can't be blamed if she didn't, I guess. Why should a mere noncom care a hoot about some missing planes?''

"I asked her the same thing, sir. But she only mumbled something about how she hates to see them get away with it.''

"It? What it? Them? What them?''

Lieutenant Raines shrugged again. "I don't know about the it. She called the them, 'sidewinding, lard-ass sons of bitches,' sir.''

"Well, Raines," he said, impassive, "it's good to see that you can talk American after all."

"I don't usually use language like that, sir."

"Oh, but you should. Nothing flushes the system faster than a good, healthy 'sons-of-bitches' now and then. A great purgative. And 'lard-ass' is especially therapeutic."

"You're teasing me and my prim ways, aren't you, Major Kaufmann?"

"I guess so. But don't take it personally. I never get personal when I'm being personal."

"Begging the major's pardon, but she told me you were weird. And I see she's right."

"Which she?"

"All of this stuff has made me, well, rather uneasy. I felt it should be discussed with a key field-grade officer who would take a serious look at it. It would have to be an officer who has a sense of duty—who isn't like all these other fat-bellied nincompoops."

"So?"

"I went directly to Captain Maude Reynolds, who is a personal admin assistant to G-2 himself, and who was a classmate of mine at Penn."

"The Old Girl Network at work, eh?"

"And I asked her who is the best, all-round responsible and diligent junior member of the G staff and she said you are, except that you're a bit weird around the edges. She said G-2 thinks so, too. She overheard him tell Ike—ah, General Eisenhower—that you are a major league oddball but he wished he had fifty more like you and maybe we'd start getting some real intelligence work done. And General Eisenhower asked G-2 why you shouldn't be promoted to something really muscular now that there are so many vacancies and G-2 said that it would be a waste of time, since you have so many points toward discharge you'll probably be home before Halloween."

Kaufmann thought for a time, studying the petunias. Then he pushed back his swivel chair, arose, went to the coat rack, donned his cap and turned, preacher-solemn, to regard the diffident Lieutenant Raines.

"Come on, Raines. I owe you a drink, whether you like it or not. Not at the Casino. I've managed to snaffle an apartment of my very single own. You'll like it. It has beige drapes. I understand all women like beige drapes. And it's far from the madding crowd."

She stood up, wary. "I must advise you that I'm engaged to a tank officer, sir."

"Please, Raines, I'm inviting you to have a drink as an expression of my gratitude for your having told me that I'm loved in the councils of the mighty. I was not planning to rassle you into bed. Besides, the sheets won't be changed until tomorrow."

He took her elbow and led her into the corridor. En route to the Paternoster he gave her a sidelong glance.

"Penn, eh?"

"Yes, sir."

"Then you are what amounts to a Philadelphian. That means that you and Maude Reynolds and I—born and raised as I was in the elm-shaded Victorian splendor and usurious mortgages of nearby Ridley Park—are sisters under the skin."

"Weird is the word."

THURSDAY
6 September 1945

3

The drinks with Raines had proved to be indecisive—a gentle sparring whose only discernible result was an easing in the lieutenant's wariness and a frequent, defensive mentioning of "Larry," the man who drove tanks. Even so, it had been a pleasant interlude, lifting Kaufmann's mood and suggesting that they might become friends.

But first things first, he reminded himself, and impelled by this injunction he mounted his jeep the next morning and drove to the Bahnhofsplatz, where he turned toward the river and, after twice losing his way in the wilderness of rubble, splintered trees and fallen power poles, eventually located the morgue. This sad little clinic, borrowed from obsequious German medical bureaucrats who claimed, straight-faced, never to have belonged to the Nazi Party, was where USFET Headquarters temporarily housed, prior to shipment Stateside, those among its personnel who showed up mysteriously, violently or feloniously demised.

A pudgy army nurse eyed him charily as he approached the reception desk. "Help you, Major?"

"I'd like to talk to the officer in charge."

"May I ask why?"

"No."

Her eyes narrowed. "Then leave your phone number and I'll have him call you."

"Since I am on top secret business for AC of S, G-2, USFET, I suggest that your O in C call the general direct. The general, who is fiercely efficient himself, detests delays caused by others, and he's waiting for some answers from this office. Be sure that the call is made on a scrambler phone. Otherwise court-martials for violations of Top Secret Security"—his voice capitalized the words—"will most certainly follow."

The steely little eyes wavered. "We don't have a scrambler phone."

"Then you have a problem, don't you." He turned for the door.

"Sir," she said, pushing back her chair and standing, "why don't you let me see if Captain Olsen is available. I'll be only a moment—"

She disappeared through a frosted glass door, behind which soon came sounds of muttered conversation. They ended when a youngish man in a not-too-white lab coat peeked out.

"Help you, Major?"

"I want to ask you questions. Privately and without interruption."

"Come on, come in."

The nurse, pouting, pushed past them and took up uneasy station in her chair again, leaving Kaufmann with the captain in a tiny gray room made beautiful by a tin file cabinet, a tin desk, three tin chairs, and a wall calendar whose message re Egelheimer's Enema Solution was a rhapsody in blue ink.

After they took seats, Captain Olsen examined Kaufmann with soft brown eyes enlarged by magnifying spectacles of the kind worn for close work by doctors and dentists. "What can I do for you, Major—"

"Kaufmann, G-2, USFET. That nurse of yours is a pain in the ass."

"Isn't she, though? I'd have her transferred in a minute if I wasn't afraid she'd tear my balls off. But, alas, like death, taxes, and my ex-wife's lawyer, Nurse Fuller just goes on and on. Even the Germans jump when she says boo."

"Don't they hurt your eyes?"

"Who? The Germans?"

"Those magnifying glasses you're wearing."

Olsen removed the spectacles and replaced them with a pair of hornrims he took from his lab coat pocket. He sighed. "Well, now. That's better. I wondered why your face was so wide at the top and so narrow at the bottom."

"Military Police reports say you're doing an autopsy on an officer name of Bianco. Major Ernesto M."

"Just finished it this morning, actually."

"G-2 wants to know what he died of."

"Cerebral hemorrhage."

"That's it?"

"Isn't that enough? I mean, dead's dead."

"I had just been talking with him. He'd seemed in good health."

"Oh, he was, he was. Strong and twangy as an ox everywhere but that blood vessel in his head. It exploded on him like a rotten hose. And there he was, dead all over."

"No traces of poisons, or anything like that?"

Captain Olsen shook his head. "Nope. And believe me, if there were a trace I'd find it. Toxicology is one of my main zooms. Funny you should ask, though. The cops did, too. They suspected somebody might have slipped the victim a mickey."

"How do you tell if someone's been poisoned?"

"Well, there are a lot of ways. Each poison leaves different clues. Arsenic, say, you tell from stool. Cyanide, color of the mouth and face, along with certain smells. Strychnine contorts the body. That kind of thing, right on down a long nauseating list."

"All poisons leave traces?"

"Most known poisons. Some more than others. Arsenic, for instance, can be found in the remains hundreds of years after death. Even in the soil after the body's turned to what preachers call dust. Strychnine, morphine, atropine, scopolamine can be found for several years. But some disappear very fast—mostly hypnotics, or sleep-inducing agents, which can be gone without trace even before the victim actually dies. But homicides by poisoning are pretty easily established if you've got a good toxicologist and chemical analyst on the job."

Kaufmann stared absently at the tin file cabinet, thinking. Then: "Did you analyze the food Bianco had eaten?"

"Of course. That's basic. Also the food he hadn't yet eaten—the remains of the sandwich on his luncheon plate. Both clean as a whistle."

"You're sure?"

"Absolutely. Pathologically and forensically speaking."

Kaufmann's eyes came around to give him a lingering stare. Olsen, despite his air of gee-whiz affability, was obviously unabashed by the presence of superior rank out of Ike's pantheon. He returned the examination unblinkingly.

"Do I detect doubt in your tone, Herr Doktor?"

"Not doubt. Uneasiness."

"What does that mean?"

Olsen hunched a shoulder. "By every practical measure available to the practical medical scientist, the late Captain Bianco died of natural causes. Part of his body simply gave out—instantly, unexpectedly. Yet that's the source of my uneasiness, I think. He was very healthy. The rest of his brain, the rest of his body—the heart and its plumbing, and so on—were textbook peachy. My inner voice tells me he was not the kind to have a cerebral hemorrhage. Anybody can have a cerebral hemorrhage at any time in his life, of course. But something simply tells me Bianco wasn't one of those anybodies. Know what I mean?"

"I'm bothered the same way."

There was a moment of silence.

"There were no signs of anything unusual at all, Captain?"

"Nothing at all. And because I felt uneasy I was especially careful in the process—the entire process. The only traces of violence or disruption were old ones: a knife laceration on the right thigh that had healed after stitching at least a year ago. A trace on the left arm that suggested a long-ago bullet graze. A scar on the right knee that had to date from childhood. Several heavy acne pits on the back of the neck. Internally, nothing. Chemical analysis, done here and in the Wiesbaden Air Force base hospital to speed things along: negative all the way. So, you see, despite our own inexplicable misgivings, Major Bianco, Ernesto M., died a natural death and the certificate will so state and his next of kin are being so notified and I'm so bored with this frigging place I'd like to go out and get pissy-assed drunk. Care to join me?"

"No thanks." He glanced around. "But I can see why this place oppresses you."

"They told me my office and lab would be ready at the 234th Base Hospital three weeks ago. It still isn't ready, and, mark my words, we'll be well into World War Three and I'll *still* be here in this rotten little Nazi pro station."

"Is that what it was?"

"Who knows? I tend toward extravagant statements. Especially when I'm bored."

Kaufmann pushed himself clear of the chair and, resettling the cap on his head, said, "Do me a favor, Olsen?"

"What might that be?"

"Use the time that weighs so heavily on you to think of ways in which our healthy Major Bianco might have been murdered. Let your imagination run. Push forensics to the outer limits. You come up with something, no matter how outlandish, call me. I'm in the USFET directory."

"Sure. Sounds like fun."

The captain walked Kaufmann past a stony-faced Nurse Fuller to jeepside in the shrapnel-pocked street. They traded sloppy salutes, then Kaufmann drove off in a cloud of blue smoke.

Autumn in Germany can be spectacular, and this day was so beautiful it hurt. Even the broken buildings, indecent with their splintered beams and toilet bowls dangling from tortured piping and framed pictures of Onkel und Tante crooked against exposed slabs of flowered wallpaper, suggested a sunlit Utrillo, and the countryside beyond, despite its vooming columns of army vehicles and its streams of refugees and displaced persons and German POWs wandering home, was an Eden of textures and colors that had no names. Kaufmann thought of his own country—the soft, rolling hills of southern Pennsylvania and the whitewashed houses dating from the Revolution and how he and his compatriots had trashed it with billboards and power poles and flickering neon, how historic byways had been lined with shaving soap rhymes and empty pop bottles and jettisoned condoms and cigarette wrappers and fields of rusted, junked cars. He missed it so badly his chest ached, but he wished he could be more proud of the way it looked.

What had his old man said so many times? Man is the only creature in the universe that craps in its own nest—and Americans are more manly than anybody.

He pulled the jeep into the choked driveway of the Air Force Annex, a rambling yellow thing strewn through a grove of ragtag trees, and parked it in a spot marked *General Office Only* on the theory that generals of the neighborhood were already on the golf course or squash courts. Besides, he had a basic philosophy that applied in this, as well as in most military situations: Screw them all. Sideways.

The receptionist here, a tiny WAAC sergeant, was a lot more cordial than Nurse Fuller had been. "Hi, Major. Want to sign up with the U.S. Army Air Force?"

"Not today. Actually I'm here on some business for the AC of S, G-2, over USFET way."

"Gee, sir," she said, "are you one of our spies?"

"I didn't have enough college credits. One more course in invisible ink and I could have made it."

"You belong in the Air Force. You're a guy who can kid around. We like that in our officers."

"I realize that she's probably on duty, but I have to see one of your staffers now."

"Who might that be, sir?"

"A tech sergeant name of Maggie Sunderman. She's assigned to Documents Processing, I think."

"O.K., let me check." Her merry brown eyes scanned an organization chart taped to her desk top, then she picked up a phone. "Give me DocProc, please." Pause. "Hi, Sergeant Williams, Main Reception. You have a tech sergeant Maggie Sunderman working there?" Pause. "O.K. Thanks."

She returned the phone to its cradle and gave him another smile. "Sunderman's at chow right now. Mess Hall B. Take the drive around this building and keep on until you get to a bombed-out chapel. Right there, go across the little bridge and B's on your left."

"You belong in G-2, Sergeant Williams. You're a very helpful young woman. Spies like that in their receptionists."

"Thank you, sir." She laughed.

He returned to the jeep and drove off on the specified route, but as he was crossing the narrow little bridge he met another jeep—this one heavily stenciled with Air Police markings and bearing a very large corporal with Air Police stenciled on his shiny helmet and an Air Police brassard on his left arm. The corporal was not at all pleased by the obstacle Kaufmann represented, and he said so.

"Hey, Major. Back up and get out of my way." His heavy features were florid.

"Hey, Corporal, who the hell are you talking to?"

"I got an emergency, Major. I'm in a hurry. So get the hell out of the way. Sir."

"What kind of an emergency?"

"None of your goddam business. Sir. Now back that

sumbish up and get out of my way or I'll haul you in for obstructing a policeman in his line of duty. Sir.''

"I was going to offer my help. But now you can stick it up your tooty. Corporal. And for the record, what's your name? Corporal. And your unit? Corporal.''

"Ransky, George P. Wiesbaden District, Air Police. Now get out of my fugg'n way so I can get to a phone.''

Kaufmann threw in the reverse gear and the jeep whined its way off the bridge. He watched, annoyed beyond words, as the corporal sped down the lane, jeep fishtailing in the gravel, to disappear around the bend.

He found Mess Hall B as described and went through the front door and into a large room aromatic with fried onions, coffee and Lysol. The noon rush was over, the tables sparsely populated by noshers and gabbers. He stood for a time, examining sleeves and faces for a tech sergeant who looked like a Maggie.

"Excuse me, Sergeant,'' he asked the prettiest one, "would you perchance be Maggie Sunderman?''

"No, sir. She left a bit ago. The mess sergeant came and told her she had a phone call at her quarters.''

"Is that far from here?''

"No, sir. Down the path outside, around the pond, and it's the building on the right. Building Forty-two.''

"Thanks. Bon appétit.''

He followed the directions and in Building 42 found the door labeled *T/Sgt Sunderman* in GI stenciling, and, nailed in a tidy joke directly below, a tin sign: *Men's Room*.

Sergeant Sunderman didn't answer his knock.

She was there, though.

Next to her bed, nude, except for panties and the GI dogtags on the chain around her neck.

Half sitting, half kneeling, a grotesque parody of prayer, her head and arms in an open footlocker.

Much blood on the bed, a pool of it on the floor around her. He felt her neck for a pulse. There was none.

He stood quietly, his gaze wandering slowly from detail to detail. He observed the exit wound between her shoulders, and, stooping, he could see a chest wound. It appeared that she had been shot in the chest, presumably by the .45 caliber GI pistol on the bed.

But why were her head, shoulders and arms slumped into that footlocker, which contained only underwear, pajamas, first-aid kit, a hair dryer, three C-ration tins, a can of PX tomato juice and a box of crackers?

Why were her dead hands clutching a C-ration can of pork and beans?

Why did he have the impression she was trying to tell him something?

He arose from his crouch, crossed the room and sat in the chair at the window. He waited a half hour for Ransky's cops to show. They never did, so he called the MPs on the phone in the hall.

TUESDAY
11 September 1945

4

Lt. Raines apparently had at last gotten through, because at 11 o'clock of an ordinary Tuesday her phone rang and Colonel Daley's secretary said the boss wanted her up there and would she please bring her file on the detention of Luftwaffe personnel or whatever it was that she'd mentioned in her memo of 22 August. She gathered the material irritably; she'd been trying so hard and long to get somebody to listen to her, the fact that somebody was now receptive threw her all out of plumb.

Inexplicably, and contrary to her contempt for self-deception, she sought to believe that her general peevishness had nothing to do with Major Kaufmann.

He was an unsettling fellow by any measure. After word of mouth had proclaimed him to be a snazzy intelligence officer, all cool and professional and replete with commendations and medals, he had proved to be, upon direct engagement, a genuine, platinum-plate, motor-driven screwball. Not so's you'd notice it right away, of course. He had quite a presence, in a somber, calm-eyed way, and his voice revealed education, self-confidence and just enough world-weariness to put him in there with, say, William Powell in those Thin Man movies, or maybe Ronald Coleman, or even her namesake, Claude Raines. All sort of dry-cleaned and clipped and suave. But then, right in the middle of a sensible, well-considered commentary he would come out—still somber, deadpan—with some goofy bit that would suggest a Bing Crosby–Bob Hope "Road" film.

After thinking about all this, she had settled on two reasons why Kaufmann distracted her. First, her father had been an entirely humorless man, given to periods of brooding and withdrawal—decompressive reaction, probably, to his angry and fruitless search for work in Depression-stunned Cleveland—and, probably in consequence, she had always been uncomfortable with, even suspicious of, men who joked around.

Of men, period.

Which melded into the second reason.

As a teen she had experienced what seemed to be a normal amount of daydreaminess and eroticism—hardly ever given overt expression, naturally, because her mother had warned her severely about the nastiness that can derive from "our animal natures." So her fantasy boyfriends were almost always modifications of the knights portrayed in the well-fingered volume of King Arthur and His Knights of the Round Table given to her at Christmas of 1932 by Goodwill Charities. Her heroes were uniformly noble of stature, and classically handsome, with long straight noses, cleft chins, large hazel eyes—serious, of course, but with a hint of jauntiness under restraint—and wavy golden hair that curled just so at the inviting nape. Because she was drawn to the theater (make that the movies), these dreamboats spoke in a theatrical baritone, vowels Englishy, consonants crisp, and when they mentioned love it was always in elevated syntax, most usually murmured against her ear, the way David Niven would do it. Through it all each would, in his own knightly way, perceive, honor, and help her to obey the

strictures against her "animal nature," the real-world result
being that her libido received hardly any physical exercise.

Until Sandy Metzger, the drama teacher at Randall High,
that is.

She'd been cast as the female lead in *Heart Heat*, a mystery drama written and directed by Sandy himself for the
senior class play. "As an actress you can be anything you
want to be," Sandy assured her in a private rehearsal at his
place one February night, "and what you must want to be
in this scene is a very proper woman suddenly so caught up
in mindless lust she is a patsy for blackmail and murder.
So when Henry takes you in his arms, react, for God's sake.
Don't just stand there and let him maul you. Maul him
back. Tear at him. Just before the blackout the audience
must see that your crotch is on fire. Here, let me show you.
Put your arms around me." Two hours later, she had staggered home, numb from lips to knees, half consumed by
guilt and half exhilarated by the acts that had caused it.
There had been a few subsequent "training sessions," and
the three nights of the play had broken all attendance records, thanks to her seething scene with Henry and the resultant shock waves that raced through conservative
Randalltown. Her mother had never really forgiven her "ex-
hibitionism." In the rage that followed her own eventual
discovery that Sandy had a wife in Erie, King Arthur and
his buddies had flown into the back-alley trashbin. But her
consolation was the understanding that she could, indeed,
be anything anybody expected her to be. So, after all this,
it was outrageous and incomprehensible that Kaufmann, who
was in no way appropriate to her long-term goals, could—
without intention, probably without even the slightest
awareness—represent Sandy Metzger II.

Damn.

Well, as she had with every other rotten surprise in her
life, she'd find a way to handle it. But right now she had a
more urgent problem.

When she was ushered into Colonel Daley's towering
presence, a squat, blue-jowled brigadier general was at his

side. Or, more exactly, at the window, rocking back and forth on his heels, hands behind his back, chest emblazoned with aviator's wings and ribbons, stars twinkling on his porky shoulders. Not sure which officer she should salute, she clicked her heels, OCS style, and threw a highball at the autographed photo of Douglas MacArthur on the wall roughly between them.

"Lieutenant Raines, reporting as ordered, sir."

"Ah, yes, Raines," Colonel Daley cooed, as he always cooed when higher rank was within earshot. "You're surely aware that this officer is Brigadier General William T. Vickery, chief, Special Aviation Projects. He stopped by to say hello to me, his, ha-ha, greatest admirer, and while we were chatting he expressed an interest in meeting you."

"Pleasure, sir."

The general, speaking around the wet stub of a cigar clamped between his large jaws, said, "At ease, Lieutenant. Take a seat."

She sat on a chair, file folder on her proper lap.

The general pointed the cigar at the folder. "Is that the material on the Luftwaffe people?"

"Yes, sir."

"What does it say?"

"Would the general like to read it, sir?"

"The general doesn't like to read anything, Raines. Tell me what it says. And keep it short. The general doesn't like orations, either."

"In carrying out my regular duties, sir, I discovered a peculiar pattern. Somebody has been screening aircrews from among the Luftwaffe personnel still in our detention camps and sending them to a new and unlisted camp near Dijon. When I asked for explanation or clarification from the pertinent commands, I received none. I wrote a report to G-2, USFET, and to A-1, 8th Air Force, at Wiesbaden, mainly just to be sure somebody knew about it." She was now at the threshold of the Tech Sergeant Maggie Sunderman complication. She fell into a silent watchfulness, inwardly cursing the heat she felt in her cheeks. The bane of her existence was her tendency to blush, often without apparent cause. Right now, though, there was cause enough: she was deliberately withholding information from a general officer, and her gamble was that he'd neither tumble to that fact nor even pursue the whole damned matter any further than needed to close it out. And, beyond that transcendentally important reason, there was this annoying sidebar issue: his manner and looks. He was one of those men who look at women as if they're zoo exhibits. Besides, his hair was slicked down with pomade, and one of her first lessons at Llewelyn Theater Practicum (*four hours a week; lab fees, $15*) told her that if the script called for a tyrannical tycoon she'd better give the character shiny, plastered-down hair. The fact that this was a real-life tyrannical tycoon—in officer's pinks and greens—was unmistakable.

So let him use those cute little silver wings to go fly a kite, eh?

The general and the colonel waited. Then Vickery waved the cigar and grated: "That's all?"

"Yes, sir. As short as I can make it."

General Vickery's eyes turned to the ceiling in exasperation. "Young woman, don't you realize what's going on? We have just won a war against the Nazis. As victors, we are presently in a process of socially acceptable plundering. Within the proprieties established by the Hague Convention, we can steal the Nazis' factories, know-how, formulas, cash—whatever the hell we find useful. Hell-oh-dear, we're right now packing up and shipping Stateside every bottle-glasses German rocket scientist we can find so that maybe we can learn how to build those V-weapons the Nazis used to blister the Limeys with. Our Intelligence people are shipping straight to guess where, special delivery, that Kraut General Gehlen, who headed up the Abwehr's Foreign Armies East and all the spooks who spied on the Russkies for him. Nazi airplanes, U-boats, tanks, artillery—military hardware right on down to condoms that feel like you're riding bareback"—Colonel Daley tittered and clucked his tongue here—"are right now on their way to the U.S. of A.

for deep-dish analysis. And you get all steamed up over a few Kraut flyboys who are probably being wrung out for what they know? Please, dear, stop playing detective and go back to your paperclip shuffling.''

Her face turned incandescent. In some unlikely reflex, she looked to Colonel Daley for whatever amelioration he might devise to soften the general's insulting treatment of a servicewoman. She could have spared herself the effort. Colonel Daley's expression bespoke amused toleration, as if General Vickery had just straightened out a bratty child.

She placed the file under her arm and stood to attention. ''Will that be all, then, sir?''

''I guess so. You got anything, Daley?''

''Oh, no, sir. You've wrapped it all up most neatly, I'd say. We in Personnel often fail to get the Big Picture, working as we do on a single aspect of the military effort. I'm sure Raines will no longer meddle in affairs that aren't her province. I'll see to that, of course.''

''You ought to have some orientation classes for your people, or something. Can't afford to have tootsies sitting around, not knowing what the hell the real soldiers are up to. Who knows? They learn a little something, they just might be of some help. Right?''

''Right, General. Very right.''

''O.K., Raines. You're dismissed. And stay the hell away from Air Force matters, you hear?''

''Yes, sir.'' She saluted and strode from the office, certain that her face was leaving a trail of steam. Under her breath, she muttered, ''Stick it up your heinie, Fatso.''

She was even angrier when she reached her office. After throwing the file on her desk, she dialed his number.

''Major Kaufmann's phone. Sergeant Willard speaking.''

''Is he there, Sergeant? This is Lieutenant Raines of G-1 Personnel Records.''

''No, ma'am, he's out right now. He told the Duty Desk he'll be in Frankfurt and Wiesbaden, returning before five this p.m. Can I give him a message?''

She thought for a moment. It wouldn't do to leave her

bachelor officers' quarters number because it might look social, and she didn't want anyone—sergeants who answer phones, Duty Desks, whatever—to get any wrong ideas.

Damn, damn, *damn*.

"No, thanks, Sergeant. Just ask him to call me at my office tomorrow. Extension twenty-three-three-thirty-two."

She hung up and sat staring at the wall for a time.

General Vickery paused at the door to his staff car. Leaning, he peered in at the corporal behind the wheel. "Take a little walk, will you, Price? I want a few private words with Colonel Daley."

The man yawned, swung out of the car and sauntered down the tree-lined drive. Arrogant son of a bitch, Vickery thought, watching him for a moment. Now that there was a demob on, every frigging enlisted man, from yardbird to thirty-year topkick, was acting as if he'd just been elected to Congress. Which wasn't too far off the mark, come to think of it. They might not have been elected *to* Congress, but they had the next best thing, what with Congress kissing their asses—blindly, indiscriminately—in the name of re-election. So what the hell else could you expect, eh?

Daley coughed against his fist, gently, a schoolmarm soliciting the principal's attention. "Something up, sir?"

Vickery's gaze, indifferent, just short of contemptuous, turned to the colonel, who stood squinting in the afternoon sun's glare, smile prissy, uniform exuding a faint air of old sweat and Old Spice.

They went back a long way, the two of them, to the first war and Spads over Chateau-Thierry and the Argonne. They were shavetails then, fresh out of Kelly Field and still under the misapprehension that heroism, if survived, was the route to the top. What Vickery hadn't realized was that heroism is expected, it's what the soldier is paid to deliver, and to achieve apotheosis in the military one must be not only heroic but also chic. He had shot down his share of Fokkers and received a proper and discussible wound in his right calf and a respectable number of ribbons, but officers with fewer victories and less time at the front got a lot more press and faster promotions, thanks to Stateside social connections or muscular bank accounts. And after the Armistice and into the twenties and thirties, when the army was cut to nothing and there wasn't enough money to buy gas for the few obsolete puddle-jumpers left to fly, he had been frozen in rank as a first looey, the exec officer of a maintenance squadron in Middletown, Pennsyl-goddam-vania. But this asshole, this Daley, had wobbled all over the French sky, shooting at everything and hitting nothing and cracking up four of the squadron's planes, finally getting sent to Blois and reclassification, losing his aviator's wings and any reasonable hopes for promotion, only to demonstrate that if your family owns California you can rise, not only above the disgrace but into the War Department's Washington zoo. As a soldier, Daley would make a good streetcar conductor, but the army had kept him on and eventually promoted him to colonel, the highest rank available to a back-alley Washington bean-counter with connections. Daley was a nothing, and the only person this side of Yokohama who didn't know that was Daley himself. But even horse manure has its use, Vickery reminded himself now, and so he got on with the shoveling.

"What do you know about this Colonel Donleavy, Herb?"

"The fellow who's just been named to understudy G-2?"

"That's the one."

Daley's slitted eyes became indirect as his mind rummaged through possible answers. "Well," he said after a time, "the man's a comer. He's risen pretty fast, as I recollect. The usual field stuff—Infantry School, the obligatory tour with troops, some infantry division or other, then a quick sidestep into War Plans, State Department Liaison, some European embassy work as an attaché, I think, a faculty stint at the War Department Intelligence Training Center at Camp Ritchie, and eventual assignment to the General Staff as an intelligence research chief. Now, apparently, when G-2 himself has been ZI'ed, Donleavy will replace him. Which means Ike will have somebody very much like himself advising him on intelligence matters. Donleavy's Washington tour showed him to be very social, very, ah, political. Always at the right parties, always seen in the right restaurants with the rich and mighty. That kind of thing.''

''Does he come from money himself?''

''Heavens, no. Son of immigrants, poor as Job's turkey. Came up from ROTC in some dreary land grant college in the midwest. But he's smart, I hear. Great at analyzing complex situations, stating them in simple language. You know. The kind of thing the top dogs dote on.''

Vickery thought about that for an interval.

''May I ask why you're interested in Colonel Donleavy, sir? I mean, I can ask around some more—''

''That's precisely what I don't want you to do. We haven't even had this conversation. Know what I mean?''

''Of course, General.''

''But there's one thing I want you to do. Very quietly. I want you to keep me advised on Donleavy's comings and goings. I want you to tell me about anything unusual he does or says. I want to know everything about the son of a bitch, and I want to know it when it happens.''

Daley's pale face showed surprise. ''But—well—you realize, don't you, sir, that I'm in G-1. I have no way to keep close tabs on anybody in G-2. I mean, really—''

''Come off it, Herb. You're shacking up with that WAAC captain who's slated to be Donleavy's secretary, the one with the red hair and big tits who's been answering phones for the District Constabulary commander in Bad Nauheim. Hell, you pitched her for the Donleavy job yourself.''

Daley had the look of a boy whose daddy had just caught him reading a dirty book. ''Well, I must say, sir—''

''Oh, knock off that offended-innocence crap, will you? You've been pranging that broad since London, and I've got invoices that show you've spent eleven grand on love nests, one right in Hyde-goddam-Park, complete with maids.''

"I don't see where any of that is your business—"

"It sure ain't, Herb. But I'm going to make it your momma's business if you don't give me what I need. And you know how your momma—the lady with all the millions—is going to take that. Especially in view of your engagement to the daughter of her best friend."

Daley appeared to be trying to swallow a basketball. "Why—why are you saying these things, General? Why are you being like this? I thought I was your friend—"

"Of course you're my friend, you horse's ass. And you're going to help me, the way friends are supposed to help each other. I'm just reminding you that you'd better keep honest and diligent about it."

"Through *blackmail*? I mean—"

"Blackmail, hell. A string around your finger that says, 'Keep in good with Momma today, Herb. Tell Vickery what your WAAC mattress has picked up around her shop.' "

The colonel's misery was abject. "Why? I mean, why do you want to know about Donleavy—"

"Let's just say I don't like the way Donleavy has ass-kissed his way into Influence Country, and I'm going to fix his wagon. O.K.?"

"The way you've fixed me. Right, General?"

"Hell, no, Herb. Not that way. I *like* you."

Daley peered off at the mountains, his face puckered. "I'd like to go now, sir. May I be dismissed?"

"One more thing. I want a couple people ZI'ed—sent home for separation. One has beaucoup points. Name is Kaufmann. A major working for G-2."

"As I say, I'm not in G-2—"

"You'll think of something. The other is that broad Raines. I don't like the way she and Kaufmann have been trying to plow on my farm, and I want both their asses out of Europe. Call me when you've done it—and route the call through Frankfurt Zentrum, patching through to Wiesbaden, then to my line, codename Hotdog. Got that?"

"Yes, sir."

Vickery turned and called down the road. "Price, get your GI ass back here and crank up this goddam flivver. I got work to do."

FOR YOUR EYES ONLY!

File No. 373841B   11 Sept 45

To: Brandt
From: Gladiator

Subject: Operation "Tailspin"

1. Sunderman and Bianco have been negated—
   Sunderman by suicide, Bianco by cerebral
   hemorrhage.

2. Minor complication: Maj. R. L. Kaufmann, CI
   officer, G-2 German Desk, USFET, apparently
   energized by the fact that Bianco died while—or
   shortly after—conversing with him, has begun a
   freelance investigation of certain aspects of
   "Tailspin."

3. 1st Lt. Molly Raines, G-1, USFET, having
   apparently stumbled on POW ploy, has been
   writing memos and asking questions.

4. While Raines is a mere busybody, Kaufmann is
   extremely capable and well thought of in Theater
   intelligence community. Shall we bring him in?
   Please advise.

FOR YOUR EYES ONLY!

FOR YOUR EYES ONLY!

File No. 233784C   12 Sept 45

To: Gladiator
From: Brandt

Subject: Operation "Tailspin"

1. Imperative that Kaufmann and Raines be blocked or neutralized. Please handle soonest. Most urgent.

2. "Licorice," on station in Dijon, has exploited social overtures made by Maj. Gen. F. M. Bascomb, War Crimes Investigations, and will accompany him to Udine, Italy, area, for interviews with Louis P. Stahl, American oil magnate and movie producer. Stahl, in Udine to check his real estate holdings, is notorious as a behind-the-scenes adventurer who shuns the limelight or the slightest invasion of his privacy. Even so, "Licorice" hopes to establish an amiable relationship with Stahl via Luigi Fortunato, Italian film celebrity and an old friend and business associate of Stahl. "Licorice" hopes to exploit Stahl's knowledge of Udine-Friuli area.

FOR YOUR EYES ONLY!

FRIDAY
14 September 1945

5

Captain Nick Anton, late of the 222nd Bomb Group, United States Army 8th Air Force, and now the leading beer drinker and solitaire player of the Nassauer Hof, an ornate 19th-century hotel that served as both architectural keystone and spiritual lodestone of the 17th Replacement Center and ZI Staging Base, Bad Schwalbach im Taunus, examined his tongue in the mirror, then, after regarding his face as a general mass, sighed and said with considerable despair, "The Red-eyed Baron."

It had been a bitter night.

He had been at his table by the front window of the hotel lounge, shuffling the cards for the thirty-first game of the day, when through the plate glass he'd seen Sammy Reynolds coming down twilit Adolf Hitler Strasse in one of those huge black Mercedes-Benz touring cars favored by Nazi Gauleiters. Sammy was in the back, very drunk, of course, and flanked by two women who, given helmets instead of the flowered hats they wore, could have been taken for Nazi Gauleiters. The driver was Frank Thomas, who

had served since D-Day as Sammy's wingman in the 87th
Fighter Squadron, and who had, like Sammy, become a
double-dip ace with ten kills and a footlocker full of medals, and was this day, again like Sammy, googly-eyed drunk.
Anton could tell this by the way the big Mercedes climbed
an azalea embankment and came to rest in the Kurpark
across the street, and by the way Frank rolled out the door
and onto the grass.

Joyful at seeing familiar, wonderful old faces again, Anton had run to the scene and there was much back-slapping
and Sammy's elaborate introductions of what sounded like
Frawlein Shitz and Frawlein von Superman. It turned out
that Sammy and Frank were on their way to Fürstenfeldbruck, an air base near Munich, to try out some captured
Kraut fighters—those new things that had no propellers and
were moved around by blasts of air, like squizzering dime-
store balloons. They had heard he was doing some rotting
away at Bad Schwalbach and had decided to take a Thursday
en route to look him up and say howdy, and here, by God,
they were, thanks to the generosity of fun-loving Frawlein
von Superman, whose daddy, a former Gestapo chieftain
now on permanent vacation in South America, had left her
the car.

Civilian women weren't allowed in the Nassauer Hof, so
Sammy and Frank had patted the Frawleins on their ample
backsides, returned the car keys, and stood mid-street, waving and throwing kisses as the ladies drove off toward
Wiesbaden. Then they'd come here to his quarters, a
second-floor room, large and airy, on the balcony overlook-
ing the fountain and pool in the rear courtyard, and launched
a heavy-caliber drinking party. Sadly, the hotel was occupied mostly by G-2 creatures—weary old spies and grubby
counter-intelligence agents who were awaiting reassignment
or shipment home—and most of these were ground army
personnel, intolerant of flyboy ebullience and tales of aerial
derring-do, illustrated by much sweeping of hands through
arcs and zooms and rat-a-tat-tats. After Sammy's third nar-
ration of a spectacular escape from thirty Messerschmitts

while upside down twenty thousand feet over Mannheim, four of the guests—a major of artillery, a captain of infantry and two second johns from 3rd Armored—had picked Sammy up, carried him to the balcony and thrown him into the air above the fountain, crying, "Let's see you fly now, you brag-ass son of a bitch!" When Sammy returned to the room, dripping, a hellish fight had broken out, not with fists but with pillows from the various nearby bedrooms, and it had required a squad of MPs, groping through a blizzard of feathers and water-filled condoms, to end the festivities.

Sammy and Frank were this morning en route to Fürstenfeldbruck under guard and Nick Anton was confined to the hotel, thanks to the chickenshit light colonel who served as overseer of the Nassauer Hof and its transients.

He had one clean uniform—his Class A's. The green jacket and pink slacks and knit necktie and brass thingumbobs made him look like a bit player in *The Student Prince*, he thought, but after a shave and further contemptuous remarks before the mirror, he had to admit to feeling almost human. He was adjusting his tie when the little Kraut kid who served as bellhop and runner announced from the doorway that he had a visitor and would he please go to the hotel lounge? The Herr Major Kaufmann, a very important-looking Offizier from Hauptquartier in Frankfurt, was waiting at table three.

Kaufmann looked like one of those brass-hat bastards who talk with clenched teeth and never get ruffled and carry briefcases, even in latrines. He never smiled and was so cleaned and pressed he squeaked. But he might be—just might, oh God please let him be—a way out of this godawful boredom, this day in and day out of solitaire and watery Kraut beer in this nowhere goddam excuse for a Saratoga Springs.

"What can I do for you, Major?"

"Sit down, Anton. Drink or something?"

"You wouldn't happen to have a gallon or two of Johnnie Walker Red in that briefcase of yours, would you?"

"Hung over?"

"Funny you should ask."

Kaufmann reached for his briefcase, set carefully beside his chair. "It's not a gallon and it's not Scotch. But it's a flask of rather decent cognac and if that waiter over there will get us some glasses, I think you might revive."

"For a headquarters bastard you're a nice kind of bastard."

"How did you know I was from headquarters?"

"Even the Kraut bellhop guessed that one. All you joadies look alike."

Kaufmann nodded, seeming to give that serious thought. When the drinks had been poured and Anton had managed to light and survive the initial assault on the first Lucky Strike of the day, the visitor looked out the window and said, "Your two-oh-one file says you are multi-lingual."

"I shpik savan lengviches, und of zeese, Anglish ze bast."

"The record shows French, German, Dutch, Italian, Spanish, Polish and Russian—thanks to a daddy who took you and your mother with him on his duties as an overseas executive of Standard Oil."

"I've got a good ear. I pick up fast. Most kids learn languages fast. And I went to good schools."

"So ist es wahr, dass Sie dienliches Deutsch sprechen?"

"Keineswegs. Heute kann ich gerade genug um mich verständlich zu machen."

"Sind Sie erfahrener Flugzeugführer?"

"Eigentlich Bomberpilot. Ich bin sowohl theoretisch wie praktisch aussergewöhnlich begabt."

"All right. You can brag equally well in Russian?"

"I suppose. Why? And who the hell are you to come around, asking personal questions about my speaking habits?"

"I'm a counter-intelligence officer with G-2, USFET. I am shopping for an officer who might give me a hand on a rather sticky matter involving Germans."

Anton blew a stream of smoke at the ceiling. "So here we go. This is why somebody snaffled me out of the 8th

Air Force and stuck me in this goddam jail. I was minding my own business, happily grubbing through life as a B-17 conductor, and all of a sudden I'm needed in Berlitz.''

Kaufmann studied the brandy in his glass. ''A minor correction, Captain. All of a sudden, now that Germany and Japan have both surrendered, almost all B-17 pilots are unemployed. Those who have enough missions or service points are allowed to go home. Those who do not are being held in the armies of occupation for whatever service is deemed necessary. Some are still flying in various capacities, of course, but most are grounded. I can tell you, for instance, of at least three bomber pilots who are today serving as billeting and mess officers in obscure Tyrolean villages.''

Anton felt an inner draining, as if someone had pulled a chain somewhere behind his fancy brass buckle. ''You're joking, of course.''

Kaufmann shook his head.

''Mess officer? Like in tablecloths and KP?''

Kaufmann nodded.

''So what's on your mind, Major?''

''Let's take a walk. We can be overheard here.''

''I'm confined to quarters.''

''I've arranged to have that order lifted.''

Anton was impressed. ''You got clout, eh?''

''Bushels.''

''Would I be working for you?''

''Come on. I'll tell you about the first step.''

They crossed to the Kurpark and followed its walks to the hulking, filigreed Kurhaus, then through the arcade of the Weinbrunnen and finally to the music pavilion lagoon, where they took a bench. The war had treated most of these things with relative kindness. There was a general seediness, what with weedy flowerbeds and untrimmed walks and a marked need of paint everywhere. But there had been only a few air attacks—these apparently limited to strafing runs by Smilin' Jacks emptying their guns on the run for home—and so the damage was mainly a matter of bullet holes in masonry that could be caulked and painted over in a morning, whenever caulking and paint became once again part of life in the cindered Reich.

"You've been poking around in my records, then." Anton was still vaguely irritated by this.

"Did you know that you are among a mere handful of American-born pilots of multi-engine military airplanes who are fluent in several languages?"

"Gloryosky."

"The fact is, very little poking around was required. You stand out like a wart on a baby's behind. A few others on the list have been discharged, or are fighter pilots, or in the Far East, or too old, or too something. You are an expert—so expert you were held in the States as an instructor, rather than being sent to the 8th Air Force, as were most of your contemporaries. And only after much fussing, including letters of intervention by your old man, who apparently holds markers on some Very Important Politicians, were you cleared for overseas."

"Arriving in time to see the end credits rolling down the screen. And now fate sets me up for a job counting salt shakers and onions in some billet in Kraphaus am Rhein. Oh, pain. Oh, woe. Oh, sorrow. Oh, shit."

Kaufmann brushed some lint from the jacket of his immaculate uniform. "Well, you've got gainful employment now if you want it."

"You need multi-engine, I guess there's some flying in this here job of yorn."

"My rough planning calls for some. How much is still unclear."

"What kind of equipment?"

"Bombers. Which kind is still to be determined."

"Unclear. Still to be determined. Don't you G-2 hotshots ever know anything for sure?"

"Certainly. We know for sure that we don't know anything for sure."

"When do I report for work?"

Kaufmann leaned over, flipped the catches on his briefcase and withdrew a packet with Top Secret stamped in red across the binder. He took out a sheaf of mimeographed pages and handed them to Anton. "Right now."

The flier fingered the pages gingerly, rolling his eyes in mock anxiety. "Oo. I'm afraid to look."

"Are you always like this, Anton?"

"Like what?"

"Silly."

"You bet. You don't think any truly serious person would be able to stand the army, do you? Armies and wars are the silliest idea ever to hit the cosmos. To endure, a soldier must match or exceed the silliness he sees around him. That is the secret of my success as a warrior. You are free to share in it if you wish."

"Get your gear and put it in the G-2 jeep parked by the hotel hitching post. Those papers advise you and authorized personnel that you've been tapped for special duty with Postwar Planning Branch, American Military Government."

"What in hell is that?"

"That's you and me, actually. For now, at least."

"Where am I going?"

"To school. A very private school near Dijon, where you'll be learning how to be a German flight officer languishing in an American prisoner of war camp."

"Now *you* are being silly."

Kaufmann stood, took up his briefcase and nodded toward the hotel. "Let's go."

Lieutenant Raines met him at the Transient Officers' PX near the Bahnhofsplatz as arranged, and they stood by the raingear racks, riffling through field coats and slickers and pretending small talk between acquaintances.

"Are you all right, Raines?"

"I think so. I'm still having the creeps over the Maggie Sunderman thing. I keep looking over my shoulder."

"There's been a development there. While I was being questioned by the MPs, I picked up a hint that Maggie wasn't exactly what she was supposed to be. Or, more accurately, she was more than what she was supposed to be. I did some listening. Maggie was a special auditor, doing a special audit on Air Force hardware."

"An auditor? Maggie?"

"Yep. On secret orders, yet. She wasn't assigned to USFET—or even the Air Force or its European ancillaries. It seems she'd been imported and planted, very special delivery, direct from Washington."

"You're joking."

"Why does everybody think I'm joking? Do I look comical or something?"

"It's just a saying."

"Well, I'd appreciate it if you'd stop using it around me."

"Sure." She sought to apply some balm, asking with a touch of concern, "Did the police question you for a long time?"

"This was the second violent death with me in the picture, so they were curious, of course. But I had a lot of backup from receptionists and other locals, so they were pretty quick to decide what they'd already decided to decide, to wit: Maggie Sunderman, having decided on suicide, lay on her bed, shot herself once in the chest— Detective Fallon says women who shoot themselves rarely shoot themselves in the head because it ruins their hairdos or something—and then, deciding she'd made a booboo, tried to pull a first aid kit from her footlocker. A wasted effort, to be sure. Using a GI bandage on a wound like hers would have been like patching a blown-out truck tire with john paper and library paste."

"The whole idea's preposterous. She was too perky, too alive, too droll and smart and cute. If she committed suicide, I'm a . . ." Raines groped unsuccessfully for a figure.

Kaufmann nodded. "I agree. I think she was murdered. Shot while lying on the bed. The killer tried to make it look like suicide, leaving the pistol and what not. But Maggie hung on long enough to make a try for the phone in the hall. She didn't make it. She fell into her open footlocker and died."

"Did you tell the police that, Major?"

"Odd thing, that. I bumped into an AP who was roaring away from the scene in a jeep. He said he was going for help. I waited for a half hour, but no police showed and I had to call them myself. Which is another odd thing. If I could call from the hall phone, why couldn't the AP? Why did he have to go running off to find the cops? When he is a cop. And as a cop, he has a radio in his jeep. So what was all the horse manure about 'going for help'? I later called Wiesbaden Air Police to learn more about the guy and they said they'd never heard of him."

She shuddered, but said nothing.

He said, "I'm going to request your transfer to G-2."

She glanced at him, curious. "Why?"

"I want you to work in Central Registry, where they keep dossiers on Nazi bigshots, spies, war criminals, and other all-round good fellows. I want your personnel experience to be working on personnel I'm interested in and I don't want you wandering around town where I can't keep an eye on you."

"Do you think I'm in danger?"

"No more than Maggie Sunderman was, I suppose."

"That's got to be the creepiest thing I've heard in weeks! Thanks so much for cheering me up, Major Kaufmann."

He took a field jacket from the rack and held it to the light from the window. "Do you think this is me?"

MONDAY
17 September 1945

6

Kaufmann had spent most of the weekend with the MPs and the CID—answering their questions, giving depositions, explaining himself and his world to beefy men with stained teeth and cynical expressions who were openly disappointed when they could find no way to cause him lasting pain. None are entirely innocent in the eye of the preacher, rooted as he is in the concept of Original Sin, or of the cop, intrinsically a moralist who, by witnessing so much depravity day in and day out, inevitably inverts to the amorality in which the man who is not a liar and thief is the exception that must be identified and proved. So, as an Original Sinner in the adjacency of a felony, Kaufmann had found himself struggling against the basic judgmental forces of the universe.

After advising him to remain generally available, the criminal investigators had freed him to go about his business. And just what his business was remained tantalizingly unclear, since he was still operating on a soldier's uneasiness and on hunches whose origins lay in a trio of suspicious deaths. It was now past time to give these ethereal naggings some substance, and toward this end he had recruited Hair's-breadth Harry Anton, prototypical daredevil ace, and Molly Raines, a Louisa May Alcott eyelash-batter with brains. Hardly an impressive host, but he had learned ages ago that a slingshot well used can be more effective than artillery. The key element, of course, lay in that term ''well used''—and it was an element that was entirely up to him to provide.

He began where he'd always begun: with the files. In this case, unhappily, he had no idea which files pertained, so he went to Central Registry and took out the root folders— Balkans, General; Balkans, Unrest; Balkans, Politics; Balkans, Economy; Balkans, German Invasion of; Balkans, Resistance Groups; Balkans, Soviet Influence; Balkans, Miscellaneous; Balkans, Links with Udine-Friuli Provinces and Alpine Italy; being just to the northwest of Trieste, the latter were, in the Army's wisdom, lumped in with the Balkan Desk. For convenience, and to allow himself an excuse to be away from the eerie silence of his office, he did his reading at a table beside a window in a corner of the great file room. In a segment on the Soviet involvement with the partisans in Northern Italy he came upon references to ''sunrise.'' References only; no discussion, no expansion, no explanation, the mere word. It hung there, as if something previous and something subsequent had been deleted. A kind of suspension of syntax.

He stared at the word for a time. Bianco had mentioned ''Sunrise.'' Last winter's attempt by SS General Wolff to turn over his command to American agents in Bern. His own attention at the time had been focused exclusively on the location and capture of General Gehlen, so he'd only skimmed the daily advisories on ''Sunrise'' and had even then considered it to be a flash in the pan. Wolff was a political hack, an opportunist, and if Dulles thought he would get anything substantial from that Nazi kook he was pumping clouds.

He checked, but the Operations Files held no folders on

"Sunrise." Nor on "C-rations," that mysterious term that had crept into Maggie Sunderman's discourse with Raines. Ditto on "Balkan Personalities." Annoyed, he stared anew at the enigmatic code-names. Then, as sudden as a hiccup, an idea. He turned to the index and "Contributor Names."

Ha.

The missing "Sunrise" segment had been written by that old chow hound, Bianco, Maj. Ernesto; OSS, Bern.

He was sitting there, wondering why Bianco had feigned a lack of knowledge on the Dulles– "Sunrise" incident when he had been invited by the Central Registry Chief to author a file insert on it. He was mulling over the significance of this when Pfc Adeline Muncy, AKA "Poopsie," approached his table, blinked her bespectacled green eyes and whispered—they tended to whisper in Central Registry because, apparently, to do so strengthened the facility's effort to resemble a library—that he had a phone call at the main desk.

It was the duty sergeant, a retired halfback named Timkins. "Hey, Major Kaufmann, guy's trying to reach you."

"What guy?"

"Medic name of Olsen. He says he wanted you to come to his office—you know where. He's got something you might want to know about."

"Did he say when to come?"

"Just the fasted the bestest."

"O.K. Any other calls?"

"One other, sir. A Lieutenant Raines, Personnel. She says it's nothing important—she'll call back tomorrow."

"Right. Thanks."

"Oops. Just a sec, Major. Your line's lighting up again." There was a click.

He waited.

"You still there, sir?"

"Yep."

"It was Colonel Donleavy, the G-2's special aide. He wants you to come to his office at sixteen-thirty hours."

"Did he say why?"

"Colonels never explain anything to sergeants, sir."

"To majors, either."

"Yeah. I guess so." The sergeant chuckled politely.

"Put me down as off the compound for two hours. I'm going to see Olsen, and he's downtown."

"Yes, sir. And don't forget sixteen-thirty."

"Right, Ma."

He hung up, and stood, thinking.

The after-lunch traffic was horrible, what with a convoy of six-by-sixes and three flatbed tank transporters that had hung up at the Opernhaus intersection of Reuter Weg and the Bockenheimerlandstrasse, but at last he made it to the clinic.

The Valkyrie queen was still at her desk.

"Captain Olsen is expecting me, Fuller."

She was much more cordial this time. He could tell, because she spoke without narrowing her eyes. "I know."

Olsen was reading *Stars and Stripes*, feet on the tin desk, magnifying glasses on his nose. "Hey," he said, looking up. "Is that you, Kaufmann?"

"How come you're reading the newspaper with your binoculars?"

"The news is awful. I'd only get more depressed if it was actually in focus. But I should keep informed, you know. So I compromise."

"You are one mad doctor."

"Let's go out and get drunk."

"Is that all you think about?"

"No, I think about sex, too. But also without any measurable results."

"If that's why you want to see me, I'll have to say no. It's my time of the month."

Olsen sighed in mock disappointment, then opened the center drawer in his desk and withdrew a manila mailing envelope. "Friend of mine is on the staff of the Wiesbaden base hospital and works part time as medical examiner—

coroner to you—and he was on duty the night they did the autopsy on that young woman noncom found shot to death in her quarters. A—ah—''

"Tech Sergeant Maggie Sunderman."

"Right. Well, he and I had split a bottle of Haig and Haig the night before, and I told him about you and your problems with those police grubs. I wasn't going to tell him because I'm one guy who can keep a secret, but he pried it out of me because I'm very vulnerable to Haig and Haig and he was really impressed that I was friends with somebody in G-2 who speaks German and all that, because the only people around him were brag-ass fighter pilots and a corps of teetotaling nurses wearing chastity belts."

"What's your friend's name?"

"Bill Riley. First looey. Helluva good forensic man."

Kaufmann took out his pad and made a note. "So what is all this to me?"

"Well, although I must stress that I'm no common gossip, I told Bill of our conversation and your concerns and like that, and how you asked me to keep on the lookout for anything that might pertain to the Bianco case. When he was getting ready to do the Sunderman autopsy he saw your name in the police report, and he thought that, since you and I were collaborating on Bianco, we might find his findings re Sunderman to have some linkage. Anyhow, he took these pictures in the hopes they'd be useful." He handed the envelope across the desk.

There were three glossies, eight-by-tens. They provided three views of a naked female derriere—a pair of buttocks that would have been quite handsome if it hadn't been for the harsh examining-table lighting and the twin bruises at the apex of their upward sweep.

"Maggie's?"

Olsen nodded. "Yep."

"So?"

"So she'd been brought in as a suicide. Bill says she warn't no suicide nohow."

"How does Bill know that?"

Olsen retrieved the photos and placed them on the desk. Using a pencil point, he designated the bruises. "These abrasions and contusions were fresh. They occurred at about the time of death."

"Maybe she got them while rolling off the bed."

"Wrong-o. To leave marks like that, Maggie's rear end had to have hit the board floor with glancing force. Those marks, along with embedded pine splinters and GI cotton panty fibers, and with an abrasion on her shoulder and a bump on the back of her head, suggest strongly that somebody threw her down violently a very short time—Bill guesses less than ten minutes—before she was shot."

"Sexual assault, maybe?"

"Wrong again. No evidence on or in the body of any recent sexual activity. Investigation suggests she was surprised while preparing for a shower, was knocked down, held on the bed, and shot once at close range by the pistol found at the scene." Olsen nodded at the envelope. "Bill put the MP investigator's report in there with the pix. He stole you a copy. I read it, too. Yecch."

"This Bill sounds like a real wonderful fellow. Would you please tell him I owe him a bottle of Haig and Haig?"

"With pleasure. He is indeed a fine man." Olsen added, "Except that he cheats at gin rummy."

He had five minutes to spare before his meeting with Colonel Donleavy so he dialed her office.

"Lieutenant Raines."

"You rang, madam?"

"Hello there. I appreciate your returning my call, sir."

"Is somebody there with you?"

"No. Why?"

"You sound as if you're talking to the King of England."

"Well, I respect you—"

"But how about in the morning, after I've given you my body?"

She made a small laughing sound. "You're the limit—"

"So what's on your mind?"

"I wanted you to know your request to have me transferred to G-2 as associate librarian, Central Registry, has been turned down. My boss, Colonel Daley, won't allow it. Just like that. The request came through and he said no."

"Did he give a reason?"

"He says AR Number-Something requires my immediate shipment Stateside." She sighed. "I'm sort of disappointed."

"So am I. More than somewhat." He thought about this for a moment. "By the way, Raines, are you all right?"

"All right?"

"No strange events? No taps at the door? No footsteps in the night?"

"If there have been, Major, I've been sleeping too soundly to notice. You wouldn't believe how soundly I've slept the last couple of nights. I hit the sack at twilight and go right through until reveille. I've never done that in my life."

"Good. Just let me know if anything bothers you."

"I'm fine. Honest."

He rang off and went down the corridor to Colonel Donleavy's office, which was only slightly larger than Radio City Music Hall. The WAAC—the sign on her desk said she was Captain Benet—gave him the kind of smile one would expect to see on the face of a redhead whose job it is to guard the gates of the Source of Incredible Power. She told him to go right in, the colonel was expecting him.

He went in and saluted the large man behind the mahogany aircraft carrier in the far corner of the room. "Major Kaufmann reporting as ordered, sir."

"Ah, good, good. Glad to see you, Kaufmann. G-2 speaks very warmly of you, and I'm happy at last to make your acquaintance. Sit down." He waved toward a huge wing chair that faced the desk.

"Welcome aboard, sir. You've joined a good bunch." He sat, almost disappearing in a sea of leather.

Colonel Donleavy turned the crags of his amiable face toward the window, his eyes searching for a way to lead into whatever it was he had on his mind. Kaufmann had seen the expression a thousand times on a thousand faces in the thousand years of his army service. Appearances told him that here was a good fellow, but he wasn't yet ready to make up his mind. He'd been fooled before.

The colonel apparently decided to dispense with small talk. "Colonel Daley of G-1 has informed Colonel Roop of G-2 Personnel that, under AR Forty-three-seventy-six, as modified eleven September, you must be ZI'ed. Immediately."

Despite himself, Kaufmann blinked. "Sent home for discharge? Whether I want to go or not?"

Donleavy nodded his big head. "It's the latest ruling."

Kaufmann received immediate new insight as to his difference from other mortals. Any reserve army officer with a milligram of good sense and healthy ambition would have done a buck-and-wing all over the colonel's fancy desk at the news he'd be going home. But Kaufmann recognized only surprise, depression, and a vague sense of betrayal. "Well, is all this final, sir? I really don't want to go home yet. I've got something going here."

"You mean Lieutenant Raines?"

Kaufmann gave him a sharp glance. "Begging the colonel's pardon, but just what the hell does the colonel mean by that?"

Donleavy laughed lightly and held up a disarming hand. "Easy, Kaufmann. No offense intended. It was a little joke, actually. I saw how you tried to arrange Raines's transfer. I've also seen Lieutenant Raines. And I wouldn't blame you in the least for, what's the term—hanging around?"

"I wanted her transfer, Colonel, because I needed help on something I was working on. I wanted Raines because she's proved to me she's smart and a savvy documents researcher." He shrugged, a sign of irritable surrender. "But that's all academic now. Both she and I are about to be ZI'ed."

The colonel did some more looking out the window. After lighting a stubby Meerschaum and puffing up a minor fog bank, he said, gray eyes on the Frankfurt horizon, "That's what I want to talk to you about. The thing you've been working on. G-2 would like to know exactly what it is. If you're going home in the middle of something, we'll have to know which strings to pick up."

"To tell you the straight, Colonel, I don't really know what I've been working on. It's an elusive series of impressions, hunches, vibrations, and I was trying to focus the damned lens. Something's going on in the Balkans, the Adriatic coasts, Northern Italy. Partisan unrest, indiscriminate killings. My feeling is that the insurrections are Soviet-inspired, and are tied somehow to criminal capers within our military forces. This idea stems from two ill-defined and widely separated events: first, a G-2 field report that somebody in the Udine area is black-marketing Air Force ordnance—heavy bombs, actually—and, second, an impression, shared by the late Tech Sergeant Margaret Sunderman, that a major misappropriation of aircraft took place, probably at the 15th Air Force Foggia maintenance depot. And now I think Sunderman's death, as well as that of Major Bianco, was murder. Murder linked to the widespread partisan unrest."

"Why do you think that?"

"Again, sir, I don't know. When I tried to talk to Bianco, he got dead. When I tried to interview the sergeant, she ended up on a slab. Somebody's been cutting us off before we tumble to something. I simply know it. Proof I haven't got."

"The Air Force's General Vickery has made it amply clear that he doesn't like the way you were poking around in Air Force matters. Why is that?"

"You tell me, sir."

"Lieutenant Raines suspects it's a classic case of turf protection. Vickery's people are interrogating Luftwaffe aircrews for special technical knowledge and they resent the hell out of ground types like us breaking into the act."

"Raines told you that?"

"Not in those words, of course. She's so prim and proper

I kept wanting to shake her gorgeous shoulders and tell her to spit it out.''

"She's like that." After a moment's pause, he was compelled to ask, "Did she tell you what I was working on?"

The colonel laughed softly. "She went beet-red and would say only that she's promised you to talk to no one about anything until you give her permission. She told me that unless I pulled rank and gave her a direct order to the contrary, it was nothing doing. How do you like that, eh?"

Kaufmann nodded slowly. "I like that, Colonel."

"Don't get any wrong ideas. I'd have ordered her to tell me in nothing flat. But I preferred to hear it from you. Even so, she's a rare bird. Everybody in this goddam army talks too much. No wonder you wanted her to work for you. And I can't understand why General Vickery wants her ZI'ed. She's too useful to be put to pasture." The colonel peered into the pipe bowl, made a face, and placed the Meerschaum in the sawed-off artillery shell serving as an ashtray. "So, then. Any recommendations as to who should follow up on your, ah, impressions?"

Kaufmann, because he was soon to be out of a job anyhow, permitted himself a small humph. "Well, sir, there just aren't a hell of a lot of people left around here. Rahrah boys from the ROTC Class of 1945 you've got lots of. But experienced, intuitive intelligence operatives? Famine. When you eventually take over as G-2, you're going to be a lonely tiger in charge of a litter of fun-loving puddy-tats, I'm afraid.''

The colonel nodded sorrowfully. "I can't argue with that. But give me a recommendation anyhow."

"You couldn't do any better than Vince Ludwig, ops chief of CIC's special team, Frankfurt. The fact that he's very good could be a problem, though. The chief of CIC won't be ready to let him go without a fight."

"You think Ludwig's worth my going to the mat over?"

"Yes, sir. I suspect that Ludwig would jump at the chance, because he shows signs of being bored with his lack of work right now. And if Chief, CIC, gets his back up, maybe you can persuade the Theater Commander to arbitrate.''

This turn in the conversation, Kaufmann realized, had two basic implications. First, Colonel Donleavy was paying homage to his performance record by inviting his recommendation, and it was flattering. Second, Colonel Donleavy was obviously giving importance to his suspicions, and that was more than flattering—it was reassuring. He felt a sudden inner aching, something akin to homesickness. This work was all he really knew. As the old saying had it, he'd found a home in the army. And, to compound the irony, just as he's being kicked out the back door, a new, approving stepfather comes in the front door.

Ah, well.

"I guess that's about it, Major Kaufmann. Your orders will be cut in a day or so, and you'll have a fourteen-day delay en route—a two-week vacation on the way to embarkation at Camp Lucky Strike at Le Havre. Meanwhile, G-2 and I personally regret your leaving. It's a real loss to us.''

"Thank you, sir.''

"G-2 says he's watched your work. And he's learned that when you have hunches they always pay off somehow.''

Kaufmann, recognizing the end of the meeting, stood up. "I've been lucky, Colonel. Now I have to worry about being so lucky in the civilian world.''

"I think you'll make out just fine as a civilian.'' Donleavy stood up and offered his hand. "In any event, you have my best wishes. And G-2 says he'll drop by before you leave. He has a Croix de Guerre to pin on you. For your work with the French Resistance. De Gaulle is grateful.''

"De Gaulle is grateful and Vickery is annoyed. I see some irony there, sir.''

"Irony? I see a big pain in the ass all around.''

Kaufmann saluted, did an about-face and strode through the door.

* * *

Well, to hell with it.

Now it was back to Philadelphia, where nobody but his parents would even know he'd been away.

Or would rejoice at his return.

Meanwhile, he'd be fretting over the wisdom (idiocy?) of his decision not to tell Donleavy—or anyone at USFET—about his setting up Nicky Anton, flyboy extraordinaire, for a secret penetration of the Great Luftwaffe POW Snatch.

Well, give it the two weeks, see how far Anton gets.

Then recall him, pull him out of the cold, a day or two before boat time. Wouldn't hurt anything, might help.

TUESDAY
18 September 1945

7

Nick Anton was not much given to self-analysis, but if he had been he most certainly would have discovered that aviating was his only abiding love. His mother had died when he was ten and his father had gone into a subsequent bitter overdrive, living with various women in all the major capitals and remaining forever aloof to mailboxes, except on birthdays and at Christmas, when the boarding school brass of the moment would hand him stilted greeting cards enfolding lavish checks "for walking-around money, love, Dad." The abandonment, first by his beloved mother and then by the large, taciturn, tobacco-puffing man, was crushing. Thus his all-too-ready laughter, his prankishness, his hair-trigger zaniness—insulation of a kind from the nagging need to weep. Only when aloft, surrounded by the immensity of the sky and secure in the rattling, droning, oil-smelling womb of an airplane, did a sense of belonging—of a reason for being—take form. It had taken form in Switzerland, during his junior year at Alpenheim upper school, after Otto Lanz had given him a ride in his bright red biplane, a Bücker Jungmeister, and, Dad, forever seeking to flush away his own inner pain via a vomiting of money, had readily agreed to spring for flying lessons.

He loved airplanes entirely, with something close to sexual passion, and they loved him back, always responding to his caresses, forgiving his transgressions, being there when he needed them. Even this brute of a machine, this JU-88, a twin-engine sonofabitchin snarler that shook and clanked and groaned and wheezed, that wanted always to drop its tail and to drift aport and throw raw oil from its starboard engine stacks—this plane, too, was trying to do its best for him.

"Watch the nose," Lawrence cautioned in his earphones. "This aircraft has a tendency to stall on turns."

"But that's the good part. Are all Junkers flying machines this godawful hard to drive?"

"I've flow the 52, that washboard trimotor the Germans used for transport and paratrooping, and the 87 Stuka. They had their faults, but this thing is nasty."

Lawrence was a light colonel from the USAAF Technical Studies Section, an organization that often collaborated with Theater-level intelligence. He was a pedantic type, full of his own importance, whose manner hinted that it was much beneath him to lead an anonymous somebody in threadbare Luftwaffe toggery through the protocols of this tired old bucket of bolts. They'd been introduced beside the plane, which still wore black crosses and the Nazi Hakenkreuz, by Mr. Donnelly, the Dijon resident manager. From the beginning of Lawrence's walk-around briefing, delivered in strained German and in the haughty manner of a professor with unassailable tenure, Anton didn't like him. But flying was in the offing, and Anton was ready to kiss the behind of a hog to get into the air again, so he sucked up to Lawrence with the Gee-I'm-such-an-earnest-pupil routine that had made him the darling of grammar school teachers. Fortunately, Lawrence occupied the observer's seat behind him, so he was spared the need to look at the man.

"Where did we get it?"

"It was forced down near Mainz last spring and sat in a field there until one of our salvage teams picked it up."

"Maybe it acts this way because the Krauts bent it when they set it down."

"We were very careful with the rehabilitation. It's probably a brat. They come off assembly lines like that sometimes. No reason to be any different from any of the others. But they show up brats."

"I still feel like I'm going to get my ass blown off, tootling around the French sky in a Nazi-marked bomber." He dropped the right wing and eased into a descending turn.

"We're doing this all the time. Testing German planes. Besides, what's to be feared? The war's over. We've grounded any airplane, from fighter to bomber, that isn't needed to carry alcohol and prophylactics. If we're shot at, it'll be by some drunken stormdoor-salesman-turned-lieutenant on some officers' club trapshooting range."

Anton glanced about the adjacent sky, a reflex check on traffic. "About time for you to get on the horn for landing clearance, Colonel. My arms are tired from rassling this clunk, and I gotta weewee."

"Awkward, this business of your not speaking English except in the privacy of this cockpit. Tedious."

"You ought to see it from here."

"We're both tired, I'm sure. But my orders are to be certain that you're familiar with this kind of airplane."

"Orders? Who gives you orders?"

"On these temporary assignments at Dijon, Mr. Donnelly gives me my orders. All I know about you is that you're an American agent being trained for a secret operation, and I'm supposed to be sure you can handle a JU-88."

"Do you know my name?"

"I'm not supposed to. But I pick up things. So, yes, I know."

"Only Donnelly's supposed to know my name."

"I happened to overhear him talking about you on the phone to Frankfurt. But I'm used to these kinds of things. Your secret is safe with me."

"No big deal, I guess. Make your call, eh?"

Colonel Lawrence made his call-in and Anton took them into their downwind leg. Dusk was coming on, and rain clouds filled the eastern sky, lightning flickering in their bowels. Anton eased back on the throttles and the big engines hushed, propellers thrashing and throwing splinters of glare caught from the lingering twilight sun.

Lawrence fell silent, and Anton, feeling the colonel's examination, went easily but deliberately through the pre-landing procedures, from cowl flaps through boosters to carburetor filters. He had completed the landing-gear-down movements when both engines died.

No warning, no belching of smoke, no clatter.

A gentle cough from the port engine and an instantaneous falling of instrument needles. Nothing more.

Anton's gloved fingers began to flip switches. "We've got a holy-cats emergency going, looks like."

"Any juice at all?"

"Nope. No flaps, no feathering, no nuthin'. This here flying machine has had complete cardiac arrest."

"How can that be?"

"On this tin lizzy, anything's possible."

"We're too low to bail out."

"Ain't we though."

"What'll we do?"

"Repeat after me: 'Our Father who art—' "

"Come on—"

"Relax, Colonel. This may be an ugly old clunk, but she loves me. She may be dying, but she'll stay true to me to the end."

"The field's off the port wing. You try a dead-stick turn, as tail-heavy as this thing is, you've got us a guaranteed spin."

"Field, hell. I'm going to take a trip down the highway."

"You're going to land on the road? I see three trucks and four cars right where we want to touch down."

"Let's just hope they see us—and get out of the way.

Because I'm not gliding, I'm diving. Anything less and we'll go in tail first.''

"For God's sake! This is—isn't there anything else we can do?''

Anton, concentrating on the problem of keeping the highway in proper alignment, fought the urge to give the colonel a sidelong glance. "Hey, buddy, relax. Ain't you ever been in a forced landing before?''

"Not with a bunch of vehicles and a village coming at me.''

The autumn colors, bisected by the chalky road, came up with a teetering rush, and, after an agonized split of time, there was a slamming and the chirping of tires. The Junkers squealed, metal on metal, metal writhing, metal snapping, and dust clouds rolled from joints and crevices and seams, and an entire plexiglas sheet poinged from its casement in the nose. Anton held to the control column with all the muscle he owned, and his boots kicked and slid in their frantic attempts to rudder against the incipient sidewise skid.

"Oopsy-daisy." Hauling back on the yoke, he managed to leapfrog a six-by-six truck cruising sedately and unaware toward the hamlet ahead. With the same momentum he cleared an oncoming jeep and a staff car, then tried some mechanical braking when the wheels returned to their mad spinning on the road surface. It was a bad idea.

"We're beginning to swing!" the colonel shouted.

"Hold on. I think I've lost it.''

The big ship slued to starboard and entered the village's main drag sideways, leaving its tail section against a house, its nose casement against a tree, its landing gear hopscotching along the macadam. The cockpit and bomb bay area, along with wing stubs and engines, continued to slide for the length of the street—a trash pile gone mad—as GIs and housewives and refugees and whores and school kids and postmen dived into gardens, through doorways, under fences and over walls.

Eventually there was silence.

Anton pushed away a sheet of fuselage metal and, peering into the dust-fogged interior, saw Colonel Lawrence, still belted to his seat, wincing and dabbing at his swollen nose.

There was a sound outside, and he peered over the cockpit rim to confront a red-faced woman, stubby and round under her peasant's apron.

"Bonjour, madame."

She spat on the crumpled wing. "Boche pig!"

It had been the same old hurry-up-and-wait crapola, as usual. The Institutional Army. Tradition à la mode.

Anton, staring out the dirty little window at the roaring rain, tried to count the times he had experienced this in the army, or in the "Ahmed Fohces," as they were starting to call it on the radio, a la-de-da name for the grunt and groan that had existed since Caesar's legions and before. How many times had he stood like this, lonely, waiting, always waiting, gazing unseeingly at some alien landscape?

And now at Dijon it was happening again: alone in a farmhouse, silence all around, in a medieval nowhere that once had been a major OSS training and operational base and now was a ghost community, with only a few specters remaining to wander the melancholy lanes.

And he hadn't see a hell of a lot of those, either.

He had been driven under cover of night from Bad Schwalbach to this lousy little stone house by a dour MP corporal who was embarrassed to chauffeur a raggedy-ass Luftwaffe captain in a stained uniform with thread-ends where insignia and decorations had been torn away by GI souvenir-hunters. Kaufmann had forbidden Anton to speak English under any circumstances, so the entire trip had been made in sullen silence, which seemed to be a small loss where this sourball two-striper was concerned. If exigencies compelled him to speak English, he was to use only basic terms, heavily larded with German inflections. Kaufmann had led him through these half-assed rehearsals and seemed generally satisfied that he would be an adequate representation of a German flying officer, captured, according to the

sealed "Eyes Only" documents the corporal was carrying
to Donnelly, after bailing out last April during a bombing
attack on a U.S. 7th Army infantry battalion moving through
Oberbayern. The travel orders—ostensibly cut by Headquarters, 217th Military Police—said that he, Captain Hel-
mut Thoma, was being shipped to Dijon airfield for
interrogation by Army Air Force technologists and members of the Strategic Bombing Survey and would be held in
custody by the local MP detachment while not undergoing
questioning. Kaufmann, sly wretch that he was, had slyly
followed Holy Procedure and sent top secret "Information
and File" copies of the fake Thoma biography and the
transfer orders to G-1 Prisoner of War Records Division,
USFET, Frankfurt, and to the corresponding Air Force office in Wiesbaden. Something would shake out, he'd said.

"When it does," Kaufmann had said, "we'll know better
how to put you into penetration. Just be sure you find some
way to keep me informed of where you are and what's going
on. I'll do anything I can to facilitate things, but you're the
one who'll be doing the moving around. You know where
I'll be; I don't know where you'll be. That puts the communix ball in your court. It won't be easy, is my guess, but
I'm counting on your ingenuity, your inventiveness."

Anton had submerged his consequent sense of aloneness
in a sea of aviation study. Throughout the seemingly interminable drive to Dijon he'd read the manuals, studied the
photos and analyzed the cockpit schematics of all the major
German types. This afternoon's introduction to Lawrence
and the ensuing JU-88 contretemps had represented the cul-
mination of his cram course.

The close call in the village street had apparently been
taken in stride by most of the villagers, the local French
bureaucracy, and the mysterious administration of this
abominable limbo into which Kaufmann had thrown him.
There had been a couple of hours in the local police station
and a taut little interview with a trio of French army officers
who were, no doubt about it, sick up to their ears of foreigners and more than anxious to get this Lawrence fellow

and his crazy German prisoner out of their lives. When Mr. Donnelly appeared and assured the officials that all damages would be paid by the American government, Anton and Lawrence had been permitted to leave. Lawrence had turned to him as they stood by the cars and, speaking through the wad of cotton he held to his face, said, "I'll never do that again."

"Do what?"

"Throw the switch on anything I'm not flying myself."

"I don't get you."

"That was a trick airplane, designed to test how well you react in aerial emergencies. I flipped a switch beside my seat and took away your power."

"You did that?"

"I did that."

"Well, you asshole, why didn't you flip the switch back on? Why did you let me kill my airplane?"

"I did flip the switch back on. It didn't work. And now my nose is bent."

"What a shame. Here: Let me put it back in shape."

So saying, he had lifted Lawrence skyward with a fist launched from near his right ankle, and there had been a nasty scene in which four MPs, yelling "The Kraut's trying to escape!" pounded across the cobblestones like the Notre Dame backfield, and if it hadn't been for Mr. Donnelly and his wallet full of credentials, Anton, instead of riding off in a GI Chevrolet, would have died on the spot.

God.

How had he fallen into this stinko deal?

He lit another cigarette and was about to undress and shower when someone tapped on the door, firm but polite.

"Herein."

A woman, blonde, lean, slightly square-jawed and bland, peeked around the half-open door. Her German was easy, with Westphalian inflections. "Captain Thoma, I'm Karla Wintgens. I really am sorry to intrude, but I thought you might perhaps answer a question or two. May I come in?"

So, then. Here it was. The shakeout. The break Kaufmann had told him to wait for. Kaufmann's spurious top-secret "For Information and File" travel orders had obviously landed at USFET and were now producing results.

"Well, I am very busy right now," he said. "I have this cigarette to finish and two more windowpanes to stare through before I take a two- or three-hour shower."

She smiled a courteous smile and stepped into the room's dim light. She was wearing a plaid skirt, a white blouse, a tan cardigan, nylon stockings and walking shoes. Give her a string of pearls and she'd look like one of those snooty girls' school dames, the kind that would come floating down from Westchester or Connecticut on house-party weekends, proper and board-like, with a "dahling" here and a sloe gin fizz there, arrogant and sexless.

"I'm glad to meet you," she said, holding out her hand. He shook it, thinking as he did that maybe she expected him to brush it with his lips, in the European fashion. Her eyes, large and translucent blue, gave no clue.

He motioned to the sofa. "Sit down?"

She sat, regarding him with a kind of curiosity and smiling that odd little smile.

"Who are you, and what are you all about?" Anton had never been much for small talk, a characteristic that had evolved from his liaisons with women in the limousine and horse-farm circles into which he'd been thrown. There the girls had acted like Olivia de Havilland, sweet and demure as all hell, awaiting some lisping, lavender-laced romance with some Leslie Howard of the moment, when in reality, down under all the hanky-waving dear-me's, they were Tugboat Annies, able to cuss the ass off a water buffalo and ever ready to haul a guy into the barn and tear his drawers to shreds. He had lost his virginity to a double-standard phony like this—she'd been almost twice his age—and when subsequent affairs varied only in dialogue and not in substance, he saw no valid reason to play the Tenderly Articulate Lover—even if to do so for three minutes would guarantee a night-long squirm in the sheets. If Miss Personality of the Debutantes' Quilting Club wanted to romp, she knew where to find him; if she wanted conversation, she could call Ashley Wilkes.

"Actually," this blonde said, "I was affiliated with the OSS until just this past Tuesday, when orders came through reassigning me to the Presidio in San Francisco. I report there in fifteen days, with a three-day delay en route in London."

"Sounds as if you've got it made, dear."

"Perhaps. But I like it here in Europe. I'm a European by birth. Munich, as a matter of fact."

"You're a German?"

"I was. But I'm a naturalized American now. My paternal grandfather was Jewish, and we left Munich when Hitler came to power in 1933. Father was more aware than most of the trouble ahead for those whose families bore non-Aryan strains."

"So what's on your mind?"

"I've been working in German POW Repatriation these past few weeks—a kind of fill-in thing while my orders to the States firmed up—and I came across your file. I noticed that you, too, are from Munich and are scheduled to be returned there once your technical interrogation is ended." She crossed her legs and brushed a hand down a nyloned calf. They were nice legs.

"And?"

"And I thought you might do me a favor." Her smile was soft, a tad sad.

"That depends. I'm not exactly a free spirit these days, you know. As a member of the Nazi Party I'm not sure I'll be in any position to do anybody any favors."

"Your Fragebogen says you joined the Party in 1933, as a schoolboy. That doesn't make you a war criminal."

"Nobody's making that distinction these days."

She nodded and sighed. "I understand. But this would seem to be a relatively easy matter. Simply looking up somebody and letting them know that my father died last year. I was hoping to have a chance to return to Munich and handle it myself, but obviously I won't. And I understand you'll be repatriated in a matter of days.''

"That shows you know more than I do. I've begun to feel that I was doomed to spend the rest of my life here. Who's this somebody you're talking about?''

"My aunt. Frau Emilie Weis. She lived on Ismaningerstrasse, not too far from the Maximiliensbrücke. I hear that part of the city was not too heavily bombed, so it's likely she's still there.''

Anton sniffed. "Obviously you haven't seen Munich lately.''

"True, but friends tell me the park, Embassy Row—Bogenhausen, and so on—were not hit so badly. I ask only that when you have a chance you will look, and if she's there, hand her this note.'' She took a small envelope from her cardigan pocket and held it toward him.

Anton took the message and went to the window and peered out at the dusk. The wind had picked up. The rain was crashing along the cobblestones in angry swirlings, and the trees, tossing, let their autumn leaves dance away, brown and orange confetti.

"Why don't you ask the Red Cross to do this?''

She cleared her throat delicately. "I did. But they wanted me to use one of their message forms. That's too cold, formal, for what I have to say to Auntie.''

He was silent for a time, watching the storm, listening to the roar of the rain. Then, without looking at her, he said, "Take off your clothes.''

She stood up, flustered, her blue eyes showing the beginnings of anger. "Why should I do that?''

"Because we're going to take a shower together.''

"You—you expect me to—''

"Every privilege has a price, dear. But I'm not going to charge you anything. I am instead going to give you a very pleasant night on that bed there.''

"Well—I must say—''

"Say what?''

"I'm not *that* anxious to get in touch with my aunt."
"Suit yourself, sweetie."

Toward dawn she made her way through the rain, bent against the wind, the GI raincoat over her head, sidestepping the turbulence in the gutters, the cascades thundering from the roofs. When she reached the hay barn, Folsum, who was on duty, let her in, holding the batten door against the storm. She went directly to the office hidden behind the false middle stall and lifted the phone, asking Zentrum for the 'M' line.

" 'M.' "

"Karla. He's as Nazi as they come."

"All right. Hitch him to the chain and send him along."

FRIDAY
21 September 1945

8

Because he liked Kaufmann, G-2 had authorized a division farewell party, originally scheduled for the officers' club at Schloss Kronberg, the late Kaiser Wilhelm's summer palace in the Taunuses. But Colonel Donleavy ordered a change of venue when he discovered that the savings would be dramatic if he entrusted the arrangements to the Farben Casino mess officer. Since Donleavy was anxious to buttress his image as Ike Incarnate, he'd seen this as an opportunity to invite wider participation (and thus create more happy faces and personal popularity) at a lower net cost.

So here it was, party time, and Kaufmann stood beside the concert grand, glass in hand, partly listening to the instrument's tinkling as managed by a foppish Hessian named Putzi Fritzinger, partly trying to ignore the baseball predictions spittled into his ear by a drunken colonel and partly watching gravely as Lieutenant Raines chatted her way through the legion of swillers—several of whom he actually recognized—come to drink his health in G-2's free booze and to lament his leaving.

The cacophony at last became unbearable and so he left
the colonel (who did an immediate about-face and, without
a pause for breath, continued his recitation of major league
statistics for a smiling and uncomprehending Putzi) and
made his way to the terrace. The air was clearer there, and
the night was starry and crisp, and the crowd's gabbling,
while as loud and lubricious as that inside, seemed muted
by the unechoing void above. But he yearned to be rid of
this noisy and smelly circus and to be thoroughly unconscious in his bed in the Transient BOQ, even though it was
as comfy-cozy as a waffle iron.

Since moving day for a soldier is a matter of stuffing a
sack and walking out, it had been fairly easy to leave Lieutenant Raines a luxury to remember him by. He had arranged, by bandying Colonel Donleavy's name about at the
Rents and Requisitions Office, to have her moved, effective
his transfer to the BOQ, into his Vom Rath Strasse apartment in the many-acred spread of Farben parkland, whose
perimeter was delineated by barbed wire and checkpoints
and whose interior residential zones looked as if they had
been designed by that fun-loving gang from Stonehenge.

The way things looked now, Raines's departure for the
States, pending under one of Colonel Daley's obscure ARs,
was still at least a month off—an eternity for a transient
between assignments. So she might as well have a bit of
luxury. Fancy, private digs would be his going-away present
to her. To a Nice Philadelphia Lady, with thanks from a
Nice Philadelphia Man.

The party was now mercifully nearing its end, what with
most of the freebies having been consumed. As always at
events of this kind, Kaufmann found himself to be depressed in direct proportion to the levity around him; a pick-
me-up at day's end was one of God's gifts, but premeditated
group drunkenness could send him into true sorrow. Red
faces, damp and slack and spouting gratuitous grossness,
invariably created visions of doomed Romans, jitterbugging
bare-assed while the Huns incinerated the suburbs. And he
would grieve.

Colonel Donleavy came out of the crowd, gave him a slightly tipsy Rooseveltian smile and said, "So then: you're leaving next Wednesday. Anything you need?"

"I don't need anything, sir. But I think you and G-2 need something. You need to kneel beside your bunkies, fold your little hannies, close your eyes and pray that you get some help. Stalin is winding up to snap our girdle, somehow, somewhere."

"Well," the colonel said, wariness creeping into his beaming expression, "the war's over, and we're a little too relaxed, maybe, but hell's ass, Kaufmann, you sound as if you were the only man in the whole United States Army who was out of bed and answering phones."

"I know I'm not the only man tending the store, sir. There's you. G-2 himself. Ike, maybe. A few more. But that's it. The rest are chasing girls and tennis balls."

The colonel delivered him a moment of silent, thoughtful inspection. Then he sighed a bourbon-scented sigh. "I was impressed with you and your careful manner when we met, Kaufmann. But you are not careful enough. You have failed to research me adequately. If you had, you'd know that I do not like sarcastic smart-alecks."

"Colonel, I assure you that I'm not being disrespectful. I am guilty only of hyperbole. We both know in our heart of hearts that the American military establishment in Europe—everywhere, actually, but in Europe particularly—is going to hell in a handbasket. The demobilization is virtually out of control. It's not demobilization, it's demolition. In fact, even that word's not strong enough. We are rapidly becoming a stage-prop military, and the struggle for Europe is just beginning."

Colonel Donleavy waved a hand of weary warning. "Please don't go into one of those threat-from-the-East speeches. I've heard so many of those from so many people I don't think I could handle another. Of course we're disarming ourselves at precisely the wrongest time in history; of course we're acting like a nation full of horse's patoots. But it's a matter of taxpayers' money. It's not my fault—not really anybody's fault—that with war's end Congress sees no need to keep on a war footing. And Ike's ad hoc committee on cost reduction has put out a blanket order the G-level operations economize and remove any vestige of waste, inefficiency or lavishness.''

"Most respectfully, sir: Just yesterday, outside Pforzheim, forty-three acres of jeeps and half-tracks—all brand new, not a scratch on their paint—were burned to ashes because it costs the taxpayer less to burn them than it does to put them on a ship and send them home. I submit that that's pretty goddamned wasteful in view of the fact that Congress is getting ready to pour umpteen billion dollars into devastated Europe, much of it in the form of new utility vehicles. And I furthermore submit that it would cost the taxpayer less to have a couple of G-2 guys investigate and forewarn than it would eventually cost him to pull all his unsuspecting fellow citizens and allies out of Stalin's prison camps. Sir.''

The colonel sighed again, a deep sigh that hinted real regret. "If I were permitted to so address a person of lower rank, I'd say you are a royal pain in the ass, Kaufmann. But regulations forbid it, and so I won't call you a royal pain in the ass. I'll just subtly let it be known by my expression that I consider you to be the royalest pain in the ass I've seen in years.''

"I appreciate that, sir. It's very kind of you to leave it unsaid.''

Colonel Donleavy, the chronic diplomat, sought to bridge the developing tension. Amiably, brows lowered in pretended severity, he said, "G-2 may love you, Kaufmann, but I suspect you are a wolf in wolf's clothing.''

Kaufmann, being heavily ballasted with Irish genes, was a strong believer in the power of coincidence. Yet more than mere ethnic mysticism was at play here: time and again his biography had been nudged this way or that by an uncannily propitious confluence of one seemingly insignificant or irrelevant force with another. And here it was again.

"No, sir. I'm a tractor-treaded jerk.''

"Why do you have that silly look on your face?"

"I've just been reminded of something I've completely overlooked, Colonel."

"You are impossible to follow sometimes. What are you talking about?"

"Sir, I simply must find Lieutenant Raines. May I be excused?"

"With pleasure."

Kaufmann muttered something polite, then re-entered the dying bacchanal inside. Pausing by the piano, he craned, trying to spot her blondness in the sea of olive and brass.

Ah. There.

In the corner, pale, tired, and enduring the boozy wit of three second looeys and a captain, whose eight admiring eyes sought unabashedly to penetrate her uniform.

Approaching the group, Kaufmann said, "Circle your wags, Captain. This lady and I will make Fort Apache alone." He underscored his command of the situation by taking Raines's elbow and, with Charles Boyer inflections, murmuring, "Come wiss me to ze cash bar."

She seemed vaguely pleased by his intervention. As they moved into a backwater in the ebb and flow, she said, "Well, Major: How are you enjoying your party?"

"Right now I'm filled with self-disgust."

"What's wrong, sir?"

"I've been racking my brains, tearing through every volume available, studying every dossier in Central Registry's catalog, and talking to every face that might know something about Northern Italy, the Balkans, Sunrise—even Sunderman's mysterious C-rations. I have become an absolute perishing expert on the Udine–Friuli area, on Tito and the Jugo and Greek partisans. I am as familiar with that part of the world as anybody in this headquarters. And I am a Number One, Kansas City cut, prime rib of nincompoop."

"Aren't you being a bit hard on yourself, sir?"

"I dismissed Wolff, and I completely forgot about the Public Relations Division."

"I don't understand—"

"Raines, I need to rassle up that Central Registry enlisted clerk—you know, Poopsie. I need her to dig out some files. Do you think your Personnel records will tell us where she's quartered?"

"No need. I know Poopsie well. She picks up my interoffice stuff with Central Registry. Twice a day. Brings me coffee and Danish every ten a.m. Nice girl. She lives in the enlisted womens' Kaserne on Ziegelstrasse."

"Where did she get that dumb name?"

"She's great at finding things—digging out the poop people need for research. We all got to calling her Poopsie. It's one of those office nickname things."

"So get the Compound OD to contact her and get her to meet me at Central Registry."

"What do you want Poopsie to do? I'll have to give the Officer of the Day some idea, and arrange with the G-2 duty officer to sign you both in."

"I want her to run, not walk, to the cabinets that carry the files on guerrilla operations, Northern Italy, and the dossier for Wolff, SS General Karl, Mediterranean Theater. Then I want her to put them on that reading table by the window and I want her to sit quietly and watch disapprovingly as this idiot reads every word, and if he calls for more, she must run again, and then again, and again, and again until he tells her to stop."

"SS General Karl Wolff?"

"Two F's. Next thing: Can you get Poopsie into PR's Official Military History Archives Section—you know, that cobwebby thing next to the basement mailroom?"

"That's Colonel Gruber's province, sir. I'm not sure that Colonel Gruber would appreciate a midnight visit to one of his offices—"

"You let me worry about Fatso Gruber. Just get Poopsie into the Archives and have her look for anything on Sunrise or C-rations."

"C-rations? You think Maggie was using a codename when she—"

"I've been thinking that all along, but until now I haven't

tried to link C-rations with Wolff. A light bulb's just turned on, and I think there is indeed a link. And now that a peace is waging, the documents I need might have been moved out of Central Registry and into Fatso's PR archives, there to await use in all those self-praising war memoirs soon to be written by our chieftains.''

As they made for the door he continued to fuss inwardly over his inexplicable myopia. He had been so preoccupied with the Balkans, so pressured by his hitherto trustworthy intuition, so busy playing detective in a murder mystery and infiltrating POW camps and installing Raines and seeing to a welter of similar wheel-spinnings, he had smothered the one solid angle Bianco had delivered right up front: General Wolff himself. How—by what mechanism, and through whom—had Wolff contacted Dulles in Bern? How had Dulles implemented Wolff's rescue from the Italian partisans and their firing squad? There was a link, and it was missing. And it was a link designed and forged by Wolff.

C-rations, maybe?

He sought to mitigate. He had not altogether ignored the Wolff angle. He had indeed tried to link the name with his inquiry. But this attempt to lessen the pain of his stupidity failed, of course; the pragmatist in him joined with the demon of self-honesty to remind him that he'd been trying to hitch Wolff to the wrong horse.

As they approached the lobby, a busboy, a smallish youth with thick blond hair and thin dark acne, emerged from a copse of potted palms and touched Kaufmann's arm. He cleared his throat, diffident, unhappy. "Eggsguse, zir. I must a vord mit you haff."

"Make it in German, please. It'll be easier on both of us, I think."

"Thank you, sir." The young man glanced uneasily at Lieutenant Raines. "No offense, but what I have to say—"

Kaufmann signaled her with her eyes and, in English again, said, "Run on, Raines. I'll meet you at the Compound OD's office."

When she had gone, Kaufmann returned to the busboy. "So then, young man, what's up?"

"Sir, I am Hermann Epp. I am employed regularly by the American forces personnel section to work here in the restaurant and bar. My Fragebogen has, of course, been cleared by your Military Government and if you need references—"

"Just tell me what's on your mind. Then I'll decide what to do about it."

Epp looked over his shoulder, and Kaufmann thought he saw real anxiety in the motion. "Sir, I am—was"—a stricken look here—"a friend of Anna Krim. I—" He faltered, his voice thickening.

"I'm sorry. She was a nice girl. I liked her a lot."

"I know that, sir. Anna spoke of you often. How kind and generous you are—"

"So what can I do for you, Hermann?"

"Anna began acting a bit strange toward the—last days. I was worried about her. She had something going on with some man, and I saw a change in her."

"What kind of change?"

"She was always, well, so easygoing and lighthearted. She had many troubles, Anna did, what with having lost her parents in the air raids and her two brothers in France, but she could always find something to be grateful for or to laugh about. But the lack of money began to hurt her badly— she was taking care of her invalid sister and her two little kids—and there was never enough to—I helped out where I could, but busboys don't make much, and—" He spread his hands and shrugged.

"So what happened?"

"So Anna became quiet, sad. She didn't want to talk about it. She just sort of clammed up. I knew something was going on, so I followed her several times, on the job, after hours, too, and she was meeting this man. Not in the romantic sense. He was much older than she was, and an ugly customer, too, I'll tell you. They'd just stand on a street corner, or in the park, and talk. Then he'd leave and she'd go home—if that ratty, water-filled cellar she lived in could be called home. I finally asked her about it and she seemed to get scared and at first she told me to mind my own business.''

"At first?''

"Yes, sir. But just three days before she died she seemed to be even more excited—nervous, but, well, kind of excited, I guess you'd say—and she asked me to do her a favor, for what she called her own protection. She wanted me to follow her again and take a picture of the man.''

"You did this?''

Hermann pulled an envelope from his mess jacket pocket and handed it to Kaufmann. "It's not very good, but you can see his face. They were talking, standing by a kiosk in the Taunus Anlage.''

That they were. Kaufmann studied the man, a lean, saturnine fellow who towered over the girl in the pathetic raincoat and wooden clogs. "Did Anna ever mention this man's name?''

"She called him Herr Klug. I don't know if that's really his name or if she was just being sarcastic, him being so 'clever' and all. She said he was a writer for that scandal sheet, *Zing*, and he needed an American uniform to get in the officers' mess and interview some war hero. He was going to pay her five hundred Occupation Marks—those 'Im Umlauf gesetzt in Deutschland' things.''

"And this happened?''

"I guess so. I followed her down to the canned goods locker that day. He was there. I watched from the garbage can assembly area.''

"You saw him in a uniform?''

"No, sir. I was afraid he'd see me, so I left. But I know Anna had provided him a uniform, borrowed by Louisa Zimmermann, a friend of hers who does housecleaning in the bachelor officers' quarters in the compound here. Anna sneaked it through the checkpoint in her totebag. The MPs never really check things, you know.''

"Anything else?''

"That's about all, sir. Except that I have the feeling Anna was too upset over something as silly as getting a uniform for a journalist. My hunch is she knew, or felt, maybe, that that officer, that Major Bianco, was going to be killed and she was beginning to feel like an accomplice."

"You're a very perceptive young man, Hermann Epp."

"I may be wrong."

"Sure. But I doubt it."

"Anna told me that, if she ever got in any kind of trouble over all this, I was to tell you, the only important American she knows and trusts." Hermann sighed tremulously. "Well, she got in trouble, all right."

"May I keep this photo?"

"Of course, sir. Just don't tell anybody where you got it. I don't want Herr Klug paying me a call, too."

"You think he killed Anna?"

"Certainly, sir. And Major Bianco, too. Don't you?"

"Tell you one thing, Hermann. This photo has just earned you a hundred marks."

"I don't expect to be paid, sir—"

"That's why you're getting a hundred marks. Along with my very sincere thanks."

Poopsie waved a hand at a file folder and a dossier packet on the table. "There you are, Major."

"Is that all?"

"The dossier on Wolff and the file on the partisans. There is nothing else on either subject. And there's absolutely no trace of anything called 'C-rations.'"

The file was skimpy. He leafed through it twice, a matter that took no more than a few minutes. Not skimpy. Lacking. Stinko. Zilch. In the Wolff dossier—a wad of biographical material and some routine sidelights on his military career—only a G-2 "For Information Only" précis of an OSS summary was helpful. But not very:

"WOLFF, SS General Karl: Son of a German jurist; owner of a failed advertising agency; one-time liaison officer betw. Adolf Hitler and Heinrich Himmler; principal figure in secret peace negotiations, Italy, Switzerland, early 1945. Subject expressed readiness to surrender all German forces under his command in the eastern Mediterranean area and claimed to have enough influence to induce Field Marshal Kesselring, commander of the German forces on the western front, to surrender his troops as well. This is direct opposition to Hitler's no-surrender, scorched-earth policy. Negotiations pursued by OSS/Bern (their file: 'Sunrise')."

He closed the files and returned them to Poopsie. "Thank you. Pretty lean pickings."

She tried to be helpful. "Maybe War Crimes has some files, sir. They keep a lot of stuff over there. I'll check with them tomorrow if you want me to."

"All right. I appreciate your help. And I'm sorry I had to drag you over here tonight."

"That's O.K., sir. I wasn't doing anything."

"So go get some sleep. And thanks again."

She disappeared into the hallway shadows and as he stood up he paused to consider Raines, who had sat mutely at the end of the table throughout his little exercise in futility. His appraisal was like that of a used-car salesman sizing up an incoming tire-kicker.

"Are you all right, Raines?"

"Yes, sir. Why do you ask?"

"You look like hell."

"Well, now—I—" Her pallor turned a shade toward red, and she seemed to be shocked by this bit of news.

He saw her unhappiness, and because he was not one to hurt another human being gratuitously, he sought now to repair the damage. "You don't really look like hell, of course, but you do look a little green around the gills. Are you sure you feel all right?"

"I guess so. I just can't seem to get enough sleep these days. I go to bed early and I sleep a lot, but I'm always tired, sleepy." She yawned.

Because he could never do otherwise in the face of a yawn, he yawned, too. Out came his trusty pad and pencil.

"Here," he said. "Go see Captain Olsen at this address. Tell him I want him to give you a physical."

"I just had a physical a month ago, Major—"

"I don't care if you had one this morning. See Olsen. That's a direct damn order, Raines."

"Yes, sir."

"Come on. I'll see you to your quarters."

She gave him a glance from under sleepy lids. "May I ask a question, sir?"

"Shoot."

"Why do you bother with this business of Wolff and stolen planes and C-rations? I mean, you're going home in less than a week. Why don't you let somebody else worry about all of it?"

"Because, Raines, I'm a cornball. I've very fond of my country and it burns my patoot when ingrates and jerks and Greedy Guses try to undermine or cheat it. And, more to the point, when they steal a U.S. Army airplane, they're stealing my dear old dad's money, my money, your money. And we all work too goddam hard to let some conniving sons of bitches, foreign or domestic, slide our money into their pockets. And I don't let somebody else worry about it because I look around and don't see too many others who want to worry about it. So every minute I'm here—until the very minute I walk up that gangplank at Le Havre—I'm going to keep plugging. Unless somebody kills me, that is."

She shook her head, annoyed. "Don't even joke about such a thing."

"Joke? Why in hell does everybody insist on making me a joker? I'm a very serious fellow, and everybody wants to make me a joker."

"You're always making jokes, and you know it. You may keep a serious face, but you're always making jokes. Rotten little jokes."

"Why are you so mad all of a sudden?"

"I'm not mad. I'm tired and I want to go to bed."

"Most women like my jokes."

"Well, not me."

"Why are you so threatened by jokes?"

"Why the hell should you care?" She yawned again.

He yawned again. "Watch your language, Raines. You were a very proper young lady when I met you. Now you're talking like a stevedore."

"I say why the hell should you care?"

"Because I like you. You're a nice person. You're a dedicated officer. And something's happening to you."

"Just take me home, will you?"

TRANSCRIPT FOR ALPHA'S REFERENCE FILE ONLY

Phone conversation, "M" Line

"Hello."

" 'Seed,' this is 'M.' "

"Stardust."

"Deep Purple."

"What's up?"

"I've just had a call from 'Alpha.' He has given me an order to pass along to you."

"What does he want me to do?"

"Kill Kaufmann."

"Why? He's going Stateside. I attended his going-away party just last night."

"You know better than to ask why. Just do it."

"Any special way?"

"Discreetly."

"Well—"

"I'll call you if there's anything else."

SATURDAY
22 September 1945

9

"I need some help, Vince."

"What kind of help?" Ludwig sipped thoughtfully from his towering stein of Stateside Budweiser.

"I'm working on something that's verboten in official G-2 channels. I have to make an end run."

"I heard you were on your way home."

"Not for a week or so. Meanwhile, I'm trying to save the world from the dreadful midnight of Armageddon and the subsequent Day of Judgment, in which the wheat will be separated from the chaff and you sinning bastards will be up to your kiesters in fire and rhinestones."

"So what can I do to escape The Wrath?"

He handed Ludwig the photo of Klug. "Know him?"

After a moment of silent appraisal, Ludwig said, "No."

"Next question: Can you get me a file from Allen Dulles, chief of OSS in Bern?"

Ludwig gave him a sidelong glance. "Dulles is returning to the States. OSS is being disbanded. The Bern mission, as we've come to know and love it, is closing down, pal."

"So if I hurry I can see the file before they burn it."

"I'm afraid you're too late for Dulles. And my Bern link is about to vaporize, too."

"Damn."

There was a pause, an interval given to the soft music murmuring from the bar radio. Considering him in the back-bar mirror, Kaufmann decided that Ludwig's bony face, with its dark, restless eyes, portrayed the clichéd CIC man.

The 970th Counter-Intelligence Corps Detachment was the Theater headquarters group for what the Germans called "Eisenhower's Gestapo" and what the army elite called "the GI Mafia." It was, of course, neither, being a rather tiny organization charged by the War Department with ferreting out and arresting or "turning around" those spies, hoods, saboteurs, seditionists (both foreign and domestic) and other low-lifes too grubby and, well, dangerous for the more august security agencies to deal with. Because the CIC was on a daily eyeball basis with Europe's trash, it was inevitable that the Corps itself began to collect bad notices—living testimony, as it were, to the apothegm re fleas being caught by lying down with dogs.

Thus it was axiomatic among the military polloi that if you wanted to score importantly on the black market, or to legitimize your looting, or to acquire the absolute best in liquor and sexual diversion, the best first move was to call up your neighborhood CIC man, who was reputed to deliver anything at all, for an obscene price, from his ill-gotten, incredibly opulent purveyance. The fact was that CIC, having its share of heroes and bums, was no better or no worse than any watchdog instrumentality, but this reality never seemed to catch up with the libel, and after a time most CIC agents learned to live with—even began to enjoy—the mystique and glamour society appends to those of sinister reputation. In Frankfurt things were not helped by the fact that the 970th's offices were located in the Farben Building on the same floor as G-2's; instead of endowing the CIC with a touch of social acceptability, the adjacency did no more than further elevate the patrician noses of USFET's Pharisees.

Since Kaufmann had often elected to crawl under the rocks in his efforts to thwart the Nazi Abwehr, he had come to know and appreciate certain CIC agents he'd found among the bugs squirming there. And one of the best was the man who now sat on the barstool next to his own: Special Agent Vince Ludwig, presently operations chief of the CIC's Frankfurt municipal detachment, which was headquartered in a shrapnel-pocked brownstone on Mylius Strasse, a few blocks south of the Farben Compound, and which was famed for its collection of exotic potables. The most famous were the chocolate malted milkshakes that had been served in celebration of Memorial Day, 1945—served in a broken city on a broken continent where there had been no ice cream for a violent eternity.

Ludwig's shrug showed he had come to a decision. Lighting a cigarette, he said through the resultant cloud, "Why don't you talk to Tom Ballentine? He's a heavy-caliber OSS gun who worked the Bern mission since the beginning. He might have some ideas."

"Where do I find him?"

"Heidelberg. He's been asked to shut down the mission there. I had lunch with him two days ago."

"Can I use your name?"

"I'll do better than that. I'll give him a buzz and tell him to expect you."

"Appreciate it. Anything I can do for you in return?"

"Yeah. Introduce me to Ava Gardner."

"You realize Ava and I are an item, don't you?"

"I plan to steal her away from you." Ludwig took a concluding sip of beer. "Something you can really do, though."

"Name it."

"Let me use you as a reference. I'll be applying for membership in whatever agency replaces OSS."

"Sure. But I'm surprised. I thought you'd be only too glad to get out of this rotten business."

Ludwig stubbed his cigarette in an ashtray labeled "Es lebe unser Führer Adolf Hitler." Pointing to his reflection in the mirror, he said, "Can't you just see that man there coming home from his day on the assembly line at the Titanic Thingamajig Corporation in Ashtabula? Stepping around tricycles in the driveway and asking the little lady what's for supper?"

"I'll admit that stretches the old imagination a bit. But why don't you just stay in CIC? Until something comes up. I have a definite feeling you'll be getting a nice job offer from higher up. Your talent's too good to be wasted."

"Bad idea. They're already trying to turn CIC back into soldier boys. Without a war, CIC will be no more than a bunch of GI Joes, counting cadence as they march off to ring doorbells and arrest AWOLs. Me, I'm a Clark Kent." Ludwig sighed, pushed away from the bar and nodded toward the door. "Come on upstairs. I'll call Ballentine from my office."

Kaufmann steered the jeep across the temporary Main River bridge and a rubbled corner of Offenbach and then achieved the southbound Autobahn, which, happily, remained fairly intact between Frankfurt and Mannheim, thanks to a war in which both sides thought the highway might be useful one of these days. One of these days had come and gone, and the Germans had guessed wrong, discovering to their ultimate chagrin that the artery they'd protected so strenuously, to keep the Reich's economic and military blood flowing, was now surging thickly, twenty-four hours a day, with Ami convoys overladen with cigarettes, candy, booze, prophylactics and horny soldiers looking for places in which to apply them all in whatever order might randomly unfold.

The open door soon clogged again, and as he slowed to match its pace his mind went to Vince Ludwig's doleful rejection of the American standard: happiness in an elm-shaded house full of wife, kids, pets and the material effluvia of a steady job down at the sash weight company. Life after war's death was a subject that he had, until now, denied much thought; for the past four years virtually every waking moment had been given to the effort of outwitting and eluding millions of people whose waking moments were given to the effort of killing him, so daydreams of levels that were split and grass that was crabbed in urbs that were subbed were, perforce, few and far apart. But in Vince's mirrored face, heavy and lined and no longer young, he had seen something of his own—and evidence of an inner understanding that there would never, ever, be any going back.

How do you keep them down on the farm? How do you keep them believing in God and the Boy Scouts and Ipana's Smile of Beauty, after they've seen Dachau and Buchenwald and Hiroshima?

So what would he do with his life?

Leave the service and suffocate in the civilian world's endless bogs of hypocrisy and boredom and schlock?

Remain in the service womb and wonder for the rest of his days if he could have climbed the outside mountain?

He heard the questions in his mind, but they were followed by the world's longest pregnant pause.

The Opel was still there, behind him. It had held an unwavering position about a quarter-mile to the rear ever since Darmstadt. The constancy, the deliberateness, were the giveaway. Otherwise the car would have been lost in the flow, which was mainly live, mostly muddy, and entirely inscrutable.

At Mannheim, the Autobahn degenerated, becoming a ragged path across a tortured prairie of craters and snaggle-tooth ruins, and eventually a Military Police checkpoint blocked the fork whose crumbling tines led to Ludwigs-haven on the Rhine's west bank and, to the east, to Heidelberg. Actually it was two checkpoints—one for U.S. military vehicles, the other for civilians, both pedestrian and wheeled, and this, he saw, would work to his advantage.

He directed the jeep into the military lane where, immobilized by the crush ahead, he turned off the motor, bit into a Zagnut candy bar Raines had given him as a bon voyage gift, and opened his copy of *Yank*, peering over it to watch the thin line of civilian vehicles inching along a few meters to the left. His tail had two choices: to go through the checkpoint like all the other non-military traffic or to turn off the Autobahn into local Mannheim streets, which would cause him to lose Kaufmann and whatever it was he was trying to learn by watching him.

The Opel nosed into the civilian lane, and Kaufmann had turned through less than half of the magazine when the line moved forward sufficiently to put the tacky sedan directly alongside.

The man at the wheel pushed his cap forward and hunched down in the seat, and Kaufmann, amused, wondered if he had flattened his ears, as a stalking cat does when making small and invisible.

Pretending to be completely lost in his reading and chewing, he watched the Opel clear the checkpoint and, after a moment's hesitation, move off in a cloud of blue smoke with the westbound Ludwigshaven traffic.

Kaufmann closed the magazine, started the motor and, flanking the knot of GI traffic, eased forward to the MP shelter, where he flashed his G-2 credentials and was waved through with a curious glance from the duty sergeant.

As he made for the blue hills to the east he wondered why he had not been surprised or shocked. Then, thinking of the jaded Ludwig again, of his own years in the back alleys, he saw that there was little left to truly surprise or shock him again.

He said aloud, "Take it from me, Phony-Corporal Ransky, you'd never make it in the Wiesbaden Air Police. As a tail you make a good chorus girl."

10

He stood on the open balcony in the shade of huge autumn-tinted trees he couldn't identify. Across the river, on the lap of the Königstuhl, the ruined castle brooded through yet another of the 27,000 afternoons that had passed since Conrad of Hohenstaufen, Count Palatine of the Rhine, had given the place its final inspection, paid off the contractors and taken over the deed.

"Beautiful town, eh?" Ballentine handed him a drink.

Kaufmann nodded. "There's no place like it."

Heidelberg had been spared by Eisenhower, partly because it would make a good headquarters for the U.S. 7th Army, partly because it was a genuinely world-famous historical site, and partly because it was just so damned beautiful anybody who'd even think of trashing it ought to have his buns kicked. Say what you want about the town as a hotbed of Nazism, a prime generator of German pomp and arrogance, and the home of that eerie amalgam of priggishness, pedantics and mayhem called "the University"—few places on earth could manage to look as pretty at any time, in any weather, and during any phase of the moon. And in the center of the prettiest part sat this chic north-bank villa, not too large, not too small, not too ancient, not too contemporary, occupied by a portly fellow *Time* magazine would probably call "graying, grumping, gracious and grandiloquent Thomas L. Ballentine."

"They're tearing down everything we've built so carefully since the war began," the graying Ballentine grumped grandiloquently. "They speak piously—no, make that superciliously—of what they call a continuum of resources and policies via a unification of services now provided by many agencies. I grant you that there is a good bit of redundancy in the mix, but in the total American war machine OSS stood alone in the demanding, esoteric and labyrinthine art form known as the gathering of positive intelligence, and it's entirely irrational to dismantle this great agency when so many of the others are mere appendages to the archaic structures devised by antediluvian militarists and are consequently expendable in the pragmatic sense."

Was he expected to respond to all this? Kaufmann said, "Hm."

"It's plain ward politics, that's what it is. Harry Truman, the archetypal ward-heeler and pawn of Missouri bossism, has inherited the presidency and is determined to leave his stamp on history, even if it's no more than changing the wallpaper in the White House bathrooms. He and our OSS chief, General Bill Donovan, are not, of course, on very cordial terms, what with the general's education, military celebrity, personal wealth and social prominence. And—"

This was too much for Kaufmann. Staring off at the castle, he said, "The way I hear it, Bill Donovan is a king-size, ultra-right-wing horse's ass whose main talent is alienating those who could help him the most. And I also hear that Harry Truman is a very ballsy guy who knows a lot about government."

There was a taut moment in which the only sounds were the breeze in the trees and the muted traffic on the Neuenheimerlandstrasse below. Then the sound of soft laughter. Ballentine's laughter.

"Ludwig said you're an up-front sort of guy. A rather huge understatement, I'd say."

Kaufmann gave him a glance, curious.

"I hope you'll forgive me, Major Kaufmann, but I had to try you out. After my years at our embassies in Helsinki, Moscow and Bern, with all the genuflecting and hem-kissing and dissembling, I've become a curmudgeon—absolutely intolerant of time-wasting pussyfooting. I've found that the quickest way to take a man's measure is to say something which you know he will consider outrageous, incorrect, or witless. In this case, Bill Donovan is in no way a horse's ass, as you put it, but he is indeed eccentric and has little aptitude for parlor politics and he has indeed very few friends in the U.S. and British intelligence communities. This sad fact, coupled with President Truman's very real need to update and streamline our intelligence-gathering machinery in the face of Stalin's bellicosity, has put Donovan—and the rest of us in the agency—on the way out." He paused. "But more pertinent to this moment is the fact that I've discovered you to be a man who likewise detests indirection and hyperbole and is therefore ready for substantive discussion. Right?"

"My very words."

Ballentine gave him a quick, amused glance; then took a lingering sip of his drink and made an appreciative sound. "So why does Bern interest you, Mr. Kaufmann?"

" 'Sunrise.' How did it break open, how did it close?"

Ballentine's pale little eyes considered him. "You don't know? It caused quite a stir for a time. A lot of traffic on the cables, inter-agency advisories. That kind of thing. Where were you?"

"Up to my eyes on the Gehlen thing. I plead guilty to a too-casual reading of my routine mail. I skimmed the advisories, acquainting myself with Sunrise's essentials, then popped back to Gehlen when I saw no apparent relevance to what I was busy with. So, while I know what Sunrise was about, I don't know how it happened. And right now I'm interested in how Wolff, the SS main gear for Italy, got in touch with you guys at Bern. I can't imagine that he just drove up to your office one nice afternoon and said, 'Hi, I'm Kurt Wolff and I wonder if you've got a minute to hash over a little surrender thing I've been kicking around.' "

Ballentine rested his ample rear against the filigreed railing and smiled, a touch condescendingly, Kaufmann thought. "He used an intermediary, of course. It was last February. Baron Luigi Parilli, an Italian industrialist and papal chamberlain, made contact with our office in Bern. He said he was acting as messenger for SS General Wolff, who—in return for personal amnesty in war crimes charges being laid against him—was ready to arrange the unconditional surrender of all German and Italian Fascist units under his command in the Mediterranean area. There was a lot of jockeying around, a lot of gibble-gabble between lesser intermediaries—I can't remember all the details because I was working on something else at the time—but eventually Wolff and Dulles got together for some talks in a most secret place—Ascona, a village near the Swiss-Italian border, as I recall—and it turned out that Wolff thought he could also talk Field Marshal Kesselring and other members of the German high command into joining him in such a surrender."

Kaufmann broke in. "Hitler had decreed no surrenders at all—a scorched-earth battle to the last German. Wolff, Kesselring, the others, would be committing high treason."

"To be sure. But Wolff acknowledged that Germany was finished and Hitler had become all talk, no substance. And he was convinced that the German troops, even the most fanatical, would call it a day if he and the high command gave the order."

"So why didn't the war end last February? Why did it go on until May?"

"Touché. Why indeed? The answer, I regret to say, is that President Roosevelt still cherished the idea that, if he and Generalissimo Stalin could become personal, trusting friends, postwar international stability would be virtually guaranteed. In short, the president wanted most urgently to avoid hurting Stalin's feelings.''

Kaufmann sniffed. "Stalin has no feelings.''

"Whether he does or does not is irrelevant. President Roosevelt perceived him as having feelings. And so, when Stalin learned of the Wolff talks, the generalissimo obviously feared that the U.S. and Britain—in direct violation of long-standing agreements with the Soviets—were planning to make a separate peace with the Nazis, thus freeing millions of Germany's remaining troops to concentrate on the war against Russia. He became enraged and sent Roosevelt a blisteringly insulting cable, denouncing the president as a double-dealing sneak and demanding that either the talks with Wolff cease or the Soviets be included in them.''

Kaufmann nodded. He had learned long ago that the one thing guaranteed to give Stalin the dreads was any hint that the Western Allies would make a separate peace with Hitler.

"Well," Ballentine said, "his paranoia effectively lengthened the European war—perhaps even the war against Japan—by several months. Wolff and Kesselring were ready to pack it in, but Stalin's cable so rattled Roosevelt he ordered us in Bern to cease and desist—to break off all further talks with Wolff.''

Kaufmann blinked. "I swore I'd never say this, but now I have no choice: You're joking.''

"It's a fact.''

"Well, if Roosevelt was so antsy about what Stalin felt about things, why didn't he invite the generalissimo to take part in the talks with Wolff? Hell—''

"Excellent, perceptive question, my boy. But no cigar. When Dulles suggested such an invitation Wolff got very angry, claiming that his troops—no German troops anywhere—would ever sign an unconditional surrender with the Russians. The Russians, he said, are the Germans' hated natural enemy and his people would die before willingly sitting down to talk surrender with Communists.''

"So Roosevelt was left with two choices: either kiss Stalin's katooty or exploit Wolff."

"And he elected the former."

"Shee-it."

"That's the word I myself applied to the situation when I learned of it. There's more, though."

"Oh?"

"Stalin apparently went into a tantrum. He decided on a show of force—a demonstration of his ability to cause trouble for us good guys—and there began some very heavy and bloody uprisings in Northern Italy, Yugoslavia and Greece. The red partisans went on a rampage and they're going on to this day."

"You mean the unrest down there is Stalin's vengeance for talks with Wolff that never came off?"

"True, to a point. Stalin was indeed retaliating in advance for a betrayal we had no intention of making. Which, in turn, ticked off Roosevelt—"

"God, I should think so."

"—And the president ordered the Wolff talks to resume. Which they did. And so Stalin ordered his North Italian partisans to kidnap and execute Wolff."

"But Dulles ordered OSS agents to rescue him."

"Right. You know about that, then."

"I talked to one of your guys. Bianco. He was on the team that pulled Wolff out of the fire."

"Mm. The upshot was that Wolff's Mediterranean armies surrendered about a week earlier than the rest of the German armed forces."

"Meaning we gained a week of peace in Italy and are still paying for it by way of Stalin's hell-raising."

"And this is only the beginning, I'm afraid. There's no telling how long—or on what scale—Stalin's vengeance will be worked on us."

"You want to bet it's forever? As long as the old bastard lives? As long as his politics live?"

"I'm not so gloomy as that, Major. Stalin has more to

gain by being nice to us than he does by being mean to us. He'll come around.''

"That's Western logic. Stalin thinks Eastern.''

There was a lull in which the future drifted, dark and silent, across the sun-dappled balcony.

''I'd like you to guess a bit for me, Mr. Ballentine.''

''In what way?''

''I've been curious about the unrest in the Balkans, in Italy. I've asked around for some clues as to what's behind all of it. Stalin's vengeance, you say, and I can accept that, even though Stalin's Eastern logic defies me. But what I'm really curious about is why my asking questions of people in my own army might have caused two of them, a captain and a tech sergeant, and a third person, a German waitress, to be killed. Why a general officer would get all upset over my looking for some answers. Why somebody has put a tail on me—and might well be planning to kill me. Can you guess at why these things are so?''

Ballentine went to the roll-around bar, and his eyebrow asked Kaufmann if he wanted another Scotch. When Kaufmann shook his head, the big man poured himself a refill, tasted it, then placed it carefully on the sculpted railing beside him.

''I have been immersed in international intrigues for many years now, Major Kaufmann. There is little that I haven't seen or participated in by way of chicanery and political scam. And the single greatest legacy of those years is an understanding that men will do anything, up to and including murder, to acquire power over other men. Whether it be economic power via money and property, or political power via the buyable ballot or the violent revolution, there is nothing—absolutely nothing—so heinous as to be left off the list of techniques. Look at the Warsaw Ghetto. Or Dachau. Who is killing your interviewees? Who is bullying you personally? You need only to find the one—or three— in your own army who stand to gain from the Balkan-Italian unrest. Is there someone who will be enriched? Is there someone who will gain political power? Which of the someones see your questions as threats to the success of their intentions? You don't need guesses. You need detective work.''

This, Kaufmann thought testily, *has simply got to be the world's greatest windbag. He's used a hundred words to say "It beats the hell out of me." Give him ten years and he'll be elected president. Or at least a senator.*

"Where do I find Baron Parilli, Mr. Ballentine?"

"Rome, I'd say. Although most of his financial interests are in the north. It was one of the reasons he was so anxious to help General Wolff end the war."

"Then he wouldn't stand to gain anything from the partisan unrest thereabouts, eh?"

"I think you could say that. But it's all rather academic. Parilli really doesn't know anything of value. In the Wolff thing he was an intermediary, nothing more."

"One more question. Does the codename 'C-rations' mean anything to you?"

" 'C-rations.' " The big man gave this some thought, after which he shook his head. "No. It's meaningless to me."

"Well," Kaufmann sighed, "I have no time left for all this crap anyhow. I'm going home soon."

Ballentine gave him a quick glance. "Then why are you asking all these questions?"

"Your guess is as good as mine."

"I must say you're an odd sort."

Kaufmann nodded. "I must say that, too."

"Well, then. Anything else I can do for you, Major?"

He held out his glass. "I've reconsidered. I'll have another nudge of Ballentine's Ballentine's. For the road."

11

The one for the road had been a mistake.

He'd had nothing to eat that day but the candy bar Raines had given him, and the whiskey hit him suddenly and hard. He had barely got the jeep headed for the Old Bridge when he became giddy and felt as if he might be sick.

All of which made him careless. As he pulled the jeep to the curbing of the Neuenheimerlandstrasse, he was only slightly aware of a black car coasting to a halt behind him. And he was entirely surprised when hands seized him, a needle pricked his neck, and he was dragged from behind the steering wheel and placed, not too gently, in the front passenger seat.

"Steady there," he thought he heard himself saying, "you have just placed my entire weight on some rather tender equipment, which is unaccountably at cross purposes with my GI shorts. Unless you alter my position, it's possible that future generations will be devoid of Kaufmann progeny."

He felt a shove. "Talky bastard, aren't you?" he thought he heard someone mutter in accented English.

"I consider myself rather taciturn, actually. Obviously I'm still under the influence of that Crown Prince of Pompous Prolixity, Thousand-word Ballentine. I'm not like this in real life, though. My mother, a fan of American films, likens me to Gary Cooper. Yup, nope, and all that. But my father, who is a Flying Dutchman wandering the melancholy seas of untenured Academia, has said many times that he wishes that I'd just shut up. I suspect that you are in my father's camp. In my father's camp are many mansions. No, make that manhandlers. No—"

The gauze, translucent at first, thickened suddenly, and the day diminished, becoming a twilight in which sound and motion took on a heaviness, the kind of weighty palpability they had presented when, as a boy delirious with scarlet fever, he would roll from his tangled bed and try for the bathroom. The sound of the jeep's motor snarling into acceleration was a drumfire, a string of tiny firecrackers detonating individually against his brain pan; the jouncing on the pitted street brought pain to the most minute and disparate corners of his body. The passing images, right and left, were a badly focused, poorly lighted slow-motion film viewed from the wrong end of binoculars.

He heard his voice again. "Where are you taking me?"

The captain behind the wheel—where had he seen that face before?—laughed softly and said, "You are indeed an unusual fellow, Major Kaufmann. Most men would have been solidly asleep by now. You sit there like a field marshal, making speeches and asking questions."

"I know who you are. You're Klug. Anna Krim's killer."

"Is that what she called me? Klug?"

"You have a big thing about wearing American uniforms, don't you, buddy."

He amassed what was left of his will to turn in his seat and roll free of the jeep, a task that compared with moving Spokane to the Jersey Shore. Worse, the effort was only partially successful, since he discovered, with his head hanging mere inches from the blur of macadam, that his left leg had been roped to the jeep frame and if he didn't somehow return to the upright at once his brains would draw a new highway centerline.

He would not have made it if Klug hadn't seized his jacket with a free hand and hauled him back aboard.

Kaufmann, speechless with shock and aware suddenly that the close call had somehow begun a clearing in his mind, slumped in the seat, struggling against the limpness that persisted. He tried counting backwards, but the lingering fog refused to let him choose a starting number. He tried to count forward from one, but he couldn't summon up what came after seven. Time was what he needed, but time was what he lacked. Closing his eyes and deepening the slump, he feigned unconsciousness.

"It's about time," he heard Klug say. "You could drug a concrete cow faster than this son of a bitch."

Watching the road through slitted lids, Kaufmann began to recognize things. They were on the road that hugged the north bank of the Neckar, heading east toward Hirschhorn. He had driven this way several times in the war's closing weeks. Was it the last part of April? After the wind-up of Operation—what was it? Bongo. Operation Bongo.

Other images, memories. The train station in the terrain cut at Ridley Park. The lake nearby, frozen in the winter, great for skating and chasing Allison Gregory, senior class queen, who would pretend to struggle when you got her down in a snowbank but who was really doing her own groping. Tommy Dorsey at Sunnybrook, and swaying by the bandstand while that skinny Sinatra kid crooned something special just for you and the Betty or Tillie or Annie or Whosie hanging on you so close you wished you'd worn baggier pants. Camp Ritchie and the clapboard barracks and the pseudo-Nazi interrogators and the rotten night problems in the mountain rain, freezing your ass off and squishing in your boots. London blackouts, Normandy hedges, French Communists pretending to be friendly, Gestapo agents pretending to be Frenchmen, friends pretending to be French

Communists, Frenchmen pretending to be Gestapo agents. Sneaking, listening, whispering, tapping keys, crawling, climbing, running, shooting, stabbing, arguing, laughing, crying, screwing, hiding, worrying. Lots of worrying. Lots of all of it. Mom: What would she say if she'd seen him that night in the Wehrmacht brothel in the Montmartre? Pop: What would he say about anything? Anything at all? Chocolate cake. Huge, black-brown. God, what he'd give for a piece of chocolate cake. A vanilla malt, four feet high. A hoagy. One of those on a crisp loaf you could buy only in southside Chester, beside the Delaware River, a yard long, filled to the roof with meats and cheese and sweet onions and lettuce and tomatoes—fresh goddam tomatoes, red and running with juice—all of it sprinkled with oregano and that special Philly kind of olive oil that didn't taste like oil at all but like a clear, twangy gravy, for crissake.

Something else, too. Something more recent. Fresher.

Something very important.

The jeep. The side of the jeep. Flat, dented, dusty. The trenching shovel, clamped there against the dusty dents. The highway inches away, and the eyes watering and the dusty jeep showing its trenching shovel through the teary fright.

Clamps.

Not locks, chains, lashings. Clamps. Flip-open clamps.

He let his right arm dangle over the side, rolling his head like a sodden commuter on the 5:15 to Westport.

There.

Flip one. Then move hand slowly to the rear. Hold onto the goddam shovel handle and flip Clamp Two, all with the one hand and while your eyes are slitted and the train wobbles through Stamford.

Concentrate now. Easy does it. Grasp the shovel handle firmly in your right hand, like so. Then ease the shovel from its mount. (See Paragraph 7, Page 9, Army Field Manual 987, ''The Lifting and Swinging of Trenching Shovels, Model 1943, as modified, from Sides of Dusty Jeeps While Recovering from Drug Injections.'')

"What are you doing there?" Klug's sidelong glance was full of angry surprise.

"I'm now applying Paragraph Eight."

Kaufmann swung the shovel with the strength left to him, which didn't seem to be enough and most certainly would, when spent, no longer support his laboring heart, thus sending him into an infarction, or whatever that dirty word was that doctors used when talking about The Final Gasp. Meanwhile, the shovel was clanging against Klug's head, sending his captain's service cap spinning into the windy void and laying open the skin from temple to nape, so as to fill the slipstream with a red mist and a combined scream and curse from the gaping mouth, which showed the gold of an upper partial knocked loose from its mountings.

Such detail was an aberration, a flicker of perception in a drifting fog, and the rest was a montage of imprecise snapshots, laid before him and then withdrawn in a split of time, like those memory tests given to agents prepping for a paradropped tourist mission: Klug sagging against the wheel; a violent swerving and the chirping of tires in torment; the oncoming trees; the fountain of dust and the flying branches and the crazy bouncing and the terminating slam against an incredible oak, huge, dark with autumn leaves, adamant.

The silence. A terrible quietness. Not even a bird calling, a leaf rustling.

Then a soft sound. The sly dripping of oil and fuel.

A hissing.

Not hissing. Breathing. His breathing.

Panic gathering. A reaching, a tugging for his knife, the pocket knife with the gleaming blades and the nail file, given to him by his mother on Christmas, 1938, and which had opened V-mail and C-ration tins and cranky windows and had whittled away boredom and presided at bivouac mumblety-peg games.

And which now cut away the rope from his ankle and allowed him to stagger to the pine-needle mulch of the wooded slope and to lie for a time, staring at the wreck and the mannikin-like Klug, shoved against the crushed wheel and the bent-in dashboard and the broken glass of the windshield, mouth open and streaming red on the ruined face, eyes glazed in their sightless staring at the Odenwald's mellow hills.

Eventually he came to some decisions, basic to his current condition and whatever future remained to him.

First things first.

He managed to return to the wreck, where he unpinned the captain's bars from Klug's uniform and replaced them with his own major's leaves. His wallet and AGO card and trip ticket went into Klug's jacket pocket, and Klug's went into his own for future reference. These would surely tell him nothing momentous, being fake as they surely were, but fakeness had been known to reveal something of its own origins and therefore prove to be tangentially useful, and so what the hell, why not?

He found his Zippo, the one he'd bought at the Fort Benning PX when he'd been sent down there for parachute training, and clicking it into a flaring, he muttered, "So long for now, Major Kaufmann, you dear, dear boy. And so long for good, Captain Klug, you bad, bad man."

12

An MP escorted Anton to a Nissen hut—one of those round-top tin things that defined the word ugly—on a farm outside Dijon. A long table bisected the main room, and a solitary bulb, shaded by a metal cone, cast a cheerless circle of light on a bald bird colonel who sat at a microphone, pretending to read a file. To the rear, dim in the shadows, a staff sergeant fussed with what looked to be a dictation machine.

"Sit down, Thoma," the colonel said in accented, but excellent, German. He waved at the folding chair across the table from him. "Close to the microphone, so the recorder can pick up our voices."

Anton sat, politely alert, as Kaufmann would have wanted him to. (Germans are a very formal people, Kaufmann had said, and one must be careful never to be relaxed and familiar in a meeting.) Kaufmann's faintly pedantic manner had proved to be one of the more vexatious parts of this trick. Anton had lived and schooled among enough Germans, in Germany, to know precisely how insufferable Germans could be. All he had to do to come across as an insufferable German was to imitate that dirty prick, Heinz Volkmann, who had been as obsequious as a headwaiter when the professors were around and a goddam Tyrannosaurus rex when they weren't.

"You have been brought here," the colonel said, "to answer some questions—some special questions."

"I'll do my best, Colonel. I have nothing to hide."

The colonel got right to the point. "On your Fragebogen you admit to membership in the Nazi Party. You've detailed your rise through the various levels of the Luftwaffe and have given a basic picture of your military service—the Battle of Britain, the Italian campaign, et cetera, et cetera. But what are not clear, of course, are certain, ah, more intimate aspects of your political persuasions."

"Does the colonel mean I am about to be condemned to death?"

"What makes you ask that?"

"We were told by our superiors that capture by the Americans meant questions, torture and eventual execution by very unpleasant means. I am assuming that my time has come, that you are preparing to pass judgment."

"Does that idea frighten you?"

"Frighten me, sir? Hardly. I am a German flier. I am not frightened by difficulty, death. I have lived with them for years. They are old companions."

"And you are also a Nazi. It is an honor to die for the Third Reich, eh?"

"If I may be allowed to correct the colonel: It is an honor to die for the Fatherland. The Nazis are finished, the Fatherland is eternal. I was a Nazi in the early 1930s, as a schoolboy. The Hitler Youth, the Young Pioneers, that kind of thing. I was no politician. I was simply going along with the crowd. But my Germanness, my love for the Fatherland, is constant, inborn. It is a matter that has nothing to do with political parties."

The colonel sighed, visibly irritated. "God, how tired I am of hearing that same old tune. Every German I've spoken to in this godforsaken business has never been a dedicated Nazi—only a frigging innocent doing what was socially acceptable."

"I don't know about every German, sir. I know only about this German."

"What do you think of the Russians?"

Anton hesitated, truly surprised by this sudden turn in the questioning. How would Heinz Volkmann answer? Smoothly arrogant, of course. And with the straight party line.

"The Russians are Germany's natural enemy, sir. As they are for you Americans. You will have to fight the Russians someday. They are sworn to destroy you."

"Tens of thousands of former members of the Wehrmacht, the Luftwaffe, the Kriegsmarine, are waiting in line these days to enlist in the American army for the war they see us Americans soon fighting against the Russians. Are you aware of that, Captain Thoma?"

Was he ever. He and Suzi (Was that her name?), who had pretended to be French but was really a Polish DP and who had pretended passion for him but was really hungry and cold, had been held up for nearly ten minutes in their dash for that crummy little pension on that rainy day in Mainz, when he'd gone politely AWOL from Bad Schwalbach. The street had been a mass of released German POWs, all in polyglot uniforms dyed blue, crowding the entrance to the American Military Government office, demanding enlistment forms to sign, insisting they'd heard on the radio that the U.S. was accepting non-Nazi Germans in its armed forces for the coming assault on the USSR.

"I am not surprised, Colonel, sir."

"Why are you not surprised? I am. These men have survived years of bloody fighting. They are weary to the bone. They have been released to homes that are mere rubble, to families that have been decimated by concussion, shrapnel, flames, starvation. And now they want to sign up for more of the same, in the very army whose soldiers have caused their agonies, their losses."

The speech had been memorized, Anton was sure. It had

been delivered in a rhythm not unlike that to be heard in Sunday pulpits, and it had been about as convincing. In fact, this entire episode suggested tired repetition, a presentation that had been rehearsed to flatness, given over and over again.

"As you say, Colonel, sir, they have little else. They have lost virtually everything but their lives. Their losses can be attributed mainly to the Communist international conspiracy. It's only natural that they dream of vengeance."

The colonel consulted the file. "Your home is Munich. That city was bombed by American planes, not Russian."

"To be sure, Colonel, sir. But you Americans have also been victimized by the Communist conspiracy. You have been duped into seeing Germany as your enemy, when your enemy is actually the Soviet Union. Most Germans understand that. They despise you for what you have contributed to their misery, and they won't soon forget it. But they hold the Russians accountable."

The colonel's gray eyes narrowed and he leaned forward, not too far, so as to appear threatening, but far enough to emphasize what he obviously thought was an expression of bitter challenge. "And the Communist conspiracy is really the cause for your having bombed London, those other English cities? You were getting at the Russians by bombing English women and children?"

Anton shrugged, the way Volkmann would have. "The Führer gave the English every opportunity to avoid such treatment. He told them openly that he had no quarrel with them—that all they need do was to mind their own business, stay off the Continent, and allow us Germans to settle our political and economic disputes with France, Poland, Russia—the others. But the English chose instead to war against us, kill our men, bomb our cities. The English earned what they got."

"So, then," the colonel said dryly, changing the subject again, "you are a flier." His glance flickered over the folder. "A multi-engine pilot. Heinkel 111s. JU-88s. You like to fly?"

"Of course, sir."

"Do you wish to continue flying?"

"More than anything, sir."

"As a military pilot, or what?"

"In any capacity, anywhere. Flying is all I have, sir."

"No surviving family? No, ah, betrothed?"

"No one, Colonel. I am a man alone. Flying is all I have, all that counts with me."

"That is why you don't fear our plans to kill you?"

"Precisely, sir. If I can't fly, I'd be dead anyhow."

There was a pause, a fleeting thing, like one of those beats in a theatrical presentation, when an actor signals a change of pace or attitude. And during this tiny interval Anton realized he had given voice to a long-sublimated truth. Flying was indeed all there was in his life. No person, not even the once-adored father, now a mere figment, a non-presence, could compel his interest or relieve his aloneness; no material thing could stir his inert ambitions. Only flying. Really, truly, there was nothing else.

"Very well, Thoma, that will do for now."

"May I ask a question, Colonel, sir?"

"What is it?"

"Why am I, a bona fide prisoner of war, being treated this way—to mystery, interrogations, execution?"

The colonel looked past Anton's shoulder and called in English, "Corporal, please escort this officer to his quarters."

Anton stood, clicked his heels, making a Luftwaffe-type half bow, then about-faced and marched out with the MP.

The silence held for a time, then the colonel turned in his chair and called out again. "You are dismissed also, Klingel."

A second lieutenant came out from behind a partition, making for the door. The colonel said as he passed, "Thank you, Klingel, for your help. You are a good interpreter."

"Thank you, sir. Thoma spoke quite clearly and his German is that of an educated man. Incidentally, the earphones can be left with the machine there.''

When they were alone, the colonel turned to the staff sergeant. "So, sir, he's the last one. What do you think?"

The man with the sergeant's stripes placed the earphones on the table beside him. "Karla's right. He should do nicely. Take him to U and sign him up. Time's very short.''

"Yes, sir. Anything else?''

"No, that will do for now. Good day, Colonel.''

"Good day, General.''

13

Kaufmann had learned when he was ten years old that you should never stand around when you have a chance to run. Especially when you're innocent.

He had been on a hike with Rog Benson and Walt Pinchard. In a large field near Essington, the grass became littered with golf balls and they were stooping to look them over when a squad of driving range attendants came running to nab what looked to be a trio of ball thieves. Rog and Wally had taken off, but he, innocent, stood his ground. After a four-hour wait, during which he'd stood in the range office, bare-ass naked, while the bastards searched his clothes for golf balls and made jokes about his wienie, his father arrived to persuade the county cops that there really wasn't enough evidence of attempted larceny. On the ride home, Kaufmann-the-boy had vowed silently never to trust in innocence when a hundred-yard dash was an option.

And that was precisely why Kaufmann-the-man had elected to plant his personal belongings on a body in an incinerated jeep. It was much safer to run and hide as a

dead man than it was to explain to the police that he was
an American officer who had been kidnaped by an unidentified assassin whose employers most certainly would chase
him down again once they discovered Klug was dead and
dear-boy Kaufmann wasn't, or to stand around to sell the
fact that said Kaufmann's having been at the scene of at
least two other recent homicides was entirely coincidental
to this most regrettable and mysterious of contretemps.

He had lain in the cover of nearby underbrush, patching
a bad cut on his left forearm with bandages from the jeep's
first-aid kit and watching when the driver of the black sedan
came upon the wreckage, looked around a bit at the smoldering site, then haul-assed. Moments later Ransky came
by in his Opel, took one look at the fire, and voomed out
of sight. A GI six-by-six finally rumbled onto the scene and
the driver used a walkie-talkie to summon up the MPs, who
arrived in a rather surprisingly short time to walk around
importantly and say cryptic things into squawking radios.
After an ambulance made off with the charred body and the
wreck was marked by warning lights, he worked his way
through the woods to an intersection down the hill and eventually hitched a ride on a GI bus whose driver was taking
the vehicle to Heidelberg for maintenance and who had
much fun razzing Kaufmann's torn and bloody appearance.

"God, Captain, when you take a broad into the woods
it's an Olympic event, eh? Ha-ha."

"Shee-it. I thought we were on an innocent little picnic
in the woods with possibilities. You know. But I no more
than put my hand on her knee and she was Max Baer,
knocking hell out of me, screaming and waving a knife you
wouldn't believe it was so long. No more German women
for me, pal. They *all* belonged to the S-goddam-S, you ask
me."

He persuaded the driver to drop him off at the corner of
the ritzy side street at the foot of the Heiligenberg where
Emma Rupert headquartered her many enterprises in a noble brownstone. Emma was a failed nightclub singer who
had discovered that more could be made by selling night-

club singers than by being one. She had become a theatrical
agent during Hitler's political puberty, supplying perform-
ers for cabarets from Lübeck to Kitzbühl. As war approached, she diversified, first by catering tony girls for
private performances that rarely required singing, then with
a move into more esoteric areas, such as hot goods fencing,
underground railroading of rich political refugees, firearms
and explosives supply, currency laundering, phony pass-
ports and visas, and counterfeit ration stamps, ID cards,
drivers' licenses and Wehrmacht Soldbücher. She had become a Third Reich legend, cherished wherever dastardly
deeds were plotted by needy dastards. Need a car thief? A
building torcher? A safecracker? An Eskimo chanteuse? A
transvestite to tapdance on a Brownshirt's buns? See Emma.

Happily, this day her door was answered by Lisa, her
lover of many years, who had taken a liking to Kaufmann
during last winter's Operation Bongo, when he, on an over-
night, in-and-out OSS collaboration gone awry, had been
sheltered for three weeks in Emma's own bedroom. It was
the only place Emma's bigshot Nazi clientele would never
enter, thanks to the understanding that he who violated
Emma's personal privacy was he who would be denied Emma's
professional accommodation. She was known by G-2 to be
unabashedly avaricious and thoroughly apolitical, and so
Kaufmann had been directed to contact her in case the mission was blown because she'd be likely to honor the five
thousand American dollars he could put down on the total
of fifteen G-2 would pay at hostilities' end. The prediction
had been correct, since Germany was in a state of collapse
and most of the Nazi high-rollers were on the run, leaving
Emma casting about for ways to meet her outrageous overhead. A short-term sharing of Lisa's digs while an amiable
and well-heeled Ami spy hid in hers was not Emma's idea
of hardship.

"My God, Putzi, dear lad, what has happened to you?"
Lisa's large eyes showed genuine shock.

"I fell afoul of a jealous husband." He took her outstretched hand. "Good to see you, Lisa."

"And it's good to see you, too. Even if you do look like the wrath of God."

"It seems as if I only come around when I need help, eh?"

"No matter. As long as you come around. Come in. Emma is in the solarium, poking about in her geranium pots. She will be delighted to see you."

She was, too. She came at him, arms spread, her portly figure and flaring kimono suggesting an elephantine Dracula homing in on a swig. "Putzi! My darling Putzi! What a perfectly marvelous surprise!"

"You're looking well, Emma."

"And you look like living hell." She lifted him off his feet and bussed his ear. "Are you going to visit us again?"

"That depends on you." He tried not to reveal that her embrace had very nearly collapsed what remained of his ribs.

Emma made a mock-accusing face and clucked her tongue. "You are still trying to be a spy? You should know by now that you're not cut out for such work."

"So *that's* what's wrong."

She laughed and gave him a fond, renewed inspection. "I know better than to ask how you came to be in such tattered condition. Cuts, bruises. Poor darling."

"Even my aches have aches."

"Get those ratty clothes off. We'll attend to all of it. Lisa, fill the tub and fetch those surgical things in the hall closet. And the tape. The way he's holding his ribs he'll need a lot of it."

"I need everything, Emma. I'm on my own in a rotten little business, and I need a new ID. I need clothes, papers, a car, maybe some weapons. I need a place to stay and the use of a phone. I need money, too."

"My God, Putzi: Where's your army in all this? Have you deserted?"

"No. It just thinks I'm dead. I have to stay that way for a while. If I can manage it, I'll resurrect and reimburse you across the board. But right now you have nothing but my promise.''

She swept an arm in dismissal. ''That's good enough for me. Besides, business is good again, and I still have some of that ten thousand your cute little messenger brought to me last June. Your credit is excellent around here, young man.''

''You'll let me stay with you, then?''

''In the guest suite. Our honored guest. The phone works, too, by the way.''

''Right now I need that bath.''

She took his arm and led him from the plant-filled room to the corridor. She waved toward the far end. ''You know where the bathroom is.'' Glancing at Lisa, she said, ''Help him off with his things, dear. Right down to the buff. We've got a major cleaning job here.''

''No need,'' Kaufmann said. ''I'll handle it myself.''

''Darling, you know you needn't be uncomfortable with Lisa.''

''Since I was ten years old I've hated to have people watch me take my pants off.''

''Life in the army barracks must have been difficult for you,'' Lisa said sympathetically.

''Let me count the ways.''

''When we're finished you can help yourself to the wardrobe, darling. Suits. Jackets. Slacks. Sweaters. Most standard men's sizes. Take what you need.''

''I always wondered, Emma: Why do you keep all those things in that room?''

''You can't imagine how many times the Gestapo asked that same question. The answer I gave them was that some of my most important clients like to start the evening with big girls dressed like men.''

''They believed that?''

''Why not? It's a fact.''

He shook his head slowly. ''No accounting for tastes.''

''And it's no easy matter meeting them. Have you ever tried to find a large girl who looks good in a tuxedo?''

"I can't even fine a large tuxedo that looks good on me."

"But the main reason I keep those things is because other clients need new clothes to get across various borders, to flee irritable police. I think you know what I mean."

"Do I ever."

Emma sent his uniform to her tailor for salvage and replaced it with a brown English tweed jacket and tan gabardine trousers of vague but passable fit. A white shirt, green knit tie, and a loden Tyrolean hat, complete with silver horn and upright brush, and he was a somber Bertie Wooster, off on an Alpine weekend.

At the door she said, "Would a girl improve your disguise? I can arrange for one in no time at all—"

"No, thanks. You've done enough as it is."

"You're sure you've had enough to eat?"

"I'm full as a tick."

"I still think you're rushing things. You've been pretty badly mauled. You should rest up a bit."

"I can't afford the time, Emma."

"Any idea when you'll be back?"

"No. I have to go to Frankfurt. Establish some lines of communication with people I can trust. I'll be keeping close to the ground, so it might take some time." He paused, remembering. "I meant to ask you: Have you ever seen the man in this photo?"

Emma took the snapshot, studied it briefly, then gave him a worried glance. "This is Artur Bikler, a very evil man."

"B-I-K-L-E-R?"

"Mm. Avoid him. He's said to be a professional killer, and very touchy."

"Is he German?"

"Who knows? The word is that he's a former Gestapo agent, but no one really knows."

Kaufmann returned the photo to his wallet. "All right. So I'm on my way."

"The Mercedes will probably need some fuel. But those

papers show the car to be legal and you to be involved in UNRRA support work for the U.S. military government and so you should have not trouble. Any official Tankstelle will accommodate you. As I told you, there's a 'Stelle just down the road from my hunting lodge. Ask for Karli, the boss there. He's an old friend of mine, and he has keys to the lodge. I don't know what you'll do for a phone, but the lodge is otherwise supplied for trysts, et cetera—"

"I'll work something out, Emma. And I'm very grateful."

Emma's heavy face softened. "Take care of yourself, dear lad. You've been a—well, a friendly friend. It meant a lot to us that, even with all your own troubles, you fixed our electric flatiron, the leaky kitchen faucets—"

"You saved my life last winter, Emma. You and Lisa. The least I could do was fix your flatiron."

He gave them a wink and went down the walk to the car.

Cruising north on the Autobahn, he gave some serious thought to the most immediate of his remaining problems, all four hundred thousand of them.

He could remember seeing—not seeing, but sensing—the black car's roll to a halt behind him at the curb. Bikler had appeared then to tranquilize him, taking the wheel for a drive to the mountains and, no doubt, a staged accident featuring a jeep ride over a cliff.

The black car had been driven by somebody wearing a tan fedora. So when Bikler failed to show up at the wreck, the fedora would have to assume the burning body was Bikler's and that Kaufmann was still alive. The same assumption would have to be made by that peripatetic and enigmatic military policeman, Ransky.

Only the good guys would think he was dead. The bad guys would keep after him.

Which was not the main problem.

The main problem was to determine who were the good guys and who were the bad guys.

TRANSCRIPT FOR ALPHA'S REFERENCE ONLY
(Warning: Use No Dates or Participant IDs!)

Phone Conversation, 'M' Line:

"Hello?"

"Alpha?"

"Moonglow."

"My Reverie."

"So how did it go, 'M'?"

"Kaufmann has been canceled."

"All right. Any problems?"

"No problem. Just another irritating complication."

"Which is?"

" 'Cutie-pie' bought it, too."

"How did that happen?"

" 'Sweetums' and 'Cutie-pie' staged an auto wreck.
But 'Cutie-pie' got caught in the crash, too. Hell of a
fire."

" 'Sweetums'?"

"He's okay, 'Alpha.' Holed up in Hoechst."

"Tell him to stand by for further orders."

"Sure."

"And watch Raines. If she becomes a problem, can-
cel."

"Very well."

"Now get off the line. I'm busy."

FOR YOUR EYES ONLY
Destroy After Reading

URGENT CABLE

(Code Zinger)

To: Brandt
From: Gladiator

Kaufmann dead in auto crash.

FOR YOUR EYES ONLY
Destroy After Reading

URGENT CABLE
(Code Zinger)

To: Gladiator
From: Brandt

Reur urgent undated, this code: Keep watch on Raines.

SUNDAY
23 September 1945

14

Anton sank into the curve of the canvas beach chair and squinted disapprovingly at the sun-brilliant nowhere around him. The camp, or whatever it was, crowned a ridge that rose like a wrinkle in the apron of the violet Alpine wall behind him, and off to his left, a river, turgid, brown, snaked indolently southward across the hard-scrabble plain toward a distant smear of sea. Despite the chugging of a generator behind the kitchen shed and the rhythmic tapping of a hammer somewhere, there was a stillness, the kind of hush that comes to arid, stuccoed hamlets shuttered against the noonday glare.

He closed his eyes, feeling the alien world around him, virtually immobilized by loneliness. He sat, waiting for the seizure to pass.

A step sounded and, blinking, he met the sunglassed gaze of the colonel who had interviewed him in that hut near Dijon—when was it? The night before last?

"Good day, Major Thoma," he greeted him in accented German. "Welcome to Stage One."

"I had the idea I was the only living soul for a thousand miles. Where are we?"

"Later for that. Right now you are expected to attend a meeting at Stage Two. Did you have a pleasant flight last night?"

Anton sniffed. "How pleasant is a flight as the only passenger on a C-47 whose windows are blacked out and whose seats are benches along the fuselage wall? You are perhaps expecting me to commend you to travel agents?"

"Come with me," the colonel said, ignoring the sarcasm.

"Where are we going?"

"To that car. There, beside the mess hall."

"Where is the car going?"

"You ask too many questions, Major. Why don't you simply wait until things are explained?"

"Because I have a childlike curiosity about the world and its mysteries. Because I thirst for knowledge. Because I am sick and tired of all this goddamned secrecy that you and your smug-ass American pals have forced on me."

"No need to get angry, Major Thoma—"

"I am a prisoner of war in a war that's long since ended. I have answered all your questions. Cooperated with you. Given you no problems whatsoever. I should, by all the rules of war and common decency itself, be repatriated and allowed to go my way. But you wake me up in the middle of the night, blindfold me, toss me onto a prison plane and fly me for hours to this asshole of creation, where I sit alone and stare at rocks and sunbaked sheds. You misjudge me. I'm not angry. I am purple-faced furious. I am so frigging mad I'm ready to bite the ass end out of that car of yours."

"You are the last. That's why you've been alone."

"The last what?"

"Get in the car, Major. It'll all be made clear this afternoon."

As they rode, driven by a staff sergeant with blue jowls and a red nose, Anton realized that his main uneasiness—

make that the real source of his very real anger—was the fact that, as a good guy, he was altogether on his own. Since his recruitment by Kaufmann in Bad Schwalbach, his existence had been that of a ranch animal—always cared for, but never in a position to go helling off across the range, squalling to the world of his presence.

Specifically, he'd had no chance to message Kaufmann about his midnight switch to this crazy place. The Wintgens woman, a bucking bronco who had practically reduced his corral to splinters, had left him toward dawn and he had been incommunicado, fed on trays, for the remaining day. By nightfall his frustration had become so unmanageable he had scrawled a note of resignation, which he addressed to Kaufmann and placed on the table. He was about to go out the window when two MPs came to drive him to the airfield. He'd had no chance to retrieve the note before they took off. Well, too bad, within an hour he was on an airplane, a blacked-out C-47, droning off to God-knows-where. And that meant, as far as he could tell, that for Kaufmann, for the Army itself, for others of the real world, Nicholas Anton— scion of wealth, possessor of beauty and charm, winner of ten Boy Scout merit badges, and lover first-class—was gone without a trace.

Alone? Mama mia, was he ever alone. . . .

He had been brought to what was apparently a country estate overlooked by a regal, melon-colored villa stair-stepped on the flank of a foothill of the incredible crags to the north. About a mile to the south was a cluster of farm buildings, and slightly apart from these, sited on the rim of a vast meadowland, was this very large structure, a shed, actually, as large as a hangar and slyly camouflaged with netting and fake foliage. At one end of the interior gloom was a small stage, with a podium to the right and a projection screen in the center. The air, while dim and cool, was heavy with tobacco smoke. Some of the men chatted in German, but their voices were low, like a congregation's before the organist starts things off. Anton estimated that at least a hundred and fifty men, all in stripped-down uniforms of Luftwaffe blue, sat at the long tables, reminding him of those Hollywood prison films where the prisoners are at mess, or whatever prison meals are called, just before James Cagney starts banging on things with a tin cup.

There were ashtrays on the tables, and a pad and pencil before each man. He sat at the end of the second table from the stage, and if he turned slightly on the bench he could see most of those in the room. His gaze went methodically from face to face, along each table, down the rows to the end, and it was only after he had begun the examination again that he realized he was looking for a face he might recognize. After all, you spend some years in Germany, you get to know some Germans.

Long faces. Round faces. Sharp faces. Amiable faces. Mean faces. None familiar. Nor, obviously, did his face ignite any memories, fond or otherwise, because no one gave him so much as a narrowed eye.

There was a stir, and the lanky American colonel, less the sunglasses he'd been wearing on the ride over, came out of the shadows and stood beside the podium. He waited, stiff, wordless, until the room came to silent order. When he spoke, it was in German.

"You and I have been acquainted since Dijon. Until this morning, it has been necessary for me to remain anonymous. But now I can tell you that I am Colonel Albert Dreher. I have been assigned by the American high command to serve as plans and training officer for a very special operation in which, it is hoped, you gentlemen will play a key role." He paused, and Anton suspected it was for dramatic effect.

"First, some background. During your detention as prisoners of war most of you have been permitted access to newspapers and radio broadcasts, and so you are generally aware of what has gone on since the end of hostilities between your nation and mine. Japan has been defeated, thanks in great measure to the atomic bomb. Adolf Hitler is dead, the Nazi party is smashed, and the ruins of Germany are occupied and governed by the armed forces of the United States, Britain, France and the USSR. To all appearances, and in the minds of most of the western world populations, the war is over and the reconstruction process is under way. Unfortunately, as you and I—pragmatic soldiers, all of us—are only too sadly aware, appearances are rarely a true reflection of the underlying reality. And the reality today is, gentlemen, that the Soviets are planning, with the help of domestic Communist parties, to overrun and absorb Europe, all of Europe, from the Norwegian Arctic to Mediterranean Spain, from the Gibraltar strait to the Greek Aegean. Their plan exploits the extensive penetration they have already made via Communist or radical blocs in the various European governments, national or local or both. France, for example, the keystone nation in western Europe, expects its next national election to bring a legislature whose majority will be overwhelmingly left-wing, with the official French Communist Party dominating. Such governments, existing or forming from Denmark to Italy, are already preparing to beseech the Red Army to cross the Oder-Neisse Line—agreed upon at the Yalta Summit conference—and move in to quell the riots and general social unrest they themselves will create in the vacuum left by the rapid repatriation of U.S. troops. The entire coup will be accomplished without violence where possible, but with military action where needed.'' Another pause.

Because the assembly was one of Luftwaffe personnel, some informality could be expected; all airmen, even the most tyrannically disciplined German airmen, tend to be a spontaneous lot. So a buzzing filled the room, and many meaningful glances were exchanged.

Dreher went on. ''The Soviet plan is abetted by what amounts to a hemorrhage in the U.S. military capability in Western Europe. Until recently there has been a virtual dismantling of the American army, thanks to domestic demands that U.S. troops be returned home. But with its discovery of the projected Communist coup, the American high command has stemmed this rout—with much care to continue the illusion of rout, so as to avoid precipitating Soviet military actions. The repatriation of highly trained technical troops, specialized individuals, and the professional cadres of seasoned combat units, from aviation units to infantry and armored divisions, has been quietly delayed. Meanwhile, fresh troops from the States are replacing those who have already been sent home." He paused again, unabashedly dramatic this time. Then:

"But these efforts are not enough. We Americans need help. We need the help of all right-thinking Germans. We need your help, gentlemen."

The buzzing became a kind of soft rumbling.

Colonel Dreher held up a quieting hand. "I'd now like to introduce the ranking German officer present. Generalmajor Siegfried Oskar, former commander of Kampfgeschwader 98, Frankreich West, and a member of the Luftwaffe since its establishment in 1935."

The man was tall and blond in the Nordic way. He was very impressive, stiff and haughty in the half light, shoulders squared, uniform creased, boots glistening, his codfish eyes searching the assembly as if expecting quail to rise there. His voice was a resonant bass.

"Thank you, Colonel Dreher. You men are at ease and may smoke if you wish."

Anton noted that nobody took up the invitation. They weren't all that cutesy, flyboy informal when confronted by a Goth who spoke in cultivated Heidelberger cadences.

"I need not make any impassioned political speeches," the Generalmajor said. "We have had too many of those over the past few years. We are not politicians, we are military airmen. German military airmen. Even so, each of us is fully aware of the political and economic disaster that has befallen the Fatherland and each of us needs no reminder that the catastrophe is directly traceable to the international Communist conspiracy." Generalmajor Oskar paused. He, like Dreher, was not above reaching for a little dramatic pizzazz.

"And each of us"—Oskar's tone turned suddenly harsh—

"has been privileged, on a hand-picked basis, to continue the Fatherland's struggle to rid the world of the Communist menace. The United States leadership, despite the military collaboration with the USSR that has been authorized under the so-called Western Alliance—and, until recently, the Lend Lease pact—has come to recognize that its real enemy has been, is, and will continue to be the Soviet Union. That despite the ill-conceived, often heinous excesses of a national government dominated by unsophisticated, self-serving and unconscionable Nazi Party politicians, the struggle of the professional German soldier, sailor and airman has been that of an honorable advance guard standing against Asiatic savages in behalf of civilization itself."

Anton sighed silently. For one who promised no political speeches, this li'l darlin' was a street-corner lulu.

"Thanks to this new appreciation of the realities on the part of the United States and its allies, certain well-defined measures are being taken. One of the most important of these is to enlist surviving apolitical military leaders and seasoned professionals of the Wehrmacht, the Luftwaffe and the Kriegsmarine into what is still a most secret organization known as 'the German Legion.' "

Another buzzing.

"And the German Legion's mission, its honor and privilege, will be to lead American forces into 'Aktion Achtung,' the mightiest pre-emptive military action in history—the decisive and conclusive dissolution of the Stalinist forces which, even at this moment, are planning to advance across Europe and forever seal its people and treasure behind a Red Russian wall."

The buzzing became a shuffling and a murmuring.

"And we, gentlemen"—the Generalmajor's voice was thick with excitement—"are the first to be chosen for this sacred duty. We, gentlemen, as the aviation cadre of the German Legion, will serve as the vanguard, the initial assault force, of 'Aktion Achtung?' We'll be the very first to strike the Russian swine!"

There was a clamorous explosion as the assembly pushed

free of the benches, stood erect and broke into a wild cheering.

If I hear a single "Seig Heil," Anton groaned inwardly, *I will absolutely throw up.*

The Generalmajor's basso profundo rolled across the room, demanding order at once, and the assembly subsided into a kind of giddy attention, many of them leaning forward across tables, the picture of sucking-up beaverness of the most eager type.

"The German Legion will, of course, be integrated with the armed forces of the United States and therefore will be financed and equipped with American materiel. Those of us who perform meritoriously will be granted certain privileges and perquisites, to be listed and explained later. We will not lose our identities as Germans, however. Our language—oral, written and mechanically communicated—will remain German. Our direct commanders will be Germans working in collaboration with their American opposite numbers under tactics and strategies established by the American general staff. Our uniforms will conform to American design, but they will carry distinctive insignia and feature identifying caps and footwear. When we march, it will be under the United States national flag, with a special unit ensign flying below or to one side of the traditional place of honor. We will remain Germans, but we will serve as a shock-troop spearhead for the American armed forces."

Another eruption of teary-eyed beer-hall patriotism melded into an a capella rendition of "Deutschland über Alles," and Anton stood with the rest of them, mouthing lyrics he couldn't remember and pretending to be having a spiritual orgasm. But all the time his mind was telling him that this was an enormous, tasteless joke and in a moment the M.C. would come bouncing and laughing across the stage to signal the skit's end and introduce the chorus line. At anthem's end, Generalmajor Oskar got everybody seated again and went on:

"Since we are aircrewmen, we will be flying. And what

will we be flying?" He called to someone in the gloom. "The first slide, Prosser."

The screen lit up with a three-view plan. "The Boeing B-17G, gentlemen. The Flying Fortress. America's much-vaunted heavy bomber. This is the machine with which we will be equipped. Its crew numbers variously from nine to eleven men. It has four Wright radial engines of 1200 horse-power. Maximum speed in excess of 300 miles per hour, American, 480 kilometers metric. Weight, 60,000 pounds American, 28,000 kilos metric. It has an operational ceiling of 30,000 feet, or about 90,000 meters. Its tactical radius is 700 miles, or 1100-plus kilometers when carrying its full load of 6000 pounds or 2800 kilos. Its armament consists of eleven heavy machine guns, some mounted in electrically operated turrets in the nose, topside fuselage, and belly, some hand-operated by crewmen. It is a very tough ma-chine, gentlemen, as any of our brothers in the fighter squadrons would be the first to tell you."

Generalmajor Oskar cleared his throat and clutched the podium with both hands, staring about the room in the man-ner of one who is filled with his own importance. "We will be forming an expanded squadron composed of eighteen aircraft, each with four officers—pilot, copilot, bombardier and navigator—and six ratings—engineer-gunner, radioman-gunner, two waist gunners, tail gunner and belly turret gun-ner. I will serve as command pilot on flight operations in full unit strength. Administration and training supervision will be conducted by myself and my adjutant, Oberleutnant Kohl, overseen by Colonel Dreher, our unit's U.S. Army liaison. The squadron will be divided into three flights of six planes each. The flight leaders are Hauptmann Kruger, and Oberleutnants Michel and Oppermann. All mechanical maintenance and ordnance work will be conducted by an American field unit commanded by Captain Johnson. A medical officer will visit as needed. Officer personnel will be quartered in the buildings adjacent to this one, while ranks will be tented, under camouflage, in the orchard at the end of the lane and will be fed from field kitchens.

Officers will dine at the villa, hours to be posted. This structure''—he waved a hand toward the ceiling—''will serve as the hangar for the aircraft to be used for aircrew familiarization and, at the proper time, transition flight training. The squadron's remaining aircraft are under cover and being kept in a state of readiness at USAF installations nearby until such time as we can begin squadron exercises.''

Generalmajor Oskar paused for another bit of drama, settling for an earnest gaze into the radiant faces of the front-row sycophants.

''It cannot be emphasized too strongly,'' he said in the staff officer's traditional negative syntax, ''that 'Aktion Achtung' is not to be discussed with anyone outside the Legion itself. It is a most secret undertaking. Security is absolute and violations will be dealt with most severely. No one is allowed to resign, request a transfer or absent himself without leave. Absences or desertions are cause for summary execution. Those who are injured or authentically ill will be hospitalized in a wing of the villa, but malingerers, too, face the firing squad.''

Another pause. Then: ''Questions?''

The room remained silent as, of course the Generalmajor, steeped in the German military, damned well knew it would. But Anton was Anton, and so what the hell. He stood at attention, clicked his heels, and barked, ''Sir.''

Generalmajor Oskar stared at him. ''Well?''

''With the Herr Generalmajor's permission, I'd like to ask, please, just where are we?''

Anton sensed the suppressed shock around him and was not surprised by it. He was, however, very much surprised by the Generalmajor's reaction, which was a protracted, evaluating stare that eventually became a frosty smile.

''Let's see. You are Major Thom, I believe.''

''Thoma, Herr Generalmajor.''

''Your question is an entirely logical one, Thoma. Logical, in the sense that you and your colleagues have all been brought here in hooded aircraft and quite naturally wonder where you have landed. But our precise location must remain a secret for the time being. Our American hosts believe it is possible that one or two of you will think things over, decide that Legion service is not for you, and try to escape. Only after an interval in which such cases have been identified and dealt with will the remainder be oriented and given aeronautical charts of this area."

"What if somebody changes his mind after the charts are distributed, Herr Generalmajor?"

Oskar gave him a lingering inspection, thoughtful, a touch of annoyance beginning to show. "We are German officers and soldiers here, Thoma. Each of us has been hand-picked on the basis of technical skill and demonstrated patriotism. I personally believe our American hosts are wasting valuable time. They don't fully understand—as you and I do— that there will be no defections from the German Legion." He peered out at the assembly. "Isn't that so, gentlemen?"

The answering roar was stupendous, and the singing began again, this time the tune being "Wir fahren gegen England."

Only the lyrics were changed, spontaneously, into "Wir fahren gegen Russland."

Anton's depression was absolute.

Good God-amighty. These people are serious.

MONDAY
24 September 1945

15

"G-2. Captain Reynolds speaking."

"Hello, Maude. This is Molly."

"Oh, dear. I was about to call you. I hear Major Kaufmann was a friend of yours. I wanted to tell you how sorry I am."

"Thank you. We were collaborating on something. You were right. He was a very smart and dedicated officer. And a nice man. Really very nice."

"Indeed he was. But as they say, it's the good ones who go first."

"Seems so."

"Is there something I can do for you, Molly?"

"Yes. I'm going to bring by a packet. A file of notes. I'd like you, personally, to keep them in a safe place."

"Well, sure. But—"

"You can read my shorthand, can't you?"

"It's about the best I've seen. Anybody could read your shorthand. Why?"

"If anything happens to me, I want you to be sure that G-2—the general himself, in person—gets the packet."

"Molly—what's this all about? *Happens* to you? What in the world are you talking about?"

"I can't explain now."

"You sound— Come right on up with your packet. You need a jolt of that hellish brew the general calls coffee."

"All right."

Back in her office again, she went through the day with great deliberateness, handling each chore with a calculated fussing that made work and killed thought. But thought was a life of its own, and when it insinuated itself into the business of being busy she would confront it, as if it were an animal, and, with whiplashes of will, compel it toward the cage that held her hatred of this place—this gloomy office, in this crumbled city, in this benighted land.

Things had been so much simpler, more single-mindedly endurable, when there had been a war. The war, for all its noise and filth and death and those other tritenesses that are so stupendous and immutable they rise above being trite, provided a kind of insane sanity to any situation in which she had found herself. Sun-blind, sweating in an interminable Texas parade; freezing and wet on a rolling, top-heavy clunk of a ship in the bitter North Atlantic; lonely and bored in a damp London night; tired and dirty and hungry in a wandering, blacked-out truck in the snowy Ardennes; resentful—make that angry, always angry—over the incomprehensible readiness of otherwise decent men to run their hands over her, to punch, to fondle, to mutter obscenities in her ear, and, worst of all, to assume that because she was a woman she was less than they, a fractional soldier whose denominator was a tomboy determination to make up for her lack of dangling genitals; all of these could be sublimated, explained away if need be, by the fact of the war. War is bestial, therefore warriors do bestial things. Think no more. Just do what you can to help them win the war, goddam it.

But this imprecise mourning, alone in one of the tin-and-glass cells of a yellow-brick monstrosity on a forsaken steppe of ruin—the sole official rationale for her imprisonment here being the supposition that this stack of papers ought to be moved to that stack so that they both could be transferred to that cabinet over there—this was the bottom, the worst of it all, and she had no cause to believe she could endure it another instant without tearing her clothes and wailing.

Colonel Donleavy had told her. He had come into her office, the day's first visitor, and, leaving the door ajar so the crews outside could hear, announced that, since she was known around headquarters to be a friend of Major Kaufmann, she should be informed, along with the next of kin, that he had been killed yesterday afternoon in a traffic accident east of Heidelberg. There had been some ritual words about Kaufmann's being a good man; the colonel had squeezed her shoulder, then closed the door behind him. And that was that. Let's see: Should Stack Three go on Stack Five?

But that was not that. Obtruding thought told her (before she could will it into the cage) that, for all the short time she'd known him—what was it? Two weeks? Three weeks?— she had understood that more than duty was involved in her relationship with Major Kaufmann. She had readily admitted to herself that she was made ruttish by his ballsy proximity; conversely, intuition told her that, for all his masculine posturing, his supercilious teasing, he considered her to be more than a potential lay. Indeed, of all the men in her life, past and present, Kaufmann was the only one—other than her darling, wretched, poverty-stricken father—who had liked her as a person, not as a winsome bubblehead. He was the one male, among all those she knew or remembered, from junior high school through the off-campus basement training sessions at Llewelyn to the entire US-by-God-Army, who had looked beyond her face and boobs and butt and seen her value. Nothing said. She simply *knew* that he had liked her and respected her. He had accepted her as his equal.

And, other than her father, he was the only man she could truly miss. Mourn, even.

If she had a regret, it was her inability to shoot straight with him, to come across with the truth about the Maggie Sunderman file. Kaufmann had died without knowing what she knew about all that, and somehow the knowledge of this made her almost physically ill. He deserved better than the calculated deception the Sunderman thing represented.

As consolation, she told herself again that she had escaped incipient disaster. The simple, chilling fact was that Kaufmann had portended negation—a voiding of everything she was, everything she strove for.

But it still hurt like hell.

She sighed.

Trade-offs. Everything in the world requires a trade-off, for God's sake. Isn't there any end to the need to make trade-offs?

The phone rang.

"Lieutenant Raines."

"Captain Olsen here. Your friendly neighborhood medic."

"What can I do for you, Captain?"

"I want to see you. Talk to you about your physical."

"I don't really feel up to it this afternoon."

"You've heard about Kaufmann, then."

"I've heard."

"A real darb, eh?"

"Yes."

"All the more reason we should consult. I don't feel good about your not feeling good."

"It's just that—well, I don't care—I just can't get worked up over x-rays and blood tests right now."

"Come on. Lots of guys die in traffic accidents, and, after all, he wasn't your husband or anything."

"Well, he was a darn nice guy, which is more than I can say for most of the people in this man's army."

"Hey. I'm a nice guy. What say you and I go out and catch a little drink in some dark place and we can talk about how nice I am?"

"Stick it in your ear, Captain."

"Don't hang up. I was just kidding. Seriously, Raines, I think we ought to talk. Come on down to my office, and just to assure you my intentions are purely professional, we can have Nurse Fuller sit in on the discussion."

"I can't stand that woman."

"Great. Neither can I. So we'll keep her out of the discussion. Right?"

"Well—"

"I give you a direct order, Lieutenant: Get out of that dreary office, get into a GI bus, and get some fresh air on your way to a change of scene and a friendly face."

"All right. I'll be there as soon as I can."

They sat in the gray little room, with its gray cabinets and disgusting wall hangings, and Captain Olsen fussed with the file folder in which he had placed her medical portrait, adjusting his eyeglasses and trying hard to look like a Norman Rockwell cover.

"Structurally, Lieutenant Raines, there's absolutely nothing wrong with you. You are, in terms of framework, pump and plumbing, in better shape than most creatures that have wandered past my stethoscope over the years.

"I should hope so. You're a coroner."

"Medical examiner. And only in the army. In civilian life, I have a private practice in which I do all sorts of neat things. I'm a life-saving and grumpy-but-lovable family physician. Would you believe I'm so well thought of in Milwaukee my patients actually pay their bills? Well, most of them."

"So you called me all the way down here to tell me I'm O.K. and to brag about your past?"

He took off his glasses and jabbed them at her. "You have nothing wrong with you. But yet you do."

She sighed. "That's a marvel of medical diagnosis if I ever heard one. Is that the kind of thing they pay you for in Milwaukee?"

"There's edema in your lungs. Fluid is forming there."

"Why?"

"I think you're being poisoned."

She blinked. "Poisoned?"

"Like in Agatha Christie."

She showed confusion. "I don't understand—"

"Being as I am a very unbusy medical examiner I have a lot of time to read, to see what's going on in the military sawbones trade. And being on the perimeter of Theater Headquarters, I have access to some of the best, most up-to-date medical information in Europe. After giving you your physical and perceiving lung edema that shouldn't be there, seeing as how you're otherwise as healthy as a cow—make that race-horse—I went to said medical information and, voilà, a clue. I won't belabor you with the chemistry, Raines, but my reading in *The Medical Intelligence Bulletin* tells me of a new toxic substance, called 'Zenog,' which is said to have been developed in Rumania and which, as an inhalant, can produce all the symptoms of a cerebral hemorrhage without leaving the slightest toxicological trace. I don't mind telling you that this excited me, because Major Kaufmann had asked me to watch for clues to the mysterious death of Major Bianco, and this thing seemed to fit to a T."

"But you say I seem to be generally O.K.—"

"Let me finish. The inhalant is said to have a derivative that lends itself to oral administration. It can be put into pills. Or, even more slick, it can be dropped as a powder into food or drink. A thousand-horsepower mickey that sends the mickeyed off to the hereafter with lungs full of stuff that looks exactly like pneumonia."

"So?"

" 'So,' you ask? My God, woman, with pneumonia, people drown in the fluid that forms in their lungs. Like the fluid that's forming in your undeniably gorgeous lungs. I'll bet my last tongue depressor that somebody's been slipping you a daily-dose Zenog mickey. Not so you drop dead dramatically, thus sparking official consternation, but to make you expire routinely, an olive drab Camille."

She stared at him. Then: "Well, who—why?"

"Where do you eat your meals?"

"At the company grade officers' mess in the Farben Casino, mostly. There's a little kitchenette in Major Kaufmann's—my—apartment, but I hardly ever use it."

"Snacks? Dinners downtown? At Kronberg?"

"Well, yes. Now and then. But only now and then."

Captain Olsen shrugged. "All right. My point is that you've got to start watching your intake like a hawk. Don't eat anything, anywhere, unless you know where it comes from and, even better, unless somebody else is eating it, too."

"That's a pretty tall order."

"Think of the alternative."

She waved her hand, a signal of her gathering helplessness. "I just don't understand any of this. Who'd want to kill me? I'm not a threat to anybody."

From the doorway behind her: "You're a threat to me. In fact, you bother the hell out of me."

She started, an involuntary jerking motion that lifted her completely off the chair. The voice—cool, amused—had moved her as if it were a truly physical force. Heat and cold gathered in her face instantly, simultaneously, and she turned quickly about.

"As you see," Kaufmann said, somber, "I'm not dead. Only slightly Tyrolean."

"I—"

"Eh?"

"I—"

"Well, speak up, Raines. We have no time for your sputtering. There's lots of work to be done."

She balled a fist and struck him with all her might below his left ear.

"Ow."

"You son of a bitch! You bastard!"

To the grinning Olsen, Kaufmann said, "You saw that, of course. She struck a superior officer."

"Superior, my heinie!"

"What's your problem, Raines?"

She couldn't help it. She began to cry.

"You absolutely ruined my day, you dirty rat!"

16

While Olsen was in the examining room with Raines, checking on what he called her "brakes and wheel alignment," Kaufmann made use of the military phone. He got the USFET board to connect him.

"USFET MP Command. Sergeant Samuels speaking."

"This is Detective Lieutenant Coburn, 7th Army CID. Working a thing with Detective Fallon, your headquarters. Can you rassle me up your Corporal Ransky?"

"We seem to have a lousy connection, sir. Ransky? You say Corporal Ransky?"

"Yep. Ransky, George P. Tell him I have a message for him from Fallon. He'll know what it's about."

"Hold on a sec, sir. I'll see if he's on duty."

He held for a full minute.

"Still there, sir?"

"Yep."

"I can't find a Corporal Ransky on the roster here. You sure you called the right headquarters?"

"Military Police Command, USFET."

"Well, that's what this is, all right. But we don't have any Corporal Ransky with us."

"That's funny. He was supposed to be helping Fallon. Doing an undercover thing as an Air Policeman in Wiesbaden. Might possibly be assigned direct to General Vickery."

"Hold, please."

This wait was for three minutes.

"Sir, I've checked with General Vickery's duty officer and with Base Personnel's duty desk. There just isn't any Ransky of any rank listed in this headquarters command— or any other MP or AP command in Europe, according to the files."

"You sure?"

"Absolutely, sir. Sorry."

"Thanks for your trouble, Sergeant. I must have got a bum steer somehow."

Well, then. Corporal Ransky not only did not work with Detective Fallon, he didn't exist at all.

"Egad."

They drove along Reuter Weg, north toward the Farben Compound, as if there was nothing unusual in a handsome WAAC lieutenant riding in a big black Mercedes sedan piloted by a Tyrolean Dapper Dan. Although the ride was meant solely to accommodate her return to quarters, it was a kindness that seemed to make Raines uncomfortable.

"Where did you get this car, Major?"

"I am not a major, Raines. I am George Coburn, a social worker out of Baltimore, Maryland, currently assigned to the United Nations Relief and Rehabilitation Administration—UNRRA, to you—and, in that capacity, supervising an aspect of the care, comfort and repatriation of displaced persons in war-shattered Europe. I am a card-carrying do-gooder, and I can prove it by the counterfeit papers I am carrying in my counterfeit leather wallet in my counterfeit Austrian jacket."

"So where did you get this car, George?"

"It's a loan from a lady friend in Heidelberg. As are the counterfeit UNRRA tags it wears on its elegant bumpers."

"She must be some lady.

"There are no others like her. Which is simultaneously a blessing and a sorrow."

"And she must think a lot of you."

"To know me is to love me."

Raines fell silent.

"I heard what Olsen said about your being poisoned, Raines. I suspected as much."

"That's why you ordered me to see him?"

"Mm."

"Do you have any idea who might be doing this to me?"

"I'd rather not toss around my hunches. I want you to continue to act as you have been. Changing your pattern might tip somebody off, compel them to kill you by other, faster means. And your murder would really screw up my plans."

He felt her quick, angry look.

"Well, now. I certainly don't want to put you out in any way—"

"Come on, Raines. Don't be a jerk. I need your help, so I'm trying to keep you alive. And you're alive only as long as you're not lying dead on one of Olsen's slabs."

"Gee, that's pretty deep stuff."

He steered the car around a mountain of rubble yet to be cleared, then followed a stream of jeeps and recons that made for the Ike-ian fastness ahead. His disappointment in himself was huge, heavy. He had in no way intended to annoy this archetype of the womanly virtues, this representative classic female, stacked in precise conformity to the GI's criteria for brick outhouses with awnings. None appreciates the American woman more than the American man who has been abroad, as he recalled some barracks philosopher having once declared, and Raines, with her innocent eyes and glossy hair and brilliant teeth and Sunday-school aroma of soap and fresh linen, was for him the polar opposite of Emma's and Lisa's perfumed Old World carnality.

Her husky voice, sounding the nuances of American naivete, evoked the Saturday night Dipsy-Doodle at the malt shop, mommies calling in their kids from the twilight playgrounds, the Little Wife ordering hamburger and Popnut Scrummies and *Photoplay* magazine at the A&P—the essence of American femalehood, good and true—and, even while sitting beside her here, no more than a foot away, he missed her with a sudden passion that was both indescribable and inexplicable.

"It's very good to see you again, Raines."

Whatever this thing he was feeling, she must have heard it in his voice, because there was no sarcasm in her answer. "You've already seen how glad I am to see you."

"And I've got a sore jaw to prove it."

"I shouldn't have hit you. I'm very sorry. Honest."

"That's all right. It was thoughtless of me to come back from the dead without first arranging a séance or something."

The silence between them resumed, and when the time came he pulled the car into a cul-de-sac a block away from the line of concertina wire that marked the compound's outer perimeter.

"O.K.," he said. "You'll have to go the rest of the way on your own. I'm not ready yet to try out my phony credentials on the Compound's security system."

"No big deal. The walk will do me good."

"You know where to get me. The Tankstelle on the Idstein road, where the railroad crosses the bridge. Left up the dirt road to the top of the second hill. The hunter's lodge there. No phone, but you can leave word with Karli, the gas station manager. Meanwhile, if I have to get in touch with you about something special, wherever I am, I'll call Olsen, and because he's part of law enforcement he can relay me to the military net, including the phone in my—your—quarters. And, by the way, you're welcome to the fifth of Old Grandad stashed in the water closet. I hid it there because Bertha, the maid, is a booze taster—she sips whatever she finds sitting around and will be passed out on the floor when you get home of an evening.''

She shrugged. ''I'd rather you pick it up sometime, if you don't mind. Liquor isn't a thing I like around, even in the john seat.''

''As you wish.''

''What can I be doing for you in the time I have left?''

''I need file stuff, backgrounders. If you can, try to get me a bio on Thomas Ballentine, until recently with OSS in Bern. There won't be an OSS file, of course, because that agency kept its personnel stuff tight and internal. But he's a product of American royalty, so there's sure to be something in *Who's Who*, or whatever. Also everything and anything on Artur Bikler—B-I-K-L-E-R. He was a Gestapo agent, and Central Registry most assuredly has a dossier on him. And above all, keep an eye on any and all correspondence regarding German POWs, any messages emanating from Chaumont or Dijon or Air Force interrogations of Luftwaffe people.''

''Anything particular?''

''I've got a friend working at Dijon, and it's been ten days since I heard from him. He's a sneaky wretch—likes to play spy—and so there's no telling how he might get word to me. So anything out of Dijon, let me see it.''

She nodded, her face solemn in the afternoon light. ''I can handle G-1 stuff. Dijon, the G-2 stuff, I'll ask Poopsie to give me a hand.''

''Be sure she doesn't know it's for me. Poopsie strikes me as the type who'd call for the white jackets if she thought you were corresponding with a ghost.''

''What's your first move from here?''

''Heidelberg. I'm going back there this evening.''

''Well, be careful.''

''Sure.''

They sat there for a suspended moment, face to face, a pair of unemployed bookends, trading stares, trying to think of things they would probably not think of until later. Around the corner, beyond the mountain of rubble, traffic thundered and clanked and beeped, intensifying the back-water quiet into which they had drifted. A shaft of evening sunlight fell fully on her, and he saw that there were tiny gold flecks in the blue of her eyes, a discovery of unaccountable sadness, a poignancy akin to that which derives from ancient flowers found in the pages of long-forgotten Bibles.

She raised a hand, and the tips of her fingers brushed lightly along his bandaged jaw. "It was awful of me to sock a guy who'd been hurt in a car crash. You forgive me?"

"No. I plan to sue for damages."

She stirred, and came closer, and her lips, smooth and slightly damp, touched his. "First payment," she whispered.

"The next is due in twenty seconds. In the back seat."

She shook her head slowly, her smile faint and sad and sweet, like Joan Fontaine's when the king's courier brings word of some ironic turn in the battle. "I never neck in back seats of cars."

"Neck? Who said anything about necking? I don't want to neck. I was to have your baby."

Laughing softly, she pushed away, opened the car door, and stepped to the pavement. "Take care of yourself, Mr. Coburn."

"George. My friends call me George."

"All right, George."

"Is it true that you're engaged to a tank officer?"

"Not anymore."

She turned and walked off, her skirt swinging in that outrageous way that causes preachers to stagger from their pulpits and run off to lives of debauchery on obscure Pacific atolls.

17

General Vickery suffered severe ambivalence on those rare occasions he visited Schloss Kronberg. He was exalted by the relentless beauty created by ancients who clearly understood arches, slants and verticals, and yet he was simultaneously repelled by the profligacy implicit in all of this having been created for the summer vacations of Princess von Somebody-or-other, a leaf in the German royal tree whose massive trunk was the Hohenzollerns, a dynasty whose primary occupation was to copulate with the right people. Tens of hundreds of acres of rolling meadows and lush forests and crystal streams given over to the indolent whims of some agate-eyed broad solely because she had developed in the womb of a certain woman who had been pranged by a certain man in a certain succession of prangings emanating from certain long-ago feudal chieftains. The Hohenzollerns: with nothing to do but wear plumes and boots and look Olympian between attempts to manufacture heirs and some socially acceptable bastards. The Hohenzollerns: paid astronomical sums to strut and prang in a string of palaces supported by taxes extracted mainly from dirt-poor clods who feared to bitch because somebody, at some ancient time, had insinuated that the family was in daily touch with God Himself.

Not that William P. Vickery was against the idea of great wealth and its privileges, or even God. He was merely resentful of those individuals whose great wealth and privileges derived from ancestral orgasms. Seated now at a table on the Kronberg terrace, ignoring the crowd of officers gabbling inside and staring off at the autumn-softened sweeps, he reminded himself that eventually he was going to have a spread like this and the power that went with it, but, unlike those limp-wristed lordlings of feudatory wealth, he was working for it, taking risks for it, and, when it came, he would deserve it. Would see a bona fide, achieving goddam oner in his shaving mirror.

"Hello, General."

He looked over his shoulder. "There you are. Have a seat."

Ballentine pulled a chair to the tiny table. "Germany has much marvelous scenery."

The general sniffed. "Too bad it was wasted on the Germans."

"Well, maybe we can pack it up and ship it to the States. Everything else is being sent there it seems."

"Except our own stuff. We destroy our own tanks and planes because it's too expensive to return them Stateside. Then we turn around and send back shiploads of German tanks and planes." He sipped at his martini. "Want one of these?"

"No thanks. I'm working tonight."

"Since when did that ever interfere with an OSS man's drinking?"

"Since I almost got my empennage riddled one boozy night in Lisbon. You wouldn't believe how sober something like that can make you."

"What are you working on?"

"The usual."

"I mean, what part of the usual?"

"I'm trying to get a bug into Colonel Donleavy's apartment. That house on the Bad Homburg road is a hard place to work, what with the high walls and his hired hands living on the premises."

"Can't you buy one of them?"

"I could try. You can buy any German today. But I prefer not to. Donleavy's one of those men who inspire confidence and loyalty, and nothing's a bigger pain than a German housemaid who's loyal. She tends to become earnestly protective, so while she's accepting your bribe she will be alerting her boss to the fact that you're bribing her."

"Lousy world. Can't even trust traitors anymore." The general puffed noisily at his moribund cigar.

In a kind of reflex imitation, Ballentine ignited a cigarette. Exhaling a cloud, he asked the question. "So what's on your mind, General? I can't imagine your having me come all the way out here just for drinks and chitchat."

There it was again, Vickery noted. That sound in the world's voices. That tone of sarcasm and defiance and contempt for the military man's dedication, discipline, and, yes, goddamn it, patriotism. It could be heard almost anywhere these days. Sherman had it wrong: peace is hell.

"Two things. First, how are things coming with the ground troops?"

"All right. We've got the appropriate number of people and their gear. General Grover says they're all airborne and all combat-seasoned. They're being moved into position and they're all briefed on the need for absolute security. The major problem there is, of course, not being able to give them a D-date or time, so they've got to be kept at maximum alert, and it's tough to manage."

"Well, if anybody can manage it, Grover can. He's one rag-ass son of a bitch. It's fundamental, though, that he and his people understand that no message traffic—radio, written, or courier—bounce off or through G-2. Troop messages must go only through you or, in emergencies, through my Hotdog line. No one in G-2 must be allowed in."

"Grover understands that. He's a cool hand."

"As for the D-date and time, we're depending on our Dijon penetration for that. Until we get word from that channel, we're just going to be compelled to assume any today, any tomorrow is it."

"That's another thing that makes me uneasy. Our Dijon person is very scanty on reports. We need more word, faster. And we seem to be getting nothing out of there."

"Well, as the saying goes, 'Don't shoot the piano player; he's doing the best he can.' "

"What's your second item, General?"

"I need another surveillance."

"Who is it this time?" Ballentine's question held weariness and gathering exasperation.

"Colonel Daley, in G-1. He's shacking up with Donleavy's secretary, and I've got him reporting to me on what she says when they're beddy-bye-bunky. But I also want to know what Daley's saying. Both in the sack and in his office."

"You want two bugs, then."

"That's right. One in his bedroom and one in his office. With daily transcripts to me." Ballentine examined his cigarette. "Isn't Daley a friend of yours?"

"And I hope to keep him as a friend—by making sure of what he says when he's not to my face, as the saying goes."

"Friend or foe, you are really given to listening in on people, aren't you, General."

"What's that supposed to mean?"

"You're putting my communications people hard against the wall. There are only two of them left, now that Tremaine has been ZI'd."

"Well, I can't very well use Air Force people. So, one way or another, you'll have to take care of it."

Vickery decided at this moment that he did not like Ballentine. While it was true that he had never liked any man who was tall and handsome because he was himself short and ugly, there was an additional reason to dislike this fellow. Ballentine was always looking around. His eyes seemed never to settle down. Even when the man was looking at you, talking directly to you, he was taking in everybody and everything else for a hundred yards around—not out of mere curiosity but out of a desire to dump you and head for a more interesting conversation. Gertrude, his ex-wife, had been like that. One of the most infuriating things about an exceptionally infuriating woman. Too bad she couldn't have gotten together with this shifty-eyed son of a bitch. They'd have made a matched set. Banging away, head to head, each of them looking around all the while for somebody more interesting to screw.

"Why are you smiling, General?"

"Was I smiling?"

"Well, yes."

"That music they're playing in the dining room. It reminded me of a woman."

"You must be fond of her, whoever she is."

"Ah, indeed I am. She did the nicest thing a wife ever did. She left me for Freddie Holman, a West Coast Packard dealer."

The OSS man, obviously unable to find anything to say, glanced at his watch.

"By the way, Ballentine, did Kaufmann say anything important that last time you saw him?"

"Not really. He apparently was onto the Bern connection and was trying to link up with Allen Dulles—just as you suspected. I delivered him the wind-and-whiskey treatment, and he went away, discernibly confused."

Vickery envisioned a jeep, crushing itself against a tree and erupting flames. "Has your man Fallon talked to the medical examiner yet?"

"Yes. The body was returned to Frankfurt for processing and shipment Stateside. The examiner, a captain name of Olsen, says incineration was extreme, but he was able to determine that the cause of death was a broken neck."

"I think we ought to keep watching that angle. I don't want any postmortem surprises from the late Major Kaufmann."

"Fallon is a good man, General. A first-class investigator

and trouble-shooter. He's great insurance against surprises of any kind.''

"So I hear. But Kaufmann was also a prime pain in the patoot. He was the kind of guy who would leave little messages around.''

Ballentine, looking irritated, consulted his watch again. "I'll let you know as soon as we have the bugs in place.''

"All right.''

The big man stubbed out his cigarette in a silver ashtray, stood up and, with no further word, crossed to the terrace doors and disappeared inside the vast house.

Vickery sat for a time, listening to the otherwise excellent string quartet and its contralto vocalist struggling to make musical sense of "Mairzy Doats." The sun had set, and the twilight was cool and damp, and he felt a tiny current of what he recognized as homesickness. Which was odd, since he'd had no real home to speak of for some years now, only a dreary succession of dreary military posts from the Rio Grande to the St. Lawrence and back again. No geographical ties, no family, no personal relationships worth anything. Only Queen Gertrude the Restless, and the roachy clapboard houses on a million Officers' Rows in a million sunbaked nowheres. Yet there was this feeling, a sense of missing something, something sweet and unnameable that might have been. Eons of scrabbling and climbing, of conniving and striving and sweating, so that he might eventually sit alone at a table in a decaying medieval brick pile, friendless in a godforsaken country filled with tears and wreckage and bones.

Daley and his mistress strolled out into the evening, and their eyes met his, so there was no way to avoid them.

"This is a pleasant surprise, General." Daley beamed, exuding false jolliness. "I believe you and Captain Benet have met?''

Vickery nodded. "Once. The day I visited G-2 to raise hell about Kaufmann and that what's-her-name broad.''

"It was terrible, what happened to Major Kaufmann,'' Captain Benet said earnestly, patting her magnificent red hair, blinking her enormous blue eyes, and exuding gin and jasmine. "Such irony. His going through a war, only to die in a traffic accident. Terrible."

"Yeah."

An awkward pause, and then Daley cleared his throat and said theatrically, "Our meeting like this is really a very big coincidence, General. I was planning to call you in the morning with a bit of news. And now here you are."

Resigned to their intrusion, Vickery waved at the chairs opposite.

They sat.

"So what's your news, Daley?"

The colonel gave his WAAC a sad little smile, then, turning a serious gaze to the general, announced, "I'm being ZI'ed. I'm going home. Effective the day after tomorrow."

"You can't do that," Vickery blurted.

"I have no choice, sir. Orders from the Pentagon. I'm being sent to the War College."

"You? The War College?"

"I feel just terrible about it," Captain Benet put in. She added, too hurriedly, "Of course, Colonel Daley will be missed by a lot of people here."

Vickery sent a narrow-eyed glare at Daley. "It's your mother again, isn't it."

"I don't understand, General. My mother?" Daley gave Captain Benet a nervous glance.

Vickery shoved a fresh cigar into a corner of his mouth. "Every time you start to be useful in this man's army," he said, chewing angrily, "your mother gets you transferred. I swear to God: that woman must have something on every topside staffer since Ulysses S. Grant."

It was Captain Benet's turn to stare narrowly at Colonel Daley. "Who is your mother, Harold?"

"Nobody, really. A little lady with blue hair. Beads on her bosom. Smell of lilacs."

General Vickery's special talent was to think quickly in a pinch. "Colonel, do me a favor. Go in to the tobacco counter and fetch me three nice cigars."

"They don't sell your brand here, sir."

"Then get me another brand. Dollar jobs. No cheapies."

"Very well, sir." Looking frustrated, Daley stood up and strode from the terrace.

Captain Benet made a business of listening to the viola's solo on "Poor Butterfly." When she spoke, amusement was in her voice.

"Begging the general's pardon, but it looks to me as if the general deliberately sent Colonel Daley away."

"Right, Captain Benet. The general did precisely that."

"Will the general permit me to ask why?"

"Because the general thinks the captain is one hell of a devastating dish."

"Sir?" She pretended confusion.

"Three things are guaranteed to devastate me. You got all three: red hair and big knockers."

"Sir, I don't know just what to say—"

"How about dinner tomorrow night?"

"Sir, Colonel Daley has asked me to—it's his going-away thing. A party for him at the Farben Casino—"

"All right. The night after next."

"Well—" Her blue gaze lingered on his chest full of ribbons and silver aviator's wings before moving on to his silver stars.

"I'll send a limo for you. Where are your quarters?"

"I have an apartment on Reuter Weg—"

"My guy will find you. Seventeen-thirty hours. We'll have dinner at my place in Wiesbaden. Then the movies at the General Officers' Club. Mitchum's playing in *The Story of GI Joe*, or some such rot. After that, nightcaps at the Zum Schwarzen Bock."

"Sir—" She was trying hard to blush but wasn't making it. "I hesitate to—"

"Come on, Benet. How often does a captain have an affair with a general? Eh?"

18

Kaufmann was not at all sure he enjoyed being dead.

There were army burdens, such as having to get up at a certain time and having to be here or there and to do this and to wear that, from which it was a delight to be freed; then there were army pleasures, such as not having to make decisions as to what time to get up and where to be and what to do and wear, that he sorely missed. Those contradictions again. They were not to be escaped even in the hereafter. And in balance, he found there was not balance, since the disadvantages of being dead outweighed the advantages.

Where, for instance, does a dead man get his mail? And the parents who have been sending much of that mail: How does the dead man spare them the pain? How does a dead soldier—no longer eligible for pay and too moral to take up stealing—buy his food, shelter and dry-cleaning? He might borrow flimsily from flimsy equity carried by such as Emma, to be sure. Borrow from soldier-type friends like Raines and Olsen? Unacceptable. They themselves were liv-

ing just this side of penury. So, if one isn't earning money
and has no heart for borrowing from needy friends, what's
one to do?

One gets even.

Preferably with a bombastic fat-cat who puts drunk-
driving pills in a visitor's hooch.

And thus these hours of lurking in the drizzle of this raw
September night.

The villa's windows, soft glowings in the mist, told him
nothing. There had been no activity to be seen, inside or
outside, and the only sounds were those of distant traffic
and the dripping from the bushes around him. He had managed to infiltrate the grounds without incident, counting two
guards en route to this cover, which was within earshot of
the villa's front door. One guard post was at the driveway
entrance, the other under the porte cochere, a happy condition, since immobile guards were really no guards at all
for a man with his experience. However, this happy development was negated by the discovery that there was a third
guard—a man who huddled in a garden toolshed and chain-
smoked cigarettes. This fellow had a direct view of the garage, Kaufmann's target, and so it was impasse in this
squishy limbo until the household was buttoned down for
the night and the guards—as guards are wont to do in the
wee hours—got careless.

Emma had given him a raincoat, one of those vomit-
colored plastic things so common among Germany's war-
time civilians, and, settling against the trunk of an elderly
elder, he pulled this closer to him, a reflexive but futile
move to counter the chill. Eventually he dozed, and in that
half world it came to him that he had to be unsalvageably
insane to be crouched alone in the fog of an alien land,
waiting for God knows who to do God knows what, God
knows when. Other men, more rational, were in warm
rooms, warm in their bellies with food and drink, and
warmer still, if they were truly rational, in the arms of
steamy women.

Raines. Now there was a steamy woman if there ever was one. Steamy, without knowing it, that is.

There had been women in his life—quite a few, he reminded himself now, not without smugness—and with this relative experience had come expertness, a happy admixture of abilities, first to command what happened for however long and then to go mad at the rightest, most explosive of times. A Clausewitz of the sack, so to speak. But there never before had been a Raines. Never anyone, even at the peak of his adolescent horniness, who could destroy him with the merest, most tangential touch of lips. The most exciting thing that had ever happened to him, hands down and bar none, was the little peck she had given him this afternoon, a tiny collision of damp smoothnesses, electric in their momentary clinging and leading to instant tumescence and racing visions of swollen boobies and bouncing buns on a shadowed tangle of sheets. If her slightest acceleration could send him into such witless lusting, what in hell's own name could she do to him with a wide-open throttle, eh? He'd never live the hour through. Never.

He smiled in the darkness.

At four minutes to midnight, tires crunched on the driveway gravel and headlights flared on the villa's flanks. Kaufmann, oddly refreshed by his snooze, was able to follow the progress of a huge gray Horch sedan as it glided to silence under the porte cochere. The car's lights went out and, after an opening and slamming of doors, a trench-coated hulk that had to be Ballentine hurried into the house, followed by the porte cochere guard and two men in black coats and slouch hats. The chauffeur stood by the car, fussing with a windshield wiper.

Kaufmann waited.

After a time, the guard assigned to the toolshed came down the path and, lighting a cigarette, asked in German, "How did it go tonight, Fritz?"

The chauffeur yawned noisily. "Boring."

"Same here. Quiet. Wet and cold. And I'm dragging, I'll tell you."

"Well, Freddi's due to relieve you in a few minutes."

"You're not done yet?"

"Not yet. The boss wants me to drive those two Italian creeps back to the Heidelberger Hof. Why in hell he didn't put them up here, I'll never know."

"Maybe he doesn't like the smell of garlic."

The two laughed, sharing this huge joke.

After an interval another man came from the house. "Hey," he said. "Where did this rotten mist come from, eh?"

"You're two minutes late, Freddi."

"So have me arrested."

"Well, get your ass into the hut. I'm turning in."

"All quiet?"

"As a tomb. Fritz will be taking the visitors back to the Heidelberger Hof. Nothing else is going on."

"All right. See you in the morning."

Freddi disappeared into the darkness beyond the garage and the other guard went into the house, leaving Fritz to resume his tinkering with the wiper blade.

Kaufmann, reassured by the tableau, eased his way through the undergrowth and, skirting a flower bed, eased silently up to the toolshed. The smell of cigarette smoke was strong. Listening, he heard Freddi's stirring inside.

So see the guardhouse. See the man inside the door. See the man watching the main house with a pair of night glasses. See the pistol on the table at his elbow. See the man fall, wheezing, when you deliver a chop to his throat.

Taking Freddi's pistol and binoculars, Kaufmann moved quietly toward the house. Holding back in the darkness, he stage-whispered, "Hey, Fritz. Fritz. Come here."

"Is that you, Freddi?" The chauffeur's voice was hushed, surprised.

"It's me. Come here a second. I need your help."

Fritz came, saw briefly, and was conquered. Kaufmann caught him by the scruff and dragged his limpness into an azalea bed, where the unconscious Freddi lay, breathing noisily. A rope taken from the toolshed made them secure, and gags of cotton wiping cloth made them silent.

Kaufmann hid his face in the shadow of Fritz's cap and slid behind the steering wheel of the waiting Horch.

At one-ten the two men in black coats came out of the house and climbed wordlessly into the back seat. Ballentine stood in the doorway, watching and saying nothing. He seemed to be displeased.

Kaufmann started the motor and, with no further fuss, put the car through the turn-around and drove down the hill, waving as he passed the guard at the gate.

The rearview mirror told Kaufmann at once who his passengers were: Gregor Koslov, a notorious NKVD gadabout with a Central Registry dossier a mile long, and Luigi Fortunato, the Roman film director of Communist persuasion who had figured tangentially in one of Kaufmann's probes of Hitler's Abwehr staffers in Rome. Small frigging world, eh?

Since his Italian was much less than perfect, Kaufmann understood only part of what the boys in back discussed so rapidly, softly, and irritably on the return to the Heidelberger Hof. Mainly that Ballentine was a tyrannical wretch who, like Louis Stahl, typified the foreign snots who were making life miserable for the NKVD these days. The Undine region of northern Italy was mentioned, too, but in what context was unclear. And something about airplane junkyards (*Junkyards? Had he heard right?*), that would cause Ballentine to poop a brick if he knew about them. Then they became silent, and they left the car at the hotel entrance without so much as a glance at him or a nod of thanks for the ride. Communist ingrates.

Thus dismissed, Kaufmann made directly for Kanal Gasse, a lane of puddled misery just off Mannheim's riverfront. He parked at the door of Rudi Altmeier's garage and pulled the chain that rang the bell in Rudi's upstairs digs.

Rudi, one of Emma's cadre of miscreants, had traded quietly and lucratively in the disguise or disposition of stolen vehicles—from hansoms to half-tracks—since Kaiser Wilhelm's abdication in 1918, and Kaufmann's acquaintance with him dated from one day last winter when Rudi, whose command of English ended with "How do you do?", needed a translation of the maintenance manual for a U.S. Army Chevrolet staff car taken prisoner in the Battle of the Bulge and subsequently traded by an especially concupiscent SS colonel for three nights' worth of Emma's services. Emma had asked Kaufmann to lend a hand, and Rudi had been impressed with Kaufmann's linguistic savvy, and grateful.

"You," Rudi said through both of his teeth. "I never thought I'd see you again. Especially in the middle of a rainy night. Don't you Americans ever sleep?"

"Sorry to get you up like this, Rudi. But I'm in a bit of a thing right now and I need your help."

The old man shivered in the garage's dankness and pulled his tatty bathrobe closer to him. "Of course. Why else would you be here?"

"That car outside: I need to fence it."

Rudi peered through the dirty window. "Willi Guntermann's Horch, eh?"

"You know the car?"

"Know it? I fenced it for Bolko Zeimer, before the war. He had stolen it from Albrecht Bongarz, the department store tycoon. I repainted it and sold it to Willi, a weird little rodent who became a millionaire by pimping for the uppercrust Nazis in Heidelberg. Bongarz saw the car on the street one day and recognized it despite the new paint. He reported it to the Polizeiamt, but he was a Jew, and a rich one to boot, so nobody did anything about it and Bongarz himself soon disappeared. You know how it was back then."

"Yeah."

"So where did you find the car?"

"It's been used by a fat-cat Ami, a former spymaster who's now pals with Commies. He did me dirty, so the

Horch is vengeance. I need to turn it into money. I'm broke."

Rudi shrugged an ancient shoulder. "The car's a specialty item now. I mean, hot's hot, but this car, with its, ah, colorful background—past and present—is blazing."

"Somebody will want it."

"Sure. But the price won't be much."

"How much?"

"I'll have to look at the car before I can say."

Kaufmann swept an arm toward the door. "Be my guest."

After an hour of dickering, Kaufmann closed the deal. For the car: seven thousand of Rudi's bona fide American dollars and a ride back to Heidelberg, where Kaufmann had stashed Emma's Mercedes before beginning the night's caper. For a lady's sable coat found in the Horch's backseat cloak chest: another twelve hundred. For a pair of Zeiss binoculars, a pristine Luger pistol and a Leica camera, all of which had been stashed in the trunk: an additional thousand.

He had—in a single stroke, so to speak—moved from pennilessness to the rim of stinking-richhood. Throw in Emma's housing accommodations and available sedan, and Raines' and Olsen's help, and he was hardly your run-of-the-mill dead man.

All in all, though, being alive was better.

TUESDAY
25 September 1945

File No. 2385098F   25 Sept 45

To: Brandt
From: Gladiator

Subject: Operation "Tailspin"

1. "Chocolate" has met with "Fudge" and
   "Caramel." "Fudge" was helpful, although
   arrogant, as usual. He served as spokesman,
   although "Caramel" outranks him.

2. "Fudge" claims there is no substance to report
   that the Soviets plan a westward movement
   beyond lines agreed upon at Yalta and Potsdam.
   He says his contacts in Moscow pooh-pooh
   rumors that left-wing chiefs in France and Low

Countries have received Stalin's assurances that he will fill vacuum left by U.S. and British demobilization. He says Stalin has great respect for new atomic bomb and will make no moves that might cause Truman, who proved his readiness to use it against Japanese, to use it against USSR.

3. "Fudge" and "Caramel" have agreed to meet again.

FOR YOUR EYES ONLY

FOR YOUR EYES ONLY

File No. 445723   25 Sept 45

To: Gladiator
From: Brandt

Subject: Operation "Tailspin"

1. I am not at all sure we can count on "Fudge's" claims in this instance. While he has proved to be a very reliable informant in previous cases, I have doubts here due to peculiar role played by "Caramel." It is simply not normal to have "Fudge" doing the talking in the presence of "Caramel," and intuition tells me "Caramel" is using "Fudge" as his ventriloquist's dummy—feeding us a line.

2. In short, if "Caramel" says Stalin has no plans to move west, I tend to expect Stalin to move west.

FOR YOUR EYES ONLY

19

It had been a real downtown drag, pretending to be a novice on an airplane for which he had an instructor's rating.

His main problem was to perform well enough to please Generalmajor Oskar without doing so well that his depth of experience as a B-17er would show—the kind of fix Tommy Dorsey would be in if his life depended on how well he pretended to be a trumpeter trying to qualify on the trombone. Dorsey blows an occasional bad note, Anton bounces a wheel here and there; simple in concept, blue hell to pull off convincingly. Which was underscored again today when the engines were still, the brakes had been set, the practice crew had spilled out on the runway, chattering and trading insults, and Generalmajor Oskar turned in the copilot's seat to deliver him a protracted stare, full of curiosity.

"I must say, Thoma, that you show exceptional adaptability. That was quite a demonstration, the way you sped through the emergency procedures when I announced a fire in your Number Three engine."

"Thank you, Herr Generalmajor."

"How do you manage so well?"

"I read the manuals, Herr Generalmajor."

"You are an excellent pilot, Thoma. So many of the others are ham-handed, impetuous know-it-alls. Of all the check rides I've given this month there have been precious few in which the pilots have escaped my wrath."

"I do my best, sir."

"I could use a hundred more like you."

"Thank you, sir. And, if you'll pardon my saying so, Herr Generalmajor, it's quite obvious that you yourself are an excellent flight instructor—and an even better check pilot."

Oskar's pale eyes went from curiosity to surprise. "Oh? And how do you come to that conclusion, Thoma?"

"Little things, sir. The way you go about the cockpit procedures—easy, familiar motions. Your coolness."

"Coolness?"

"On that touch-and-go landing. When I bounced hard, and, in the lift-off, that burst of crosswind cocked my wing and dropped my tail, I came very damn near to digging in a wingtip. The temptation to take over must have been very strong, sir, because your ass was on the line, too. But you kept your hands off the controls and let me muddle through. That's a very cool check pilot at work, in my estimation."

Anton knew that he had presented the Generalmajor with a pesky question. As a Nazi fundamentalist, cynicism would be a staple of Oskar's personality, impelling him naturally toward the negative, suspicious view of the society around him. But thanks to one of the Nazi psyche's many paradoxes, it would also be difficult for him to turn away from flattery in any form. So now, with his distrust of others' motives being counterweighted by his thirst for approbation, the Generalmajor was forced to make a decision: Was this Major Thoma a mere ass-kisser, or was he in fact an astute airman, candidly complimenting a professional peer?

"Would you care to join me for a drink Thoma?"

Ah. Question answered. "I'd be most pleased to, Herr Generalmajor. At the villa bar?"

Oskar freed himself from the narrow copilot seat and stood, crouching under the cockpit's low ceiling. "No. My car's outside. We'll go to my quarters. We can talk better there."

"Might I change first, sir? This flying gear's a bit gamy—"

"I'm surprised that it makes a difference to you, Thoma. You seem to have a certain, ah, earthiness about you, what with your bluntness, your foul mouth. That kind of thing."

"If I'm to socialize with the Generalmajor I should at least see to it that I look my best."

"Don't overdo it, Thoma."

"Sir?"

"I know that you're trying to ingratiate yourself with me. Just don't push too hard. Understand?"

"No, Herr Generalmajor."

"I think you do."

The afternoon's flying conditions had been marginal, what with a gusting wind, a lowering sky and intermittent showers. By evening, the rain was lashing and cold, and the villa and this guest house, so impressive in the sunlight, took on a dark oppressiveness.

The Generalmajor stood at the window, sipping his cognac and staring out at the sorry twilight. "What did you think of the war, Thoma? I mean, really."

"It was all politics, sir. And I take little interest in politics. As a soldier, I simply went where the politicians told me to go, did what they told me to do."

"And thought what they told you to think?"

"Usually, sir. It was—easier—that way."

"Which, of course, makes you a good Nazi."

Here we go again, Anton thought irritably. Another Nazi hard at work on self-justification. Another infallible superman about to whitewash a boo-boo.

During his school years, Anton had seen virtually every shade of the Nazi ethos, and among the most vexing was the Nazi's inability to admit a mistake. The Generalmajor

and his genre were absolutely crazy about themselves; as-
tronomers to zookeepers, they considered themselves to be
the world's leading experts in all things. Paradoxically, they
would often invite questions from lesser mortals. But this
was no real paradox, since their intent was not to inspire
debate but to parade (and probably to recertify in their own
minds) their superiority. Which was precisely how Anton
had found the temerity to stand up and ask his questions in
the first day's briefing; he knew that, by looking somewhat
the jerk, he would be making Oskar feel keen, and he also
knew, from experience he'd had with professors of Oskar's
ilk, that Oskar would be secretly grateful.

Thus life was difficult for the infallible Nazi who failed.
Hermann Göring, the Luftwaffe chief, had, early in the
war, boasted that if ever a single aerial bomb fell on Germany, his name was Meier. When important German cities
became smoldering trash pits, thanks to the RAF, Göring
spent most of his waking hours inventing scapegoats and
never fully recovered from his diet of crow.

Now here was Generalmajor Oskar, faced with the fact
that the National Socialist idea, a political philosophy he
had outspokenly championed since 1933, had proved to be
a colossal bummer. What to do? Do what Göring did, what
everybody else does when confronted by his own bad
guesses: make excuses and point fingers. Oskar, it seemed
obvious, had a pressing need to prettify, if not justify, his
bad guess of 1933. The German Legion presaged an epochal collaboration between Germany and the United States.
If he was to make the most of this opportunity, he would
have to devise a persona that would be socially acceptable
to the Amis. So what the Generalmajor wanted now was
not Anton's Nazi testimony but an opportunity to rehearse
before a live audience his new role as an apolitical Soldat,
a mere patriotic military technician—born of and steeped in
the classic German "Gott mit Uns" tradition—who'd been
led down the garden path by Machiavellian zealots.

Still, Anton knew, he would have to go warily. Oskar,
for all his carefully hidden diffidence, remained a very dan-

gerous fellow. Sure, Oskar needed to be on his best behavior, to project the image of a nice fellow who had at last been liberated from the sins of others. Yet, as a long-time Nazi, Oskar knew many ways to appear righteous and altruistic while kicking the shit out of somebody, and he wouldn't hesitate to use them if he thought his new initiatives were threatened.

"I think I was a good Nazi, sir. I tried to be. I believed in the Führer and his plans for the Fatherland. But the theatrics of it all wore on me. As I say, politics aren't my dish, and so I wasn't apt to go crazy at the rallies or get all excited when the band played the Horst Wessel Lied."

"It was more important to be a good soldier."

"Indeed, sir. And I've always prided myself on being a good soldier. I am, as a matter of fact, one hell of a soldier and flier."

Oskar lit a cigarette and blew smoke at the portrait of a fat woman in medieval dress that hung above the mantel. He asked a question. Casual, quiet. "Would you like to get away from this place for a few hours, Thoma?"

"I'd like to get away from this place for good, Herr Generalmajor. But, unhappily, it's forbidden—potentially fatal, actually—even to think of such a thing. By your own order."

"What if you and I were to pop into the Opel and run into town for a look at the girls?"

"That would be fine, sir. But only if you were to lift your order and all other the others to go, too."

"You mean you'd only go if the others could go with us?"

"Not with us, sir. That would not only be impossible, it would be a bore. Most of the others are very tedious types, for my money, and I'd give a lot to escape their company for a while. Even so, I could not enjoy myself if I thought you and I were the only men with such permission."

"What if I simply ordered you to accompany me to town for a bit of socializing?"

(Ah, Anton thought. The crux. The Generalmajor had been struggling with the problem of atrocities. He was seeking some lines of usable dialogue vis-a-vis the soldier's inability to question orders from legally appointed superiors.)

"Then I'd go, of course."

"But you wouldn't enjoy it."

"That's correct, sir. I am most uncomfortable in the face of double standards, hypocrisy. And under the circumstances, your order would be both."

"What if I ordered you to kill somebody? Would you do it? Would you follow my order?"

"Yes, sir."

"Blindly?"

"Not at all, Herr Generalmajor. I'd assume that the Generalmajor had valid reasons so to order. The person to be killed—man, woman or child—must certainly, in some way, pose a dire threat to the Fatherland, because good German officers do not knowingly order the execution of innocents. And the Generalmajor is a good German officer."

Oskar studied the tip of his cigarette, his lips pursed in the manner of one who is deep in thought. Outside, the storm intensified, making howling sounds in the thrashing trees, banging a shutter somewhere, seething against the windows. The lamps dimmed briefly.

"I have decided to appoint you as my second-in-command, Thoma," the Generalmajor said.

"I am honored, sir."

"I made the decision as you were preparing to land the B-17 this afternoon. For all your rough edges, you have a certain, ah, style. You have the courage of your convictions. You show evidence of being a thinker. Even so, you are ready to follow legitimate orders. And you are loyal to your fellow officers, even though you are not particularly fond of them. But most important, of course, you are quite clearly a better pilot than any of them."

"Thank you, sir. As your second-in-command, what will be my duties?"

"To lead the squadron. You will be command pilot on the mission against the Russians."

"You will not be accompanying us on the raid, then?"

"No. I was planning to be command pilot, as you know, but the Amis have asked me to serve as chief German adviser in their tactical headquarters, and as coordinator of radio communications with you and your people."

"I see." A pause. Then: "Do you expect the Amis will accept my appointment?"

"Of course. They have given me complete authority to design the interior composition of the Legion. They retain the authority to tell the Legion what to do—and when, and how. They set policy, I devise the structure. They establish the strategy, I collaborate with them on the tactics. Your appointment is my decision alone."

Anton decided that it was time to ask the Big Question. Since the answer was critical—crucial—he tried to be disarming, projecting idle curiosity, indifference. "These Americans, Herr Generalmajor: Who are they, and what do you think of them? Really, I mean."

Oskar turned from the window. "What makes you ask?"

"They seem a little strange to me. Not merely foreign—alien—but strange, in the sense that they might have something more in mind than what they've been telling us. Do you know what I mean?"

"I can't say that I do, Thoma."

"That Colonel Dreher, for instance. From my first interview with him in Dijon, he's given me the creeps. It's as if he's a mortician, measuring me by eye, trying to decide if I'm a standard suit size."

"The Americans—almost all of them—are little boys playing soldier, Thoma. Their basic idea—a pre-emptive attack on the Russians—is good, and has my complete, enthusiastic support. Yet Colonel Dreher and the group in charge of Aktion Achtung like to play spies. They like to tiptoe around, pretending deep intrigues and sly plots and dark deeds. It's almost laughable, the way they posture and play-act. But for me—for the German Legion—they are means to an end. And so I endure them. As you should."

"Well, forgive my seeming disagreement, sir, but I don't trust them. They're all sneaky bastards, to my mind."

"Certainly. And they're using us. But we're using them, too. We are using them to avenge the Fatherland. Don't you forget that."

"Which brings up the question, sir. Just when does this vengeance take place? We've been familiarizing ourselves with our one B-17. Each crew has flown a few clear-day VFR practice hops. But if we're going to do a long-distance bomb mission we've got to start some formation stuff. Lead navigator stuff. Instrument stuff. Lead bombardier stuff. Right now we're a bunch of solo artists. We've got to have some heavy rehearsing with a full complement of planes, and damned soon, it seems to me."

The Generalmajor took a final, somewhat overly dramatic pull at his cigarette, then flipped the butt into the fireplace and released twin bursts of smoke through flaring nostrils. "The time has come, obviously, to give you a few more details on our proposed aerial operation. It is a tricky thing, but now that our crews are familiar with the airplane they should have little trouble."

Anton remained silent.

"This Friday a truck convoy will take our crews to Lucia, a village on the Swiss-Italian border. Twelve of our complement of eighteen aircraft have been assembled at an abandoned airfield near there. They—"

Anton broke in, incredulous. "My God, sir—how in hell do the Amis expect to keep anybody from noticing a parked squadron of heavy bombers?"

"It's a very remote, seldom used airfield established, prewar, on an Alpine plateau, by the Italian Air Force. Most aircraft avoid the area, thanks to its adjacency to risky air and risky Alps, but even those that might pass over would have trouble spotting our machines. They have been extremely well camouflaged."

"No camouflage netting can effectively hide an airplane for long. And twelve of them? Really, now."

"We needed very little netting, actually. Only enough to obscure the B-17 outlines within a rather extensive desert of junked aircraft of all descriptions. The Italians used the field as a depot for the cannibalization of damaged or otherwise useless airplanes. I myself failed to see the 17's from the air, even when I knew they were there among the junk piles.''

''Who put the planes there? And where are the other six?''

''A small cadre of Ami maintenance crews brought them in by rail, disassembled and under tarpaulins on flatcars, two or three at a time. The twelve machines had been written off Ami headquarters records as destroyable surplus. The six others are en route, disassembled and in flatbed truck convoys, from various points in the Adriatic area, where they had made forced landings during the war and have since been rehabilitated by Captain Johnson's itinerant salvage crews. Ground delivery is necessary because ferry flights are too chancy. Somebody, somewhere, might have become suspicious. With the Ami armed forces as permeated by Communist spies as they are, we simply can't afford any suspicions. It would, of course, be catastrophic if Moscow were to get wind of what we're up to here. And that's where the tricky part comes in. That's why we will be having no squadron-strength rehearsals. The first time we fly formation will be on the raid itself. Even one rehearsal would tip our hand.''

Anton gaped. ''No rehearsals at all?''

''Our crews are seasoned airmen, Thoma. They will take off from the open runway at Lucia and rendezvous at a specific altitude and at a specific point en route to the target. They've done it many times, in other aircraft, other places.''

''Talk about doing things the hard way—''

''As I say, we can't afford to be spotted too soon.''

Anton thought about that. Then: ''So how many people *do* know about us, sir?''

''A handful of Ami brass hats and technical people, all on a need-to-know basis. We Germans. And that's it.''

''Presumably Harry Truman is among those Amis?''

''Colonel Dreher tells me it is the Ami president himself

who will be giving the actual attack order. By coded radio to the communications room at Lucia.''

A girl in a maid's uniform made a polite sound at the archway and announced dinner. The way she looked at Oskar suggested that her duties extended beyond those of housekeeping. The way Oskar looked at her confirmed it.

"Ah. I'm starved. How about you, Thoma?''

"I'm really not very hungry, sir.''

Anton, truly uninterested in the push-and-shove of applied politics, wasn't likely to have a heavy question about Oskar's assurances that President Truman would be personally pulling the handle on Aktion Achtung.

But he barely tasted his meal, thanks to precisely that question.

Either Colonel Dreher was a lousy student of government or he was a bullshitter of some dimension.

The war was over. A peace was on.

And even in Anton's indifferent understanding of the U.S. political process, only Congress could authorize major wars. Presidents had no power to start heavy-duty conflicts on their own.

And, practically speaking, wars of any kind, authorized or not, couldn't be started without vast and intricate preparations—an intricacy that precluded the secret organization and supply and briefing of a major pre-emptive strike. In a nation whose Congressmen used raw emotion and diarrheal speech as their power base, word of a military initiative involving millions of men and billions of dollars would inevitably get around.

So then, if Truman couldn't legally or secretly prepare to attack Russia, what was with this Aktion Achtung crap?

Curiouser and curiouser.

WEDNESDAY
26 September 1945

20

"Captain Olsen speaking."

"Kaufmann. Are you alone?"

"I'm splashing in the tub with three Hollywood starlets. It's what I do every one-thirty a.m."

"Sorry to call you this late."

"What's up, your Deceasedship?"

"I want to ask a favor."

"I'm really good at that kind of thing."

"I'd ask Raines to do it, but she's obviously on somebody's watch list."

"Worse. She's on somebody's kill list, you ask me."

"I'm working like hell on that. They won't get her if I have anything to say about it."

"So what can I do for you?"

"I have a letter. To my parents. I want you to mail it to them. In one of your envelopes, your APO. Like that."

"Glad to. Mail censorship's been lifted. So why not?"

"I can't let them go on this way. You know. Grieving."

"Where's the letter?"

"Under the seat cushion of your jeep."

"When did you put it there?"

"You were at dinner at the Edelweiss Klub tonight."

"You're following me around these days?"

"Only when I have a letter to send."

"Weren't you taking a chance? A lot of USFET staffers hang out at the Edelweiss. Somebody might have seen you."

"I paid a parking attendant to stash the letter."

"Deucedly clever."

"There's something else you can do, Olsen. I want you to call Lieutenant Raines in her office tomorrow morning—this morning. Early. Before she takes her daily POW summary to Central Registry. Tell her that when she delivers the summary she should ask Poopsie for the dossiers on Gregor Koslov, an NKVD agent, on Luigi Fortunato, an Italian film director, and on Louis Stahl, the American oil and real estate baron—"

"That super-rich mystery man? The guy with the Homburg and the beard?"

"Yep. He's very publicity shy, so there might not be much on him. But his name's come up, and I'd like to read whatever's available on him."

"Okay, then what?"

"Tell Raines to read whatever Poopsie gives her, then return to her office. Request a jeep from the motor pool, and during her lunch break, drive to the Hauptbahnhof. Stand in the main concourse for five minutes. If I don't show up in those five minutes, she's to go back to her jeep and return to work. O.K.?"

"Sure. Secret agent stuff, eh?"

"I suppose."

"Anything else?"

"That's it for now. Tell Raines to be careful."

While he waited, a light rain misted the windshield and the oncoming winter made its presence known in his knees and calves and on the end of his nose. To keep his mind off the discomfort, Kaufmann mulled his ages-old question of treason and why men commit it.

In his collegiate days, and in his subsequent army tour, he'd been both bemused and confused by those members of the American Communist Party he had met. For a penniless loser shivering in an alley in Cleveland or Boise, there might be some logic in giving the finger to the Star-spangled Banner. But what practicing hedonist, aware that his right to life, liberty and pursuit of nooky is formally guaranteed by a generally benign and undemanding government, would be attracted by the grubby gray rigors of a Stalin-style tyranny? What hatred or ambition was powerful enough to enable those fat-cat pinkos he'd known to sign on with a system that openly warred on everything they were? The appeal of Nazism was easier to understand, because Hitler legitimized, made socially acceptable, the worst aspects of human nature; Adolf recognized that there's a Nazi lurking in everyone, and for proof one need only to drive in rush-hour traffic and feel the universal rage to be first, or to get even, or, if it could be made legal, to kill the stupid bastards who are getting in your way. But Stalinism was contrary to human nature, demanding that everybody—geniuses, strivers, idiots and drones alike—share the wealth (except for Stalin and his pals, of course, who shared equally with the masses whatever was left of the wealth after Stalin and his pals took what they wanted from the top). The Russian people were magnificently brave and industrious and loyal. Yet loyalty itself was both their strength and their vulnerability. They might detest their government because its brutalities were alien to their inborn nature; but it was *their* government, by God, and woe unto him who threatened or ridiculed it. Moreover, the typical Russian felt smugly superior to foreigners—to outsiders of any kind, actually. Given all this, it seemed to Kaufmann that any American had to be nutty indeed to become a disdained outside evangelist for a Russian gangster.

It was just such a nut that he was up against in this current unpleasantness, he suspected. If the American military presence was presently a Three Stooges shambles, the NKVD and its formal intelligence ancillaries in Western Europe were little better off. Few native Russians were capable of passing as natives of France, Germany, Britain or the United States, and those few were reserved for only the most delicate, consequential assignments. So it followed that the Soviets' subversions and espionage penetrations west of the Oder-Niesse line would depend almost entirely on local Communists and military turncoats. So whatever was impending via the missing Luftwaffe POWs and garrulous OSS officials and mysterious Italians and exotic poisons and assorted assassinations, both attempted and accomplished, it was virtually certain that American traitors were involved.

Traitors?

Who?

And what was the nature of their treason?

He thought of the old story in which a mother, realizing her kids were being very quiet in the next room, called, "All right, you two: whatever you're doing, stop it."

Of all the nutty people he knew, who were the nuttiest?

And the quietest?

He was forming a list when Raines came around the curve, heading south on Reuter Weg, sitting high and determined behind the jeep's steering wheel.

She was really very pretty. He noted her pallor, and it pained him. He hated to put her through this kind of hoop, but it was better to jazz her around a bit now than eventually to lose her altogether.

He started the motor and released the hand brake, waiting, studying the traffic. She had almost moved from sight to the left when his ploy paid off to the right.

A dark green Maybach convertible sedan materialized behind her, threading its way purposefully through the lunchtime flow, closing in on her, not so near as to be obvious, not so far as to lose her. He nosed the Mercedes into the stream, taking cover in the lee of a large produce van, sidling to the left now and then for a glimpse of the Maybach's driver. It was no go. The green car's canvas top was up and fastened and its windows were shaded by visors, so the driver—apparently a man wearing a fedora—remained a dim silhouette.

The parade moved without delay to the Bahnhofsplatz, where Raines pulled the jeep into a slot between a pair of GI six-by-sixes, and the Maybach parked nearby. Kaufmann found his own place across the square and waited until the Maybach's driver, a lanky fellow in one of those long leather coats favored by Wehrmacht officers, dismounted hurriedly, resettled the hat on his head, and followed Raines into the sooty shadows of the station's rubbled lobby.

Bingo. It was the same man, in the same fedora, as the one who had driven past the jeep wreck on the mountain road.

Kaufmann gave a moment to the Maybach. Wiesbaden-Hesse license plate, probably stolen or fabricated. The driver had left the doors unlocked. The glove compartment and map pockets were devoid of ownership ticket, maintenance records, or anything else of informational value.

He drop-kicked a tire star behind the Maybach's left front wheel. When the car was backed away from the curb and over the cluster of steely needles, a disabling flat was sure to follow. After another circuit of the sedan to be sure he hadn't overlooked anything helpful, he went inside the station.

True to her instructions, Raines was in the main concourse and was standing patiently beside one of the fluted columns, glancing occasionally at her watch. The lanky man had posted himself near the message kiosk and was pretending to read a newspaper. Between them was a current of humanity—shuffling, snuffling, burdened with cardboard suitcases, bulging knapsacks, tattered shopping bags and melancholy lostness; beyond them, the steamy thumping and clanking of a shifting train, the distant hooting of a locomotive whistle, a metallic voice blattering incomprehensibly of why nothing would be running anywhere this day or maybe even tomorrow.

Kaufmann sat on a bench near the main entrance, flanked
on both sides by wraithlike transients who smelled un-
washed and who said nothing, choosing to stare unseeingly
at the passing formations of like wraiths. He hated railroad
stations; they were rotten places of mute apartness and sad
eyes and ancient, caked, coal residues that grayed walls and
dimmed lights. Nothing truly happy ever happened in these
vaulted barns. Even when reunions were made with outstretched arms and squeals of delight, tens of scores of others around them, separated by no more than inches of steam
and coal smoke, were dying the silent deaths of leave-taking,
and the sorrow would be felt by the rejoicers, no matter
how determined their exuberance, and so even these flickers
of jubilation could never be what they might have been in
other places, other times. Unaccountably, his mind went to
the flier, Anton, a man who must have endured a thousand
such places as this, judging by the aloneness that showed
through his persistent ebullience and his too-quick grin and
defiant tomfoolery. Now *there* was a man who was hurting,
by God. There was a man who, sure as hell, spent each of
his days coping with a personal, built-in, lifelong railroad
station. Where was he now? The lack of word should be
taken positively; in the trade, no news was good news if the
silence occurred in an acceptable time frame. Anton had
entered the dark side a little over a week ago, so he was
still due some elbow room.

But wherever he was, he was in some metaphorical train
station, hurting, and he'd be hurting precisely as much as
in New York City or Burpville, Indiana.

When the five minutes were up, Raines again followed
her instructions and strode briskly toward the lobby and the
square beyond. The man in the fedora did not do as expected, however; instead of making for his own car and the
resumption of his tail job, he followed her only to the lobby,
where he closed in, seized her elbow, whispered briefly in
her ear and half pushed, half dragged her toward the Maybach.

Kaufmann stood in the crowd swirl at the entrance, watching with great interest. His initial plan had been simply to bait the hook with Raines and see who nibbled. Then, when the Maybach appeared, he'd decided instead to step in for a serious talk with Herr Fedora. What better time than when Herr Fedora was on his haunches, cussing up a storm over a pancaked tire?

"So then, it's off to work," Kaufmann thought aloud.

"Bitte?" a soft voice asked beside him.

He turned, startled, to confront a short round woman with missing front teeth. She wore a ratty thin coat, and a shawl was tied over her gray head. Her right hand held a satchel, from which a huge sausage end and a stick of bread protruded. Her faded blue gaze was curious but polite.

In German he said, "Sorry, madam, I was thinking aloud."

"I though you were talking to me. Do you always think aloud in English?"

"I'm on my way to lessons. I have a date with my tutor."

She shook her head and ambled off, her ragged shoes making flopping sounds on the pavement.

The man was shoving Raines into the Maybach's driver's seat. After pushing her across to the front passenger seat, he slid behind the wheel and slammed the door. Kaufmann stood fast, watching the car back into a turn that halted when the tire emitted a roaring hiss.

Chat time folks.

He strolled down the walkway and pulled open the Maybach's driver's door. "End of the line, pal."

"Ah. At last. I've been looking all over for you." The man's English was harsh with Slavic accents. "And you, obviously, have been looking for me, what with your using the lady as bait, your immobilizing me with a tire star."

"Let the girl go, or I'll shoot you where you sit."

"We're at impasse, I'm afraid. I am holding a pistol against Fräulein Raines's elegant ribs."

"Let her go, or I swear, I'll drill you."

The man began a comment, but his mouth suddenly spurted blood and the air next to Kaufmann's ear cracked nastily.

"My God," Raines shrieked.

The man slumped against the steering wheel, shuddered deeply, then was still.

Kaufmann stared, astonished, at the round little woman with the shawl, who stood beside the car, smiling her toothless smile and unscrewing the silencer from a Colt automatic.

"Who the hell are you?"

She slid the automatic into her satchel, nodded a polite good-bye, and swung into a dark blue sedan that now voomed to a halt beside her.

"Damn," Kaufmann said, watching the car speed off.

Raines was very flustered, and he led her to the shelter of the Mercedes, where she sat beside him in the front seat and did some heavy-duty trembling.

"That man was going to kill us."

"Yep."

"Why? I mean—who was he? And that horrid little woman—who was she?"

"I don't know."

"What are we going to do about that man?"

"There's nothing we can do about him."

"We can't just leave him lying there in that car."

"Why not?"

"The police—"

"They'll find him sooner or later. And there's nothing to connect us with him."

"Somebody might have seen us with him."

"Lots of people saw us with him. But if any of them were in the mood to report us we'd be up to our satchels in cops by now. Anybody who saw us is trying to forget he saw us. Talking to cops only brings trouble these days."

"So what are we going to do?"

"First, you're going back to the compound, turn in your jeep, and go back to your office. Second, you are going to drop in on Poopsie again and ask her to see the general file on Soviet agents, unidentified, Western Europe. They've got such a file. I know. I've worked with it several times. Look through it and see if anything there connects with—even reminds you—of our Sleeping Beauty in the car over there. Third, I want you to get me copies of the service records of some U.S.-type people. I'll give you the list. Their complete biographies, military and civilian. Since you're in Personnel, that should be no problem, and you can package them up with the stuff you're getting me on Ballentine, Koslov, Fortunato and Stahl. And fourth, I want you to call Olsen and see if he can finagle the autopsy on the guy in the car. Olsen can probably work up enough clout to at least get in on the ID process. If he gets a line on who the guy was, have him call you so you can tell me when I call you tomorrow night."

He was deliberately loading things on her—mainly of necessity, but in good part because it would break her preoccupation with her narrow escape. "Are you getting all this?"

"Yes."

He took the wallet from his jacket pocket and, fishing, found the list. "Here. Try to get as many of these bios as fast as you can. No particular order. Also, check them all in *Who's Who in America* in the G-2 reference room—just for the hell of it. Who knows who's in *Who's Who*, eh?"

"The Shadow knows," she said, suddenly snappish.

He gave her a fond smile. "There's hope for you yet, Raines."

She considered him out of the corners of angry eyes. "You're a real prick, aren't you."

"Why, Raines. Such a thing to say."

"You used me as bait. The man even said so."

"I didn't enjoy it. But yes. Yes, I did." He gathered righteousness about him. "We're trying to save some civilization around here, you know."

"How do you know what we're trying to save? But more than that, how do *I* know what we're trying to save? All I know is what you tell me, and that isn't very much. I don't mind saying, mister, I'm having a lot of trouble right now, trying to believe anything you tell me. And that's a living fact. Take it from me: any guy who uses his own girlfriend as bait for murder is a sick, sidewinding S.O.B."

"I didn't know there was going to be a murder, Raines. I had to pull somebody out of the woodwork, somebody that could lead us to more information. Obviously somebody had to be watching you in the hopes of finding me, so what's more logical than to have you bring them to me so I can see who they are? You've got to remember, lady, that I'm an investigator. And investigators investigate."

"You could at least have told me what you're trying to do."

"Sure, and have you leave a trail of nervous wee-wee all across town?"

"I don't wee-wee when I'm nervous, damn it. What is it with you men, anyhow, always trying to make women look like hand-wringing, whimpering little idiots?"

"You were scared out of your mind just now, and you've got to admit it."

"Of course I was, you ass. It's not every day I see a man get his brains blown out while he's getting ready to blow my brains out."

"Well, you sure as hell would've tipped the guy off somehow. The only way to get him was to keep you acting naturally."

"Let me tell you once and for all, buster: you want my help, you'll level with me all the way. No more cute tricks, no more half truths. If I'm in a fight I want to know all the rules and have all the tools."

"And another thing, Raines. Just what is all this stuff about my 'girlfriend'?"

"Oh, stick it up your big fat bazoo."

She swung out of the car, slammed the door, crossed the plaza to her jeep and roared off in a cloud of tire smoke..

TRANSCRIPT FOR ALPHA'S REFERENCE FILE ONLY

Phone conversation, "M" Line

"Hello."

" 'Alpha'?"

"Sweet Sue."

"Margie."

"What is it, 'M'?"

"Kaufmann's alive."

"What? How do you know that?"

"This morning Raines asked for the files on some of our people, alerting 'Doll.' 'Doll' called 'Seed,' who told 'Sweetums' to tail Raines. She went to the Hauptbahnhof, tailed by 'Sweetums,' who, in turn, was tailed by 'Seed.' Raines was taken by 'Sweetums,' and Kaufmann appeared, apparently planning to rescue her. 'Seed' says that, as he watched this little scene, an old woman walked up to the car, shot 'Sweetums,' then escaped in another car, leaving Kaufmann and Raines with their mouths open."

"Who in hell was the old woman?"

"I simply don't know, 'Alpha.' "

"Where did Kaufmann and Raines go?"

"He drove her back to the Farben Compound. She got out of the car and walked through the main gate there. Kaufmann drove off south, but 'Seed' lost him in the traffic."

"Damn."

" 'Seed' apologizes."

"Fat lot of good that does."

"Mm."

"Well, tell everybody to keep their eyes open. When Kaufmann shows up again, kill him. Summarily. By any means. We're beyond the discreet stage, I'm afraid."

"That Kaufmann's a slick one, all right."

"He's very dangerous to us now."

"Odd thing about that, 'Alpha': I don't think he really and fully understands how much of a threat he is."

"Well, we don't have time for such philosophizing. Just kill the bastard."

"Consider it done."

21

Evening was settling over the Hessian hills as General Vickery turned the L-5 into an easy power glide toward the big base at Rhine-Main. The engine burbled softly, and the slipstream was rich with the perfume of high octane burning evenly and efficiently. One of the great perks of Air Force generalship was the availability of some kind of airplane to fly whenever the hell he felt like flying. (Which was all the time, of course, but his determination to avoid abusing the time-honored military philosophy, Rank Has Its Privileges, served as a silent governor that limited his pleasure flights to two per week.) He could have flown just about any ship on the line this particular afternoon, but the wonderful, old-fashioned sense of seat-of-the-pants aviating it served up led him to choose the L-5, a two-seat high-wing utility puddle-jumper. Everybody liked the L-5, from briefcase couriers to Ike himself.

There was a moment in which he remembered the Spad, a fleeting surge of nostalgia for the pug-nosed biplane which, as the hottest fighter available to the American Expeditionary Force in War One, wasn't a hell of a lot more oomphy than this little rattler. Twice as much horsepower and a pair of Vickers machine guns, mounted under the upper wing directly in front of the cockpit, made it considerably more of a weapon, of course. But it glided like an anvil, and, thanks to the rotten gas of those days, its engine was likely to conk out at the most embarrassing moments—in the middle of a take-off, say, or while coming in for a strafing run on a Heinie airfield. He couldn't recall ever having flown the Spad without worrying about something. Yet he missed the little sumbish. For him, flying one of today's four-engine jobs was like driving a moving van full of pianos, and in fighters like the P-47 Jug, or the P-51 Mustang, or the twin-tailed P-38, you were so busy watching dials and listening to radios and working vectors your sense of flying gave way to a sense of being strapped into a 400-mile-per-hour juke-box. So for the pure fun of flying, the L-5 was a comparative dreamboat.

He shifted the cold cigar to the other corner of his mouth and said, "Air Force thirty-two-oh-two for landing clearance."

"Roger, thirty-two-oh-two," the headphones told him, overly polite. "You're cleared for the south end grass utility strip. Request you taxi to Small Craft Transient Hangar for tie-down there."

He fed a touch of throttle, and the hose lifted, and he banked left from due west into the downwind leg. The smoky smear of Frankfurt came around, golden brown on the twilit horizon, and then the purple vastness to the east, and eventually, with power reduced, the final approach. Sighing, teetering slightly in the shifting currents of the oncoming night, the little brown ship settled into a faultless, bounceless, three-point return to earth, and the general chuckled, knowing as he did that a lot of hotshit Boston Charlies were watching this old son of a bitch from out of the primeval past. *General Vickery was a World War One ace? You better goddam well believe it, pal. Did you see that landing, for crissake?*

The L-5 waggled to the flight line, its engine snorting, its propeller wash flattening the grass, and three mechanics hurried out to help it through its final turn into tie-down position.

When the prop had ticked into silence, the line sergeant did a bit of fawning. "Good flight, General?"

"Yep."

"Here. Let me help you out."

"Get your hands off me, goddam it. Who do you think I am—Whistler's mother? I'll get out of my own goddam airplane on my own goddam steam."

"Yes, sir. Sorry, sir."

Vickery gave the crestfallen man a closer look. "What's your name, soldier?"

"Boggs, sir. Sergeant Avery P."

"Well, Boggs, I appreciate your courtesy. And you're a man who likes and respects airplanes, if the shape this little sucker's in is any measure. But I'm very goosy about people treating me like an old man. I might be old, but I'm not old, if you get my drift."

"Yes, sir, I sure do. I shoulda known better, sir."

Vickery stepped to the turf and looked around, squinting against the orange western glare. "Where's that goddam driver of mine?"

"Here she comes now, sir."

The GI Packard bounced regally across the autumn-browned grass and came to a halt in the plane's long shadow. Vickery, ordinarily insistent that his driver open the car's rear passenger door and stand at attention until he'd entered, in this instance went directly to the car and climbed in behind the warm and ample Captain Benet, who sat at the wheel, stiff and solemn and soldierly.

Before slamming the door, he said, loud enough for the ground crew to hear, "Take me to my office, Captain."

They drove off in a flurry of salutes, and after they had left the base and were on the main road to Wiesbaden she said, over her shoulder, "Don't you want to come up here with me, dear?"

"Hell no. Generals don't ride around in the front seats of cars driven by female officers. It doesn't look right."

"I'm not your driver, I'm just doing you a favor. Besides, Ike rides up front in jeeps driven by Kay Summersby. I've seen him do it."

"Ike isn't a general, he's a politician. He wants the troops to think he's a reg'lar guy. Besides, Kay looks sweet and virginal and all business."

"You mean I don't?"

"With those boobs? With that ass? My god, woman, be realistic, will you? Hell, all you have to do is stroll down the street and every guy for eight blocks around creams his drawers. Why do you think I get in the car without you holding the door for me? You stand beside my car just once and I'll be derided by the whole United States Forces in Europe as that impotent old fart who thinks it might help things to import a chauffeur from Hollywood and Vine."

She smiled the easy smile which, he knew from last night's covert observation in the upstairs dressing room of his Wiesbaden villa, she spent much time practicing before a mirror. "We know different, don't we, Willie? Impotence is not your problem."

He grinned sheepishly and groped in his trench coat for a fresh cigar. "I told you not to call me Willie."

"I think Willie's a cute name. I think you're cute."

"You're full of more crap than a Christmas turkey."

She laughed, and it was a pleasant sound.

"Speaking of cars, did Ballentine ever get a lead on his? That pimpmobile that was stolen from under his nose?"

"Yes, sir. Some fence or something in Karlsruhe recovered it and sold it back to him."

"What a world. Guy steals a stolen car, gets it stolen from him, then buys it back from a guy who deals in stolen cars. The world is certifiably mad."

"Mm."

He got his cigar going, and through the cloud he asked, "How'd things go in your office today?"

"Colonel Donleavy had a big, long meeting. Which kept

me taking and transcribing shorthand all afternoon. And which caused your sleep-in driver to show up late for your landing this evening. Your sleep-in driver is truly sorry, darling.''

''What kind of meeting? Who with?''

''The colonel is very upset over what he sees to be a leak. He had the entire G-2 staff in, and he really read the riot act. He said that some things that are very much top secret around the shop are showing up in Soviet intelligence summaries—that stuff he learns one day is showing up in the Moscow summaries two days later.''

''He gets Soviet intelligence summaries? How?''

''Moscow moles, our embassy nets—that kind of thing.''

''Did he give some examples?''

''Well, two congressmen visited on a so-called fact-finding tour for the Armed Services Committee last week, and Ike sent them down to us for a detailed briefing on Operation Nursery, that thing I told you about.''

''The sedition those fugitive Nazi bigwigs are planning?''

''Mm. Down in Munich. Well, there's some worry in the States that Nazism isn't really dead, and the committee got wind of the Nursery case and wants to know just what it means. The fact of their visit and what they were interested in appeared in an NKVD summary the day before yesterday, and Donleavy is very unhappy about that.''

''I can see why.''

She gave him a glance in the rearview mirror. ''You aren't snitching to the Russians, are you, dear? I mean, I tell you a lot of things out of school—''

''Very funny.'' He made noises with his cigar. ''So what does Donleavy propose to do about the leak?''

''He's instituting a new system of classified document distribution and control. Sign-outs for everything, red tabs, initial slips—that kind of thing. And summary court-martials for all transgressions. I have never seen him so mad, actually. 'Any infractions of our security provision by members of this staff will be treated as criminal acts,' he said. Boy-oh-boy.''

''So what we're doing now is a criminal act?''

She laughed. "Well, after all, darling, you *are* one of our generals. If we can't trust you, who can we trust?"

Vickery studied the cigar's coal for a time. Then: "Has Donleavy clued in G-2 and Ike on this leak business?"

"Of course. He dictated several memos to me and I personally delivered them to the two gentlemen."

"Has Ike reacted?"

"He was very spiky about the Nursery leak. He said in an answering memo that it's of the utmost importance to keep an eye on the Munich Nazis and to round them up no later than next March. He said they may be kooks, but kooks or mainstream, he wants everybody eligible for trial at Nuremberg to be rounded up by April one."

Vickery sniffed. "Which, translated, means Ike guesses it'll take him about a year to get ready for his retirement and subsequent run at the presidency. He won't leave Europe without some kind of fireworks—some kind of unmistakable evidence that he's conquered the Nazis finally and forever."

"You're a real cynic, aren't you, Willie."

"You bet your sweet buns I am. Show me a human being and I'll show you an angle-shooter. Some human beings just manage to look better—more noble and benign and altruistic—while they shoot their little angles, that's all."

A silence followed. She drove, and he watched, and the evening settled in around them. As she entered the cobblestoned, tree-lined Allee and slowed for the turn into the villa's driveway, he asked a question. "What does Donleavy really think of the Russians? Aside from all his puffing and blowing in staff meetings, that is."

"I don't have any doubt that he hates them. Under all that easy-going suaveness, that cool, button-down, one-world liberalism, there lies a veddy, veddy hard-case Republican, you ask me. If I was a pinko, I'd never trust him out of my sight."

"What are you, baby? If you're not pinko, what, then?"

"Me? I'm a Roosevelt Democrat. A wild-eyed, cheerleading, banner-waving New Dealer. How about you?"

"I'm not old enough to vote."

She laughed again. "Come on—what are you?"

"I'm serious. I'm so horny right now I feel like a fuzz-faced junior high schooler. That's what you do to me, baby. You make me too young to vote."

"Well, then. Come into the house and we'll see what we can do about that, eh?"

After Benet and the general disappeared arm-in-arm into the villa's great gray bulk, Ludwig removed the distance lens and rewound the film.

"We've spent the whole frigging day on Vickery," he said aloud, yawning. "I'm tired of looking at the sumbish, and I want something to eat."

"Vickery is up to something," Ransky said. "And we're going to find out what. Blackmail pix might do it."

"With him, I wouldn't bet on it." Ludwig buttoned the case, placed the camera on the seat beside him, fired up the Opel and turned its nose toward Frankfurt.

TRANSCRIPT FOR ALPHA'S REFERENCE FILE ONLY

Phone conversation, "M Line"

"Hello."

" 'Alpha'?"

"Charmaine."

"Diane."

"Yes, 'M,' what is it?"

"Vickery and Benet are shacking up."

"Oh? You're sure?"

"I'm sure."

"Interesting development. Although I must say I'm not surprised."

"Just thought you ought to know."

"All right. Thank you. Anything else?"

"That's it for now."

"Good-bye."

22

He waited on a park bench fashioned of granite, an artifact which dated from the long-ago, when clement weekends would bring out strolling armies of papas in bowlers and celluloid collars, haughty mommas with loops of beads on their brocaded bosoms, and flat-faced brats in the obnoxious pupal stage of that piggish priggishness (or was it priggish piggishness?) they would eventually exhibit as inflexibly Teutonic adults. He had selected the site because she was sure to pass here, there being no other path leading directly from the trolley stop to that part of the great gray Kaserne allotted to USFET enlisted people of the female persuasion. In the bargain, it was poorly lit and sparsely traveled at this time of night, conditions well suited for what he had in mind.

It irritated him to delay once again a return to Heidelberg and a probe of what he saw to be the target of greatest potential reward. But his years in the espionage sewer had taught him never to wade, always to step from discernible stone to discernible stone. Never make for Square Two until you've put your full weight on Square One. Never enter a room without first counting the exits. Never take on an enemy before you're taken in by friends. Never forget to remember. Never do this, never do that. Blah, blah, blah. Now, at this most unlikely moment—and yet in a kind of mad, juvenile relevance—his mind rang with that grotesque college drinking ditty, "Never make your move to the Y before you tell her you l-o-o-o-ve her."

Night had brought a cold wind, and the stars, which earlier had suggested diamond dust on velvet, were gone behind a layer of nimbus that seemed to traverse the sky, racing and rolling darkly, just above the treetops. Fallen leaves, dry and dusty, skittered across the cratered parkland, and the solitary streetlamp at the end of the promenade seemed unable to throw light beyond its own dirty globe. It was a cheerless place and time, and he thought of home and supper smells and loving faces and he wanted briefly, of all things, to cry. He hadn't really cried since he was a boy, since that morning he'd found Trixie, his beloved Boston bull, dead of old age at the foot of his bed. But now he wanted to cry and he wasn't sure why.

What a lousy world.

The trolley arrived finally, a box of pale light and muted clankings. After a pause in the streetlamp's glow, it ground off to the north, leaving her behind, a shadow moving with purpose along the promenade.

He stepped into her path and said, "You are a traitor, Poopsie."

"What? Who is it?"

"You have betrayed your country." The night produced a resonance, transforming his voice so as to suggest the echo-chamber preface to a radio spook show, warning hollowly of dire events, and he felt his lingering blues meld into mild self-contempt.

"Who *are* you? And what the hell are you talking about?"

"You know who I am." (Portentous cello music here, the creaking of a door.)

"So let me see your face, pal."

He moved closer to the light. Slowly, because it pained him to employ such tactics. He was at a very serious turning point in a very serious business, and it was annoying to be compelled to resort to Inner Sanctum theatricals. But being dead left him no choice.

"*Kaufmann?* They said you were dead—"

"It's all over for you, Poopsie. It's time for us to talk about your treason."

"What the hell's going on here?"

"I've got you. You're done."

"What is this bullshit?"

"You put a killer onto Raines today. She asked for some files, and you told Ballentine, and he sent a guy to kill Raines. I set up the test, Poopsie. And you failed. You revealed yourself as a black-marketing traitor." This was hyperbole, of course, since he had no real idea just what Poopsie's role was in this thing or how far her influence ran. But he had her. And she knew it.

"You've also been slipping Zenog into Raines's coffee. You're a naughty, naughty girl."

Poopsie was no easy mark. She pushed past him and made for the barracks again. "I don't know what the hell you're talking about. I don't know any Ballentine."

He called after her. "Ballentine will soon find out that we good guys are onto you. And if we don't put you away, Ballentine will."

She paused and looked back at him. "Of course you're not dead. You're stark raving. And you've just escaped from that asylum they've been keeping you in."

"If you want to stay alive, Poopsie, come back and sit on this bench and talk. Depending on what you tell me, I might be able to make an amnesty deal for you."

"Up yours, lint-head."

He watched her walk off.

"You have until oh-seven-thirty tomorrow morning," he called. "I'll be waiting for you here."

He watched until she had disappeared into the gloom of the Kaserne gate.

He missed Raines terribly.

Her anger and disappointment, so intense, so undisguised during the rotten scene in the car, was an inner stinging that refused either to abate or to overwhelm his shame at having exploited her naivete. And now this added thing. This confirmation of her mortal danger.

He tried to call her, first from a booth on Henckel Gasse, then from Olsen's military phone. The civilian line couldn't connect with the Vom Rath Strasse apartment, and Olsen's office was dark and locked. He decided to try again from Karli's Tankstelle.

He turned north from Wiesbaden and took the road for Idstein, driving fast, headlights and fog lamps etching the two lanes of macadam and the flanking forests in a chalky glare. The car was good, for having been through war. Its motor rumbled, unmistakably Mercedes; it glided over clefts and potholes with the serenity of a liner nosing through harbor chop; it sped through curves as if it were on rails. He hadn't driven for pure pleasure since his school days, and, despite his preoccupations, his gathering rage and frustration, some of that enjoyment came back to him now, faint, teasing. He sought to lock onto the sensation, to expand it into a total involvement that would, if only for a minute or two, mitigate the pain of this huge, war-shaped hole in his life—a chasm with boyhood's fey innocence on one side and an old man's paranoid cunning on the other. He knew that he had been cheated of something terribly important, but precisely what he had lost and how he had lost it would remain forever beyond definition—like a blind man's knowing that while yesterday had a sunset, its exact colors will never, ever, be known to him.

This depression of his stemmed first, he knew, from the flare-up with Raines, second, from having wasted four hours on researching General Vickery, and, third, from the melancholy fact of Poopsie's sins. Raines and her anger he could handle, because it was definable, reasonable: he had used her, and she rightfully resented it, and yet he could, thanks to his own honest repentance, and given time and patience, eventually rebuild the relationship. Her good will was of great importance to him for the fulfillment of his professional mission, sure, but mainly he cared because of her wonderful face and all-American disposition.

And because of that wonderful kiss.

Poopsie? The absurd little tableau in the park had placed her in a fatal checkmate. The mysterious Ballentine probably knew by now that Kaufmann had survived the assassination attempt and he would therefore be unmoved by Poopsie's report of Kaufmann's appearance. But Poopsie, obviously no dummy, had to understand that if she told Ballentine that American intelligence knew of her work for him, she would be signing her own death warrant, as the cliché had it; to cut her out as a possible squealer, as a vulnerability he couldn't afford, Ballentine would have to eliminate her. Yet if she went the other way and confessed her transgressions to her army bosses, as Kaufmann had demanded, she would face life in Leavenworth or execution by firing squad, depending on the mood of God and the court-martial panel. Kaufmann's gamble was that she would choose the lesser of evils. Leavenworth offered a chance at some kind of life; Ballentine offered nothing at all.

He slowed to make the turn-off at the Tankstelle. The place was dark. Karli was no doubt off in the arms of the plump and amiable blonde who blithely and simultaneously dispensed gas to his patrons and breast milk to her infant daughter. He used his key to get to the phone, but there was only a lonely, unanswered ringing at the other end of the line. Nor did Karli's message spike offer anything.

The depression deepened.

Emma's idea of a hunting lodge was typically Emma. The blacktop driveway arced to the summit and a splendid view of hills and the distant Rhineland, obscured now by night and the descending weather. The house itself, a pile of rock and timber arranged into a modest twenty rooms, give or

take a library or two, sat on the crest and loomed appro-
priately Gothic. Emma had acquired it from SS Standartenführer Oswald Oppermann as his payment for her hastily
contrived and unsuccessful attempt to relocate him in São
Paulo. These days Oppermann was busily lying to a battery
of war crimes probers at Oberursel.

He parked the car in the circle beside the fountain and
trotted up the stairs to the side veranda, where, after much
fussing with the set of keys Emma had given him, he let
himself into the solarium. As he stepped into the hallway
and flipped on lights and made for the study, which, Karli
had assured him, was the least creepy of the godawful rooms
in this Frankenstein's castle, he suffered a sunburst of anger—an unreasoning and entirely unexpected explosion of
blind rage. He was so tired of, so fed up with, so pissed off
at those sons of frigging bitches who had destroyed half the
world and caused him to be here, in this hideous pile, he
wanted to fall to the gaudy parquet and kick his feet and
pound his fists and screech. Oppermanns existed everywhere: here in Germany, there in France-England-Sweden-
Italy-China-Russia-Denmark, ad nauseam and ad infinitum,
right on down to Gizmo Junction, I-o-way, and he was so
sick of them he wanted to puke all over this expensive floor;
he was one of them, everybody was one of them—the whole
shitty world was filled with Oppermanns, whether they were
Gestapo creeps or ruthless bankers who built houses like
this or pious religionists who built churches to honor themselves or salesmen who lied or husbands who cheated or
wives who connived or kids who stole. What had happened
out there, somewhere in the cosmos, to materialize a world
that would aid, abet and applaud all these on-going crimes
against God and man? Who—in Hell or elsewhere—had arranged to turn what could have been a paradise into such a
putrid dump? What, in specific, had happened so as to allow a sweet, wonderful, lovable, gorgeous, intelligent,
witty, gracious and modest kid like this here Kaufmann fella
to place the Girl Next Door in mortal danger just so he
might put the finger on one more version of the already

countless versions of Oswald Oppermann? Toward what end? To make this Kaufmann fella feel self-righteous, sanctified, worthwhile, respectable and squeaky clean?

"The world is one big asshole." The pronouncement, spoken aloud, echoed through the oaken cavern.

In the study a lamp glowed by the sofa, and she was reading. She put down the file and gave him that steady-eyed special of hers.

"Did you just say something out there?"

"I've been talking to myself a lot these days."

"It's cold. Could we have a fire?"

"What are you doing here?"

"I came partly to deliver these personal histories you asked for. But mainly I came to apologize. Karli let me in. He's a dilly, that one."

"Apologize? For what?"

"For my tantrum."

"Tantrums are in this season. I was just having one of my own."

"You need my help. You do not need my whining, my bitching."

"I need you, Raines. There are no words for how much I need you."

"So then build me a fire."

The storm had finally broken, and rain lashed the casements and lightning flared across the hills. She turned, a faint readjustment in the featherbed warmth.

"Are you asleep?"

"Yes."

She laughed softly. "Listen to that out there. It's like one of those Karloff movies. The old haunted castle, the thunderstorm, the creakings in the wind."

"If you hear spectral voices calling, put them on hold. Better yet, tell them we're busy tonight and will get back to them."

"I'm developing a real case on you, Major Kaufmann, sir."

"Who could blame you?"

"There isn't anything better than what we have right now."

They lay quietly for a time, considering this truth.

"Raines?"

"Mm?"

"What are you going to do with your life?"

"I'm not sure yet. Why?"

"I've been giving the question a lot of thought lately. About me, my life. After the resurrection from my current death, that is. And I'm not sure either."

She coughed lightly. "You'll make out fine, whatever you do. You have what it takes."

"How can you know that? I don't know that."

"You're looking from the inside out. The light's against your windows, and you see the streaks of dirt. I'm outside, looking in. The smudges can't hide the nice things in there, in you."

"Are we going to be married sometime?"

"I don't think so. I've got to concentrate too hard on some goals, and the kind of concentration I'm talking about is too selfish, too hard-boiled, to accommodate a husband."

He gave her an amused glance. "You? Selfish, hard-boiled? Horse manure."

She didn't answer immediately.

Why did he keep feeling that she was about to tell him something—about to speak, but deciding not to? A nagging thing, it was. Even in their love-making there had been a persistent sense of her holding something back. A something, larger than a hunch, that spoke of a wall between them, nebulous, undefined, but as substantial as quarry rock.

"I see," he chided. "You're my Pensive Pal."

She returned from wherever her mind had been. "I know that I'm as naive as anybody can be without diapers. It really bothers me sometimes—actually gets in my way. Self-confidence isn't my strong suit, no doubt about that. But that's exactly why I'm going to have to work so hard. Harder than most people."

"Work on what?"

"Money. Money to buy freedom from the kind of poverty that killed my father. That demeaned my mother and me.

That required the two of us to live on hand-outs from supercilious Gotrocks who salved their guilt over inheriting all their clout from Uncle Fudd and Auntie Boob by giving Mom and me the crumbs from their butlers' pantries."

Real bitterness came through, Kaufmann noted. He sought to lighten things a bit. "You want money so you can get even with the Gotrocks? Become like them?"

She didn't hear the kidding in his tone. "No, I want money because it assures me that I don't have to associate with, depend on, anybody I have contempt for. Do you have any idea what it's like to accept old clothes, two-year-old canned goods, a roll of fifty pennies from a snooty preacher who pontificates in his pulpit Sundays, all soulful and righteous, and weekdays diddles little boys in the church cellar? Money buys me distance from creeps like that."

(*Whoops*. The Killarney Telegraph again. That inexplicable awareness of things beyond awareness. That mysterious—no, make that mystical—phenomenon, part of his life since his first breath, in which a flicker of intuition, a vaporous hunch, a gossamer insight, would dart into his consciousness and out again, leaving a maddening, elusive afterglow, like the luminescence that follows ships in nighttime seas. What had she just said? Something she'd just said had touched on revelation. But what? The tiny internal explosion, a mental flashbulb, had illuminated a thought in the darkest corner of his mind, only to return instantly to black, leaving him with the understanding that he had seen, then lost, something of extraordinary importance. *Damn*.)

"How do you plan to make your money?"

"The theater."

"Come again?"

"I majored in drama, the theater. That's my degree. I've worked with some great people through the WPA, writing, producing, acting. Mainly acting. Even some movie work. I had bit parts in two army training films. And I actually had lunch once with David Sorenson, who was visiting our WPA theater project." She coughed again.

"The famous movie producer?"

"Of course there was a bunch of us, but I shook hands and chatted with him for a minute or two."

"Wow."

"He told me to come see him when the war's over. He said I'm pretty awkward, but that can be coached away, and I have a great face, he said."

For a moment Kaufmann, jealous, felt a confused sense of the impending loss of something he didn't even own. He sought, with only partial success, to be diplomatic. "That proves Sorenson's got taste, all right. But the way I hear it, the theater is a very dicey way to make money. Big success comes hard and fewish."

"Sure. But the odds are lowered if you know the right people. And that's what I'm going to work on."

"If you were so broke, where'd you get the money for college?"

"I won a scholarship in high school. I'm pretty smart."

"So when are you going to start showing it?"

She gave him a defiant little razzberry.

"Well," he said eventually, "I suppose you're right. With marriage you don't really know what you're getting. You risk inviting just another creep to get close on a long-term basis. Still, money—lots of it—usually makes its own prisons. Makes it harder to run away, get lost, if life starts boring in."

It was her turn to glance at him. "You've got something against money?"

"Not at all. In fact, I expect to make a big bunch of it someday. At least, I'm going to work on that. But my motive's a bit different from yours, I guess. I see money as a tool for getting things done. You see it as medicine to quiet your anger, your fears. It seems to me there could never be enough money to do that."

"Well, we all follow the rails we've been set on."

"I hope we keep in touch after you're rich and famous." She kissed the end of his nose. "You can count on it."

"Meanwhile, though, you're in considerable danger."

"So are you. What's that old saying? 'We begin dying the day we're born'? Something cheery like that."

He sighed, then laid it on her. "Poopsie's been poisoning you. I've arranged to have her stop. But there are others who won't stop. They'll keep trying to get at you."

"Poopsie? She's—?"

"In your morning coffee and Danish."

"How do you know?"

"I went with a hunch. It told me that the snacks she brought you every morning were the only stuff you were taking in on your own—that wasn't served up in GI chow halls, or similar facilities. So that was half of that little test that browned you off so much. I asked you to ask her for some touchy files. If she was really involved, two things would happen. First, she'd tell her people, and second, her people would try to polish you off quick—no more of this natural death crap. And that's what happened, and that's why I asked her about it tonight."

"Why would she do such a thing?"

"I don't know yet. I expect to learn that tomorrow. My guess it that Poopsie has the money hunger. Like you."

"You make me sound awful—"

"Somebody's stealing army planes for reasons I'm still trying to find out. They've killed Bianco and Sunderman and Anna Krim because they knew too much. Now it's our turn—you and me. Only they wanted your death, like Bianco's, to look natural, to keep the police heat down. Poopsie's job was to mickey you into pneumonia."

"You mean she just up and admitted trying to kill me? Just like that?"

"Not just like that. But sort of like that."

"So where is she now? What did you do to her?"

"Nothing."

"Nothing? Well, holy cow—"

"I'm waiting to see what she does now."

"What if she just runs and hides—"

"Where she tries to hide can tell us things. Who her friends are, and like that."

"You're using her as bait. The way you used me."

He gave her a quick look through the dimness. "I thought we weren't going to mention that again."

"I told *you* not to mention it. I plan to bring it up whenever you get out of line."

"Now who's being a prick?"

He'd meant the question as a little joke, but there followed a lingering pause, a time of silence in which she seemed to be deep in thought.

"You knew this when you came in tonight. Why did you wait so long to tell me?" she asked, her voice low.

"Selfishness. I didn't want to ruin our making up. To get in the way of the most wonderful night a guy ever had."

Again she was silent.

"What's wrong, Raines?"

"I don't know. I'm suddenly very lonely."

"How can you be lonely when I'm holding you like this?"

"I don't know."

In the humid darkness, a pause. An extended interval, with her breathing soft and moist against his cheek.

She stirred finally. "Do something for me?"

"I've done everything I can think of."

"Get that liquor out of my john seat."

"Wow. Now that's *really* kinky."

"I'm serious. I don't like the thought of its being there. I want you to get it out of there."

"Well, that might not be so easy for a dead man who has no USFET gate pass. Why don't you just bring it here some evening? Easier yet: throw it away, or give it to Bertha."

"I just don't want to handle it at all."

He was about to ask her why she was making so much of a lousy bottle of booze, but then he realized a tension had developed—an atmosphere, as the English would put it.

"I'll take care of it soonest, Fräulein Leutnant."

Near dawn, she shook him awake.

"What is it?" he asked, groggy.

"I've changed my mind. It'll be too risky for you to bother with the whiskey. I'll throw it out."

"Sheesh."

"I don't want you in danger for something so silly."

"Good thinking. Now may I resume my unconsciousness?"

She turned away.

TRANSCRIPT FOR ALPHA'S REFERENCE FILE ONLY

Phone conversation, "M" Line

"Hello."

" 'Alpha'?"

"Margie."

"Nola."

"What now, 'M'? Do you realize what time it is?"

"I just had a visit from 'Doll.' She says Kaufmann is onto her."

"Damn. She's sure?"

"He confronted her tonight with the Raines coffee thing. Accused her of working for Ballentine, as a black market chief, or whatever."

"That would be funny if it weren't so very damned serious."

"Well, that's what she said. He's ordered her to see him tomorrow for a complete interrogation."

"Tell 'Seed' to handle it."

"Discreetly?"

"Hell, no. As gaudily as possible. And take Kaufmann out with her. We've got to make a statement, so to speak."

"Consider it done. Anything else?"

"Call me as soon as it's accomplished."

THURSDAY
27 September 1945

23

Poopsie was waiting for him on the bench when he arrived in the park.

With her pockets turned inside out, her musette bag open and empty.

With a neat .38 caliber hole between her staring blue eyes.

The fact that her body, propped as it was against the bench, represented not a message but a trap, took no more than a millisecond to register. Yet it was barely enough to save him, because the air beside his head exploded with a vicious cracking precisely as he spun around and dropped to the turf.

Half rolling, half crawling, he made it to the defilade of weed-choked flower bed, with two more shots spanging against the stone retaining wall as he went. Lying motionless in the deep morning shadows of an ancient chestnut, he waited for another shot, determined to establish its direction, its point of origin.

But the assassin wasn't buying in. The silence continued,

and after a time Kaufmann stirred, eventually sitting up for a cautious look around.

Nothing.

He returned to the Mercedes and drove to Emma's place.

TRANSCRIPT FOR ALPHA'S REFERENCE FILE ONLY

Phone conversation, "M" Line

"Hello."

" 'Alpha'?"

"Elmer's Tune."

"Goody-Goody."

"Yes, M?"

" 'Doll' 's bought it. But Kaufmann got away."

"Oh, for God's sake. What's the matter with 'Seed,' anyhow? Can't he do anything right?"

"He apologizes."

"I'm sick of his apologies. I'm sick of his increasing unreliability."

"Well, we still need him."

"Not for long. As soon as this thing has jelled, get rid of him."

"Consider it done."

24

The radio murmuring, its gassy crooner bemoaning his sad discovery that *In der Nacht ist der Mensch nicht gern allein-ah-h-h-h.* . . .

Dishes rattling briefly in the kitchen. A trolley bell clanging in the distance beyond the casement. A car horn. The sounds of humanity striving for normality.

No major aftershock. He's been through such things before. A vague numbness, but nothing he couldn't handle.

Poopsie had been a zero and a zero she would remain, her information drifting with her ions, irretrievable in some trackless eternity.

Still, the morning's violence suggested that he was coming close to something. He was beginning to make the bad guys anxious. They were losing their cool. They were lashing out. Killing their own.

He recalled the old cartoon, in which a solitary cop, surrounded by a crowd of club-swinging thugs, snarls, "Okay—you people are in real trouble now!"

. . . und Sie wissen ganz bestimmt was ich mein-ah-h-h. . . .

He sat in Emma's tub until the hot water turned cool, sipping some of Emma's Spanish brandy and giving still more thought to the cryptographics of the biographies provided by Raines's notes and photostats.

Ballentine's history was a curious amalgam of academia and public service. There was no formal OSS record, since that agency had always been circumspect about those who filled its ranks. Most of them were civilians, many of them from Big Old Wealth, much traveled and socially influential, who went about their daily lives on the surface while taking on special secret assignments. Raines had copied Ballentine's listing in *Who's Who*, taking considerable time, obviously, since it was in her schoolteacher's handwriting on a sheaf of lined paper torn from a secretary's shorthand book: Born and raised in Fairfield, Connecticut, the eldest of three sons of Emmett Hancock Ballentine, patriarch of the Ballentine shipping dynasty and heavy-duty patron of the arts in the United States and Canada; private schooling in Switzerland and Italy; B.A., M.A. and Ph.D, each from a heavy-horsepower Ivy League institution; professor of fine arts, holder of Louis P. Stahl Chair at Llewelyn University, later head of the arts department there; chairman of the American Institute of the Creative and Performing Arts; appointed by President Roosevelt to serve as a special cultural attaché at the Moscow embassy after the formal recognition of the USSR by the United States; subsequent appointive cultural posts at the Department of State, both in Washington and abroad, specifically in London, Paris, Oslo, Copenhagen, Helsinki, Berlin, and, at war's outset, in Bern. Et cetera, et cetera, and blah, blah, blah. Significant omission: enlisted at some unspecified time by the NKVD to serve as a Soviet mole in the American OSS; cohort, probably boss, of a crew composed of Gregor Koslov, NKVD hotshot, and Luigi Fortunato, film director and Communist sympathizer, plus a thug named Bikler, now dead, plus a thug in a brown fedora, now dead, plus two thugs named Fritz and Freddi, left in a bind in a toolshed at the Heidelberg villa, plus a WAAC pfc named Adeline Muncy, AKA "Poopsie," now dead; plus who knows how many other thugs. Most significant omission: probable planner-in-chief of plot to knock off Mrs. Kaufmann's Little Angel because Little Angel was becoming a pain in the NKVD's ass, just exactly why and how still to be determined.

He turned to Raines's extract from *The 1944 Directory of Motion Picture Producers, Directors and Personalities*:

Fortunato, Luigi M.: b. Genoa, Italy, 9/21/98 son of B. F. Fortunato, restaurateur; St. Paul's School, U. of Rome, Heidelberg U., M.A. fine arts, Ph. D. dramatic arts, 1919; professor, performing arts, Llewelyn U.; associate producer, Odin Studios, 1927; assistant to Louis Stahl, CEO, Odin Studios, 1929; producer-director, Stahl Films, 1930– Film credits: *The Tyrant, 1930; Heaven is Here, 1932; Love Me Now, 1933; The Eradicator, 1935; Our Manners Show, 1937; The Kremlin Noon, 1938; Death in Munich, 1939; The Little Giant, 1940; Squadrons Aloft, 1941; The Yank, 1942; The Girl of the Underground, 1943*. Adjunct prof., Llewelyn U., 1938– International Arts Council, Venice, 1938–39; arts consultant, U.S. Embassy, Rome, 1938–39. Addr.: Star Agency, Los Angeles.

He picked up the copy of *The Giants of Film* Raines had borrowed from the PR library and stared for a time at the biography of Stahl and what were touted as very rare photos of the mysterious and elusive Louis Stahl, the lumbering, bearded, super-private tycoon, who "always" wore a gray homburg. The Stahl story was typical of Hollywood itself—part hard-headed business, part apocrypha, part dazzle, part bathos, mostly malarkey. The poor kid, saving enough to borrow more to make more to borrow more that made more until the poor boy, using somebody else's money, had bought everything between Santa Monica and Uranus. He had eleven homes, according to the vital statistics section, and one was listed as the Casa del Sol, Udine Province, Italy.

He reached for the pad and pencil on the tub-side table and made a note: *Get more dope on Stahl.*

General Vickery's army service record would be the envy of any self-respecting general: Born 1894 in Hamilton, Ohio, the son of blah, blah, blah. Graduate of West Point, Class of 1915; served under Pershing in Mexican Punitive Action; appointed military aviator, 1917; pursuit pilot, Western Front, France, 1918; awarded DSC and a perishing boxcar full of other medals, foreign and domestic, for shooting down twelve enemy aircraft and four balloons; postwar duties at many U.S. military posts; graduate of eighty skillion military schools and faculty member in a bunch of them; aviation attaché at embassies in London, Berlin, Rome and Moscow; Army War College, somewhere in there; command of Digby Air Technical Testing Center, 1938–40; assigned to Air Training Command, then to newly formed 8th Air Force, headquarters London, et cetera, et cetera. Only significant omission: incandescently pissed off at Little Angel and Little Angel's sort-of-girlfriend, Molly Raines, for reasons as yet unknown except to God, who ain't saying much these days.

He turned to pfc. Adeline Muncy, AKA "Poopsie": native of Cleveland, Ohio, daughter of blah, blah, blah; public schooling, plus two years at Llewelyn University, major in library management; left college to enlist in WAAC, 1942; service at Stateside posts hither and yon, the most interesting of which was the main technical reference library at the War Department Intelligence Training Center, Camp Ritchie, Md., before her assignment to Central Registry, USFET, last August. Gee-whiz omission: enlisted by NKVD, or others with no good on their minds, for duties unspecified, except for the slow-motion assassination of Lt. Molly Raines, would-be movie star.

Margaret Sunderman, AKA "Maggie," special agent of the Criminal Investigation Division, US Army, found dead while taking a very special look into a very special handling of Army Air Forces flying machines, ordered by a very special and as yet unidentified power source in Washington.

Military records unavailable, by very special order of the AGO, Pentagon.

Ransky, Cpl. George P., pseudo air policeman, 8th Air Force Hqs, Wiesbaden. No records to be found.

Shee-it.

He put down the stack of papers and sank deeper into the water, still aching in assorted fuselage compartments and suddenly and inexplicably disarmed of his earlier insouciance, overwhelmed by a renewed sense of forces he could not effectively resist or even define. So now Poopsie was dead. Who shot her? Who shot at him? Who was the shootist working for? Who poisoned Bianco? Who shot Sunderman, and what was the significance of the can of pork and beans in her dead hands? Who was the toothless woman shootist? Why did she shoot the guy in the fedora at the most propitious of times? Who had Bikler worked for, and why did he try to fake a traffic accident when so much shooting was in the works? What was Vickery up to? Who was Ransky? Did Ransky, overtly tied to the Air Force by both uniform and proximity, work for Vickery? If so, why? Who had ordered Poopsie to kill Raines? Why? Was Ballentine in charge of all of them, the mastermind of a master conspiracy? If so, how did he get such a polyglot group together and working in concert? Why the hell would, say, a war hero and professional officer like Vickery work with, or for, a pendant-pinko-turned-hardcore-Red? And toward what end? Where was Anton, and why hadn't he sent word—any kind of goddam word—as to what he was doing and where he was doing it? Wolff: What had he been really up to, and how come an SS bigwig like him, now lost in the bowels of the War Crimes Commission, still had clout among so many? And how did Stalin figure in all of this? Did he really have a role, or was he getting a bad rap, serving merely as a Red political herring, a big bogey providing the razzle-dazzle for what was basically a major criminal conspiracy, a black market caper of humongous scope?

Kee-rist, what a mess.

"Are you going to stay in there all day?" Emma peered

around the half-open bathroom door. "You will look like a prune if you don't soon get out of that water."

He held out his glass. "Take this brandy from me before I become a stewed prune."

She placed the drink on the washstand, then sat on the rim of the tub, smiling fondly at him. "Let me rub your neck and shoulders."

"Emma, for God's sake. I'm stark naked in here."

"I've seen it all before, sonny. And you know it doesn't impress me."

"It doesn't impress anyone else either, I'm afraid."

She laughed, and her large fingers began to knead his shoulders. "You don't have any girlfriends?"

"Thousands."

"Seriously. Isn't there someone—somewhere?"

"A lady up Frankfurt way, an American. She likes me, it seems. But not enough to get involved on a long-term basis. She has a career in mind."

Emma nodded. "I understand that. No permanent arrangements. They get in the way of business. Lisa and I go a long way back, but we've understood from the beginning that neither of us has a chain on the other."

"It has its positive side, though. My old man used to say that if a man needs a symbol to prove to the world how successful he is, a happy wife is the best there is. He liked to say that any jerk can con the world into thinking he's a big deal, but no man has to con the world—or anybody else—if it's obvious his wife is content. His point was that it takes one heroic, inventive, ambitious and solvent son of a bitch to keep a wife genuinely happy."

"No denying that."

"And marriage settles the question of turf. No poaching. Trespassing forbidden. Don't you get sore, for instance, when another lady makes a pass at Lisa?"

"Certainly. But then I remind myself that Lisa likes me better than anybody, and she isn't the type for pick-ups. How about your lady? Is she, ah, easy? A party type?"

Kaufmann sniffed. "She's so proper she wears a slip under her slip. In public, that is."

"Ah. And in private? What then?"

"None of your business."

"That means she's good. Men rave only about dull, marginal bed partners. If the women are really good, they don't say so. Poachers might try to move in. Eh?" She laughed again.

"You're a dirty-minded bawd, Emma."

"Absolutely. And it's made me a millionaire. A woman needs to combine only two things to make a fortune, or eventually to rule the world, if that's what she wants: the first is a master mechanic's understanding of the masculine crotch and the second is an aura of gentility. The trick is to make the specific men she wants to control aware of her, ah, special understanding, without diminishing her image as a woman of intelligence, quality and breeding."

He gave her a wry glance. "God, Emma, I hope you never write one of those how-to books. Every man in the world will be in the greatest of peril. Governments will fall. Civilization will totter."

"You have nothing to fear, my lad. The average woman doesn't aspire to world domination. I do, of course. But I'm not the average woman."

"I'll say."

She chuckled and winked broadly.

"Where did you go to school, Emma?"

"Ha. You know better than that. When would a woman like me find time or opportunity to go to school?"

"You sound as if you had."

"I'm a reader. After all, what is schooling but organized reading, eh? A university says, 'You want to know something about so and so? Read these books. We'll talk to you about what you read, test you to see how well you've read. And when the tests show you to be sufficiently well read on a certain number of subjects, we'll give you a paper that proclaims you to be an educated person.' Well, I just asked a friendly professor or two—clients, they were—what books to read about what. And I read them, by God, from algebra to zoology. I used every conscious, unoccupied moment to read the spots off the damned things. Nobody's given me tests, but I'll bet you your pink dinky that, if they had, I'd pass them easily.''

"One thing for sure: You make a great masseuse."

"If I set my mind to it, I make a great anything, dear."

"Speaking of your mind, how's your memory?"

"Good in some ways, bad in others. Why?"

"One night last winter one of your clients, that SS Standartenführer, Horst Something-or-other, brought along a friend. The little man with a bald head and a Hitler mustache. Do you remember?"

"Mm. Herr Gittelmann. A voyeur, preferring girls doing calisthenics in the buff."

"I heard him talking with the SS fellow. They were in the sitting room, next to your bedroom, waiting for the girls. Something he said convinced me that he was no Nazi."

Emma nodded. "Of course he isn't. He is a Soviet spy."

"Is? Not was?"

"Is."

"You know this for certain?"

"Herr Gittelmann is a Soviet spy. He is also a French spy, an American spy, a British spy—any kind of spy you name. He is entirely apolitical. He is a professional spy who will spy for anyone who gives him the right amount of money and protection. A dreadful little man, actually."

"Can you arrange for me to see him?"

"It isn't easy. And it'll cost you."

"Everything costs me. So why shouldn't he?"

"When do you want to see him? And where?"

"As soon as possible. Here."

"That tub isn't big enough for the two of you."

"Come on, Emma. One thing you aren't is a Bob Hope."

"I'll see what I can do. Meantime, climb out of there and let me wrap this towel around you. By now, even your wrinkles have wrinkles."

25

"Mr. Donnelly, this is Kaufmann in Frankfurt. Are you on your secure phone?"

"Yes, I am. Nice to hear from you, Major. What's up?"

"I haven't heard anything from or about my client."

"Major Thoma, the Luftwaffe trainee?"

"That's right. The man I sent you for aviation transition and PW indoctrination the week before last."

"Why, I thought he was with you."

"With *me*?"

"Thoma had a bit of unpleasantness here, you know. That officer we borrowed from G-2—Colonel Lawrence, the German aircraft familiarization instructor? Thoma actually struck the man with his fist. He was given a reprimand and restricted to quarters, but during the first night of his restriction he disappeared. He left a note of resignation, open on his table, addressed to you. It was quite—ah—scatological, if you know what I mean. And it was my impression that he was on his way to tell you these things in person."

"I haven't seen him or heard a peep out of him."

"Strange. Do you think he might have gone AWOL? Maybe even deserted? There's been quite a bit of that in this Theater lately—"

"No. That isn't his style."

"You're sure? He's a very difficult man at times—"

"He's that, all right. But for all his fuss and fuming, he's conscientious. I think he might have come across an opportunity to penetrate—which, as you know, was his basic assignment—and he might have jumped into a quick exploitation."

"But where, or how?"

"I was hoping you'd tell me."

"Well, if you don't know, and I don't know, that means we've lost him."

"I'm afraid there's just no other way to phrase that. Lost is the word. For the time being, at least."

"Is there something we can do to help here?"

"Just keep looking for leads. Another note, maybe. Somebody remembering something, maybe. Whatever. You get anything at all, message or call Captain Olsen, USFET District medical examiner, Frankfurt. Top secret, of course."

"Olsen?"

"Right. I'm using his phone."

"I certainly hope you find him, Major. We've put a heavy investment in him."

"You don't know the half of it, Mr. Donnelly."

"I imagine."

"Meantime, thanks. I'll be in touch."

"Good-bye, Major Kaufmann."

Damn. The inevitable complication.

He had an agent who could be anywhere in Europe.

Or, even, anywhere in the Hereafter.

If his years of work on the dark side had taught him anything, it was that agents never performed precisely as planned. Rarely, even, did they perform as hoped. The human factor. Personality quirks. The unforeseen. Absurd coincidence. The vagaries of weather. Plain luck. All of these, and more, singly or in combination, could turn an operation for the good or the bad. He remembered the agent—one of the first to parachute into the Reich itself—who made his way properly to a railroad whistle stop, caught the proper train to the nearby town where his contact was waiting, and then promptly fell sound asleep in his seat, eventually to be awakened by the Gestapo in the city at the end of the line. Hundreds of hours of complex preparation; thousands of dollars expended; a dozen men and women, from Ostend to Pforzheim, alerted and in great danger. And all for naught, because the Officer-in-Charge had given no importance to the agent's casual remark, "Train rides always make me sleepy."

So what should he do about Anton?

What should he do about old age?

Wait and see how things turned out. What else?

26

The autumn sunlight, despite its pallor, was warm, and Anton raised his face to it, eyes closed in pleasure. The crews were at chow, and he'd brought a canteen cup of soup and a slab of bread to the flight line. There he sat, his back against a fencepost, and ate in bucolic solitude, thus genuflecting before the God of Loneliness that was said to rule folks at the Top. Whether the rank of squadron commander was toppish enough to qualify for such loneliness was moot, but it was enough to justify his practical need for privacy—even an hour's worth. He wanted a chance to use his camera.

He had never been much as a photographer; lenses and filters and shutter speeds and such rigmarole were hard work, and he was essentially a lazy lout, dedicated to the easy way in all things. But Kaufmann had made him promise to use this little box, developed by OSS and produced by Eastman Kodak. It could focus itself and would take a studio-quality shot from any angle and under virtually any light conditions, or so Kaufmann said, and was the finest espionage camera in existence. But Anton had uncorked the camera only twice—once for a quick shot of the villa and another time to catch a profile of an unsuspecting General-major Oskar. Today, though, the benign sun and his own vague sense of obligation combined to overcome his inertia and his fear of being caught, and so he'd worked the expensive little appliance free of his fieldcoat lining and brought it to this nowhere, from which he hoped to get some panoramas of the airfield and its buildings.

Thinking about it now, chewing and sipping, he saw a third reason: Oskar's absence simply made him feel better about taking the risk. The Generalmajor had left an hour ago, lifting off in the snarling little Mustang fighter on what he'd called, enigmatically, "a bit of reception-committee work." The Mustang was one of three smaller ships—the others were L-5 recons—kept in the long utility shed south of the mail hangar. Oskar, who apparently had been a Lufthansa transport pilot in the '30s, had made the transition to fighters with his move to Göring's Luftwaffe. After Göring's virtual liquidation of his own bomber force over Britain in 1940, Oskar had been taken out of his Jagdgeschwader and assigned to a replacement bomber wing near Brussels. But once a fighter pilot always a fighter pilot, and Oskar used every opportunity to climb into the Mustang, which he called "an absolute, toe-curling marvel of an airplane," and wring it out in the Wild Blue Yonder.

Speak of the devil.

There was a faint drumming to the northwest, and then, like a silvery wasp, the Mustang materialized in the upper haze and darted across the field, leaving its racket to echo in the distant hills. After an interval, the echo was replaced by a droning, this from the twin engines of a C-47 transport, which descended to a direct, workaday thump on the broad grass strip. The big machine rolled to a halt near the far fence line, then flicked its rudder and turned to waddle for the hangar, an irritated, olive-drab gander, grunting and squeaking.

Anton watched as the ship fell silent and the side hatch

opened to eject a large American major general and, of all people, Karla Wintgens, the drawling, cardigan-draped Westchester County prig who had screwed like a mink and pretended to have an aunt in Munich. They stood in the sunlight, blinking, then asked a question of the ground crew chief, who pointed to the north, where the Mustang was sighing into its landing approach, its engine burbling and popping, its big four-bladed propeller windmilling.

Say cheese, folks.

He made three exposures, firing from the hip and hoping the claims for the little Kodak weren't mere bean breeze. Then, while everybody was watching the taxiing Mustang, with its blasts of sounds and clouds of dust, he moved closer, stopping in the shade of a stack of oil drums. When Generalmajor Oskar swung down from the Mustang's cockpit to trade salutes with the general and handshakes with Karla, he was able to aim the camera quite accurately and get three more shots, two while the trio chatted amiably in the Italian noonday, the third as they climbed into Oskar's Buick for the drive to the villa.

Anton met the visitors over cocktails. He feigned first-acquaintance correctness with Karla, bowing slightly and brushing her hand with his lips and sounding the appropriate words, and she played to this, coolly haughty, even though she knew he could give a precise description of her appendectomy scar.

The American was introduced by Oskar as Major General Edward Bascomb, who had dropped in for an hour or two to see how things were going with the German Legion. The general—taut, burly, sandy hair cropped close, eyes like white grapes—was sour, rude, and filled with his own importance. He spoke no German, so Karla served as interpreter, and the conversation was less than scintillating.

The general was precisely the kind of person Anton disliked most. But Anton's real difficulty with this fellow derived from the insignia he wore.

Anton realized he had seen the man before. In Dijon it was, during his interrogation by Colonel Dreher.

Back then, there had been no general's stars.

Back then, Bascomb had been a staff sergeant, fussing in the background shadows with a dictation machine.

So just who and what was this guy?

Really.

27

The man in the fedora had been identified as Alois Moller, a professional assassin known throughout the trade as "Sweetums." The toothless little woman who had shot him remained unknown.

Raines had drawn a blank on both IDs. According to her report, absolutely no paper could be found in the forty-seven miles of file cabinets maintained by G-2, the CIC and CID, MI, ONI, the FBI and MPs, and like alphabetics at USFET level. Aided by three Central Registry clerks bucking for the late Poopsie's job, she had rummaged for seven hours straight for mug shots that would even approximate the features of the victim and his killer. Nothing.

Ironically, it was that goofball, Olsen, the Friendly Neighborhood Coroner, who pulled the trick. While Raines and crew had been deep in the files, morgue photos had been couriered to him because it was his duty day as standby District Medical Examiner. The photos had been accompanied by a photostat of a 1944 Kriminal Polizei rap sheet—a veritable encyclopedia of felonies—and by a Victim's Personal

Effects list, which included one each fedora, brown, size 8
(American), and one each field coat, Wehrmacht gray
leather, large. These two items rang one of Olsen's bells,
because they had figured importantly in Lt. Raines's breathless phone conversation with him the day after her train
station adventure. Thus energized, the Mad Doctor had used
his lunch hour to jeep to Karli's gas station and leave Kaufmann an envelope containing the photos and rap sheet.

"How come everybody, even the beat cop on Schit Strasse
in Tootelberg, Austria, knows who 'Sweetums' is but we
don't have a scrap of paper on him in our entire military
file system?" Kaufmann snapped during his subsequent
phone call.

Olsen had simply snapped back. "How the hell should I
know? Am I my brother's file keeper? I just read my mail,
I don't try to understand it."

"Well, I wish our military people would start reading
their mail from the assorted police agencies. Maybe our
dossiers would get a little more up to date."

"I wish our military people would start doing a hell of a
lot of things. The most important of which is firing me and
sending me home."

"I want to borrow your jeep."

"What are you talking about?"

"I need a jeep. I don't have one. You have one. I want
to borrow it."

"Why?"

"Secret agent stuff."

"Sorry, Your Conniverinship, that's out. If you bung up
my jeep, the army will charge me for it. It's assigned to
me, and I'm accountable."

"I won't bung it up. But I'll put a hundred bucks into
escrow as payment toward anything you might get charged
due to my using the vehicle for two hours, no longer. If
nothing happens to the jeep, you keep fifty of the hundred."

"Meaning you will pay me fifty bucks to rent my jeep
for two hours? And by bucks, you mean U.S. folding, not
those Occupation funny-money things—right?"

"Precisely."

"And if you do a thousand bucks in naughty things to my fenders—"

"You keep the hundred and I give you another nine hundred."

"Where are you getting money like this?"

"None of your business. Just have the jeep ready for me by tomorrow noon. Have it gassed and ready and parked in that alley a half a block south of your office."

"It's got a Medical Corps designation on its bumper. The MPs will not take kindly to a nut in a Tyrolean suit driving around in a Medical Corps vehicle."

"That's why you're also going to lend me a blank trip ticket form from your HQ, plus a set of captain's bars, plus a pair of brass Medical Corps insignia to pin on my Class A blouse, which I plan to wear while driving said vehicle."

"You're not only dead, you're sick in the head."

"Yeah. But I'm also going to find the sons of bitches who are behind all this killing and stealing, pal."

Gittelmann would not come to Emma's Heidelberg house. She reported this fact the moment Kaufmann walked in that evening. She had made contact via a nightclub proprietor who, for a modest consideration, pointed her to a cab driver who, for a modest consideration, would carry a message to Gittelmann's landlord who, for a modest consideration, would arrange to have Gittelmann call Emma at 17:30 o'clock. Which had happened, she said, wide-eyed, and Gittelmann had promised to meet Kaufmann at 22:00 o'clock at *Zum Fliegenden Pferd*, a Gasthof four kilometers south of the Neckartal village of Nageldorf. Kaufmann was to wear a blue feather in his hat band and ask the barmaid for Herr Stossel—this instruction causing a minor crisis, until Lisa, phoning around, discovered that Lola Bingel, the chanteuse, had a bright blue boa and would, for a modest consideration, send a strand from it via bicycle messenger.

The place was one of those half-timbered, low-ceiling jobs, with age-blackened oaken beams and sway-backed

floors that hadn't been scrubbed since Charlemagne stopped
in for a quick one. A man with a wooden leg sat in a corner
next to a tile stove, playing a wailing version of "Am
Abschied reich' ich dir die Hände" on an antediluvian
concertina. Add the leaning chimneys, crooked shutters,
bottle-glass casements, and wrought-iron sconces, whose
flickerings and evil-smelling emissions created the cheeri-
ness of a bat cave, and you had something less than a
smasheroo rave in *Baedeker's*. (Kaufmann's mind, always
reaching for the pun, told him it was a Hof you had to be
Gast to stay in.) The locals apparently had no trouble with
all this; they were there in considerable numbers, nursing
beers in tall, ornate steins, puffing up a rancid nimbus on
their yard-long Meerschaums, staring at checkerboards, and
trading guttural jokes.

"I'm looking for Herr Stossel."

The barmaid, a dirndl stuffed with volleyballs, gave him
an unfriendly inspection, starting with the blue feather.

"Who are you?"

"Winston Churchill."

"Funny man, eh?"

"Come on, Sweets. Point out Stossel."

"I don't think you're very funny."

"Oh, darling, what ever happened to those dear, crazy
days when we laughed, and danced, and shared?"

"Smart aleck." She rearranged the uppermost pair of
volleyballs with a nudging of elbows. "Up those stairs over
there. Second door to the right."

He pushed his way through the smog and mounted the
stairs, and at the designated door he tapped three times.

"Herein."

The room was like the rest of the inn, made even more
beautiful by an unmade bed, a floor strewn with newspapers, and a central table, at which a fat man, glistening bald
and suety in the glow of a ceiling lantern, shoveled sauerkraut from a tureen onto the tin plate before him.

"Herr Stossel?"

"You are Emma's friend, then. George Coburn." The fat man did not look up from his chores.

"Yes."

"Why is it I don't think Coburn is your real name?"

"For the same reason I don't believe Gittelmann is yours."

"Hah. But you are wrong, Herr—Coburn. My name really is Gittelmann."

"We all have our burdens."

The fat man glanced at him from under heavy lids. "Funny man, eh?"

"The barmaid thinks so."

"You want some kraut?"

"No thanks."

"You will at least sit down, I hope. I hate to eat while someone hovers over me."

Kaufmann pulled a straight-back chair to the table and sat down. "Emma says you might be willing to serve me as a consultant."

"My fees are exorbitant."

"She says that, too."

"And you wish to continue this conversation?"

"Well, it depends on whether your consultations are any good. I have no way of knowing that yet."

"Oh, I'm good, Herr Coburn. I'm worth every penny."

"I'd like a sample or two."

Gittelmann, having depleted his sauerkraut, served himself some more. "How about this: I can identify the little woman who shot 'Sweetums.' "

"Assuming that I'd be interested, of course."

"Don't spar with me. I know you're interested. As I know that you would like to know what Luigi Fortunato, the famous film producer, is up to these days."

Kaufmann nodded reasonably. "You're right, of course. I'd like to know those things. Among other things."

"Good. Shall we do business?"

"Maybe. How do I know for sure that you're not selling

me phony information that somebody else has paid you to deliver to me?''

Gittelmann's gray face showed a faint smile. ''You can't be sure. But, as a professional yourself, you are quite aware that my business success, often my very life, depends on my reliability. I wouldn't last a week if I delivered patently false information or violated a client's confidence. I make my living serving one interest at a time, but respecting the secrets of all at all times.''

''So if I ask you a question now that unknowingly nudges one of your clients of, maybe, five years ago, you won't answer. Is that what you mean?''

Gittelmann hunched a heavy shoulder. ''Essentially, yes. But I reserve the right to make the judgment. The key is what I discern to be damaging or dangerous to you—or to the previous client. But I assure you that I will take things as far as possible—as far as ethics on either side permit. And if I can't answer fully, I will tell you.''

''You must be doing something right.''

''How so?''

''You're still alive.''

''Precisely.''

''What's the deal?''

''Five thousand U.S. dollars. Half on agreement, half on delivery of the specified information. I reserve the right to renegotiate the fee if additional questions arise.''

Kaufmann drew out his wallet and placed two thousand-dollar bills and a five-hundred-dollar bill on the table. ''Deal.''

''So what is your first question?''

Much to his own surprise, Kaufmann heard himself asking the root question—that nagging, unspecific yet fearsome unknown of such cosmic importance it seemed altogether out of comprehensible scale for a mere field hand. It was the question being asked openly only by presidents, kings, generalissimos and barbers.

''Is Stalin moving to take Europe?''

Gittelmann shook his head slowly, not in negation but to emphasize his words: "I'm not at liberty to say."

"Ethics?"

"Not vis-à-vis Stalin, but other clients—"

"So I must assume he is."

"Assume what you will, Herr Coburn. You didn't hear it here."

"And I must assume that you are working toward that end. New war. It's good for business, eh?"

"On the contrary. Armed conflict restricts me, reduces my mobility and access to sources. The threat of war is very advantageous to me, but war itself I abhor. I am therefore as much worried about war breaking out as you or the most obscure wife and mother. This is why, actually, I've agreed to talk to you in the first place. If I wanted war, we wouldn't be having this conversation."

Kaufmann sniffed. "You mean you and I are co-workers in the interest of world peace?"

"Droll idea, isn't it."

"Who shot 'Sweetums'?"

"Katrina Kolody. A freelance gun known to the Trade as 'Little Katy.' Hired by Emma Rupert to serve as your hidden escort. To keep you out of trouble. Emma, you see, fears you are a boy trying to do a man's work. She's very fond of you and doesn't want you to be hurt."

Kaufmann struggled to hide his astonishment and anger. "So for that I owe you another twenty-five hundred dollars?"

"Not yet." Gittelmann wiped his plate with a slab of bread, which he then popped into his busy mouth. Speaking and chewing simultaneously, he sounded like an orating, rooting hog. " 'Sweetums,' whose real name was Alois Moller, was the partner of 'Cutie-pie,' codename for Artur Bikler, another professional freelance killer. The pair was hired by an international cabal to eradicate certain individuals who pose a threat to something called 'Aktion Achtung.' "

"What is that?"

"Aktion Achtung—Operation 'Attention'—is a secret collaboration of certain elements within the U.S. Executive Branch and certain sanitary, or, I should say, sanitized, German military interests who see a successful pre-emptive attack on Stalinist Russia as the only route to a quick resolution of an East-West power struggle which otherwise promises decades, if not centuries, of world turmoil."

"You mean, knock Stalin out of the box now, while he's still staggering from War Two?"

"Mm."

"À la Pearl Harbor?"

"A more appropriate comparison would be Hitler's Blitzkrieg against Russia in June, 1941."

"When and where is this supposed to happen?"

"My sources are a bit fuzzy on this, but the consensus is that October 2 is the magic date."

"October 2, this year?"

"This year. Next Tuesday."

"Good God."

"It is something we must not let happen—you, for your reasons, I, for the reasons I've already given you."

"Where will the attack be made—and who are the main players in this Aktion Achtung?"

"Here's where the other twenty-five hundred is due, and here's where further answers call for renegotiation."

Kaufmann sighed. "Well, I'm in trouble. I'm running out of money."

"Emma has guaranteed your credit. She will pay what you owe, whatever the amount you agree to."

"Why in hell would she do that?"

"I really can't say. And I wouldn't, even if I knew."

"Emma doesn't have anything to do with any of this—"

"I wouldn't know."

"All right. Beginning with another twenty-five hundred of Emma's money: Who makes up this collaboration?"

"The word is that—"

The fat man's little eyes widened, seeming to fix on the doorway behind Kaufmann. He pushed back his chair and attempted to rise, his gray face now the color of wood ash. Kaufmann, because he recognized the symptoms, took the appropriate action in the splinter of a second that preceded the hellish sleet of a Schmeisser machine pistol. He rolled out of his chair, crashed to the floor and lay motionless—concentrating in an almost prayerlike intensity against the instinct that would have him clamber to his feet and run. He watched with half-open eyes as Gittelmann spun around, slammed against the wall, then slid to the floor, slugs fluttering his shirt, tearing away pieces of his coat, and reducing his face to jam. And, in a kind of dreamy detachment, he felt three bullets tear at his own clothes, two through his right coat sleeve, the third through his right pantleg. In the acid smog generated by gunpowder and dust and flying shards, in the glaze brought on by pure animal fear, Kaufmann's view of the doorway and the man who stood there, machine gun thumping, was less than clear and precise.

Yet it was good enough to show him that the shootist was none other than that ubiquitous charmer, George P. Ransky.

After an eon of clangor and tearing and splintering, the shooting stopped.

The doorway was unoccupied, except for drifting smoke and dust.

Kaufmann knelt beside the wreck that was Gittelmann, straining to hear the words that came slowly, faintly, through the spittle.

"Gittelmann—for God's sake. Who? What?"

The man's eyes were white circles around yellowing dots—two small fried eggs confronting eternity. His mouth worked, the jaw dropping, then clamping, over and over.

Kaufmann could hear very little.

A gasp that sounded like "Udine—Italy."

A grunting that sounded like "Bombers—"

A final, convulsive wheezing that sounded like "Stalin—Stal—they betray—"

Gittelmann took Kaufmann's hand and holding tight, died.

Breaking the grip, Kaufmann retrieved his twenty-five

hundred dollars, eased out of the room, and made his way down the hall.

Near the top of the stairs, a body lay. In the dim light he could see it was Little Katy, lying on her back, her toothless grin a grimace above the coil of piano wire around her swollen throat. Ransky had seen to it that she had performed her last escort service for Kaufmann. For anybody.

From halfway down the stairs came whispering, sounds of curious crowds and delighted shock.

He went to the window on the landing and, dropping to a shed roof, returned to earth.

Raines. He had to be with Raines.

He drove at flank speed through the night, shaken, intensely frightened and lonely.

God bless her. She was waiting at the lodge.

FRIDAY
28 September 1945

28

Raines had become very diet-conscious since Poopsie's death. The people who had lured Poopsie into her assassin's role could, after all, easily find a replacement. So, following Dr. Olsen's advice, Raines took her meals only at the Farben Casino's company grade officers' cafeteria. To Olsen's way of thinking, it was simply impossible for a bad guy to poison her alone out of two thousand people sharing, say, three hundred and fifty dozen scrambled eggs. Yet she had little enthusiasm for eating even here. After all, Major Bianco had expired, mid-sandwich, on the top floor of this very building.

"Coca-Cola and toast? That's all you're having for breakfast?"

Raines, surprised and trying to sound amiable through a mouthful, said, "The coffee's terrible and government eggs make me sick. Besides, I need to trim down."

Captain Benet loomed, her tray suspended over the table, her teeth gleaming like ceramic tile, her impressive bosom impressing one and all. "Take it from me, dear: you're gorgeous, and any change would be a felony."

"Thanks."

Benet nodded at a chair. "May I join you?"

"Please do."

"I hear you're being ZI'ed."

"Yep. Three more weeks, then it's off to the Land of Bilk and Money."

"I envy you in a way. It's been years since I've been home." Benet unfolded her napkin and gazed with anticipation on the cornucopia she'd assembled.

"Where's home?"

"All over, sort of. I'm an army brat. But Daddy spent most of his years at Aberdeen Proving Grounds in Maryland, and so the Chesapeake Bay area is home to me, mostly."

"Nice country."

Benet began her attack on the French toast, chewing slowly, eyes half-closed with appreciation. "You ought to try this. It's fabulous."

"Maybe sometime soon. I've been rather off my feed lately."

Captain Benet's quick glance was full of sudden apology. "I'm sorry, Lieutenant Raines. I should have realized you're still mourning your dear friend, Major Kaufmann. It was thoughtless of me to impose on you like this."

"Hey, you're not imposing. Honest. Life goes on, as the saying goes." Raines felt her face redden, the sign of uneasiness over what promised to be a sticky scene. How do you project sorrow over the loss of a friend, when you know for a fact he's lolling abed in the afterglow of a sunrise quickie you administered less than an hour ago?

Benet placed her knife and fork on her plate, dabbed her lush lips with her napkin, and sighed. "Major Kaufmann was a lovely man. I never got to know him well, but those times we spoke he was always so nice. What a rotten thing, his going that way. In a silly, needless traffic accident."

"It makes you wonder, all right. How long were you at Aberdeen Proving Grounds?"

"He tried so hard to do his duty. He was one of the most dedicated officers on the support staff."

"I understand Chesapeake Bay freezes over in the winter."

The captain took a sip of coffee. Over the rim of her cup she said, "The last time I saw him was that day Colonel Donleavy called him in to tell him he was to be ZI'ed. He handled it so well. A cool gentleman, the major."

"Sure was. What kind of soldiering did your daddy do?"

"Artillery. What I regret most is missing Major Kaufmann's going-away party. I'm told that it was simply super in every respect."

"Sure was. Where's your daddy now?"

"Retired, on the Eastern Shore. How long were you and Major Kaufmann an item?"

Raines blinked. "Item? We were never an item. Not while he was alive, that is."

"Well, I can't imagine you being an item at any other time. Eh?" Captain Benet chuckled, then quickly sobered, realizing that her mot wasn't altogether bon.

"I meant that we were just friends, duty associates, and our friendship never went beyond that."

"What a shame. My hunch is he was the kind of man who would've made a wonderful lover. Too bad you never tried him out."

Raines had no idea as to how to deal with this. She said nothing.

"Men are usually such pricks," Benet said, stabbing another piece of toast. "Of all the guys in my life, only one has ever made me feel as if he liked me as a person and not just some big broad to bounce on a mattress. Don't get me wrong: this guy's a real hairy-chested he-man kind of guy who likes to talk accordingly—you know, making a big deal out of my boobies and how, just by looking at me, he turns into an instant tripod, and that studhorse kind of crap—but that's mainly for show. Underneath all that puff and snort is a really sweet man. And you know what? I think Major Kaufmann was the same kind of guy, in a way. A lot different in looks, and age, and, well, manners. But pretty much the same. And I liked him for it.''

Raines, her cheeks burning now, glanced at her watch.

"Hey, am I making you uncomfortable talking about your friend this way?''

"Not really," she lied. "But I do have to get to the office. I'm already running late.''

"So what? If you get to the office on time you'll be the only one in the Theater to do so, believe me. Even Ike's on the golf course this morning, and Donleavy and all the G-officers are with Lucius Clay, inspecting captured Nazi lawnmowers, or something. So relax. What can they do? Send you home?'' She laughed, and it was genuine, with no meanness or cynicism in it.

Raines considered Captain Benet anew, a brief moment of re-evaluation. "You really liked Major Kaufmann, eh?''

"Sure did. I felt just awful when I got the news about him being killed and all. So I can imagine how you felt.''

Raines remembered how she'd felt, and she was able to answer straight up. "It was terrible. I didn't know what to do, or say. What to do with myself.''

"And you know something? I got red-eyed mad at Colonel Donleavy, the way he went into your office and told you about the accident. As if it was just another chore he had to take care of that day, and if he gave you a squeeze on the shoulder and Condolence Speech Forty-two-A he could forget about you and get on with his silly paper-shuffling.''

Raines gave her a look. "You were there?''

"Right outside the door. I was there because I thought you might need somebody, you know? But you didn't. You handled the news—yourself—real well. Ladylike. Sort of like Greer Garson hearing Walter Pidgeon was missing at Dunkirk, or something. Know what I mean?''

"You like Greer Garson?''

"She's a peach. My favorite actress."

"You like movies?"

"Do I ever."

"So do I."

They exchanged smiles.

Benet polished off the French toast and began to slice a pear. "What are you doing with your time, now that you're on orders for home?"

"Marking time, that's what."

"You still seem to put in a bunch of hours in Central Registry. Still trying to find out what happened to all your little German PWs?"

"I might as well. I've read all the orderly room magazines."

"Well, I've got a day of file-reading and file-sorting myself. Colonel Donleavy has a desk drawer full of stuff he wants me to organize and collate, or whatever. You know all that stuff Kaufmann was looking for and Poopsie couldn't find? Well, it turns out Donleavy had it all along, right in his desk drawer, and now I've got to drag it out, and align it alphabetically and chronologically, and then put it into that new-fangled steel cabinet he just got. I know I'm going to screw up somehow and get that damned thing to lock just when I don't want it to. And then—"

"How about if I give you a hand? I'm cleared for Top Secret, and I know the kind of cabinet you're talking about. Colonel Daley's had one for two months, and they're dillies, believe me."

"You'd do that for me?"

"Anybody who liked Major Kaufmann is somebody I like. I like to do things for people I like."

Captain Benet smiled, her cheeks turning pink. "Well, fine. That's fine. Let's get to work, then."

"Captain Olsen."

"Hi, Captain. This is Raines. I need to get a message to Mr. Coburn. Will you give me a hand on it?"

"You just missed him, Raines. He left here no more than two minutes ago, vooming off in my darlin' li'l jeep."

"Darn. Well, will you ask him to meet me at Emma's place tonight? It's super important."

"Emma's place?"

"He knows where it is."

"Consider it done, young lady."

29

How quickly the body repairs itself. The mind is slower to mend, but the heart never does, because, according to his dear, intuitive and perpetually sad mother, it is in the heart where the devil dwells. Everything bad, from burnt toast to disaster at sea, she would accredit to the Satan in man's heart—a summary judgment always whispered, brows lowered and eyes averted, as if Old Nick himself might be in the corner, resenting her special knowledge of his ways.

Kaufmann thought of her now as he dealt with the aftershock of Gittelmann's death last night. Body-wise, the trembling was gone. The mind? Gittelmann had been just one more casualty in a war that had caused millions, so there was no sleep to be lost. The heart? Already so bruised it was numb to further impacts.

Gittelmann had been a slimer. And the war had killed him. Katy: just another fallen soldier.

Life goes on.

He decided to make his try through the Main Gate. It

was the busiest of the Compound's entry points, especially at noon, and the MPs on duty there, led to believe that they were the crème de la crème, were apt to indulge in military showbiz, a preoccupation which often caused them to drop a stitch here and there. But the brass doted on glitz and continued to tog out its gatekeepers in chromium helmets, white scarves, full Class A uniforms, white spats over ox-blood combat boots and a whorehouse splattering of jewelry, tinsel, and ribbon. Rare was the man who, when thus costumed in the Patton mode, could resist the tendency to out-Patton Patton, and so security suffered.

Olsen's jeep was winterized, its sides having been covered by plywood walls and celluloid windowpanes. He gunned the jeep to a stop under the ornate canopy, flashed his AGO through the celluloid, waved an answer to the slap-crack-West-Pointy salute, and was en route to a Visitors' parking lot without the slightest MP eye contact. He found an unoccupied spot near the inner gate and, after making final adjustments to the horn-rim windowpane glasses and paste-on mustache borrowed from Emma's make-believe closet, he made his way to the Paternoster and the suite that housed Theater-level Public Relations. En route he passed, face to face in the traffic flow, Bobbie Saxon, the G-4 logistics hotshot who still owed him four dollars, Ellen McKinley, the WAAC captain who'd been drunk at one of his parties and fell asleep in his bathtub, and Colonel Donleavy, G-2's heir apparent. None of them gave him so much as a second glance, and he remembered the advice of Camp Ritchie's surreptitious-entry instructor: "You want to hide something? Put it on the piano, or the mantel. Nobody ever notices stuff—or gives it any importance—when it's right there in plain sight."

The PR duty clerk was a T-5 with a drinker's nose and breath to match. "Help you, Captain?"

"I hope so. I've been named staff morale officer of the Two-oh-fifth Surgical Relay Section down in the Stuttgart area, and my C.O., Colonel Frammus, you know, the kidney specialist from Terre Haute who had that big article in the *AMA Journal* in 1942, thinks it would be a good idea to check out the inspirational movie library you people maintain and maybe borrow some of your films for showing to our monthly staff orientation sessions held on the second Tuesday of every month in the regimental theater which has been set up in that old brewery just outside Goonsdorf and which has astonishingly good acoustics for a place with such high ceilings and so many big vats and things, know what I mean?''

"Well, I—"

"And the colonel has suggested that seeing as how so many people got all teary over Mitchum in the *GI Joe* movie it might be a good time to show them some of the regular PR stuff—the why-we-fight, and the nature-of-the-enemy reels you guys made up to make us citizen soldiers more warlike and feeling better about all the shitty things the army makes us put up with, know what I mean?''

"Captain, just a sec.'' The T-5 held up an interrupting hand. "We don't keep a film library here. Not for lending out. You might check the USO, or the Special Services Officer in your command. They can probably take care of you. But we can't. Not us. We don't do anything. We're just a headquarters kind of thing.''

"Damn. You mean I came all this way just to find out I came to the wrong place?''

" 'Fraid so, sir.''

He pretended to think a moment. "Would you at least have a list of movies currently available to ETO troops?''

"Jeez, I don't—the only thing I can suggest is that you look at the catalog we keep in our reference library. The library our news release writers use to check facts and things. The librarian might put you onto something.''

"Who's the librarian, and where's the library?''

"Sergeant Tindall. Her office is through that gate there and the second door on the left.''

He repeated the schmooz for Sergeant Tindall. Although the WAAC noncom had passed him in the hall every day of his previous life, she failed to recognize him in this context. A dead man simply doesn't walk around, asking addled questions about movies, in a resurrection that featured a mustache, horn rims, and a demotion.

She was helpful, though. She led him into the library, a large room with book stacks and reading tables, and after a bit of rummaging, placed an assortment of tomes on the checkout counter. "This is all we have on the movie industry, sir. You can sit at one of those tables, and pencils and pads are in the drawers, if you want to make notes."

"That's fine, Sergeant. I see you have a *Who's Who* on that shelf there. I'd also like a look at that."

"Help yourself, Captain. And if you need anything more, you know where my office is."

"Many thanks."

He read for an hour, concentrating on Stahl, of course. Same old stuff. The mysterious tycoon; the billionaire hermit; the man who made movies without ever, never ever, publicly associating with movie people; the world-ranging adventurer; the hunter who would endure any hardship to make the kill; rifle and shotgun marksman of legendary accomplishment; the he-man decathlon qualifier; the owner of enough real estate to make another Asia.

All this and nothing. Puffery. Speculation. Rumor. Same old pictures: some with sunglasses, others without, but always the beard, the hat. And for all of the thousands of words written on the man, only a few were demonstrably true.

After reading it all twice, he decided that, if Stahl were available for liking, he wouldn't like him.

How about the Udine?

Lots of mention of that area of Italy. What did it look like? What went on there? Why did Stahl have a home there?

The *Britannica* had a fairly good topographical map of northern Italy, including the Udine and the adjacent Balkans. He used his little Kodak to make some pictures of the map and its accompanying text.

He sat in the quiet room for a long time, thinking.

He was nearing something. But he was also missing something. He'd had the sensation the other night at the lodge, when Raines was talking. She had said something, and he had felt revelation at hand. Then it was gone.

He'd been through this process many times, this thinking, reaching, sensing, knowing without knowing. There had never been a case whose resolution had been achieved without his first enduring this bizarre agony.

He read each of the bios again. Stared at the photos.

Was there something in one of the articles—in all of them—he wasn't seeing? Some link, some recurrent beat?

If so, what, for hell's sake?

Where was the Killarney Telegraph when he needed it most?

He dared to drift past Raines's office, and from the corridor he could see her through several walls of glass, standing at her desk by the window, looking out as she spoke earnestly into her phone. She was really splendid, elegantly shaped and neatly groomed, and he remembered the night at the lodge and how surprised he had been. Not so much surprised at her explosive readiness—because, as some great religious philosopher once said, a case of the hots, like death, is no respecter of parsons—but at her having chosen him as the ready-ee. By her own proclamation she would, if she someday decided to marry, become a movie tycoon's wife (if she didn't first become a movie tycoon herself) and it didn't seem likely she would jeopardize such exalted goals by playing impulsive games of mattress leapfrog with some guy down at the office.

Likely?

As some other great philosopher once said, "What the hell is 'likely' in an assed-up world like this?"

Count your blessings, Kaufmann-baby. If a Vargas Girl gets the urge to uncoil your spring, take it like a man—and stop asking questions.

So, then, on with the rest of the mission: that goddam fifth of hooch, asleep in the deep of the water closet, that so unaccountably gave Raines the willies. Which, he'd re-alized he could present to Bill Riley, Wiesbaden's answer to Captain Olsen.

As he drove to Vom Rath Strasse 49, he realized he had a minor problem. Just exactly where did Bill Riley hang out? The Wiesbaden Air Force hospital, Olsen had said. Not good enough. He'd call Olsen while it was on his mind.

He let himself into the apartment with the key he'd kept. The place was neater than he had ever seen it. Clean, even. To overcome a vague sense of intrusion, he reminded him-self that he had willed her this house and, besides, he'd be welcome here. Even so, he kept his eyes averted from the personal things that signaled her occupancy and went straight to the phone.

He dialed Olsen's number, but Nurse Fuller's nasal ar-rogance reported that "Doctor" was at lunch.

As he hung up, he noted a discord. The phone jack in the baseboard was slightly askew. Kneeling, he confirmed his old salt's reflex suspicion: the line was bugged. The tiny cylinder inside the jack facing told him so. It had been bugged after Raines's occupancy, because he knew—for an absolute fact—that the line had been clean when he'd moved out. It was his way, to check things like that.

An interesting development, this. Curious.

He went into the bathroom and retrieved the bottle. As he sought to return the porcelain top to the water closet, his hand touched paper. Heavy-gauge paper. A manila enve-lope. Taped to the underside of the lid, whose curved edges effectively hid it from view.

Unable to control his curiosity, he turned the lid and held it to the light of the window. A handwritten legend on the envelope's face:

C-ration—Sunderman. TOP SECRET.

He stood, immobilized both by the discovery itself and by his astonishment, suspicion, and outrage.

Raines had possessed the Sunderman file all along. After

telling him directly that she had no idea as to whether such a file even existed. After knowing how hard he had been trying to trace such a document. After knowing the brutality, the vicious zealousness with which others had been pursuing the same search. After damned near being killed twice herself in the struggle.

Oh, *shit*.

There was the sound of a key in the hallway door lock, a gentle turning of the knob.

She was at the door, and he was here, unready—by every conceivable measure—for the confrontation.

Back door time, Kaufmann.

He tore the envelope from its cache, slid the lid into place, stepped quickly across the dining area, through the kitchen and into the utility room, and was about to flip the lock on the back alley door when, through the window, he saw a black Peugeot parked by the fence. At the wheel, smoking a cigarette and seeming not to enjoy it, was none other than that great spouter of ornate oratory, that silver-tongued, silver-haired, silver-spoon scion of the late OSS and present-day associate of assorted assassins, Thomas N. Ballentine. And, coming through the front hallway door, none other than the sour-faced redhead who claimed to be a detective from the Farben Compound military police department, fella name of Gene Fallon, looking furtive.

Kaufmann ducked behind the water heater in the utility room. The kitchen door was ajar, providing a limited view of the action.

Fallon stood in the vestibule, listening and seeming to sniff the atmosphere. Then he returned the set of jimmies to his jacket pocket and went immediately to the bookcases that bracketed the large window on the streetside wall. Working swiftly and quietly, he rummaged and replaced, rummaged and replaced, an expert searcher searching.

He gave a full fifteen minutes to the examination of the apartment, and twice it was all Kaufmann could do to stay out of sight as the detective moved from room to room.

Eventually, and again at his expert best, Fallon took time

to be sure everything was being left as it was before he entered. Then he turned to the door, wiped the knob with a hanky and let himself out as quietly as he had come.

Kaufmann, bottle and envelope under an arm, moved to the kitchen window. Fallon appeared in the street below and climbed into the Peugeot, which, after what must have been Fallon's brief and unhappy report to Ballentine, clacked into gear and rumbled around the corner and out of sight.

Very depressed, Kaufmann returned to the jeep and headed for Emma's lodge, driving through a sudden cold rain.

It really was a crappy world. Crappy.

30

The Taunuses were blurred and gray in the afternoon squall, and the lodge creaked and hissed as the wind-driven rain swirled about its Victorian scarps and crags. He had been drenched between car and door, even under the porte cochere, which seemed to serve more as a venturi than as a shelter, sucking the gusts through and spattering the tiles and glass with the detritus of autumn. To counter the chill, he took a shower—Karli had devised a field expedient that returned the hot water system to a semblance of working order—and climbed into a set of GI fatigues, fresh-washed by Karli's fecund lady friend. He hung his wet uniform near the charcoal heater in the kitchen, poured himself a massive dose of Fundador, and went into the library, where he dropped onto the sofa and began his reading of the Sunderman file.

Surprise and betrayal were occupational hazards he had learned to live with over the past five years. Although the aftertaste was always bitter, the recovery time shortened with each succeeding incident, so that by war's end it had become possible for him to receive a shock, then quickly divert it to a kind of mental siding, where it would sit—and often die a natural death—while he continued to busy himself with first things first.

The Raines thing was different, of course. Yet it wasn't. He had become truly slushy over her in recent days, more moved by her than by any woman he'd ever known; the fact that she had lied to him and withheld crucial case material stung like hell. So in the past several hours he'd had to come full circle in his thinking—turning passion into wariness, converting Raines from his first humongous crush into an enigmatic stranger who might very possibly be a deadly antagonist.

But go into a flap he would not. His professionalism wouldn't permit it.

She'd just killed him, but he wasn't dead. He'd deal with her later.

First item of business: the Sunderman file.

He read it three times, all twenty-one pages.

The result was the same each time.

He didn't know a hell of a lot more when he finished than he did before he'd begun.

The pages were replete with words, phrases, assorted numbers and terse references, all as inscrutable as a pharaoh's check stubs. All as revealing as that maddening title, "C-rations."

He returned the file to his briefcase and sat, thinking.

C-rations.

What did it mean? Did it, in fact, mean anything at all? Or was it simply a convenience title, arbitrarily selected, akin to the whimsical police practice of naming unidentified individuals "John Doe"?

The Killarney Telegraph said no to this last. Maggie Sunderman had been too careful, too deliberate to indulge in whim or caprice. The name signaled something. Something definite. Precise.

But *what*?

And, of course, the larger question of the moment.

Just *why* had Molly Raines lied to him?

Who, or what, had applied the kind of pressure or threat that would make that otherwise nifty woman participate in treachery? She'd studied drama at Llewelyn. A significant number of the others in his developing cast of bad guys had involvements with that school—the documents said so. Stahl, the world's richest man, had endowed the goddam place.

Who among these creeps had gotten to her?

One lies only about matters which matter, be it the little, politic lie that says the boss doesn't play favorites, to the whopper, Santa Claus Lives. So where in this spectrum did Raines's lie fall?

He dozed.

"Hi. You're early."

He opened an eye. "Who are you?"

"Raines."

"Ah, yes. Second Bull Run, wasn't it? You were a bugler. What time is it?"

"Almost four."

"My God, I dozed, all right. Three hours."

She hung her dripping trench coat on the hallway hatrack and returned to show him a face that contained a happy announcement.

"I'm glad to see you got my message."

"Message?"

"Didn't Captain Olsen call you? To tell you I wanted to meet you here this evening?"

"I didn't hear from anybody. I came here to think."

"No matter. I've got news," she announced happily.

"Was ist?" He rubbed his eyes and yawned.

"I spent most of the morning with Captain Benet."

"I imagine she's quite a catch, if you go for that sort of thing."

She laughed. "I mean we were in Colonel Donleavy's office, sorting and clearing correspondence files and minutes of meetings and that kind of thing. And guess what:

he had all the files you've been looking for right there in his desk drawer.''

He swung his feet to the floor and sat erect, trying to fit Raines's bit of ''news'' into the frame holding his new picture of her. ''You don't say.''

She nodded, excitement in her face. ''The files on 'Sunrise,' and on the Wolff surrender attempt, and on the various personalities, Cutie-Pie, Sweetums, the others. They were all in his desk drawer all along. And I had the chance to make some notes.''

''Ah. You are one hell of a bugler indeed, Raines.''

''Thank you, sir.''

''How come Central Registry File Checkout had no record of his having those papers?''

''I asked Captain Benet that very question. She was surprised that there were none. She said with Colonel Donleavy being such a stickler for proper records it was dead certain that Poopsie had made all the necessary notations on a checkout slip.''

''Did Donleavy check out the files personally?''

''Benet said she remembered him phoning Poopsie and asking her to bring him some files. Which Poopsie did. Benet never saw the files herself.''

''But Poopsie, being one of the bad guys, saw this as a nice break. If she jimmied the checkout, leaving no hint that the files were snoozing in a staff officer's desk drawer, my frenzied efforts to read them would be negated.''

''It looks that way.''

''And you've made notes on what you saw in the files. Just for me.''

''Yep.'' Her smile faded, and she gave him a narrow-eyed inspection. ''What's wrong?''

''Nothing's wrong.''

''There is so. It's all over your face. You look—mad, or something.''

''Show me the notes.''

''Not until you tell me what's eating you.''

He sighed, deciding to get it over with. ''I went to my—

your—apartment today. To get the bottle of whiskey. I found the Sunderman files. Taped in the lid of the water closet.''

"Good.''

He gave her a look. "What do you mean, 'good'?''

"I mean that's fine. Swell.''

"Why did you lie to me? I asked you at the very beginning if you had any idea as to whether Maggie had made copies of her file. You said you didn't know.''

She sat in the overstuffed chair, her face now entirely somber. "Correction: I said I couldn't *say*. I wanted to tell you from the start. You have no idea how close I've come to telling you in the past couple of weeks. But I not only promised Maggie I would keep the copies for her, I also promised to tell absolutely no one about them.''

"Well, for God's sake, woman, I'm absolutely no one.''

"And I made sure you'd find them, didn't I? I knew you were coming some time to get your damned whiskey, didn't I? As a matter of fact, I remember fussing at you last Wednesday night to go to the damned hopper and get the damned booze out of there.'' She sat forward, taut, her eyes showing the beginnings of anger.

He rolled his eyes in exasperation. "I don't even begin to understand what the hell you're saying.''

"I promised Maggie I would say nothing to anybody about those damned files. But I didn't promise her that I would keep them some place where the right people couldn't find them.'' Her anger was in the open now.

"Let me sort this out: You couldn't *tell* me that Maggie had left copies with you, but you could keep them some place where I'd be likely to *find* them. Is that right?''

"And where nobody else would be likely to find them.''

There followed a protracted, silent interval in which they traded hot stares. Then: "Your ability to keep promises and to keep your mouth shut until given permission to speak is altogether admirable, Raines—laudable, even. It is also, at one and the same time, the source of one gigantic pain in the kiester. The fact is, I think your little story is as weak as hell. The fact is, I'm having a lot of trouble believing it.''

''Well, then, that makes you one stupendous horse's ass, Major Kaufmann. If you want proof, go see Captain Reynolds, G-2's private secretary. I gave her a copy of those files for safekeeping the very damned day I learned you'd been killed in that car crash. I was damned near sure that was no accident—that somebody had killed you. And I guessed I'd be next. And if I was killed, I'd be released from my promise to Maggie. And in that case, I thought G-2 himself should see those files—get to work on their meaning.''

''Big deal. You'd give Reynolds a copy, but not me, after I turned up alive.''

She stood up, fists balled, face the color of wet brick. She exploded: ''Why you compound son of a bitch, do you have any idea how hard it was for me to trust *you*? After I saw first-hand how you *used* people? After I was one of the people you used? Just when I'd get ready to tell you, you'd put me, or somebody, through the wringer, making us patsies in your rotten I-Spy-You-Spy games. Even the naive little jerk who was so crazy about you she wanted to pop— you used and endangered her, just for the goddam hell of it. How did *I* know where I was coming down with *you*, eh? How did I know how casually you might handle information Maggie gave her life to get? Eh? Tell me *that*. I don't know bean one about that dreadful business you're in, Major Kaufmann. But one thing I do know: I don't trust anybody in it—especially you. You scare the living hell out of me.''

Another pause, strained, electric, in which the sounds of the storm echoed in the caverns of the ugly old house and seemed to intensify the chill that immobilized them.

''Maude has a copy of the file?''

''I said so, didn't I?''

''And you trust her more than you trust me?''

''You better believe it. Maude's right up front with everything. *She* wouldn't set me up to get my buns shot off by some slimer with a big hat and bad breath.''

''So it comes down to this: I don't trust you and you don't trust me.''

''That's what that lovely business of yours does to people, Major.'' She strode to the table, picked up her musette bag, took out the notes and threw them on the floor. ''There. There are your goddam notes. Take them and stick them up your hooter.''

She slung the bag over her shoulder and made for the door, eyes ablaze.

''Hey. Where are you going? I'm not finished—''

From the hallway she said, ''The hell you aren't, buster. You're as finished as anybody ever gets around me.''

He heard the gale's roaring and then the big front door slammed.

He read the notes.

He read them again.

Finished, he rested back and rubbed his eyes. The storm had died off, and the rain sounds were soft and steady against the tall windows.

He missed Raines so much his chest hurt.

Her notes had told him the meaning of C-rations, and what he must do about it.

And what he'd eventually have to do about her.

TRANSCRIPT FOR 'ALPHA'S' REFERENCE FILE ONLY:

Phone conversation, ''M'' Line

'' 'Alpha'?''

''One O'Clock Jump.''

''Stompin' at the Savoy.''

''What is it, 'M'?''

''I can pretty well guarantee that they haven't found the Sunderman notes.''

"Good. Although I have reservations about those words, 'pretty well.' "

"There are no absolutes, of course. But in this case it looks very good."

"All right. I won't quibble. How are things with 'Asp' and 'Cobra'?"

"Moving along. October two is firm."

"Excellent. 'Old Buddy' is most adamant about getting things under way before heavy winter sets in."

"Well, he needn't worry."

"Meanwhile, keep your eye on the other people. They must not see the Sunderman papers, and I simply can't believe she didn't leave some. That idea haunts me."

" 'Seed' and I are watching that angle very closely."

SATURDAY
29 September 1945

31

He hadn't stopped thinking about Raines for hours, and now that he'd concluded that she was not guilty of willful duplicity vis-à-vis the Sunderman files, he lay on the sofa, tired to the point of death, and dealt with the puzzle represented by the bug he'd found in her apartment.

The bad guys—Ballentine and whoever else—knew he was alive, thanks to Poopsie. Since they were now trying to track him down and kill him, they had most probably tapped Raines's phone as a means of getting a fix on him. The logical counter move was to use their own device to give them a Jesus crisis, a problem so urgent it would automatically become their top priority. And while they were dealing with this, he could sandbag his own position so as to make it more difficult for them to get him before he got them. He could best accomplish these ends in two consecutive steps. First, he'd throw them into an uproar by revealing via their bug how much he knew about them. That done, he'd pull a Lazarus, rejoin the U.S. Army, and then make a massive feint.

Raines would be safe for two reasons: her continued occupancy of the apartment would keep information flowing to the baddies, and this time he, not she, would serve as bait.

Plan firm at last, he decided to get on with it.

He got dressed and drove down the hill to Karli's darkened Tankstelle and let himself in. The phone was its cantankerous self, but he finally got through.

"Hello?" Her voice was muffled with sleep.

"Raines, this is Kaufmann."

"What do you want? It's after midnight."

"First, I want to apologize. To tell you I'm sorry. I have indeed treated you shabbily—misjudged you. Made a lot of mistakes. And I'm sorry."

"So you called Maude Reynolds, eh?"

"No. I didn't have to. You told me. That's enough."

"So write me a letter. I'm going back to bed."

"I mean it. I'm truly sorry for doubting you."

"All right, all right. Good night."

"Wait. I want to ask you for a bit of help."

"Oh, come on—"

"Please."

"So what is it?"

"Get a pad and pencil. I want to dictate some notes to you. Type them up at once and take them directly to Colonel Donleavy. It's of the greatest urgency that he gets them as soon as possible. No matter the time, no matter where he is—even if you have to hand them to him in the bathtub."

"Hold on."

He waited, listening to the shuffling at the other end.

"Okay. Ready here."

"I might ramble a bit, but Colonel Donleavy will know what to do with it all, and he's not expecting a prize-winning essay. Anyway, here goes.

"Classification: Top Secret, Your Eyes Only. Today's date. Over my signature, your initials. Memorandum to Colonel Donleavy, to read as follows:

"Undersigned was kidnapped by a professional assassin named Bikler, AKA 'Cutie-Pie.' Bikler was going to fake a highway crash in which I was to be killed, but I managed to escape and Bikler was killed instead. I saw this as a chance to mislead those who had hired the killer and at the same time continue my investigation, which is to determine who is stealing our aircraft and why (reference our earlier discussions). So I switched IDs with Bikler and went underground. Beyond clarifying his status, undersigned offers this report as an update.

"Central Registry documents on the 'Sunrise' case show that last February, Baron Luigi Parilli, an Italian industrialist and Papal chamberlain, made secret contact with OSS agents in Bern. He told OSS that SS General Karl Wolff—in return for personal amnesty in war crimes charges being laid against him—was ready to arrange the unconditional surrender of all German and Italian Fascist units under his command. The OSS chief in Bern, Allen Dulles, met with Wolff on March 3. Wolff said he thought he could persuade Field Marshal Kesselring and other members of the German high command to join with him in such a surrender, despite the implicit treason against Hitler. This talk was the first of several held under the 'Sunrise' codename. There was a lot of hope among our top brass that the war could be significantly shortened this way.

"But Stalin learned of 'Sunrise,' and, fearing that the U.S. and Britain were trying to make separate peace with the Germans, sent Roosevelt a blistering cable, demanding that this double-dealing cease at once. Roosevelt folded under the Russian heat and ordered OSS to break off the talks. But even though OSS did so, there were immediate reports of large-scale uprisings by Communist partisans in northern Italy, Yugoslavia, Albania and Greece.

"Faced with what was obviously Stalin's retaliation in advance for a shafting the Americans never had any intention of giving him, and persuaded by Churchill that he had nothing to lose and seemingly much to gain by continuing the dialogue with Wolff, Roosevelt decided to reopen the talks, provided Wolff would arrange to have his disciplined German troops contain the Stalin-choreographed chaos in the Balkans. Then, Roosevelt reasoned, when Allied troops had moved into the trouble spots and conditions were relatively stabilized again, he, personally, could smooth Stalin's ruffled feathers.

"But Roosevelt died in April. There was no longer any hope that Stalin would return to personal diplomacy. Worse, the Balkan uprisings had unleashed Greek and Yugo left-wing demons, and the killing goes on down there.

"Enter Louis Stahl, plutocratic hermit and king of capitalists, who sees that the time is ripe for Stalin to act on his obsessive worry that the Americans and their western allies will unite with the Germans in an eventual war to destroy the Soviet Union. Stahl reasons that Stalin will tell his West Europe Communist parties, their political clout boosted dramatically by the reaction to twelve years of Nazism, to demand a Soviet occupation of all of Europe as the only way to bury right-wingers and assure Continental stability for centuries to come. He, as the magnanimous savior, will do as invited—sending in the Red Army under orders not to shoot unless shot at. The American armed forces, virtually emasculated by irresponsible demobilization, will, he figures, offer no armed resistance to the Soviet westward movement. Nor will the war-weary British and French be able to put up any effective fight. So he will eventually pick up Western Europe—all the way to the Channel—without having fired a shot.

"So Stahl decides to stop Stalin: to precipitate a preemptive shooting war—now, this autumn—while America is still relatively strong and the Russians are still relatively weakened by their years of fighting the Germans. He bribes a few corrupt and well-placed bureaucrats in the American military to steal a squadron's worth of B-17's from the eighty-jillion airplanes scheduled for retirement, mothballing or salvage, along with the necessary armaments. He then hires a full complement of fanatic—and expendable—Nazis to fly the things over Soviet territory and drop enough bombs to convince Stalin that the Amis have enrolled what's left of the German armed forces to help them launch War Three against him.

"Stalin retaliates, and the U.S. government has no choice but to fight back. The shooting escalates, but the Amis can't use their A-bomb against the advancing Asian hordes because they'd wipe out the remaining Ami troops, too. So Stahl and his corps of embezzlers and sycophants have their war, which, they expect, will be won by America's re-aroused wealth and industrial vigor and lost by the Soviets' fatal exhaustion.

"Undersigned has come to these conclusions per notes left by the late Margaret Sunderman, CID, copies of which are available in the office of G-2, attention Captain Reynolds. Sunderman's notes include a list of the missing planes, the missing parts and the missing ordnance. They also trace their faked transfer documents to the Udine area of Italy, where Stahl owns a large site, which, if developed as an airbase, would put the southwestern corner of the Soviet Union within easy range of fully laden B-17s.

"The undersigned is convinced that the B-17's are to be flown by those Luftwaffe aircrewmen reported by Lt. Molly Raines, G-1, to have been transferred to Dijon. It's likely that they have been screened there by Stahl cohorts, enlisted as mercenaries to be paid by Stahl, and transferred to the Stahl place in Italy."

There was pause. Then: "Got all that, Raines?"

"Yes."

"Good."

Another pause.

"Are you going to Italy?"

"No. World War Three's about to start, and I've had enough. I'm sick and tired of being a target. I'm sick and tired of being sick and tired. I'm getting back in uniform and heading for Le Havre. If the Army wants to pick up this memo and run with it, it's O.K. by me. Just count me out. I've got orders for home, and, by God, I'm going home."

"Will I see you again?"

"Who knows? Your best chance of that is to get back Stateside before you, too, get caught by the new war."

"Well, you never seemed to be the kind to just walk out when things got tough—"

"Oh, yeah? Watch me."

He hung up.

TRANSCRIPT FOR ALPHA'S REFERENCE FILE ONLY

Phone Conversation, "M" Line

"Hello."

" 'Alpha,' this is 'Seed.' "

"Chinatown."

"Nagasaki."

"What is it, 'Seed'?"

"The bug picked up Kaufmann last night. He called Raines. Gave her a memo on what we're up to."

"Damn. Is he on track?"

"Close as hell, sorry to say."

"All right. I'll talk to 'M' about it. No need to panic yet."

"It's Kaufmann who's in a panic. He's on his way to Le Havre. He told Raines he's had it with being a target. He's going home."

"You believe that?"

"Well, yes. Yes, I do. He knows we're going to nail him eventually if he doesn't stop horsing around. And he doesn't stand to gain a damned thing by hanging on. And take it from me: if he's anything, he's a realist. Yes, I'd say he's packing it in."

"All right. But tell Le Havre to confirm his arrival."

"By the time he shows up there our thing will have happened. It'll all be over."

"Ask for confirmation anyhow. I want to be sure that snoopy bastard is out of our hair—out of Europe—for good."

"O.K."

"Meanwhile, keep on that bug. He might call Raines again."

"I'm not so sure. They didn't sound too goddam friendly to me. I got the idea she was giving him the gate."

"Well, stay on it anyhow."

"Right."

"Anything else?"

"That's it for now, chief."

32

One of the many disadvantages of being a general was the need to do the work of a general, which was mainly reading bushels of mail and attending the thousand meetings a month generated by the bushels of mail. General Vickery detested this aspect of his life, of course, and so he was a great delegator—doing what thirty years in the army teaches, to wit: getting somebody else to do the work, for which, if it's done well, you take the credit.

One of his responsibilities—the continuing scrutiny of Soviet air force capabilities—could not be artfully dodged, even if he'd been so inclined. He took this matter very seriously, probably because it had directly to do with airplanes and their operation, and he was a tireless student of the dispatches, memos, agents' reports, diplomatic pouch stuff and radio intelligence that dealt with the subject. And so, on this particular Saturday—Vickery and his staff always worked on Saturdays—when immersed in the correspondence dealing with a misplaced shipment of rebuilt Wright Cyclone carburetors, he welcomed the appearance of Lt.

Col. Sammy Peterson, the honcho in charge of Soviet air force order of battle. Sammy was totally inept as a bullshitter, a fact which, while endearing him to the few remaining Victorian pragmatists at command staff level, earned him the impatience (if not the contempt) of the Madison Avenue Warriors, those who understood that today's quackery, if articulated in headline-inspiring syntax, could become tomorrow's unassailable wisdom.

But Vickery, a Victorian, had learned that when Sammy told you something you were getting the pretty straight scoop, at least as far as Sammy knew the scoop, and if you wanted Sammy to make guesses or speculate on Soviet intentions and what not, forget it. Sammy would simply stand there and say, "It beats the hell out of me," or, "Your guess is as good as mine," or, on more formal occasions, "We don't have any information on that, sir."

He stood there now, file under one arm; the other arm making a half-assed salute, and looked gloomy. "Morning, General."

"Hi, Sammy. What's up?"

"This week's Soviet O.B. stuff, sir. It shows some things I think you ought to know about."

Vickery rolled the cigar to the other corner of his mouth and happily shoved the stack of carburetor papers to the other side of his desk. "Ah. Let's talk."

Peterson spread a chart and a small stack of memos on the newly created bare spot and said, "The Russian bear is out of its den and on the fugg'n move."

"How so?"

Sammy's forefinger traced a line across the chart's mishmash of legends and numbers. "See this, sir?"

"Of course I see it, goddam it. What does it mean?"

"The Soviet Far East Air Armies are rapidly becoming the Soviet Not-So-Far East Air Armies. They're moving west."

"A build-up?"

"Sure looks that way, sir."

"Details?"

"Those three air armies the Russkies were using against the Japs in Manchuria and Korea are busting up and shifting, leaving the Far East situation in charge of Colonel General Lemeshko's Pacific Fleet Air Force."

"Equipment numbers?"

"The 9th Air Army, headed by Colonel General Sokolov, has eleven hundred sixty-two aircraft. The 10th, whose boss is Colonel General Zhigarev, has one thousand, ninety-five. And the 12th, led by Marshal Khudyakov, has thirteen-oh-seven. Lemeshko's naval aircraft number just over fourteen hundred. You want figures on types and their distribution?"

"They're in those reports?"

"Yes, sir. Mainly Yak 9's, La-7's and Tu-2 bombers. Some Lend Lease stuff, too—C-47's and other transport types."

"Where are they going?"

"They're pulling out of those new fields they built for the assault on Japan—fifty-six of them less than twenty kilometers from the Soviet Far East border—and they're flying by stages to Vitebsk, Minsk, Bobruisk, and Kiev. Just as if they were reassembling for the shoot-out with the Nazi Luftwaffe. The same old steps, but to different music."

Vickery chewed on his cigar, thinking. Then: "Trouble coming, eh, Sammy?"

"In spades, sir."

"Does Ike know about this?"

"Advisories are being laid on his desk even as we speak. As they are at all G-level staffers."

"All right. Anything else?"

"Not for now, sir. We'll keep you updated."

"Thanks, Sammy."

Peterson waved a salute and disappeared into the outer office, to be replaced in the doorway by Captain Allen, who reminded him that the general was expected at the USFET base hospital at thirteen-thirty for his dental checkup.

He had just irritably waved her away when the Hotdog phone rang. The clangor startled him. The Hotdog line was so seldom used it was an event when noise came from it.

"Yeah?"

"I've got to see you."

"Where are you?"

"In the parking lot. The usual one."

"Give me ten minutes."

He hung up, shoved his fifty-mission-crush service cap on his mildly aching head, and left the office. Outside he paused at Captain Allen's desk. "Get Colonel Donleavy on the line."

She made the connection and handed him the phone.

"Colonel Donleavy's office. Captain Benet speaking."

"General Vickery here. Put him on."

"I'm sorry, General. He just left. In a kind of a hurry."

"Well, where did he go?"

"I don't know, sir. He's been in a meeting with Lieutenant Raines for the past hour. After their meeting he came out, all sort of agitated, and ordered me to make him a date with G-2 as soon as. Some big crisis or other. And then he hurried off down the hall. He didn't say where he was headed."

"When he comes back, tell him I'm coming to Frankfurt for a session with that goddam sadist who calls himself a dentist. Tell him that when I'm finished I'll stop by his office. About fourteen-thirty."

"Yes, sir. Anything else?"

"Later."

The parking lot was nothing more than an area cleared in the downtown rubble, three blocks from the Zum Schwarzen Bock, the hotel that served as a combination officers' club, transient billet, and unofficial headquarters for aviators who weren't aviating lately. There were sufficient numbers of GI vehicles there to make the arrival of another, even a Packard with a general's flag, of no particular note, and the fact that the site was a gathering place for chewers of the rag and black marketeers and planners of gaudy debaucheries made it an excellent contact zone for people with privacy on their minds.

Corporal Price no longer had to be told to take a little walk, since he'd been through this drill so often. He pulled the car into a corner spot, climbed out and, with a parodized salute that seemed to dismiss the general rather than the other way around, sauntered off for the EM snackbar, whistling *Flatfoot Floogie*. Vickery, slumped in the back seat, watched him go, yearning to kick the arrogant bastard's ass.

The door opened, and Ballentine slid in beside him.

"Appreciate your doing this on such short notice, General."

"What's so important it can't wait until our regular meeting?"

"Several things. For one, Fallon rummaged the Raines flat and didn't find a thing. No Sunderman file, no nothing."

"Damn. I just know Sunderman kept a record of her findings somewhere. And we can't afford to have Donleavy find it. He'd know we know, and too many people know already, I'm afraid."

"Well, we'll keep looking."

"So what else?"

"Brandt is getting into the act. Personally."

"Jesus. He's coming here?"

"Yes. He's worried that there's been no word from 'Licorice.' And he's worried that Grover's airborne troops will get restless and noisy in their Godforsaken nowhere."

"And by being here he thinks we'll hear from 'Licorice' quicker, that the troops will ease up, for crissake?"

"Don't ask me to explain the ways of hotshots."

General Vickery sighed, a study in exasperation. "Does Fallon have any more ideas where to look for the Sunderman notes?"

Ballentine shook his big head. "Not a one. But the Sunderman notes aside, we've got to wind up this jamboree at the earliest moment, or we'll all be swimming in one huge bowl of melted Jell-O."

Vickery glanced at his watch. "Right. We're going to

have to make some fast moves, without benefit of a full deck. I saw a Soviet Air Force order-of-battle report this morning, and time's a-wasting, believe you me. The Russkies are picking up steam on their end, and if we're to be ready on our end, we'll need to know the where and when and who at once. The days of winging it are over.''

It was Ballantine's turn to look at his watch. ''I've got to run, General. Meanwhile, maybe we can pick up a clue or two from your bugs—those we've hung on Donleavy. Or even from his nubile secretary, eh?''

''You know about that, then.''

Ballentine showed a dim smile. ''I envy you. It's a nice way to get information.''

''Frankly, Tom, it ain't all that great,'' he lied. ''She looks super, but it's like banging a Victrola. Talk? Kee-*rist*, but that woman can talk. Trouble is, she never says anything worth a good damn. She can tell me exactly what kind of gravy Donleavy had on his tie three days ago, but she can't remember exactly what Donleavy said to G-2 three minutes ago about Stalin's bowel movements. Between you and me and the gatepost, that woman's one *beeg* pain in the ass.''

''I take one look at her chest and I find I can't feel sorry for you.''

''Come on—beat it. I got to go see my dentist.''

Ballentine swung out of the Buick and, before turning away for his own car, said softly, ''There's no other way, you know. We're running out of time. If we don't have a handle on all this by the weekend, we've got to take it to the very top and ask for a foreclosure.''

Vickery nodded, having, for once, nothing else to say.

33

Generalmajor Oskar was aloft on another of his so-called familiarization flights in the Mustang, leaving Anton in charge of the preparations for the flight crews' move to Lucia. A pool of vehicles had been assembled—fifteen six-by-six trucks, a half dozen quarter-ton four-by-fours and, of course, a Buick sedan to be used at Lucia by the Generalmajor, who, for all his fulminations on the contributions of the Spartan life to the art of soldiering, was in reality a closet hedonist and would be as likely to ride around in a jeep as he would be to grow a third buttock.

Much of the morning had been given to packing bedrolls and B-bags aboard the six-bys and to talking on the special line, confirming that the squadron field kitchens and latrines had been installed at the Lucia end. Colonel Dreher reported that all of the B-17's—less the one remaining here at the villa for tomorrow's flight by Anton and Dreher and General Bascomb—had been assembled and given run-up checks by the Ami mechanics, who had been transferred a week earlier. The planes were now parked, fully bombed, fueled and combat-ready, at Lucia, under a forlorn wilderness of duraluminum trash.

The raid would be on Tuesday, October 2. The date and target had been firmly established and revealed to the crews, kept in the dark until last night as a security measure.

Kolomyya.

According to Generalmajor Oskar, it was the site of one of the USSR's largest fuel and weapons caches, assembled during and since the Red Army's climactic assault on Berlin. Their raid would be, he had told the assembled crews, akin to the Japanese attack on Pearl Harbor, and it would debilitate the USSR in the west as thoroughly as the Japanese had debilitated the Amis in the Pacific. The final course headings had been set, too, with charts and overlays issued to aircraft commanders and navigators. After assembly at 20,000 feet over the Udine plateau, the squadron would fly east-northeast across Yugoslavia and Hungary to the eastern end of Balaton Lake, then south of Budapest to the Soviet border town of Mukachevo, just beyond the Carpathian range, then due east to the target—a total air distance of some 600-plus statute miles, which was comfortably within the B-17's combat radius. The plan was to cross the target area at noon, Moscow time, in "javelin down" formation and at an altitude of 29,000 feet.

The target was a nest of bunkers and storage buildings built on a sweep of the Ukrainian plain seven miles north of the town. Three railroads converged there, at a right-angle turn in the river. Since the target was large and irregular in shape, area bombing techniques were to be used, which meant that the bombardier in Anton's lead plane would line up the target with the synchronous bombsight and the others would release their bombs when they saw his fall away. Due to the enormous stores of munitions cached in the target zone, a single stick of 500-pounders could be expected to set off sympathetic explosions of cataclysmic proportions. Eighteen plane-loads? Forget Kolomyya.

All the bombardiers had been introduced to the Norden sight, of course, and if the formation had to break up, or there were other exigencies that compelled individual bombing, the crews were ready. Once all bombs were away the squadron would make what was essentially a U-turn and fly home on reverse headings. And, although the target area was in the Soviet underbelly, and therefore relatively barren of troop concentrations, they could expect fighter opposition to be moderate to heavy, thanks to the critical importance of the stockpile itself. On the plus side, most of the Soviet squadrons in the area were equipped with obsolescent Yak-9 fighters, for which hotshot machine gunners in Mr. Boeing's Flying Fortress could be more than a match. Better yet, the bombers wouldn't be alone on the road back; with surprise lost and full pursuit under way, the U.S. Army Air Force could unleash its fighter escorts—three squadrons from Foggia alone—to intervene in behalf of the fleeing 17's. Capping the advantages was the fact that, once Kolomyya had been hit, the total U.S. Air Force would be launched against key targets from the Black Sea to Leningrad, calling for an even greater dispersal of defending Soviet aircraft.

Even so, Kolomyya represented a hairy piece of work. The bomber crews had no more than marginal chances of coming through unbent.

Which for Nicky Anton, the All-American German, was not the real problem.

The big problem was what to do about all of it, US of A-wise. Or, more to the point, Nicky Anton-wise.

He could go along on the raid of course, and do his schtick. But whose side was he really on? Was all the razzmatazz handed out by Generalmajor Oskar the real stuff—was a German Legion truly part of American secret planning, and was a pre-emptive strike against the Soviets really established policy? If so, why had Kaufmann, the sumbish who had seduced him into this jamboree, been in the dark on his government's intentions? It didn't seem likely that a Theater-level G-2 hotshot like Kaufmann would not have been privy to the Big Picture; but even if he were no more than an eager-beaver self-starter bashing around uninvited in tender areas, how come the Big Picture in-crowd hadn't derailed him at once, thus causing Nicky Anton's penetration of the German group to be stillborn?

It was obvious that an incredible amount of money was being spent on this so-called Aktion Achtung—the kind of spending that could be undertaken only by a government, or by a huge organization. But his high school civics class had taught him that America could not start a war, its president could not start a war, and the money couldn't be made available for a war, without Congressional approval derived from democratic debate. Yet none of this had happened, so far as he knew. And if the American government was not actually supplying and directing the squadron, where in hell was all the money and management coming from? And, no matter who in hell was picking up the goddam tab, what was *he* doing here? What was *he* supposed to do about all of it?

He could jump into a car, or a jeep, or a truck—even a motorcycle—and run like hell, crying wolf as he ran. But who would he be yelling to? A government, an army, that already knew and approved of what was going on? And if the U.S. didn't know, what could he warn anyone about, when he didn't know what was really going on himself? It would be like Paul Revere, tear-assing through the night, screaming, "To arms! To arms! Something's going on, but I'm not exactly sure what the hell it is!"

Worst of all, at this moment in time, as the cliché had it, he was, in his government's eyes, nothing but an AWOL at worst, a missing soldier at best, who had been assigned to a G-2 operation and had disappeared without a trace. If he did any yelling, it would be from inside a guardhouse.

"Nicky-baby: You got a beeg problem."

"What's that?"

He glanced at the office doorway, where Colonel Dreher stood smiling in that cool way of his.

"Hullo, Colonel. I was just talking to myself again."

"In English?"

"Why not? I've heard so much of it for the past few weeks I think I could teach it at Harvard."

"Harvard wouldn't let you teach that kind of English. You sounded like a Hollywood agent."

"You hang around Captain Johnson as much as I do, friend Colonel, and you'd sound like that, too." He switched to English. "Hay boddy: han' me za fugg'n poopsheet, hay?"

Dreher laughed softly. "I take it back. You don't sound like anything I ever heard before."

"So what's on your mind, Colonel?"

"General Bascomb is flying down for Tuesday's show. We're invited to lunch today. The Generalmajor and you and me. Bascomb has things he wants to discuss."

There was something peculiar about General Bascomb, Anton decided. This was only his third encounter with the man—the first being that interrogation in Dijon and the other at Thursday's brief visit here—and it was becoming clear that Bascomb, aside from his chameleon changes of costume, was unlike any general officer of his ken. In his boyhood, most of the high-ranking dudes of military, corporate, academic or government persuasion who had visited his daddy's house (wherever it happened to be at the time) were openly crazy about themselves. It was an amiable snottiness that suggested Christmas cards could be sent to them by appointment only. But this man, large, meaty, blunt, came across as an aboriginal tribal king who, having been almighty since birth and having beheaded every subsequent annoyance, gave nary a thought to who and what he was because there wasn't anything beyond who and what he was.

Bascomb sat at the table, with the window glare to his back and with the aloof Karla Wintgens at his right elbow, commenting on the rotten state of a kitchen that could transform what might have been an acceptable mousse into vomit like this. Karla, ostensibly translating for Anton-Thoma, prettied up the language a bit—not, he guessed, in deference

ence to his sensibilities, but because it was the only way she could keep her own lunch down.

Eventually, after soliloquies on Italian cooking, German preoccupation with defecation, and American automobiles, Bascomb belched, the sound of distant thunder, then got on with what presumably was the substance of the meeting. "There's reason to believe that there is a traitor in our squadron. I want to find out who he is. At once."

Generalmajor Oskar leaned forward, his face suddenly red. "Traitor? One of my men? Impossible, sir."

"That's the word I get from Frankfurt."

"We've hand-picked these people. Checked their records, interviewed them and given them psychological tests. Not a one of them shows anything but fervor for the National Socialist principle. It's simply not possible that a Soviet agent could have passed our stringent screening—"

"Oh, horseshit, Oskar. Spare me your Nazi posturing. All that's needed to make a turncoat is money or orgasms, sometimes both. Find out which of your men is suddenly fat-cat or limp-dicked and we'll shoot the sumbish and get on with creaming the Soviet Union."

Colonel Dreher cleared his throat. "Begging the General's pardon, but there is simply no way any of our men could have become sexually involved during the training period. The supervision has been absolute. Even when sex was part of the testing, the woman was an individual of demonstrated loyalty to the Führerprinzip. And, in the unlikely event that our screening failed to reveal homosexual tendencies among the candidates, there has never been a moment in which such activity could have gone unobserved."

"All right, so then you look for a horny bastard with a fat wallet. I don't care who or why he is what he is—just find him."

Anton decided it was time to enter the discussion. "May I ask, General, how you found out about this—turncoat?"

Karla translated and Bascomb stared at him as if he had just suggested that they tango. "I told you. I got word from Frankfurt."

"I mean, what was the word, and from whom?"

"You're a presumptuous asshole, aren't you, Thoma?"

Karla's translation made the word "fellow," and he worked hard to keep from smiling the smile of panic. "I mean no disrespect, sir. It's simply that the more detail we have the more readily we'll find the culprit."

"He's right, General," Oskar put in earnestly.

Bascomb popped a grape into his mouth, chewed for a moment, then spat the seeds into his hand. "I got a phone call from one of my people up there. He said he got a call from one of his people at Dijon, a disgruntled colonel named Lawrence, who said one of the Luftwaffe people we picked was a ringer. Which means we have been penetrated by an unfriendly—that we have a stoolie aboard. Our man in Frankfurt has arranged to send us a special investigator, a man with a lot of savvy in such things, to help us sniff the rat out. He's in the next room. He's been here since breakfast, looking over our personnel files." Bascomb dropped the seeds onto his plate.

Anton asked the obvious. "Didn't this Colonel Lawrence give you a name?"

"Of course. But it was only a codename. The Dijon people assigned codenames to all the Luftwaffe candidates. Our stoolie was known to Lawrence only as 'Anton.' "

Anton, his heart resettling into its customary position, asked another obvious question. "Aren't we slamming the door after the horse is gone, sir? I mean, the raid's laid on for Tuesday. We have to assume the traitor has already informed the Soviets. Since they will probably be waiting for us when we cross into their territory, don't you think we ought to call the thing off, or at least go with an alternate plan?"

All three officers and Karla, too, stared at him with open astonishment. It was left to Generalmajor Oskar to give words to their shock. "Call it *off*? Are you suddenly insane?"

"Well, with the element of surprise lost, we—"

"We will fight our way through!" General Bascomb

roared, as if he was actually going to be in the battle, instead of in the sack with Karla. "The attack will be launched as scheduled, no matter who knows what, no matter what the ultimate cost. And I must say I don't think much of your negative attitude, Thoma. How the hell you ever got to be a hotshot in the Kraut Air Force is more'n I can say."

Karla made it a bit softer, but not much. She was showing her displeasure.

"Sir," Anton said, properly unctuous, "I was merely playing devil's advocate. No one has more enthusiasm for this operation than I do. But there are some hard questions that must be asked, and I'm asking them."

"Well." Bascomb still bristled. "It's time we got on with it. Karla, tell 'Seed' to come in."

SUNDAY
30 September 1945

34

The long flat buildings of Rhine-Main were sharply delineated, as if they had been sketched with tinted inks on white
board, and out on the field three Thunderbolt fighters
snarled and bounced along a feeder runway, their propellers
blatting and flattening the grass, their pilots, perched high
and with canopies open, leaning from side to side so as to
see beyond the massive engines. Closer in, utility vehicles
and tankers, like huge grubs, nestled up to the broad-winged
trans-Atlantic transports. Amid the overall bustling, an olive drab L-5 taxied up to the transient hangar, popping and
snorting, a motorbike among tour buses.

Olsen tooled the jeep around a jam of six-by-sixes at the
main gate and pulled to a pause beside the MP shack, from
which emerged a large T-5, strutting importantly, to ask if
he could "see a little ID, maybe?"

He peered at Kaufmann's UNRRA pass for some time,
turning it twice in his pudgy fingers. "This face don't look
like your face."

"The picture was taken before I grew this mustache. And I've taken to wearing glasses."

"Why you coming on base, sirs? I expect you have some kind of business here, maybe?"

Olsen joined the scene. "Dr. Coburn here is under orders to fly to Foggia. Medical business. I'm driving him to the Operations building where they will assign him a flight. Now let us pass, please. A life may be at stake."

The man thought about all this for a time, then shrugged and stepped back a pace to throw a pretty nice salute. He waved them through and returned to the shadows of his shack to light up a cigarette.

The jeep got under way again, snorting and clouding the air with exhaust, and Olsen followed the directional signs for Air Ops. "That mustache is pretty silly, you know. And those glasses are a riot. You look like Groucho Marx with heartburn."

"Just so long as I don't look like the Late Great Me."

"Any idea how long you will be gone?"

"Nope."

Olsen steered them around a traffic circle. "Those travel orders of yours: How in hell did you get them cut, as dead as you are?"

"Lady friend of mine down in Heidelberg has access to a mimeograph machine, a USFET authentication stamp and a stack of GI paper. She could order Eisenhower to weekend KP with the gear she has down there."

"Introduce me, will you? I want her to order me to Milwaukee, Wisconsin."

"The trick is knowing all the symbols and abbreviations and diddly-dos the army loves to lard into its written orders. Nobody every checks orders, they just look at them to see if they appear to be authentic."

"Could this lady get me a mustache, too?"

"She can get you a rabbinical beard, if you want one."

"Interesting job you've got, Mr. Coburn."

"Yeah."

They parked in the transient area and Kaufmann hauled his B-bag from the rear seat.

"Don't forget this," Olsen said, handing him the physician's bag. "You can't play doctor without one."

"The last time I played doctor I was banned forever from Miss Daisy Throckmorton's nursery school."

"That's why I decided to be a doctor, actually. It was the only way to get all those irate mommies off my back. Sort of like I did in the army—enlisting, so the bastards couldn't draft me."

"Makes sense." Kaufmann held out his hand. "Sure appreciate everything. Drive carefully on the way back."

"Hey. I'm coming in with you."

"No need."

"I wouldn't miss this for the world."

"Suit yourself."

They entered the main office area, a bleak GI arrangement of plywood, tin desks, and plasterboard walls covered with ancient memorandums nobody ever read. A counter bearing a sign, "Military Passengers Report Here," barricaded an inner sanctum, where a clutch of enlisted men sat at the tin desks, reading *Stars and Stripes* or snickering into phones. Kaufmann stood at the barrier and cleared his throat. The results were hardly electrifying. One man, a private, did give him a fleeting glance, but he was probably a rookie and as yet unskilled at putting officers and feather merchants in their place.

"Could I get a little service here, please?"

The rookie turned to look out a window. The corporal at the big desk turned a page. The pfc at the water cooler poured himself a short one. The two buck sergeants on the phones spoke lower. The top sergeant yawned, rattled his newspaper and shifted his feet on the desk.

Kaufmann placed his bags on the floor, walked to the end of the counter, pushed through the swinging gate, went to the desk whose sign read "Today's Outgoing Flights," and began to shuffle through the papers there.

"Hey, pal, what you doing?" the top sergeant demanded from his corner.

"Looking for the departure time of my plane to Foggia."

"You ain't supposed to be back here. And you ain't allowed to screw around with our papers."

"Obviously you people aren't either. Leastwise, I don't see any of you doing anything with them."

"You ain't allowed back here, pal. Unnerstan? You gotta get on the other side a the counter."

"I don't gotta do anything you say, Sergeant. In fact, my friend here, Captain Olsen, is associated with the law enforcement chain at USFET, and I have a mind to ask him to arrest you for disrespect of a UN official, inattention to duty, goldbricking, and scuffing a government desk with your GI boots. Are you ready, Captain Olsen?"

"Indeed I am, Dr. Coburn." Olsen pulled a prescription pad from his jacket pocket and poised his pen. "You want to file under United Nations Punitive Code one-eighty-three-stroke-nine-oh?"

"Stroke nine-nine."

"That specific, then, eh?" Olsen shook his head slowly, clucking his tongue and making notes.

The sergeant stood up and came to the desk. His heavy face had turned a light strawberry. "What is it you sirs want?"

Olsen pointed to Kaufmann. "Just that sir."

"This sir is a United Nations medical doctor, under urgent orders to report to 15th Air Force headquarters in Foggia. There's no time to waste and I need a plane ride that way as soon as. Now if you'd please stop all this screwing around and get me aboard such a plane I might return to my usual sweet-tempered self."

The other enlisted men traded amused glances and settled back to watch the joining battle.

"We ain't got any planes going anywhere near Foggia in the next ten days. Sir."

"Oh, yes you do. You want to see my orders?"

"Even if you got orders, I ain't got the authority to assign a plane special to fly you to Foggia. Or any place else, for that goddam matter. Sir.''

"Then who does have the authority?"

"Major Kowalski. But he's in Wiesbaden right now. Won't be back until fifteen hundred hours. And his assistant, Captain Bloom, is on sick leave.''

"Who's in charge in their absence?"

"Well, I guess I'm in charge of the office here. But it'll take the base commander to authorize a plane—''

"But you have the authority to contact the base commander and ask him to assign me a plane.''

"He'd skin me alive for bothering him on Sunday about something so goddam routine—I mean, aircraft dispatch is our responsibility, and the base commander is a bear for people handling their responsibilities, and—oh, shit.''

"So it seems that the short of it is, if you don't deal with the orders I'm carrying, you could find yourself in very, very deep trouble, Sergeant. Very deep.''

The door to the flight line opened, and a porky man in flight gear entered. The phone conversations became authoritative, militarily brisk. The newspaper flew into a drawer, to be replaced by an in-box. The water-swiller was suddenly transformed into the world's fastest typist.

"Where's Sergeant Boggs?" General Vickery demanded. "Sir?"

The general unzipped his flight jacket, an angry motion that punctuated his angry syntax. "Sergeant Avery Boggs, line chief in charge of maintenance of L-goddam-Fives around this fugg'n aerodrome.''

The sergeant blinked and swallowed noisily. "That Sergeant Boggs?"

"Yes, goddammit, *that* Sergeant Boggs. I just put a half hour on that L-5 out there and I'm surprised I'm alive, the way that goddam engine kept snorting and spitting and throwing smoke. I don't think the sumbish has seen a screwdriver since Limburg flew across the Atlantic. And I want Boggs to tell me why the hell not.''

"Sir, Sergeant Boggs has been ZI'ed. Three days ago.''

"I *saw* him three days ago, for crissake. I flew one of his L-5's, right off of that turf out there." Vickery waved an arm in the airfield's general direction.

"He musta left that night then. Because Sergeant Lamb is line chief now. Has been since Boggs left."

"Well, go get Lamb. Right now. I want words with him."

"Yes, sir." The sergeant pointed at the rookie. "Go get Sergeant Lamb, toot sweet. On the double."

After the man had banged out the door, on the run, there followed a strained silence in which General Vickery glared at his wristwatch, then at the others in the room. The group, frozen, suggested the statuary on a Mafia don's back lawn.

"Who are you?" the General rasped, his stare settling on Kaufmann.

"George R. Coburn, M.D."

"Medic, eh?"

"Yes, sir. In a manner of speaking."

"What the hell's that mean? Either you're a medic or you ain't."

"Well, sir, I'm always sort of uncomfortable in the presence of a general officer. Especially one as famous as you. World War One ace, and all that. And I say dumb things at a time like this—"

Vickery's eyes softened, from furious to annoyed. "What are you up to, Coburn? I came in the door, I felt an atmosphere. Something heavy. What?"

"Sir," Olsen broke in, "Dr. Coburn is en route to Italy. Only he's having trouble getting transportation."

"Who are you?"

"Captain Olsen. Medical examiner, USFET district. I drove Dr. Coburn to the field here. He was consulting me on an important case, and it was the least I could do to make sure he caught his plane. But there's no plane."

"Why the hell not?"

"Sergeant Whoosis here won't assign him one."

"I didn't say I *wouldn't* assign him one, goddammit, sir. I said I *couldn't*."

"Same difference, Whoosis."

VIckery held up a hand of warning. "Hold it. One at a time. What's your business on this trip, Coburn?"

"I'm trying to get to Venice, actually. But I'm shooting for a ride to Foggia, because it seems a lot more likely that there'd be something going to Foggia, where we got an air force, than to Venice, where we got nothing big-time. My business I can't discuss, because it's top secret. Would you like to read my orders?"

"Hell, no. I don't like to read anything. Especially orders. All those silly doodlies."

Another moment of silence, in which everybody traded stares of varying temperatures.

"Venice, eh?"

"Yes, sir."

"You heard about my War One record, then?"

"Not only heard, sir. Read. I've read every word that was ever written about your exploits on the Western Front. You were my special hero all the time I was growing up. Twelve Fokkers and four balloons you got."

"Nine Fokkers, two Albatrosses and a Rumpler."

"Really? The books never said you got a Rumpler. That was a two-seater recon ship. Flew higher'n hell and was real hard to catch, way I read."

"Hardest shot I ever made."

"Wow."

Vickery regarded the bemused Sergeant Whoosis. "That AT-10 out on the line. Who's it belong to?"

"It's the base commander's ship, sir. He uses it to—"

"Let Coburn have it."

"Sir?"

"Are you deaf, goddammit? I said gas up the AT-goddam-Ten flying machine, put the doctor here on it, and fly him to Venice. On my VOCO." The general glanced at Kaufmann. "You coming back here? Or are you stationed in Venice?"

"No, sir. I'm stationed in Heidelberg."

"How long will you be in Venice?"

"Not sure, sir. But—"

Vickery looked at the sergeant again. "Tell the pilot to wait. Tell the base commander to give the pilot a delay en route so he can paddle around in a gondola or something while Coburn does his business. You read me?"

"Loud and clear, sir."

"Anything else, Coburn?"

"No, sir. I'm—overwhelmed."

"Aviation fan like you shouldn't have to wait around to do some aviating. Specially when you're on GI business."

Kaufmann shook his head, an outward study in astonishment, an inward study in dumbfounded relief at not being recognized. "All I can say is thanks, General."

"You, Olsen. You have a car here, right?"

"A jeep, sir."

"Drive me to the main PX. My car's being serviced there."

"With pleasure, sir."

As the general strutted into the morning light, Olsen, following, turned to wink at Kaufmann. "So long, Your Sneakiness," he said softly. "Don't get bent. I don't know what I'd do without you."

Olsen pulled the jeep to a halt at the PX main entrance. "Here you are, General. Sure nice to meet you."

Vickery said around his cigar stub, "What's Kaufmann up to?"

"Sir?"

"Don't be coy, Captain. I asked you what is Kaufmann up to?"

"Kaufmann, sir?"

"Come on, goddammit, you don't think that silly-ass soup strainer he's wearing would fool me, do you? I want to know what he's going to do in Venice."

"Beats the hell out of me, General."

"Look, it's bad enough he's AWOL, playing dead, or whatever the hell he's been doing lately, without you aiding and abetting by denying knowledge and all that kind of horseshit. But I want to know what the sumbish is up to. Don't you understand?''

"I honest to God don't know, General. All I know is, he's a helluva good guy who's working on one helluva nasty thing. And that's all I can say."

Vickery nodded reasonably and said, "All right. For the time being, anyhow. But if he gets in touch with you—so much as phones to say Happy Labor Day—I want to know about it. Understand? I want you to call me soon as he hangs up. You may think he's a good guy, but I think he's a royal pain in the ass who stands to queer something very special I got going. And if he does that, pal, I'm coming for your balls with a pair of ice tongs."

General Vickery swung out of the jeep and disappeared in the building's inner shadows.

The youngish captain came around the corner of the hangar and delivered a salute that suggested he was shooting away mosquitos. "Captain Barney Griswold here, sir. What might I do you for?"

"You the pilot of that there AT-10 on the line?"

"Yes, sir. Although I admit I'd much rather be the pilot of a Super Constellation on the Miami run."

"Handle yourself right and I might fix you up with just that kind of thing."

"Are you bribing me, sir, or preparing to give me an order?"

"A bit of both, I guess."

"Fine. I am easily bribed, and I follow orders to a T, unless they displease or inconvenience me."

"Here's the order part: you call me every day at eighteen hundred hours at the special number on this slip of paper, and you tell me where your upcoming passenger, Dr. Coburn, is and what he's doing. And you stay in Venice until I tell you to come back."

"There are worse places to stay, I suppose."

"And here's the bribe part: I pay for all your socializing while you're there."

"Socializing. That includes ladies?"

"You want to bang Venus dee Milo, put it on my tab."

"Ah. You're my kind of general, General."

"You screw up, or cross me in any way, Griswold, and you will not be flying a Super Constellation, you will be driving a donkey cart in a salt mine."

"Don't worry, General. I'm not only easily bribed, I am also a craven coward in the face of threats."

"So why are you standing around here? Get moving."

FOR YOUR EYES ONLY!

File No. EW231147f   30 Sept 45

To: Brandt
From: Gladiator

Operation "Tailspin"

1. Subject operation is at the brink.

2. Grover's people are deployed, waiting.

3. Our loose cannon is rolling, and I am watching.

4. Any ideas?

FOR YOUR EYES ONLY!

File No. MM098056   30 Sept 45

To: Gladiator
From: Brandt

Reur's this date: Pray, maybe?

35

He watched his driver, a small man named Eduardo, negotiate the straits between a donkey cart and a wood-burning truck whose handlers argued animatedly over some right of the narrow road. The afternoon's sunniness had faded to a metallic gray, and there was a touch of winter in the wind coming out of the Alpine vastness. Udine, provincial power center of ancient Aquileian patriarchs and the Venetian governors, took form on the plateau ahead—towers and pastel-hued walls and arches surrounding a castle atop a solitary hill—and even from this distance Kaufmann could feel its unfathomable antiquity. He experienced a sudden sadness, a perception of his tiny moment in the physical continuum; he would shoot his few lines, take his bow, then exit this mortal platform to join those actors yet to come and those gone on who watched from eternity's shadowy wings. It was a sensation he invariably felt in museums, or in medieval cathedrals, or when leafing through yellowed photo albums.

He guessed that this attack was an extension of the down-heartedness that had dogged him since the revelations triggered by the Sunderman documents. Maggie had been onto something big, very big. She had made many notes, and yet the entries were obscure, mysteriously phrased and seemingly disconnected, as if they had been made in a huge hurry and under strenuous conditions. The enormity of their implications was made apparent when laid against the combined canvases of "Sunrise" and "Canned Goods." Her major findings:

1. At least a dozen B-17's had been diverted from 8th and 15th Air Force inventories, and it seemed to have been an inside job, accomplished by individuals with enough rank and clout to cut diversion orders, which could be buried in the Vesuvius of orders and counter-orders issued daily by USFET and the Pentagon. It seemed, too, that at least three other planes had been retrieved from the Ukraine, where they had been forced down during west-to-east shuttle bombing flights late in the war.

2. Important quantities of aerial bombs and other armaments had been "acquired" (Sunderman seemed unwilling to use the harsh word, "stolen"), according to her study of inventory shortages, by as yet unidentified units both within and outside the Air Force. Clues suggested that this "acquired" ordnance was shipped by truck and train south through the Tyrol—in some cases under validated USFET shipping authorizations. USFET, not Air Force. (Odd, this. Significant? Probably.)

3. Agents in North Italian border towns had reported large convoys of trucks, bearing what appeared to be parts of large airplanes under tarpaulins, coming south out of Austria. Dates of the sightings always followed by a day or two the dates of the validated shipment orders for ordnance and "parts."

4. Only one person was named in the notes. Three times. Louis Stahl, the American oil tycoon and international gadabout.

And this was where Kaufmann's bulb of comprehension had flashed bright. In a kind of sidebar question to herself, Maggie had philosophized: Why would Stahl, a super-rich

oil baron, up to his eyes in the theory of free enterprise
capitalism, contrive a huge-scale enterprise which, if successful, could only benefit Stalin?

Benefit Stalin?

This had given Kaufmann a jolt. Stahl was a renowned
enemy of the Soviet Union. Maggie's studies suggested that
Stahl was spending millions to finance a plot to stop Stalin—to forestall Stalin's plan to occupy Western Europe. So
why, then, was Maggie seeing Stahl as a Stalin benefactor?

Ah.

C-rations.

Read, "Canned Goods."

And, if read "Canned Goods," the plot was revealed.

Stahl only *thought* he was starting a war to stop Stalin.
Stahl and his people were patsies. Stahl and his people,
thinking they were hurting Stalin, were, as planned by Stalin himself, actually abetting his scheme.

In the summer of 1939, Hitler was preparing to invade
Poland. But he needed an excuse to launch his attack—a
reasonable explanation that would satisfy world opinion.
Reinhard Heydrich, chief of Hitler's SS, devised "Aktion
Himmler," in which SS men, dressed in Polish uniforms,
attacked a German radio station on the Polish border and,
after gunning down the Germans on duty there, broadcasted
anti-German slogans. When the "Polish killers" vanished,
the dead left at the scene were not German radio crews but
what Heydrich called "canned goods"—Jews and political
prisoners he had selected and dressed in German uniforms.
Hitler, ostensibly "outraged" over this "heinous Polish assault" on peace-loving Germans," sent his legions into Poland that very morning.

It was the only thing that made sense in this schmeer.
Maggie had seen it, and now Kaufmann saw it.

Stahl and his people had one job: to be killed in Russia
as American invaders. They had been selected to serve as
Stalin's "canned goods."

"And I," Kaufmann muttered aloud, "have two jobs: to
put Stahl back in his cave before he gets into Russia, and

to find out who in hell selected him and his group as 'canned goods' in the first place.''

''What's that, sir? I can't handle English.'' The driver looked at him in the mirror. ''Italian, as my mother tongue. German, as you can hear, by acquisition. But English, not at all.''

''Sorry. I have a habit of talking to myself. I was just saying I've got one hell of a weekend cut out for me.''

''English is such a peculiar language.''

''It certainly is.''

Benito Mancini lived in a severe gray block of buildings off an arcade that branched from a sorry little plaza in the shadow of a glassware factory. Like his apartment, he was disheveled and smelled of garlic and stale wine. He was short and round and hairy, and he spoke an acceptable English in a voice that sounded as if it hurt him.

''There they are. I've laid them out on the table, and you can help yourself.''

''These are all you have?''

''Nowadays. I used to have some very large-scale charts of the Dolomite area, but I sold them to American soldiers who wanted to go mountain-climbing.''

Kaufmann took some bills from his wallct. ''Here you are, then. A hundred dollars, American.''

''I should charge you more, you know.''

''Why? I only want to look at them, not buy them.''

''Because you won't tell me what you're looking for. I must assume, then, that you are up to no good. That smells of police. When the cops are involved, there is danger for me. I should charge more.''

''I follow your logic, but you're wrong. I am not involved in anything illegal. I'm simply trying to satisfy a personal matter. It can't be resolved unless I find a certain place in the Udine-Friuli area.''

Mancini shrugged a fat shoulder. ''So that's your story. So I have no choice but to go along with it.''

''A hundred dollars is a decent amount.''

"I'm going to the grocery. I'll be back in an hour. If you're still here, it'll be another hundred."

Kaufmann, without comment, waved the man away. Many things about human nature irritated him, but the most annoying of all was greed. He hated greed and greedy people, sure enough, and this man typified the genre.

They were real estate plats, charted with fussy precision, and he leafed through them all, quickly the first time, so as to get a feel for how long the search might take.

It took no time at all, actually, because it was so large it leaped out at him on the first go-through.

"Ah. There you are, you rascal."

It was about thirty-five miles northwest of Udine, near a town called Cassana, which, by coincidence, he remembered as having been the site of last June's intensive search for some big-league fugitive Nazis, said to have fled Berlin for Rio by way of Munich, Udine, and Tripoli. Nothing had come of the search, so far as he could remember.

Since he still had about ninety-nine dollars on the meter, he made a leisurely business of jotting down map coordinates, dimensions, and related data, including a rough sketch of nearby road networks.

Networks was hardly the word.

There were only two roads worth noting—the main highway that ran three miles to the west of the western boundary, and the gravel secondary road, more like a farm lane, that served as the west-to-east link between the highway and the Casa del Sol, owned since June, 1935, by none other than that great American fat-cat, Louis Stahl.

All 989 acres of it.

He rented Mancini's phone to make a tenuous connection with the Hotel Lorenz in Venice, whose switchboard operator agreed, after much confusion, to ring the bridal suite.

"Hello?"

"Barney, this is George Coburn."

"You call at a very awkward time."

"Sorry. But I promised you I would call, and this is the first chance I've had."

"If you had any notion of how long and hard I've struggled to get this lady's drawers off, you'd be very ashamed of yourself."

"I wanted you to know that I won't be back to Venice tonight. Probably not for a day or two. I'm going to be doing some medical work at a village named Cassana."

"All right."

"Keep the airplane ready. Okay?"

"I may be a drunken wencher, Mr. Coburn, but I am not—I have never been nor ever will be—an ignorer of my airplane. You tell me we got three minutes to get ready for a flight to Zanzibar, my airplane will already be ready."

"Good. Meanwhile, give your lady friend my regards."

36

Late that afternoon, a bike-riding fatty in a constable's uniform assured Kaufmann that the area's highest official was a "Mee-stair Sevens," who turned out to be Special Agent Lars Svensen, the convivial blond beanpole who headed up a CIC team lost in the heart of downtown Cassana, population 723. Svensen and his people occupied a block of regal buildings that had opened as an abbey in 1521 and, during Italy's recent alliance with Germany, had served as an R and R center for overworked Gestapo functionaries. After a cursory inspection of Kaufmann's phony UNRRA credentials and the phony letter of mission signed by Dwight D. Eisenhower, Svensen had led Kaufmann on a leisurely stroll about the place. Eventually Kaufmann was able to dismiss his Italian driver, having parlayed a bottle of Hennessy cognac—acquired within minutes of yesterday's landing in Venice via Barney Griswold, ace aviator and bon vivant—into the use of a jeep and the solitary phone that connected Svensen to the army command net.

"The phone is yours whenever the occasion arises." Svensen beamed magnanimously.

"An occasion just arose, Lars."

"Just don't call L.A. unless you reverse the charges."

"This is a doctor colleague in Frankfurt. A GI doctor. And it's strictly government business."

Svensen cradled the Hennessy bottle in his arm and made for the door. "He'p yo'sef. I'm going to deflower this little virgin. You need me, just check the floor outside. I'll be passed out on it."

When he was alone, Kaufmann cranked up the set and got an army switchboard in Foggia, which patched him into Milano, then to Frankfurt via Strasbourg, Epinal and Mainz. The USFET operator connected him.

"Captain Olsen's office. Nurse Fuller speaking."

"Is he in, please?"

"Who's calling?"

"Dr. George Coburn, UNRRA. In Cassana, Italy."

"This is long distance, then?"

"Four hundred crow's-flight miles is my guess."

"Oh. Well. May I ask what it's about?"

"Put me through, please. I'm allowed only so much time on this phone."

A crackling, then a click.

"Dr. Olsen here."

"Dr. Coburn, UNRRA, in Cassana, Italy."

"Oh, yeah. Hold just a sec, Doctor. I want to send my secretary on an errand."

After a silent moment, Olsen came back on. "There. She's off the line. So what's up, my boy?"

"I just want you and Raines to know where I am. That up to now I'm okay. That I think I'm onto something big down here and, if things go right, I will be checking in with you again tomorrow."

"Great. Glad you called. And I know Raines will be, too. The little lady has just given me some exciting news. She's got a job offer in Hollywood. Some big producer sent her a cable today."

"Oh?"

"She's to report as soon as the army releases her."

Kaufmann took a moment to deal with a mixture of surprise and depression.

"Are you still there, Your Deviousness?"

"Well, it's something she's wanted very badly. I hope it works out for her."

"Such enthusiasm I hear in your voice. This is Raines we're talking about, pal. The president of your fan club. Can't you sound a bit more pleased?"

"She doesn't like me very much right now."

"Horse manure. She's ga-ga about you. And, if you don't mind my saying so, I think it's a terrible waste to have such female beauty wasted on male junk like you."

"I do, too."

"Anything I can tell her?"

"Just give her my congratulations. And tell her to keep Colonel Donleavy clued in on what I'm up to. That's in case I get tackled, or something. He'll be able to pick up the fumble and run."

"You need anything else?"

"No. Just the use of your phone now and then."

"Cassana, eh? Is that near Cleveland?"

"You can get me here at Ring Thirty-one, CIC Team, Cassana, Udine Province, Patch-through Army Net, Foggia. Got that?"

"Mm."

"I'll call tomorrow."

He returned the phone to its cradle and stared out the window at Greater Cassana, thinking. Then he went to the door and, peering into the anteroom's gloom, called, "Hey, Svensen. You still conscious?"

"Unfortunately, yes. Get your call through?"

"Yes. And thanks again."

Svensen came in and plopped into his desk chair. "I'm just glad to learn that the sumbish works."

"Why haven't you tried it yourself?"

"Well, if it actually worked, Army'd know where I am."

"I don't get it. What's your business here?"

"Ah, yes. An excellent question. My team was sent up to this shitty little village from Rome in the final days of the shooting. Rumors were that Hitler's deputy, Martin Bormann, was hiding here. As you can see, it took us all of two hours to check out every building in sight and even quite a few in Udine itself. And, as you no doubt have surmised, we didn't find Bormann. So the next day I checked in with my headquarters in the Eternal City, and guess what? Everybody had been transferred out, to where nobody knew, and the G-2 honcho there advised me to sit tight and blend with the populace until further orders. I'm still sitting and blending, and, because I am a good soldier who follows orders to the letter, I also stay somewhat tight. Which I have to be actually, because the pressures on a six-foot-three Swede who seeks to blend in with a populace of black-haired fire hydrants with garlicky breath are more than somewhat, I assure you."

Kaufmann glanced around the ornate room. "It seems to me you're doing all right. You got an office that looks like the Alamo and personal quarters that look like an old Douglas Fairbanks movie set. You got two housekeepers who look like Rita Hayworth, three teammates who look dead, and a garage that looks full of cars, gas and tires. What's it worth to you if I don't report your location?"

"Well, you may not believe this, buddy, but I do get lonesome for Indianapolis now and then."

"You're right. I don't believe you. By the way, does your jeep have a unit designation on its bumper? The wrong one could be embarrassing for me."

"I long ago had the same concern. So I hired a commercial artist who is quite gifted at making bumper templates at very short, let us say, even edge-of-panic notice. What would be your pleasure in this case, Doctor Coburn?"

"Something medical, maybe?"

"How about, say, 'UNRRA Med Team, Foggia District'?"

"Sounds good."

"Consider it done. Meanwhile, would you like to sample this Hennessy?"

"No thanks. I've got to stay alert. Heavy schedule."

They'd said their good-byes at the gate of what Svensen called his twenty-room foxhole, and Kaufmann promised to have the jeep back as soon as possible, a matter of supreme indifference to Svensen, since his personal vehicle was a red Ferrari, confiscated in the name of the United States of America from an abandoned SS garage in nearby Gemona, while his team members, when they were stirring, drove Wehrmacht staff cars confiscated in the name of Curly, Larry, and Moe.

He checked into a roadside inn shortly before midnight and, after a two-hour nap, pulled fatigues over his Class A UNRRA uniform and took to the countryside, carrying compass, night binoculars with range reticle, and a canteen of the local red wine. Following his GI compass, he walked an azimuth that led to a modest promontory, which, according to the charts, provided a panorama of Louis Stahl's home away from home. And he'd taken up station there until the chill predawn twilight, lying on his belly on the crest, above vast sweeps of pasture, forests and lakes overviewed by a main house the size of Delaware. Peering through the night glasses, he concentrated on a huge outbuilding, more than a barn, less than a cathedral, which was busily lit in the midst of this fenced-in wilderness and whose gaping doors revealed a single B-17. The plane, its olive paint dull under the ceiling lights, provided the focus for a gaggle of mechanics and several officers in coveralls, who came and went in jeeps and huddled occasionally over tech manuals.

He watched long and hard, with no significant reward.

As the sky reddened in the east, he stood up, stretched, stamped the cold from his feet and returned to the jeep, which he had hidden in a copse about a quarter of a mile from his observation post. He pulled off the fatigue coveralls and brushed down his UNRRA uniform, even wiping the dust from his shoes with a piece of gun cloth. He tested the mustache, pressing the adhesive firmly against his upper lip, and settled the eyeglasses on his nose. He considered briefly carrying his pistol but decided against it. Without a shoulder holster, he would be as lumpy as Dr. Frankenstein's Igor, and it would be a gross inconsistency if it were to be seen in his physician's bag in the shakedown he could most certainly expect.

Besides, as the world's most clumsy handgun handler, he would probably shoot himself in the dingus before the hour was out.

The jeep snorted and spun its wheels, and he was off across the open country, bouncing and grinding and fish-tailing, for the narrow road that led to the huge posts and wrought-iron gates of the villa. The dawnlight was the color of ripe peaches now, and the fields and brush and rocky outcroppings gleamed with dew, and there was a sweetness in the air, a sad redolence that spoke of faded flowers. Clutching the throbbing wheel, eyes fixed on the zigs and zags, he wondered why there was no excitement, no blood-rush of impending danger, no surging of adrenalin.

Only this—resignation.

Sorrow?

Two guards, dressed as GI riflemen. One holding up a hand, demanding a halt.

The jeep skidded to a stop, its motor idling noisily.

"Hi."

"Goodt morning, zir," the larger man said. "Zis is a reshtricted area. You are not allowedt to enter."

"This is the estate of Louis Stahl, is it not?"

"I couldt not zay, zir."

"I'm Dr. George Coburn, a physician assigned to the Foggia District, UNRRA. I've been ordered to visit your commanding officer for a discussion of certain medical matters. Here are my ID and travel orders."

The man peered at the papers. "Zis is a secret blace, Doctor. How didt you know ve vere here?"

"How did I know? Come now. From what I've been told,

I don't think there's anybody in this part of Italy who hasn't heard your airplane motors, seen your vehicles coming and going, speculated on what's going on out here.''

The soldiers traded glances, and the larger one, slinging his rifle, went to the gatepost and lifted a field phone from its pack. He spun the crank vigorously, then, turning his back to the jeep, holding the Coburn ID to the light, began a conversation that was lost in the jeep's busy mutterings. After a minute of this, he returned the papers.

"You vill vait here. An offizer comes from za villa.''

"As you wish.''

The man stared off at the dawn, saying nothing more.

The wait, only minutes in elapsed time, was an eternity for Kaufmann, who huddled in the trembling jeep, trying to draw some warmth from the motor. The soldiers stamped their feet and blew on their hands and pulled their fieldcoats closer against the morning chill. The sky grew brighter and somewhere a bird called, high up, lonely.

Eventually a motor sounded over the rise, and a GI staff car appeared, an olive-hued lump that came down the lane in a kind of angry sluing, its driver in silhouette against the rosy glinting of its windows.

Kaufmann sat erect, tense, aware that his lips were dry.

The car skidded to a halt at the gate and the driver's door banged open and Nick Anton leaned out to demand in German, "What's this all about?''

TOP SECRET URGENT
EYES ONLY

By Courier   *30 Sept 1945*

To: Gladiator
From: Mint

To confirm phone call, the following message from "Licorice," via scrambled Code Jupiter, was recorded at 04:38 hours this date:

". . . (Garbled) . . . and it is now definite that the raid will be made Tuesday, 2 October, 1945. ETA . . . (Garbled) . . . according to . . . (Garbled) . . . Out."

MONDAY
1 October 1945

37

Kaufmann blinked, working to control his astonishment, as the large soldier answered in thick, Austrian-inflected German. "This man is an UNRRA doctor, sir. He says he's here to discuss certain medical matters with the C.O."

Anton got out of the car and strode to the jeep, a portrait of Prussian irritability. "You must leaf now. Idt giffs no admissions here."

"Sorry, buddy," Kaufmann managed. "You're up against Ike himself. Want to see my orders?"

Anton snatched the papers from Kaufmann's outstretched hand and read, his face severe. Finally he looked up and, pocketing the orders, said, "Leaf za cheep here. Gedt in za car." To the guards, in German: "Good work, men."

Kaufmann did as he was told.

Only after the car had been turned around and was rumbling up the rise again did Anton speak. Presumably out of habit, or momentum, he held to German. "I never thought

I'd say this, but, man, I am very pleased to see you. We have World War Three on our hands, you know.''

"We most certainly do.''

"You know what's going on here, then?''

"Partly. But I came down to get the details, whatever photos you've taken. Everything, anything that will help us convince Ike.''

"We're running out of time.''

"All we can do is try.''

"We have very little time now—even to talk. I'm on a schedule. I'm expected back at the villa in five minutes.''

"They control things that closely?''

"You can't imagine how closely.'' Anton swung the wheel sharply, muttering, as the car slammed over a crevice in the tortured road. "How did you know I was here?''

"That's too complicated for now. I just worked it out.''

"I've been wracking what's left of my brain to figure a way to get word to you. But I've been watched. They watch everything. All the time.''

"How come you're the gatekeeper here?''

Anton snickered. "Gatekeeper, hell. I'm the squadron commander, my friend. I am a very important fellow in these parts. Perimeter defense is among my many responsibilities and the main gate is in the perimeter. If some idiot causes a fuss there, it's my job to handle it.''

"Tell me what happened.''

"I ended up in Dijon, as planned. The next day, an old man named Donnelly, who said he's a friend of yours, and some prig named Lawrence began to teach me how to be a German ace. I didn't like Lawrence, and I didn't like him a lot when he killed my airplane on me. I punched him and they sent me to my room without my supper. A woman named Karla Wintgens showed up to test me for the Nazi virus. Several days later, I was interrogated by an American colonel named Dreher. By then I was fed up with this whole business, and I wrote you a note of resignation, but the ink was still wet when some MPs stuffed me on a plane to this place. I've since made friends with Generalmajor Oskar, the Nazi in charge of something called the German Legion, who thinks so much of me he's made me boss of the B-17 squadron that's supposed to attack Kolomyya, Russia, tomorrow. And this morning, while I'm seeing to my airplane, the gate calls about a fellow claiming to be a doctor who wants to talk to me per orders of Eisenhower. And here you are, silly little mustache and everything.''

''I saw only one plane. Where are the others?''

Anton steered the car around a huge pothole and shifted into second gear to take a rise. ''In Lucia, about seventy miles from here. Hidden under the scrap at an Italian air force salvage dump. They're loaded and combat-ready; the crews—dedicated Nazis making up the so-called German Legion—are standing by; and all eighteen planes will take off in the morning to be over Kolomyya at noon, Russian time. The ship that's here is reserved for General Bascomb, an American who's apparently in charge of the whole business. I'm supposed to fly him to Lucia this morning.''

''Where's Oskar?''

''At Lucia. He's taken to flying around in a Mustang, and he went up there last evening.''

''Who else is in the house right now?''

''Besides General Bascomb, there's Karla Wintgens, Bascomb's interpreter and mistress; Colonel Dreher, Bascomb's aide and, on this morning's flight, my copilot; my flight engineer, a peculiarity named Brenner; and a man out of Frankfurt they refer to only as 'Seed,' who, it seems, was sent down by some overlord in the scheme to investigate a report that the group has been penetrated by an unfriendly named Anton. 'Seed' has spent most of his time reading Fragebogen and air fitness evaluations. He's a snooty son of a bitch, and he never looks at you directly.''

''You said Karla Wintgens?''

''Yes. Why?''

''The name's familiar, that's all.'' Kaufmann thought for a moment, then asked, ''This 'Seed'—he doesn't suspect you?''

"No. We even played a couple of games of Russian Bank last night."

"Any hints as to who the overlord in Frankfurt is?"

Anton shook his head. "Not a one."

"What kind of pictures have you shot?"

"The principals—Oskar, Bascomb, Wintgens, Dreher—some long shots of the planes, the hangars, the villa. The camera and film are hidden in my quarters."

"Nobody else is in the house?"

"Only three housemaids and two old men who work as gardener and butler. That's it."

"I was on recon earlier. My glasses showed me a group working on the plane. Where are they?"

"They left for Lucia a half hour ago. The only people left on the estate are those in the house and a platoon of former SS paratroopers who, because they serve as perimeter guards, are nowhere near the house."

"Where will the guards go after Tuesday's raid?"

"Bascomb hasn't said."

Kaufmann thought about all this. Then: "Why Kolomyya?"

"General Bascomb tells us it's a super-colossal Red Army ammo dump and weapons test center. Knocking it out will be the equivalent of Pearl Harbor."

Kaufmann sighed. "That's nonsense. I know Kolomyya. I was running a pair of Wehrmacht turncoats near there last year. It's a nothing place, militarily speaking. Or from any other point of view, for that matter."

"A lot can happen in a year."

"Not in Kolomyya, pal. Nothing happens there in a century. Besides, the squadron will never get there. It'll be massacred as soon as it crosses the Soviet border."

Anton's sidelong glance was sharp, and full of shocked surprise. "What?"

"The squadron has one job: to get slaughtered."

"Why, for Christ's sake? And by whom?"

Kaufmann gave him a summary of Reinhard Heydrich's "canned goods" scheme to rationalize Hitler's invasion of

Poland. He concluded: "Stalin's fighters will nail you all the moment you enter Soviet airspace is my guess. Or, he might even permit you all to bomb Kolomyya, then nail you."

"God. Do you think Bascomb, Oskar, the others are in on this—this plan of Stalin's?"

"Not for a moment. Stalin's using them, all the diehard Nazi airmen, as 'canned goods.' "

"Well, hell, he's got to have help from the Americans somehow."

"Right you are. It's obvious to me that some American muckamuck has convinced Stahl that the U.S. government supports him and will reimburse him in his preventive war initiative. Stahl's been sold a bill of goods, you can bet on it. But that doesn't make him and his German Legion any less dangerous. Any way you look at it, they stand to bring on a major war. Which means we've got two jobs, you and I. We've got to keep those planes from getting off the ground, and we've got to identify Stalin's American collaborators—the people who have conned Stahl."

"But what the hell—there are only two of us against at least two hundred bad guys."

"My part will be to pick up whatever film you've exposed and get back to Venice, where I have a plane waiting. My report and your pictures will be flown to Colonel Donleavy, at G-2 in Frankfurt. And I'll ask Donleavy to get Ike's approval of an air strike on Lucia. Your part will be to stall things as much as you can, then get out of the way when the air strike hits."

Anton gave him a sidelong glance full of incredulity. "You are joking."

"Why should I be joking? You say you're an important man around here. So you can take me to your quarters, pretend to deal with me as an UNRRA physician taking a survey, then boot me out the door—pictures and all."

"It's out of my hands now, damn it. Bascomb, Oskar, Dreher—they're suspicious of everything. There is no way I can take you to my quarters without first showing you to those people. They know you're here; every perimeter incident is automatically reported to them, whatever the time of day. Your visit will have to be explained in full.''

Kaufmann said a dirty word, clutching the door handle when the car bounced over a series of ruts. ''Well, we could cut and run with what we know right now. Grab the plane in Venice and fly back to Frankfurt, crying wolf.''

''Bad idea. If I don't show up at the villa on time, the security guards start a search. We wouldn't get twenty yards, let alone to Venice. I tell you, these people are very, very spiky. Very, very organized.''

Kaufmann stared at the brightening sky, his mind evaluating and estimating, and, eventually, accepting the unacceptable. ''Then there's nothing left but for me to go to the house with you and improvise. Bluff my way through a confrontation, play for a chance to get your film, and then get somebody to bring me back to my jeep.''

Anton's voice carried the sound of his gathering despair. ''God. It'll never work. Never.''

''Do you have any other ideas?''

''I was afraid you would ask me that.''

''So, Herr Hauptmann Thoma, drive on.''

The house was a marvelous piece of architecture, with splashing fountains and atriums and slants of tile roofing and Spanish-style arches and ambulatories. The war had brought poverty and dilapidation to most of Italy, but here the plantings were lush, the entrance tiles gleamed, the windows sparkled, and the carved eave brackets and outside staircase trim were of rich, dark oak.

Anton parked the sedan in the driveway circle and muttered, ''All right. It's go for broke. Follow me.''

They hurried up some slate steps, then along a portico of delicate arches and into an atrium with still another fountain and piles of greenery. Through a bank of French doors and across a foyer and into a living room in which parchment-shaded lamps glowed and flames flickered politely in a huge stone fireplace and where a large man in a major general's uniform stood, coffee at the sip, orating briskly to three men and a woman.

Where Kaufmann came to a sudden halt and said, "Oh-oh."

Where Anton, instantly aware that something was amiss, nonetheless snapped to a sharp Wehrmacht attention and announced in German officialese, "General Bascomb, sir, this man says he's a physician from UNRRA and is here to consult with us."

Where Karla Wintgens, sitting deep in the divan's cushions and allowing her surprise to show, translated rapidly in professional reflex.

Where a colonel and a captain, staring quizzically, seemed to be frozen in their chairs.

Where the orator proved to be an unholy trinity, a tin god in three persons: General Bascomb, Corporal Ransky and—as Kaufmann's shock-stunned mind told him he should have known all along—Louis Stahl.

And, even worse, where Special Agent Vince Ludwig leaned against the mantel, smoking a cigarette and drawling, "Well, now. Look who's here."

38

He had overslept.

The night had been a heavy one, with a little too much Scotch and a rather astonishing performance on the living room couch. While she had provided little information, the original need, Benet's prowess as a nymph had worked a miraculous transformation in his self-esteem, which had sagged heavily in the years since the divorce. His ex-wife's departing gesture had been a sneering laugh and a curled forefinger, and, since his body had corroborated her taunt, he forged on with living the celibate life of a declining, aging, and ugly man whose blind preoccupation had become the exercise of his professional skills—a total absorption in the intellectual *hut, twup, three* of air-force level management, supplemented by frequent physical workouts in the sky, kicking the hell out of some airplane of the moment. But in the quiet isolation of the night, he'd confronted the fact of his loneliness and unattractiveness and incompleteness, and he would stare into the gloom, hating himself and the prison built by the passing years. Benet, though, would accept none of this, and she'd actually pulled off his pants to prove how wrong he was. Even now—lying beside her in the morning twilight, considering her face, soft and rosy against the dusky pillow, cheerily lusty even in sleep—he wanted to laugh at the memory of that first merry combat. He knew that she was more clever than she let on, and he suspected she talked too much, too often, to nourish the dumb-broad fiction men had built around her as protection from the threat of her incredible physicality. A paragon she wasn't. She lived only for the moment, and there were times when she was a monumental pain in the ass. But so was he, damn it. And despite that, she liked him. She was the first woman ever to like him, not only for what he was but also for what he was not. Most important of all, she had completed him, given him back his manhood, and for all of these reasons he was grateful beyond words.

He even gave her a little peck on the nose before answering the phone, which had begun to fill the room with a ragged clanging.

"General Vickery."

"Boyd, of Communications Surveillance, sir. I tried your office, but the duty desk said you hadn't come in yet, and—"

"Obviously I haven't come in yet, for crissake. What's on your mind?"

"You asked to be advised if our tap on Olsen picked up anything offbeat or significant."

"I know what I asked, goddammit. Get to the point."

"At seventeen-thirty-three hours yesterday, there was a long-distance call from Udine to Frankfurt. It was an UNRRA physician name of George Coburn calling Dr. Olsen. Coburn said everything was all right, he was onto something big, and would be checking back as soon as he had more info. Olsen then called your office, but since you weren't in then, either, he left a message for you to call him."

"You woke me up for *that*?"

"Not exactly, sir. It's simply part of some phone activity out of the northern Italy area that bears on the Aktion Achtung thing. It's the call we recorded a short time ago—oh-five-thirty-eight, to be exact—that we think you really ought to know about. 'Licorice' put in a call to your Hotdog line, but since you weren't there, left a message in the recorder."

"What was the message, for crissake?"

"That the raid will definitely take place on Tuesday."

Vickery took a moment to think. Then: "Were those 'Licorice's' actual words—'the raid will definitely take place on Tuesday'?"

"There was some garble, sir. But here are the actual audible words: 'and it's now definite that the raid will be made Tuesday, two October forty-five. ETA'—then more garble—and 'Out.' End of message."

"Anything else?"

"No, sir. That's it for now."

"Thanks, Boyd. Nice work. Alert Grover and the boys at Fürstenfeldbruck and keep me posted." He rang off and turned to reach for his robe.

"What was all that about?" She sat up, rubbing her eyes.

"Cover up those knockers."

"Why?"

"I've got to go to work. Those things are guaranteed to keep me from going to work."

She laughed and swung out of the bed. "Last one in the shower's a dumbbell."

"I mean it, baby. I got a real heavy thing breaking around my ears."

"So you want a shower, don't you? So do I. So get your heinie in there."

A good commander makes his own reconnaissance, Vickery assured himself, knowing, even as he did, that he was rationalizing his use of the headquarters P-51. It was really unnecessary that he take a look at the Udine sector; he'd already made three flights over the area and had first-hand knowledge of the conditions there. But (he rationalized) tomorrow's action would be hectic, and a last-minute look at the scene could provide him with an edge. To further this justification, he had instructed that the airplane be fully armed so that he could update his aerial gunnery qualification while overflying the range at Landsberg on the return leg.

He was airborne at 08:13 hours, landing gear tucked in, engine throbbing, propeller thrashing in huge arcs that glinted in the hazy sunlight, climbing under reduced throttle at an even, fuel-conserving 170 mph, the vague blue wall of the Alps already visible as Heidelberg, then Stuttgart, appeared briefly in the morning mists thousands of feet below. A gentle movement of his boots, and the rudder adjusted the course, just so, and as he cleared Augsburg, with Munich a great smudge just to the left of the nose, he ID'd himself with Fürstenfeldbruck Control, then flicked his radio to the universal frequency and listened with amusement to the chatter amongst a flight of Thunderbolts that was off on a gunnery run and couldn't seem to find the target area. By the time he cleared Kufstein, the Austrian Alps and their snowy snags lay below a filmy blue sky, and the descending reaches of the Friuli, his recon target area, were a hundred miles dead ahead.

God, but it was great to be alive.

Who's an old man, eh?

39

Corporal-General-Tycoon Ransky-Bascomb-Stahl was now flashy in the pinks and greens of the American cavalry officer's Class A uniform. A government-issue Eric von Stroheim, less the riding crop and monocle, with whipcord riding pants and mirror-like boots and a looming presence. He stood silently for a time, his watery brown eyes considering Kaufmann gravely. When he spoke, it was without heat.

"You are a wily fellow, Major Kaufmann. You have cost me a lot of time and money."

"One does what one can."

Oddly, Kaufmann found himself to be more irritated than anxious. He should have recognized Ransky as Stahl from the first. He had been trained to de-beard or en-beard subjects, to imagine them fat or lean or with eye-color changes or with wooden legs or skirts instead of pants, and it was an embarrassment to discover that he had let this one get by. The only mitigation was Stahl's enduring anonymity—the scarcity of photos, the reclusive life, the walls of goons that made him virtually faceless. Slight additional solace lay in the fact that he had been uneasy about Ransky from the first, the fact that he'd sensed something discordant there.

Stahl glanced at Ludwig. " 'Seed,' take this man to the meat locker and shoot him."

He turned, and, with a summoning wave of the hand to the others, strode from the room, his shiny boots clacking on the hardwood floor. As he trailed the group, Anton managed to sneak a look back and show a brief grimace of surprised chagrin, accompanied by a hunch of his shoulders and a sly spreading of his hands.

When he was alone with Ludwig, Kaufmann said, "I don't suppose you'd let me make a break. For old times' sake."

Ludwig drew a pistol from his shoulder holster and waved it toward the doorway. "No, I don't think so. Stahl's a hard-ass. I've got to stay on his good side. Business is business."

As they crossed the foyer, Kaufmann said, "I've seen them all, Vince: idiots who euphemize their crimes as Robin Hood altruism; pigs who root around in other people's purses and bedrooms; and plain old dirty pricks who slip it to unsuspecting decent people just for the thrilling hell of it. Which are you?"

"You left out boredom, pal."

"Boredom?"

"I ran out of war. So I help make another one."

"Jesus."

"I could give you some psychological reasons, some philosophy, if it'd make you feel better."

"Don't bother."

"So. Here we are."

The meat locker was a mere shed with cold storage rooms and a straw-littered floor, three processing tables and some hooks and chains looped over the wall hangers. It was otherwise empty, and its clamminess was redolent of ancient bleeding and dying. It was a sad, foul place, and the gloom seemed to reach Ludwig, too.

"So long, pal," Ludwig said, his voice low.

Kaufmann heard the clicking of the safety catch on Ludwig's pistol, and in the animal reflex of self-preservation, he turned, unthinkingly holding up his hands as if to ward off the coming bullet.

In the kind of distortion brought on by fever, Kaufmann saw the pistol's barrel centering on his chest, and then, a perception of the reality: he had run out his string. Until this moment, even in war and its misery and fear, time had seemed unlimited; life, for all its tenuousness, had promised long years ahead in which lurked vaguely perceived but inevitable glories. A pretty mate, in a pretty house on a pretty hill, and maybe even some pretty kids; a great job with great pay; a shiny car; rosy dawns and soft twilights filled with friends to see and things to do and good things to eat and places to go. Death was an abstraction that always involved others, the more vulnerable ones. He, though, would go on and on, forever and ever, world without end.

Until now.

Oddly, there had been fear, but now, in this splinter of time, there was none.

Only a rising curiosity. An expectancy.

He actually heard the shot. He had thought he wouldn't. But there was the sound—a flat snapping, like the clap of hands.

And Vince Ludwig sagged to the floor. Turning slowly, a look of profound surprise and disappointment on his warping features.

From the doorway, she said, "Are you all right?"

"Karla?"

"Just in time, as usual."

"Will you marry me?"

She smiled. "I'm not the marrying kind."

"I absolutely adore you."

She took his elbow and directed him to a corner out of sight of the doorway. "No you don't. You're just glad to be alive."

"The last I heard you were in Dijon, waiting for a State-side boat. I almost fell over when Anton mentioned your name this morning. Then when I saw you—"

"Take your clothes off." She glanced out a slit-like window.

"What?"

"Stahl thinks you're dead by now. He also thinks that Ludwig is still alive. So we dress you up like 'Seed.' It might give us an edge."

"No kidding, Karla"—he began pulling off his uniform—"what are you doing here? And how did you get here?"

She knelt and tugged at Ludwig's boots. "No big deal. I was waiting to be ZI'd, doing odd jobs for Donnelly. Stahl showed up one day with that pilot fish of his, Dreher. Presenting himself as Major General Bascomb of the War Crimes Commission Investigation Section and flashing corroborating orders. He got Donnelly's permission to interrogate certain Luftwaffe personnel in the Chaumont cage. I was assigned as Stahl's interpreter, and while I was helping him and Dreher sort out the heavy-duty Nazis, you contacted Donnelly, telling him how you wanted to penetrate the Luftwaffe cage with Anton, AKA Thoma, to see what the hell was really going on there. Donnelly, who by then had his own suspicions, had checked War Crimes and discovered that no General Bascomb was working there. So he authorized Colonel Lawrence and me to make your insert."

She handed him Ludwig's pants. "During aviation training, bad blood developed between Lawrence and Anton, threatening the whole shaky business. But then we got a break: Stahl turned out to have the hots for me, and I was able, on my own, to convince him that Anton was the cat's ass, Nazi-wise. Since I was about to be ZI'd, Stahl asked me to take my discharge and come along with him as a civilian playmate. Donnelly authorized this, because going along with Stahl looked like a good way for me to keep on top of things." She laughed in that faint, hissing way of hers and made a joke. "Trouble is, that bastard Stahl always wants to be on top. His tonnage is killing me. And his constant hovering has made it impossible for me to radio Donnelly for two weeks.''

"I really owe you, Karla."

"Hey, don't give me that crap. I've owed you ever since you pulled me out of that fire in Rheims. So we're even."

He hugged himself and danced a little jig. "Look at me. I'm shivering. Like a wet dog. I can't stop shivering."

"You had a close one. Me, I pee my pants when I've had a close one."

Kaufmann's trembling intensified as he examined Ludwig's jacket. The shot had made a clean entry, so the blood, while heavily staining the lining, was not evident on the outside. "What are Stahl's plans?"

She grasped Ludwig's partly clad body under the arms and dragged it to an open locker. "Here. Give me a hand. Help me get him inside."

Once the insulated door was closed, they stood erect and stared at each other.

"Are you all right, Kaufmann?"

"Sure."

"Well, button up and get the hell out of here. I'll cover for you as long as I can."

"You're a hell of a warrior, Karla."

"You bet."

"If you get a chance, tell Anton to meet me in the hangar. I'll be hiding there until the plane leaves."

"All right. But watch yourself."

"What will you do if Stahl wants to see Ludwig before he leaves?"

She shrugged. "I'll think of something. I always do."

She gave him a wink, then ducked out the door.

40

Anton, deeply dejected after having heard the shot in the meat locker, was striving to concentrate on his pre-flight walk-around of the B-17, which was parked in the wan sunlight before the open hangar doors. When Karla sidled up, he considered her with eyes that showed hurt and indifference.

"I've got news for you," she said softly in English.

"Wie bitte?"

"Kaufmann's in the hangar. He wants to talk."

Anton froze, his expression a contradiction of delight and reproval. "Bist du *verrückt* geworden? Um Gottes willen, Liebling—auf *deutsch*!"

"Oh, come off it, Anton," she muttered impatiently. "I know who you are. I've known all along."

He gaped.

"We don't have time for games, pal. I know you're an American flier Kaufmann sent to Dijon to penetrate this crazy business. It's been my job to help you along the way. And don't just stand there with your mouth open—keep moving. Inspect the goddamn airplane. The others are packing their gear, but they might be watching.''

"Are you serious? You're an *American*?"

"We've got a problem."

"You're telling *me*?"

"I mean, Kaufmann's hiding behind the empty drums in the hangar. We've got to invent a logical reason for you to spend a few minutes with him."

Anton ran a hand along the rudder's trailing edge, pretending to inspect the trim tab. "So he wasn't shot by that creep, 'Seed'?"

"That shot was mine. 'Seed' bought it, not Kaufmann."

"You're right. That is news. Good news. But then, it's bad news, too. How the hell are we going to explain the obvious disagreement in bodies?"

"That's partly what Kaufmann wants to talk to us about."

"Us?"

"You. Me. We and Kaufmann have got to figure a way to put a cork in Stahl's bung."

"Stahl? What's a Stahl?"

"General Bascomb, you ass. Haven't you guessed?"

Anton tapped a knuckle against an elevator hinge. "Mama mia. Life gets more complicated by the minute."

"Switch to German. Here come Stahl and Dreher."

"Is the airplane ready?" Stahl called, his eyes squinted against the glare.

Karla translated.

"Yes, sir," Anton said. "Just about. I suggest, though, that things could be speeded up a bit if Colonel Dreher were to take the copilot's seat and run the pre-flight cockpit check. And I'd like to take a final look around the hangar and its tool room, to be sure we haven't left behind anything we'll need on the show tomorrow."

Stahl listened to Karla, then said, "In a moment. First I want to go over some things with you and the others." He swung an arm, motioning assembly under the plane's wing.

* * *

The great estate, with its impending closure, seemed suddenly forlorn in the windless morning, its windows vacant, its gardens devoid of sound or movement. The outbuildings, too, were shuttered and still, and the hangar, that monstrous shed in the lee of a hill, echoed Stahl, who spoke in the broad shadow of the B-17. He was bundled in an airman's coveralls and boots, and he spoke to Anton, Dreher, Karla and a tech sergeant who, Kaufmann assumed, was Brenner, the plane's engineer and crew chief, as if delivering parade-ground pronouncements. Anton's concern over the foul conditions forecast for the Ukraine by mid-week was argued into silence by Stahl, who said that after coming this far he was not about to have Aktion Achtung disrupted in any way by a few clouds and snow showers.

Kaufmann had listened in on all of this from the building's dimmest corner, his body still shaken by spasms of chill. In his lonely waiting the irony was especially keen: Ludwig had gone on to the greatest of all immaterialities, and the most significant traces of his having existed in substance were a holed jacket and the trembling he had bequeathed another man.

Stahl paused in his oration to look around. "Where is 'Seed'?"

Karla improvised. "He's in that outhouse behind the meat locker. He says he has a bad case of the runs."

Stahl nodded at the crew chief. "Brenner, go get him."

Karla told Brenner, "I wouldn't get too close to him, if I were you. He looks as sick as a dog. Dysentery, I think."

Brenner hesitated, looking at Stahl diffidently.

Stahl, annoyed, snapped, "I don't give a damn what he's sick of. I don't want him lurking. It makes me uneasy when people lurk, and he's a lurker. I haven't trusted him since the moment I laid eyes on him. I want him to come out here and listen to what I have to say." He took a deep breath, then added in a kind of massive non sequitur, "This thing has been in process since last July, with every waking minute of great numbers of people having been given to the planning and preparation of this goddamn epochal event, and great sums of money have been spent, and huge amounts of effort have been brought to bear on what will, in the final analysis, resolve the great struggle between the pivotal political philosophies of the ages, and I absolutely refuse to let weather or dysentery or earthquakes or lurkers or typhoons or anything else keep us from dropping bombs on Soviet territory tomorrow at noon because it's imperative that there be bombs dropped and that explosions be felt by the Russian people with all there is at stake and all the trouble we've gone to in gathering together so many American planes. And that, by God, is that.''

''Well,'' Karla parried, maneuvering for a delay, '' 'Seed's' condition could make things miserable for all of us.''

Stahl gave this a moment of thought. Then, seeming to have come to a decision, he glared at Anton. ''You and Brenner do what you must in the hangar. Fräulein Wintgens will make herself comfortable on the plane. Dreher, see to the cockpit checklist.''

Karla translated.

''Meanwhile,'' Stahl said, ''I'm going to take a moment to look up that idiot 'Seed.' ''

Damn.

Kaufmann arose from his crouch to watch through the hangar windows as Stahl marched around the building and went down the lane to the clump of structures dominated by the meat locker. His heart sank when Stahl halted behind the wooden privy, drew his U.S. Army .45 from its polished holster and fired three shots through the thin planks of the rear wall. Riveted by the tableau, he saw Stahl move around to the front of the little building, where he reholstered the pistol and yanked open the door.

Stahl stood, stiff with sudden anger, staring into the gloom of the shed. He turned, then, to face Karla, Anton and Brenner, who had come running at the sound of shots.

''He's not here,'' Stahl barked. ''Where did he go?''

''Well, I—'' Karla feigned confusion. ''He said he was going to be here—''

"Find him! Find him at once! I don't trust that man as far as I can spit. Find him and bring him to me!"

"What's going on?" Dreher came dashing down the lane.

" 'Seed' is missing. I want to find him. I want to ask that shifty son of a bitch some questions. You people find him and bring him to the meat locker. I'll be down there, making sure that other bastard, Kaufmann, is really dead."

Damn.

Kaufmann, sensing the mad racing of events beyond control, scurried to the hangar's rear door and cut through the small grove and over the stone wall, eventually achieving a full run for the locker. In his dash, legs pumping, chest heaving, his mind went aberrantly to that sergeant he'd had in basic training—the one who advised solemnly, "If you want to take your enemy by surprise, show up unexpected."

Which is what he did, in a manner of speaking. Only it was moot as to who was the more surprised.

He had just entered the locker's back door when Stahl came through the front door, and they stood at the room's opposite ends, staring at each other, wide-eyed, unmoving.

Stahl broke the spell. "You're not dead," he rasped, clawing for his pistol.

Kaufmann raced forward, vaulting one of the tables, careening the room's length, aware of Stahl's pistol glinting in the pale light, of the flash and contained thunder, of the passing bullet's heat on his cheek. They closed, and Kaufmann's momentum sent Stahl crashing backward into the whitewashed plaster. With his free right fist, Kaufmann managed a hard jab, and Stahl's head, snapping back, made a thudding sound against the wall. He went down, eyes glazing.

Kaufmann stooped, snatched up the pistol and, sensing movement in the front doorway, spun about. Brenner stood there, legs in a combat crouch, swinging a Colt from side to side as his eyes adjusted to the gloom.

"Drop it, Brenner!"

The man took a gamble and lost. He fired two quick shots, one of which tore Kaufmann's sleeve, and then he fell back into the sunlight when Kaufmann's return shot virtually lifted him off his feet.

Then Karla was at the door, shouting, "Hold it, Kaufmann—it's me!"

"Where the hell are the others—Dreher, Anton?"

"At the plane, I think. I came down here to help you. Everything's coming apart—"

"Secure Stahl with some of these cords here. I'm going to the plane. Anton may need a hand."

He did, too. Dreher, obviously alarmed by the shooting and confused as to its causes, had clambered out of the plane, to be met on the ground by Anton's roundhouse swing. Apparently Anton would have had more success if he'd tried to cold-cock a rhino. Dreher, tall, broad, solid, grasped Anton's jacket and, lifting, slammed him against the fuselage and was preparing to finish him off with a paratrooper boot knife.

"Drop it, you son of a bitch!" Kaufmann rasped, leveling his pistol.

Dreher pulled Anton close and pressed the blade against his throat. "I have a better idea, Kaufmann. You drop the gun."

Impasse followed, a momentary freezing of movement. And then a shot, that clapping sound in the dead air, from the hangar door, and Dreher dropped like a sack of meal—instantaneously, heavily—leaving Anton standing alone, looking oddly foolish.

"Jesus to *Jesus*, Karla," Anton complained, "that was one hell of a chance you took with that shot. It damned near parted my hair."

"Chance? What the hell do you mean, 'chance'? You want to see my handgun trophies?"

Kaufmann, shaken, breathless from shock and exertion, said, "All right, cut the crap. Karla, where's Stahl?"

"Like you said: trussed to the eyebrows."

"All right. Anton, you get aboard the plane and crank it up. Karla, you come and help me with Stahl."

"What are we going to do with him?"

"Put him on the airplane and deliver him to G-2 in Frankfurt, that's what. And on the way, we're going to destroy the planes at Lucia."

"Just a frigging minute," Anton said, holding up a hand. "We're going to have a problem with that."

"Why?"

"For one thing, we don't have bomb one on that airplane. And even if we did have bombs, we have no bombardier."

"I count at least a dozen machine guns."

"Who's going to be shooting all those guns? You? I'm supposed to singlehandedly turn a seventeen into a hedge-hopping fighter so's you can run from window to window like Tom Mix shooting Injuns from a stagecoach? Come on, buddy, get realistic."

"I'll be there to help out," Karla said.

"Come on, Karla," Anton snapped, "you may be an Annie Oakley on the handgun range, but we're talking airplanes."

"That's what *I'm* talking, dummy. I'm a pilot. I'll fill your right-hand seat."

"This is a four-engine bomber here, lady, not a rental Piper Cub. Besides—"

She threw out her hands in sudden exasperation. "I was flying multi-engine when you were slopping beer at a table down at Mory's where the Whiffenpoofs assemble. You think Amelia Earhart's the only woman who ever aviated?"

A moment in which Anton considered this interesting news. Then: "You're a pilot?"

"I'd show you my logbook, but I left it in my peignoir."

"You ever handle a seventeen?"

"No. But an airplane's an airplane. Give me a minute to look at the bells and whistles and I could solo the sumbish."

Anton gave her a lingering, thoughtful look. "You're a very interesting lady."

She glanced at Kaufmann. "What's the plan?"

"We stow Stahl on the plane, keep him lashed down. After take-off, we stay low. Lucia's only seventy miles away.

Keep low as we pass the airstrip. I can't handle the electronic turret, so you guys will have to circle the field so that I can pump away at it from the waist with one of the hand-operated 'fifties. My hope is to start some important aircraft and fuel fires.''

Anton sighed. ''I don't want to be a worrywart, but you realize, don't you, that while we're lazily circling Lucia so you can pot away at gas tanks, there are seventeen other planes on the ground—each loaded to the rafters—that are going to be potting away at us. Let alone whatever other flak guns they've set up there.''

''I admit it could be a little dangerous.'' Kaufmann glanced from one to the other. ''Anything else?''

After a moment, he said, ''War time, folks.''

41

Kaufmann came through the bomb bay hatch and crouched behind Karla's copilot seat.

"Do you know how to operate those waist guns back there, Kaufmann?" Anton asked over his right shoulder.

"If they're standard air-cooled Brownings, yes."

"They're standard, except for the looping feed tracks from the ammo boxes."

"I'll figure it out."

"Be sure to have your headset on and plugged into the nearest intercom jack. We may want to converse. And watch for my oxygen signals. If we make it through your Hopalong Cassidy stagecoach shoot we'll have the Alps to go over, and the sky gets pretty thin up there. And we all can expect to freeze our buns off. These helmets and coveralls are okay at most altitudes, but if we have to go way up, teeth will chatter."

"I've ridden in these things before."

"So you know about the cheap-pack parachute. How to snap it on. How to bail out. That crap."

"That's my best trick."

"All right, then. Karla, baby, read me your list."

They flew low, never more than five hundred feet above the rushing land, and there were times when the airplane's shadow, flitting over fields and trees and upland rises and dales and tortured little streams and country lanes, seemed to be a sister craft, close below, never faltering, always there. Chatter on the intercom was infrequent, terse. The war had been reborn, undeniably present, no longer a huge and obscene abstraction, and the four thrumming engines, the thrashing propellers, like great awls boring into the stuff of the sky, were pulling them toward their objective at 14,000 feet per minute.

Karla was indeed a pilot, Anton noted. For her first time in a B-17, she exhibited impressive insights, a kind of second-sense knowledge of an unfamiliar machine which, because it worked on the principles governing so many other aerial machines, was in fact familiar. She gave full respect to his command responsibilities, confining her participation to supportive motions and observations—setting and releasing brakes on the runups; watching rpms, fuel and oil pressures, cylinder head temperatures, and manifold pressures; calling out "tailwheel locked, light out, gyros" and "generators" on the take-off run; and visually checking the right main gear after the wheels were up and tucked into their nacelles. She was just plain damned generally useful.

"You climb at twenty-three hundred rpm?" she asked once.

"Yep. At IAS of one-forty."

"What's the drill on feathering?"

"If we need to feather a prop, I'll handle it. But if for some reason you have to take over, just do what comes naturally: close the feathering switch whose number corresponds to the bad engine, turn off the turbo with that handle there, close the proper throttle, move the mixture control to idle-cutoff, close the fuel shut-off valve and turn off the booster pump. And then, when the prop has stopped turning, switch off the ignition."

"No big deal."

He glanced at her, smiling faintly. "Right. No big deal."

Kaufmann wandered the length of the ship, carrying the chest pack with him, because he had never been at home in airplanes and having a chute at hand made him feel as if he had one foot on the ground. It was oppressively cold in the waist area, thanks to the open hatches required by the flexible-mount, hand-operated guns there. He checked the loadings of these and took some trial swings with each, picking up the proper leads and deflections on chalets and barns and church towers that showed briefly in the rushing greens and purples below. Twice he looked in on Stahl, who sat at the radio operator's table, tight-lipped and glaring, his hands lashed together and affixed to a fuselage spacer.

It occurred to Kaufmann that Stahl might be dealing inwardly with a never before experienced perception of his own mortality—the realization that he, too, was vulnerable to loss or denial. Poor baby.

"What's our ETA, Anton?"

"With this headwind, I'd say about eleven minutes."

"Heads up, everybody," Karla said coolly. "Ten o'clock high. The Mustang. Generalmajor Oskar's out on his morning constitutional."

Anton, from his pilot's vantage, and Kaufmann, craning from the portside hatch, sought out the silvery shadow that flitted along the underside of a string of alto-cumulus dotting the northwest quadrant.

"What's your plan, Anton?"

"Plan? What means 'plan'? You expect me to dogfight this thing, maybe? Hell, man, all we can do is what we were going to do. Fly straight in and do some strafing—and hope for the best along the way."

"What's he doing now? I've lost him."

"He's peeled off and settling in on the starboard," Karla said in her businesslike way. "It looks as if he plans to come alongside and say hello."

"All right," Anton said. "Easy does it. Look natural. Karla, turn up your collar and get that helmet lower. I don't want him catching sight of your hair. And wave at the bastard.

He'll probably call in on this preset frequency. Let me do the talking.''

"Roger."

There was some crackling in the phones and then the Generalmajor's voice came in, booming. ". . . aren't you answering me? Turn on your radio . . ."

"Sorry, Herr Generalmajor. The radio seems to be a little testy this morning."

"You're running late. Where have you been?"

"Herr General Bascomb is indisposed. It could be dysentery." Anton winked at Karla.

"I'm sorry to hear that. Give him my felicitations."

"I'd invite him to chat with you, sir, but he's in, ah, considerable difficulty right now."

"I'll see him after we land. Out."

Oskar, a lump of leather in his plexiglas cocoon, returned Karla's wave. The Mustang lifted away in a climbing turn, its belly suggesting a dirty gray shark seeking the distant surface.

"Good," Anton said. "That'll hold him for a while. Everybody try to keep an eye on him, though. We should be raising Lucia in three minutes."

"Make your three-sixty turn to the port, Anton. The portside gun feels better to me."

"Roger. But our friend in the Mustang will come down on us like a ton of wet noodles as soon as you open up."

"We'll handle that when we get to it."

They flew without further comment. The sky had turned the color of lead, and Kaufmann thought he saw flurries off the port wing. The past month had been mostly chilly and damp over Western Europe, but real winter was at hand here in the high country. They were certain to suffer some damage in the coming do, and it would be tough enough, trying to take a wounded airplane across the Alps, without having to deal with a snowstorm in the bargain.

Well, first things first.

"There it is," Anton announced. "At ten o'clock."

Kaufmann peered over the port engines at the blue-gray terrain ahead. The Alps were hulking monsters, dim and bale-

ful in the pale swirling, but closer in, on a gently curved flat-
land between ridges, he could see what appeared to be acres
of crumpled tinfoil. Two buildings of moderate size were to
one side, and a structure that suggested a control tower. Leading away from this was a ragged strip of Alpine turf, a deep
green rut in the snow-dusted litter. The B-17's were invisible,
testimony to Stahl's money and Dreher's ingenuity.

"Where's Oskar?" Anton wanted to know.

"Five o'clock high," Karla reported.

"Is Stahl still secure, Kaufmann?"

"Yep. I just checked. He's madder than a hornet. But, if
you ask me, a good bit scared, too."

"Well, so am I. How about you? Are you ready?"

"As I'll ever be."

"All right. Beginning three-sixty to port in thirty seconds."

The left wing dropped and the landscape wheeled majesti-
cally. Kaufmann swung his gun into a lead on a suspiciously
large mound of metal adjacent to the makeshift tower.

"Take me lower, Anton."

"*Lower?* I'm rubbing our belly with edelweiss blooms
right now, for crissake."

"I want to be sure I hit something."

"Shee-it."

At what seemed to be the right moment, he thumbed the
triggers. The big machine gun startled him with its violent
jerking and slamming and thundering, its cascade of empty
cartridges rolling and bouncing on the floor at his feet. But
he kept his attention on the lead, and he could see tracers
arcing into his target area.

"*Pay dirt!*"

"Hot damn, lookee that. Nice *shot*, Kaufmann!"

Flames weltered high, and the tower teetered. Secondary
explosions erupted almost at once, tossing an obscene confetti, sending out rings of concussion and starbursts of ragged yellow fire, propelling a tremendous upward boiling of
oily black smoke. The tiny figures of men running. A truck
racing the flames, only to disappear in its own flaring. A

B-17, distorted and ablaze, rising from the core, rolling slowly, then falling back into the inferno.

Karla's voice was in the phones, calm. "Three o'clock high. Oskar's peeling off for a pass at us."

"All right," Anton said. "Let's head for the hills. Watch the board closely, Karla. I'm going to pour the coal on. We'll hedgehop, so Oskar can't get in any belly shots."

Kaufmann spun about and reached for the starboard gun. He was staring aloft, straining for a glimpse of the Mustang, when the B-17 was caught in a sudden sleet of machine-gun fire. He felt the plane tilt awkwardly, like a startled animal, as the topside fuselage metal turned to lace, chunks of wing skin erupted and spun away into the void, and dust and insulation swirled in the interior winds like some vile blizzard.

Despite his fright, Kaufmann returned to his portside gun, trying again for a sighting. But he saw the Mustang the way he made his first billion dollars.

"Where'd he go, for God's sake?"

"How the hell do we know? You're the one who's back there. We're just driving this miserable mother."

"Here he comes again. Nine o'clock low."

Kaufmann managed to catch the Mustang in a lovely deflection as it came full on, left wing high, all guns twinkling. His thumbs pressed hard on the trigger levers, but nothing happened.

"Goddammit to hell!"

"What's wrong, Kaufmann?"

"I think I've got a jam on the portside gun."

He threw himself on the starboard gun and managed to blast ten angry but ineffectual rounds at the Mustang's dwindling silhouette.

A sour-smelling smoke formed a haze in the bomb bay area, and there were what looked to be electrical flashes in the shadows there.

"Feathering number four engine," Anton said. "Karla, use the extinguisher if you have to."

"There's vapor around the cowling. Oil smears on the nacelle. But I don't see any fire."

"We got smoke back here," Kaufmann reported.

"Bad?"

"Electrical, I think."

"Use one of the hand extinguishers, if you can get at the fire."

"Not yet. Oskar's coming back."

He swung the starboard gun in an arc that put the proper lead on the shark hurtling in from the lower flank. He tore off a long burst, the gun leaping and jerking as its heavy bolt racketed back and forth, the yellow muzzle blast thumping and roaring.

"I think I scratched his fenders."

"You've got to do better than that."

"Number one engine dropping in rpm's," Karla reported. "All other readings still okay."

"Here he comes again. Seven o'clock high."

This pass took out a large piece of the vertical fin and turned the left horizontal stabilizer to junk. The smoke became thicker, more acrid; the sparks leaped farther and more vividly.

"Karla, do you think you can handle this locomotive for a minute or two? I'd better go into the topside turret and give Kaufmann a hand."

"Roger."

"Watch that number one engine. Feather it if you have to. But try not to. We need all the power we can get."

"Wilco."

Kaufmann turned to see what he could do about clearing the portside gun, only to be confronted by Louis Stahl, major general, né oil tycoon, who was coming at him in what was a lunge turned partly duck-waddle, thanks to the impossible footing created by the mounds of ammo casings that rolled and shifted across the floorboards.

"I'll kill you, you rotten bastard!" Stahl shouted, groping and heaving. His gloved hands—trailing remnants of the cord restraints that presumably had been cut against jagged, gun-shot fuselage metal—seized Kaufmann's sheepskin collar and hurled him around, and Kaufmann felt the hammering of a fist on the side of his head.

"Stahl's free!" he shouted into his mike. "He's all over me!"

"Hold on, I'm coming," Anton said tautly.

"Hurry! He's got me dangling out the goddamn window!"

He did, too. The small of Kaufmann's back was against the lower sill, his torso was bent backward over open sky, and Stahl, his face cranberry red and his eyes wide and glistening with bloodlust, held a paratroop knife aloft, ready for the plunge.

Generalmajor Oskar came to the rescue.

A spatter of machine-gun fire tore the length of the fuselage, and Stahl's head disappeared, to be replaced by a red fountain. The grip on Kaufmann's throat fell away, and what was left of Stahl collapsed into a shapeless bundle in the brassy gravel.

"Godamighty!" Kaufmann gagged with revulsion, falling to his knees, eyes watering, saliva running.

He felt a touch, and Anton was there, examining him anxiously.

"You hit, pal?"

"I'm all right! Get back to the goddamn turret!"

Kaufmann staggered to his feet and held onto the grips of the starboard gun, fighting for control and clear eyesight. As untrained as he was in the way of aircraft, he could tell that the B-17 was mortally wounded. This was confirmed by Karla's unruffled voice reporting that the machine was still receptive to aileron and rudder control, but the damaged fin and elevator were playing blue hell with lateral stability, with the tendency to yaw suggesting a readiness to fishtail, skid, and spin. Things weren't helped at all when, in a mist of glycol, the main landing gear dropped out of its wells—unlocked, dangling.

"Here comes Loverboy again. Five o'clock high."

"He's all yours, Anton."

"I can't move this fugg'n turret. The track has been torn and jammed."

"Can you get out?" Karla sounded anxious for the first time.

"Sure. Move over, baby. Daddy's home."

This time Oskar's burst crashed through the B-17's mid-section, blowing away a bomb bay door, tearing the starboard machine gun from its mount, holing and gashing the fuselage from wing root to fin. Something hit Kaufmann, picked him up, and spun him around, and slammed him against the forward bulkhead.

It was the bubble of flame and the spreading rings of concussion that first caught General Vickery's eye. Something very big with a lot of pizzazz had just let go, and it was a hair to the left of twelve o'clock—at the precise location of the Lucia salvage field. He slid the throttle to maximum open setting, charged his machine guns, lowered the goggles over his eyes, dropped the nose and streaked for the action.

He switched the radio to the emergency frequency that had been agreed upon all those weeks ago.

"White Fox One to Sweet Sue Leader. Do you read me? Over."

"White Fox One, this is Sweet Sue Leader. We read you, but where the hell are you? We don't see you. Over."

"About five miles north of Lucia. Descending toward fires there. Are you on station? Over."

"Friendly troops are moving in on Beanpot, as planned. We're a half hour ahead of schedule, because some kind of hell has broken out at Beanpot, and we're hopping ahead to exploit. The fires are bright, and there won't be any take-offs from Beanpot tomorrow. Or ever, you ask me. Over."

"Good show, Sweet Sue Leader. I'm coming down on the deck to see what's going on at Beanpot. This is White Fox One. Over, and out to lunch."

What was going on at Beanpot was something remarkable to behold, General Vickery discovered. About twenty acres of seething flame and minor explosions. And, stag-

gering away from the mess, a B-17 that was being gnawed
to death by a P-51.

He rolled over into a steep spiral, bringing his machine
to the level just off the port wing of the other fighter plane.
He switched the r/t to the universal interplane emergency
frequency and pressed the button. "Hi, buddy. Why are you
so mad at our fat friend there?"

"Hey, new little friend, this is your fat friend. That sumbish is trying to kill us."

"Why would he want to do that?"

"He's a German."

"You're joking. Right?"

"Nope. Honest Injun."

"How do I know you're not the German in this little mix?"

"Look, you dumb son of a bitch, who's doing the conversing—him or us? If he's the good guy, why isn't he telling you so?"

"Anything to say to that, little friend?"

The other Mustang had begun a quick turn, and Vickery
saw the white-hot blobs of tracer bullets arcing past his canopy and heard the dry-stick cracking of their passage.

"Boy. You got a lot to say, ain't you."

He kicked rudder and eased the throttle against the stop
and went into a whistling break. The other machine followed closely, but not close enough, and, tightening his
turn, Vickery completed the break and was in the clear.

"Now, you bastard," Vickery rasped into his open mike,
"you're up against Willie Vickery, the best fugg'n fighter pilot
in the U.S. of A. I shot the ass off your uncle at Chateau-
Thierry, and now I'm going to shoot your ass off, too."

The other Mustang went into a screaming Immelmann
turn, clawing for the open sky, but Vickery tapped a bit of
rubber and fingered a bit of stick and created the perfect
deflection shot.

"Whee-hoooo."

His airplane trembled from the combined racketing of its
six heavy machine guns, and the air ahead was a storm of
tracers converging on the twisting silver dart.

"Ah, ha-a-a-a-a!"

The target rolled, belly to the sky, then broke into three pieces, which quickly degenerated into a scattering of smaller pieces, each a source of brilliant flame and roiling smoke.

"Weeeee! Fourth of July!"

The wreckage tumbled down the sky to disappear into the smoke and flame that swept the great plateau.

Vickery eased back on the throttle and brought his plane around to a gentle, curving climb for altitude. He realized he was grinning from ear to ear when he took a fresh cigar from his flight jacket pocket and, pushing his mask aside, shoved it into his teeth. He pulled alongside the B-17, examining the damage.

"Hey, fat friend. You got a hell of a case of acne."

"It could've been worse, little friend. Much obliged."

"Where you headed, fat friend?"

"Straight down, I'm afraid. We were headed for Frankfurt, but we'll be lucky if we can make it to that farm over there by the ridge."

"Your gear's bent all to hell, you know that?"

"Yep. I don't plan to land. I plan a bail-out over the big meadow."

"How many you got aboard?"

"Three of us good guys, one of whom's been banged around a bit, but he's okay. Plus a very dead bad guy. The German dude gave his pal a real short haircut."

"I don't pretend to understand what the hell you're talking about. But I'll send some folks your way. We got troops moving in on that bonfire down there."

There followed an interval of silence as Vickery lifted up and around for a better view of the farm.

Karla's haughty Westchester voice broke the radio hush: "Tell me, Willie. Are you really the best fugg'n fighter pilot in the U.S. of A.?"

"I don't know who you are or how you got aboard that there flying machine, lady, but you can bet your sweet patoot I am."

THURSDAY
4 October 1945

42

G-2 sat at his customary place at the head of the long conference table, backstopped by situation maps and flanked by flags and looking serenely in charge of everything between Frankfurt and the rings of Saturn. Here was where all the ends came together—the cables and dispatches and memos and TWXs from Washington and London and Moscow and Tokyo and Sydney and Hossesoss, Utah; the jeeps and motorcycles and Cadillacs and planes bearing the tinseled couriers of Pentagonia and the Brooks Brothers soldiers of Foggy Bottom; the anonymous angleshooters and grifters and tinhorns inhabiting the secondary informant chains of varsity espionage teams everywhere on Earth. And G-2, a crisp, mild-mannered West Pointer with stars and spangles and ribbons from waist to eyebrows, occupied the center of the web and noshed hourly on predigested tidbits from the world's grubby chicaneries. This man knew more than anybody—period—but it didn't seem to do much by way of dramatic deification; he was unattended by heavenly choirs and had his buns on the chair like everybody else in the room.

Which had always rather reassured Kaufmann, chronically fretful as he was over his own chronic mundaneness.

G-2 cleared his Establishment throat and drawled, "I rejoice over Major Kaufmann's return from the dead. How are things on the other side, Major? Is the Boss well?"

There was a moment for the obligatory polite titterings, during which Kaufmann was aware of all the amused glances. He went along with the current. "He sends His greetings, sir. Although He's still considerably miffed over that affair in Eden."

"I dare say. He'll have to agree, though, that it has gainfully employed a bunch of preachers over the years."

The laughter concluded, G-2's gaze moved to the opposite end of the table. "We welcome Mr. C. G. Brandt, the President's special counsel on European Affairs, who has been visiting Generals Eisenhower and Clay this past week and has expressed an interest in our session this morning. Mr. Brandt, do you have anything you'd like to bring up before we get under way?"

The man in the severe suit smiled dimly and shook his head. "No, thank you, General. I'm simply here as a visiting fireman. President Truman, while he's been extensively informed by your cables, is curious about some of the, ah, local details of this brouhaha. And I appreciate your accommodating me this way."

Protocol thus attended to, G-2's cool stare moved to his right front. "General Vickery, you've carried the lion's share of this commotion. Would you mind filling in Mr. Brandt? Summarizing to date?"

"Glad to, General." Vickery pretended to look at some papers in his attaché case—it was always good form to consult papers in a thing like this, even when everybody from Ike to the handyman knew that you seldom read anything more complicated than a phone book—and turned his yellow pencil so that it lay neatly parallel to the band of his airman's chronometer, which he had removed from his wrist and placed on the polished mahogany table because it looked urgent and businesslike.

"This past August, right after the Potsdam conference, there were some simultaneous events that sort of bothered me. One was the nutty, almost panicky demobilization of our forces here in Europe, with the remains of our air forces sitting on the ground and all of our ground forces—what was left of them—sitting on their duffs. Second were the reports of Soviet troop realignments that looked a hell of a lot like regrouping, restaging, for a push west. And the third was the very mysterious disappearance of some of our B-17's from 8th and 15th Air Force inventories. I kicked some butts and raised a little hell about this last part, and, sure enough, checking and rechecking showed about eighteen aircraft serial numbers unaccounted for. I reported this to Washington, and to G-2 here, and G-2, thank God, shared my curiosity about this and put some people on it, namely Mr. Ballentine, there to your right, who, as a key man in OSS, Bern, has a very fine rapport with Soviet dissidents and various Eastern intelligence types. He and another OSS agent, Major Bianco, assisted by Special Agent Fallon, of the Criminal Investigation Division, began an investigation of reports that some of these planes and their parts—as well as some Air Force ordnance—were showing up in the Udine district of Italy, where Communist partisans were particularly active against our attempts to help the Eye-talians establish orderly, working local governments.

"Meanwhile, G-2 here was getting in a lot of material that suggested agitation by West European Communist Party cells for a Red Army representation in their local peace-keeping forces, and so the pattern began to show: a Stalin ambition to move in on us and the Brits and the Frogs. G-2 told me that you guys in Washington shared our concern and that you saw a linkage between the stolen planes and Stalin's ambitions, and to launch a systematic probe of the airplane angle you sent in a special investigator, Margaret Sunderman, who, under cover as an Air Force records noncom, began a formal audit. She got too successful, I guess, because she got knocked off, as did Major Bianco. And—"

Brandt held up a finger. "Excuse me, General Vickery. May I ask a question?"

"Sure thing."

"Mr. Ballentine, did you and Allen Dulles, your other people in Bern, see a link between General Vickery's concerns and the Sunrise thing—SS General Wolff's attempt to surrender to us last spring?"

Ballentine shifted his bulk, making his chair squeak. "Absolutely, sir. When Allen was withdrawn as an active Bern participant, I was put in charge, and my first move was to contact some of my Communist sources—Luigi Fortunato, the filmmaker, others—and they confirmed that Stalin was still in a huge snit over the Sunrise thing and was determined to show President Truman that American waverings of this kind would be severely punished. They also revealed that we had some rotten apples in our own ranks who, for money, sex, other motives, were participating in the theft of material from our armed forces—stuff that was being fed to unidentified recipients in the Udine-Friuli area."

"Rotten apples?"

Vickery broke in. "Sunderman picked up on a CIC agent, name of Ludwig, who seemed to be in some kind of heavy traffic with the Soviets regarding this airplane thing. That was getting a bit close to G-2's home, so, with the okay of 'Top Dog'—President Truman himself—he assigned me, as 'Gladiator,' Frankfurt, to take charge. G-2 felt if he and his staff were to pursue the thing, Ludwig would most certainly have a way to tap in, so it was best to throw up a screen—make it look as if G-2's special assistant, Colonel Donleavy there, was investigating—while the real probe was being led out of my office, the most unlikely of places."

Brandt nodded. "I see. So this Ludwig fellow was the master conspirator?"

"No, sir. He was the, ah, master conspirator's right-hand man. We saw this early on. It takes an enormous amount of money to finance the assembly, staffing and operation of a bomber squadron, and Ludwig simply didn't have this kind of muscle—neither the money nor the clout that could divert aircraft and ordnance to the black market. Which meant he had to have very muscular help.

"Our leads finally led us to Louis Stahl, who, as you know, was one of the world's richest men and renowned as a gentleman adventurer. Unfortunately, Stahl was very low profile, a man who few people had ever seen or associated with on a regular basis, a man who abhorred publicity and made a thing about keeping his picture out of the newspapers and magazines. He was also quick to jump around, was a very aggressive risk-taker, and had no qualms about physical violence. All of which meant that, while we knew he was involved, we could never put our eyes or hands on him. Slipperiest goddam eel there ever was.

"It took our loose cannon, Major Kaufmann here, to chase the bastard down."

Again all gazes turned toward Kaufmann, a condition that made him uneasy, having confirmed within the context of this meeting that he'd become a key player in one of the most delicate games known to military science.

"How did you do that, Major?" Brandt asked coolly.

"Well," Kaufmann said carefully, "I called in a few markers from the shady side, I exploited a botched assassination to play dead and go underground, and with the help of some friends, I finally got a line on Stahl and his financing of an aerial effort out of his estate in the Udine. Pretty routine, all in all."

"And what, precisely, was his plan?"

"To trigger a major war between the East and West by sending Nazi soldiers in a token attack on a token Soviet town. To assure, once and for all and at a time favoring an American victory, the world dominance of the free-enterprise system over Communism and all other political-economic philosophies in the centuries ahead. He was the most dangerous of men: an egomaniac with billions."

Brandt glanced at Colonel Donleavy. "And you, Colonel, had to play both ends against the middle, as I understand it. G-2 says you had one of the most onerous tasks of all."

Donleavy, pleased, cleared his throat and beamed his

Roosevelt beam. "Well, sir, I wouldn't put it so strongly, but, yes, it was difficult in that I was compelled more or less to pretend to be the somewhat bumbling head of an investigation that was in fact being led with skill and vigor by somebody else—General Vickery. I was privy to much of what was going on, of course, but my main job was to pretend, as a means of misleading Stahl and his confederates within our military structure, that I was getting nowhere with my investigation. As you know, a career military officer is most uncomfortable with anything that might, even in the slightest way, make him seem to be inept, and this was the kind of shirt I was wearing. I hope, frankly, it's the last time I'm called on to perform such a duty."

"Did you know who made up General Vickery's team? Tom Ballentine, codename 'Chocolate,' Detective Fallon, codename 'Mint,' Karla Wintgens, codename 'Licorice'? That General Vickery had already tumbled to the Udine connection and had surrounded the Germans' Lucia launching base with U.S. paratroopers—ready to move in whenever the Germans trundled out their hidden B-17's and prepared to leave for Russia?"

Donleavy chuckled and shook his handsome head. "No, sir, I did not. G-2 explained to me at the outset that it would be best if I were to be kept in the dark on specifics. I might have unwittingly compromised one or all of them."

Brandt nodded. "Well, I'm sure we all appreciate your sacrifice, Colonel. 'They also serve,' eh?"

"That's right, sir. And I thank you."

"You might be interested to know, Major Kaufmann," Brandt said, "that 'Top Dog' got a special kick out of you and your dogged inventiveness."

G-2 smiled his correct smile. "What do you say to that, Major Kaufmann?"

Kaufmann gave Brandt a direct, confessional stare, the look of a man who can no longer rationalize his own stupidities. "I thought I was all alone in my suspicions. Actually, I was just sort of a hind-end Charlie in a great big crowd of hotshots, all led by General Vickery, who were running down the same alley. And, in my ignorance, I was suspecting all the wrong people. For instance, I was sure that General Vickery was a real horse's patoot, maybe selling planes to buy those fancy girlfriends of his—"

Vickery interrupted. "Hey, Kaufmann, have a heart. I got only one fancy girlfriend."

Everybody chuckled, and then it escalated into laughter when G-2 said, "That's one more than I have, you rascal."

"And I thought Mr. Ballentine was in cahoots with the Soviets when I saw him associating with Luigi Fortunato and another left-wing hood. I didn't realize he was pumping them. And I was sure of his complicity in whatever was going on when I was kidnapped and damned near killed by a couple of professional hitmen—actually hired by Ludwig—after leaving an interview with him. To get even with him, I stole his car and sold it on the black market."

"So it was you who did that," Ballentine huffed, feigning indignation. "That was my very favorite car."

"I understand you bought it back. From the guy you stole it from in the first place."

More laughter.

G-2 said, "We'll be clarifying details on this thing for some time to come, of course. But for now, unless there are other questions, I think we might adjourn."

General Vickery suggested, "I think all this calls for a drink at the Casino."

Ballentine said, "I've got a better idea. Let's all go to Kronberg. They've just received a shipment of tom turkeys and mince pies."

Brandt stood up. "President Truman has asked me to extend to all of you his personal thanks for smashing what amounts to the last serious Nazi threat of World War Two. If Stahl and his cohorts had been successful, the legacy of Sunrise—the ostensible effort to end World War Two—would have been World War Three. The president says all Americans owe you a profound thank you."

G-2 nodded his acknowledgment. "Won't you join us for a bit of refreshment, Mr. Brandt?"

"I wish I could. But my master calls."

There followed a lot of chair-scraping, hand-shaking and generalized gabble. As Kaufmann headed for the door, Brandt turned from the group and touched his elbow.

"Excuse me, Major. I wonder if you'd give me another minute or two. Privately."

TOP SECRET
Your Eyes Only!

File No: 56879b   4 October 1945

To: Top Dog
From: Brandt

Subject: Operation "Tailspin"

1. Subject operation has been completed and files pertaining to it (and its ancillary, "Aktion Achtung," which see) are to be closed and sent, along with relevant dossiers, to Historical Records.

2. *Codenames to be retired, U.S. Forces:*

   "Gladiator" for Maj. Gen. William P. Vickery
   "Chocolate" for Thomas N. Ballentine, OSS
   "Mint" for Capt. George (NMI) Fallon, CID
   "Licorice" for Karla Wintgens, G-2, USFET
   "Bon-Bon" for Margaret Sunderman, CID
   "Gumdrop" for Maj. Ernesto M. Bianco, OSS

   Codenames to be retired, Foreign National Informant:

   "Fudge" for Luigi Fortunato, motion picture producer

"Caramel" for Gregor Koslov, NKVD resident, Italy

3. Interrogation of Albert F. Dreher, Military Prisoner 445637, mortally wounded in "Aktion Achtung," has produced a list emanating from that operation which should also be noted, then retired.

Codenames to be retired, "Aktion Achtung":

"Asp" for Albert F. Dreher, SS Standartenführer
(Deceased)
"M" for Louis P. Stahl, industrialist
(Deceased)
"Seed" for Vincent L. Ludwig, Spec. Agt., CIC
(Deceased)
"Cobra" for Siegfried Oskar, Generalmajor, Luftwaffe
(Deceased)

4. Note, please, that codename "Alpha" continues to be in use, per original plan.

5. For the record, Maj. Robert L. Kaufmann, MI G-2, USFET, formerly listed as deceased, has in fact survived and has been returned to active duty.

TOP SECRET

43

The downtown officers' club was a block away from the Bahnhof, in the cellar of a brownstone whose upper stories had been vigorously tilled and mulched with 8th Air Force droppings. From the street the club was merely unprepossessing, but inside it was spectacularly ugly, thanks to plumbing and air shafts that had forced the ceiling oppressively low and to walls whose dankness had been camouflaged by threadbare tapestries featuring nude women fleeing lusting satyrs. The light was dim, the air was befouled by tobacco, stale beer and cheap perfume, and the entertainment was outrageous, ranging week by week from oompah bands pretending to be Dixieland, through baggy-pants comics, to this night's zither duet—a cadaverous old man and his frozen-faced wife who twanged away on such trendy, cutting-edge numbers as "Let Me Call You Sweetheart."

Raines sat alone at a penny-size table in a dim corner. The maître d', unctuously apologetic, had asked her to sit here, explaining that he was saving a bloc of tables for a going-away party scheduled for ten o'clock. Which worked to her advantage, actually, because the seat provided a good view of the entrance stairway while keeping her out of the midstream current of table-hopping Lotharios.

She ordered a plain soda—Captain Olsen had forbidden her to drink alcohol while still under the influence of Zenog—and settled in for the wait. Her attempt to take mental inventory of the day just finished got nowhere; the zither music, for all its corniness, was pre-emptive, and she found her fingers tapping to the beat. A pudgy captain and a boyish second looey made separate overtures, drifting past the table with suggestive leers, but each time she was able to parry the thrust with a glance at her wristwatch and an impatient preoccupation with the traffic at the entrance, a lady waiting for a tardy date.

He arrived at five after eight.

"Howdy-doody. You're looking good."

"Hi. Is that a smudge on your lip, or are you growing a mustache?"

"I decided to go legit. All my girlfriends tell me I look cute in a mustache. I like to look cute. So one thing led to another."

"I like you better without one."

"Which is sort of irrelevant, ain't it? Olsen tells me you're off for the ZI and a new career in the movies—all those handsome stars—and so, while it's nice to know you like my bare face, it's the still-available ladies who are doing the swooning."

She was disappointed. No, sad. Sorry. She had been saving the news for this meeting. She'd wanted to tell him directly, in her own way, of the cablegram offer from Sorenson. And, in a shifting of perception, she saw this as the real source of her—whatever it was she was feeling. He'd returned from Italy, from some kind of terrible thing there, and he'd called Olsen first—perhaps others. And, as hard as it was to admit, in view of the emotional effort it had cost her to keep him at a manageable distance, she could not easily deal with the fact that he saw her as someone to get around to after the important things had been handled.

He must have seen some of this. "For somebody who's just had great news, you look a little down. Are you all right?"

"Sure."

"Olsen says you should be out of the Zenog woods very soon now."

"I feel fine. I tire out a little faster than I'm used to, but what the heck—"

"When do you report to Sorenson's studio?"

"As soon as I can return to the States. And that brings up an angle you just *won't* believe: General Vickery called this afternoon. And, after grumping around—you know how he is—he said he wanted to apologize for the bad time he'd been giving me recently. And he said he'd do whatever he could to keep me here in Germany, if that's what I wanted. And when I told him about my new job, he said he'd see to it I'd get sent straight to California on the MATS Connie, whatever that is, the day after tomorrow. *Plane.* Isn't that the limit? Here I've been waiting around for some lousy boat, and now I'm going to fly to the West Coast like Lady Gotrocks." She laughed lightly.

"Why not? You're going to be a movie biggie someday. Good to get in practice, flying around, and so on."

"I can't imagine why Vickery had such a change of heart. He was so stinky to me—"

"Well, remember, with the war over, he's sort of out of a job, and guys get a little testy at times like that."

"I suppose." She gave him a quick glance. "How about you? Have you made any decisions about what you'll do?"

"Not really."

There followed a stilted pause. The zithers took up "Bill Bailey," managing somehow to play it as a waltz, and in the crowd at the bar a drunken woman began to sing along, off-key, raucous.

"Well," Kaufmann said, "I'm glad I had this chance to say good-bye. And to thank you for being my buddy in all those dark hours. I did use you pretty shabbily a time or two, but you were always ready to help, and I appreciate it. More than you know.''

Things weren't going very well here, she realized. Her plan had been to spend a few good-bye minutes with him, to be gracious, friendly, yet sufficiently distant so as to insulate herself from whatever temptations he might dish up. He knew how vulnerable she was to the physical thing. He'd seen how, at little more than a touch, a caress, her fuse would be lit. And she was damned if she would fly off to California, leaving him to gloat over a last-minute explosion. But here he was, being more polite, more distant, than she was. She was the one who had the job. She was the one who was leaving. She was the one who was saying good-bye. Yet the atmosphere here at this silly little table suggested that it was he who was dismissing her—that she was leaving because he had decided to permit it.

So what to do? Give him a punch.

''You're a nice guy, Major, but you'd be a hell of a lot nicer it if weren't for that rotten business you're in.''

He nodded. ''Rotten's the word.''

''You lost me when you used me that way.''

''Yeah. I know.''

Why did he have to look so—resigned? She groped inwardly for a defense against the swift movement of tenderness Kaufmann always seemed to stir in her. She could not, would not, absolutely must not, let this man divert her from her chosen life's path. There would be other men, at other times. Men could wait. But this man must be excised at once—sliced away, jettisoned. She *would* not throw away everything for a man who would inevitably use her again as a plank to be stepped on in his crossing of the swamp.

''Your business is so filthy, so virulent, it infects everybody it touches. Even me. In just a few weeks, I went from a naive jerk to a sly, calculating jerk. My whole life, I've tried to play straight—with everybody. I've never been comfortable with the idea that good things can come from deception. And yet there we were, deceiving the hell out of each other.''

She thought she saw the beginnings of a wry smile, a barely discernible turn of his lips, as elusive as heat lightning.

He said, "A line in an old aviator's ditty says, 'This world is a world of lies.' Nothing is what it's said to be, Raines. Everybody deceives. Hell, that business you're going into is *built* on deception—on making people believe the unbelievable for an hour or so."

"Entertaining diversion's one thing. Premeditated, lethal deception is something else."

He shrugged. "You're right, of course. I just try to make myself feel better by telling myself that when you lie to me, and I lie to you, a truth is created—like two negatives making a positive."

"That's too deep for me. Any way you slice it, your business stinks. And I don't want anything to do with it."

"I've gotten that impression."

"I didn't want to lie to you. I wanted very much to tell you about Maggie's papers—"

"I know that. And I think I knew it then, too. And I'll have to admit that your goofy scruples made you even more special in my eyes. I'm going to miss the hell out of you, Raines."

She felt a dangerous melting inside.

"I've got to go now," she said, gathering up her gloves and her sling bag.

He stood up and eased back her chair. "So long, Raines. You're a great little lady."

"So long, Major Kaufmann." She gave him a sanitary kiss on the corner of his mouth and then turned and disappeared up the ugly staircase.

He sat down and nodded when the waiter asked if he'd like a beer.

He was sipping away when Brandt materialized and, pulling up a chair, sat down, facing him.

"So that, then, is Molly Raines."

"Yep. Beer?"

"All right."

"I don't think she'll go along with you, Mr. Brandt. She's really very intent on becoming something in the movies." Kaufmann signaled the waiter.

"That's a shame. She's the kind of woman we always look for and rarely find. Smart, personable, patriotic, brave, tenacious. Native-born. Degree. Hard to find."

"She's a good egg."

They sat and thought about this for a time.

Brandt lit a cigarette and exhaled slowly, thoughtfully. He said then, "I'd like you to work for me, Major."

"Why?"

"You're very clever. Ballsy. We're always looking for men like that, too."

"You're trying to buy my continuing silence?"

Brandt's pale eyes glimmered. "What does that mean?"

"Donleavy. That whole goddam meeting with G-2 this morning was to convince Donleavy you aren't on to him."

The glimmer turned to a faint smile. "Would you explain that, please?"

"Donleavy's resume: if it's read carefully and often as I've read it, and if laid as a template against Stahl's and Fortunato's—even Poopsie's—resumes, an interesting pattern, a direction, a prognosis evolves. Born to poverty and its resentments. A struggle for an education, for social acceptance. Where? At Llewelyn University, a left-wing hotbed. Among the artsy, leftsy crowd in Rome and Moscow. Opportunity, exposure—"

"What are you driving at?"

"The bizarre part. Stahl was no hater of Stalin. He was an admirer of Stalin. Of Stalin's absolutism, of his incredibly far-reaching autocracy. He had to be. Why? How dare I claim this? The Llewelyn endowments, the financing of movies made by Fortunato—two big clues. Why, if Stahl was such a hater of Stalin Communism, did he give millions to institutions and individuals who were Stalin evangelists? Why would he spend millions of his own money in a staged attack on Russia that would, in the long run, fool nobody but a bunch of Nazis blinded by their own fanaticism?''

Brandt waved a dismissing hand. ''We've settled all that. It was a Soviet ploy to set up a Western Europe take-over. It really matters very little what Stahl's political allegiance was—whatever his motives were. He was trying to ignite World War Three, and we stopped him. *You* stopped him. End of story.''

Kaufmann shook his head, slowly, in the manner of one whose patience is being strained. ''No, Mr. Brandt, it is not the end of the story. It's the beginning.''

Brandt stared into his beer. ''Why do you say that?''

''I think I'm one of the very few U.S. security men who've ever seen the pattern. And I'm probably the only one, besides you and a handful of others, maybe, who's tumbled to its significance.''

''Which is?''

''A mole.''

Brandt sipped his beer and said nothing.

Kaufmann took a deep breath, carefully, because his ribs still hurt under their bindings. An explosion in the B-17 had thrown him hard against a gun mount, cracking a pair of ribs and, as Olsen put it, venting his spleen here and there. Things had not been helped when the parachute had dropped him through the lath roof of a chicken coop. After exhaling slowly, he went on:

''The only way those B-17's and their armament, their crews, could have been made available to Stahl was through the manipulations of some strategically placed staff officer, somebody high enough and with clout enough to pull the strings and grease the palms and smother the paperwork involved. I thought it was Vickery until I learned that Colonel Donleavy had pulled and sat on every critical paper, from Sunrise to the B-17 serial numbers. Until I saw this very morning how carefully you people at G-2's meeting avoided any mention of 'Canned Goods' or, as Sunderman put it, 'C-rations,' in Donleavy's presence. To have done so would have tipped him to the fact that you see more than just a fanatical Nazi plot to continue the Hitler war. He would have seen that you know Stalin was engineering a phony attack on himself, à la the 'Canned Goods' operation by which Hitler justified his invasion of Poland. That he—Donleavy—has to be an NKVD mole whose assignment was to use Soviet funds and resources to implement such a ruse.

"Stahl and his hirelings were a Stalin-financed front to convince Oskar and his Luftwaffe buddies that the American government was bankrolling a German spearhead of a pre-emptive war on the Russians. But the Germans didn't know two very important truths: first, that Stahl was no Nazi sympathizer, he was a self-indulgent adventurer, an apolitical soldier of fortune, an anti-establishment iconoclast whose idol, whose role model, was Josef Stalin; and, second, that their main job was to fly over Russia and get killed, leaving their American dogtags and American equipment dramatically scattered for propaganda photo purposes.

"Donleavy was the manager of the money Stalin had budgeted for this project, and Stahl was the operations man who spent it. And your job—yours and G-2's and Vickery's—has been, and still is, to keep Donleavy from knowing you know all this. You guys had to keep tabs on the German Legion, the Aktion Achtung thing, and be in a position to blow the whistle on it while convincing Donleavy that his plot failed through plain bad luck. Through some asshole like me bumbling onto it and screwing up the details, for instance."

Brandt smiled his dim smile. "Why, for heaven's sake, would we want him to think that?"

"Come on, Brandt, treat me like an adult, will you? You want him to think that so that he can continue to work amongst us as an NKVD mole. A mole we can keep a watch on and get a foreshadowing of Stalin's intentions. Watching the enemy's spies is a hell of a lot more rewarding than arresting the enemy's spies. A spy in jail, a dead spy, reveals nothing. A lively, working spy reveals many things."

"You're saying—"

"I'm saying you've arranged to have your cake and eat

it, too. You broke up Aktion Achtung and Donleavy thinks you have no idea he was involved in it. And now he will move on to whatever new assignment Stalin gives him. And you'll be watching him the whole way. Music up and out.''

Brandt took a final sip of his beer and placed the stein carefully on the table. ''Will you work for me, Major?''

''Who are you? Besides a White House hand, that is.''

''Do you need anything more than that?''

''I guess not.''

''Well?''

''I'm going to Philadelphia and mend some parental fences. I'll let you know from there. Do you hotshots carry business cards?''

Brandt took his expensive wallet from his expensive herringbone tweed and produced an expensive white card. ''Someone always answers at that number.''

They stood up and shook hands, and when they got to the street, Brandt climbed into an expensive automobile and murmured into the clammy night in a cloud of expensive fumes.

Kaufmann was watching after him when he felt a tug on his trenchcoat sleeve.

''Hey,'' Raines said, her face chalky under the street light, her breath making little puffs of steam, ''I decided I was only kidding.''

''About what?''

''I got no more than four steps down the street and I realized I've been had. I can't just walk away from you.''

''Why?''

''Because you seem to be a liberal-thinking man.''

''What the hell's that got to do with anything?''

''You'd probably look benignly on a wife who works. Who has her own career.''

''Don't count on that. I'm not very benign when it comes to those Hollywood smoothies with the restless peckers. Besides, I just got me a job offer. If I take it I'll be on the road a good bit.''

''Okay. So if I can't make a home for you, I'll travel with

you. And if I can't travel with you, I'll wait for you. In other words, you dirty rat, you've absolutely ruined me. I love the hell out of you and I can't imagine not being with you—even if I'm just a shack-up.''

He took her chin between his thumb and forefinger. "No rule in my rotten business says a rotten guy can't love a beautiful, decent, straight-shooting Fräulein Oberleutnant. But there's also no rule against said Oberleutnant toddling along to see how much fun rotten can be.''

He brushed her lips with his.

"First things first," he said. "We have a date at the Klub Fabelhaft. Olsen and Anton and some lady friends of mine are going to do some partying.''

"Lady friends?''

"Emma and Lisa, the Heidelberg banking, carpool and theatrics people. Karla Wintgens, famous aviatrix. Nothing serious. Just three or four days of riotous drunkenness and general debauchery.''

"Sounds really rotten. Lead on, Herr Major.''

His solemn face broke into a wide, adoring grin.

MONDAY
22 April 1946

22 April 1946
Code: Punkin
File: Jupiter

To: Brandt—Washington
From: Kaufmann—Seoul, South Korea

Subject: Operation "Soy Sauce"

1. Raines has reported to her new job as Sorenson
   Fellow dramatics instructor, American
   University, Seoul.

2. She has been seen chatting with General
   Donleavy (Codename: "Alpha") at a recent
   faculty party, per our Dr. Olsen, whose cover as
   visiting lecturer on forensics medicine, that
   university, seems to be nicely established.

3. While awaiting Raine's report, I will continue my personal surveillance.

4. All told, "Top Dog's" suspicions vis-à-vis North Korea are well justified.

5. Urge maximum-effort intelligence program, effective at once, since my Tokyo-Seoul network concurs with "Top Dog's" assessment, being convinced that Stalin will make his next try on the Korean Peninsula.

TOP SECRET